Gould's
BOOK of FISH

Gould's
BOOK of FISH

A NOVEL IN TWELVE FISH

by

RICHARD
FLANAGAN

ATLANTIC BOOKS
London

The paintings of fish by the Van Diemonian convict artist
William Buelow Gould, from Gould's BOOK OF FISH, *held by the*
Allport Library and Museum of Fine Arts, State Library of Tasmania, are here
reproduced with that body's kind permission.

For Rosie, Jean and Eliza,
swimming in ever widening rings of wonder

First published in 2001 by Picador, an imprint of Pan Macmillan Australia Pty
Limited, St Martin's Tower, 31 Market Street, Sydney, Australia

First published in Great Britain in 2002 in a special five colour edition (isbn:
1 84354 021 5) by Atlantic Books, an imprint of Grove Atlantic Limited

This edition, printed in black and white, published in Great Britain in 2002 by
Atlantic Books, an imprint of Grove Atlantic Limited

10 9 8 7 6 5 4 3 2 1

A CIP catalogue record for this book is available from the British Library.

1 84354 146 7

Typeset in Historical Felltype by Post Pre-Press Group, Australia
Printed by Creative Print and Design (Wales), Ebbw Vale
Text design by Mary Callahan

Atlantic Books
An imprint of Grove Atlantic Ltd
Ormond House
26–27 Boswell Street
London
WC1N 3JZ

My mother is a fish.

William Faulkner

THE POT-BELLIED SEAHORSE

Discovery of the Book of Fish—*Fake furniture and faith healing—The Conga—Mr Hung and* Moby Dick—*Victor Hugo and God—A snowstorm—On why history and stories have nothing in common—The book disappears—Death of Great Aunt Maisie—My seduction—A male seahorse gives birth—The fall.*

I

MY WONDER UPON discovering the *Book of Fish* remains with me yet, luminous as the phosphorescent marbling that seized my eyes that strange morning; glittering as those eerie swirls that coloured my mind and enchanted my soul—which there and then began the process of unravelling my heart and, worse still, my life into the poor, scraggy skein that is this story you are about to read.

What was it about that gentle radiance that would come to make me think I had lived the same life over and over, like some Hindu mystic forever trapped in the Great Wheel? that was to become my fate? that stole my character? that rendered my past and my future one and indivisible?

Was it that mesmeric shimmer spiralling from the unruly manuscript out of which seahorses and seadragons and stargazers were already swimming, bringing dazzling light to a dreary day not long born? Was it that sorry vanity of thought which made me think contained within me was all men and all fish and all things? Or was it something more prosaic—bad company and worse drink—which has led to the monstrous pass in which I now find myself?

Character and fate, two words, writes William Buelow Gould, for the same thing—one more matter about which he was, as ever, incisively wrong.

Dear, sweet, silly Billy Gould and his foolish tales of love, so much love that it is not possible now, and was not possible then, for him to continue. But I fear I am already digressing.

We—our histories, our souls—are, I have since come to believe in consequence of his stinking fish, in a process of constant decomposition and reinvention, and this book, I was to discover, was the story of my compost heap of a heart.

Even my feverish pen cannot approach my rapture, an amazement so intense that it was as if the moment I opened the *Book of Fish* the rest of my world—*the world*!—had been cast into darkness and the only light that existed in the entire universe was that which shone out of those aged pages up into my astonished eyes.

I was without work, there being little enough of it in Tasmania then and even less now. Perhaps my mind was more susceptible to miracles than it might otherwise have been. Perhaps as a poor Portuguese peasant girl sees the Madonna because she doesn't wish to see anything else, I too longed to be blind to my own world. Perhaps if Tasmania had been a normal place where you had a proper job, spent hours in traffic in order to spend more hours in a normal crush of anxieties waiting to return to a normal confinement, and where no-one ever dreamt what it was like to be a seahorse, abnormal things like becoming a fish wouldn't happen to you.

I say perhaps, but frankly I am not sure.

Maybe this sort of thing goes on all the time in Berlin and Buenos Aires, and people are just too embarrassed to own up to it. Maybe the Madonna comes all the time to the New York projects and the high-rise horrors of Berlin and the western suburbs of Sydney, and everybody pretends she's not there and hopes she'll just go away soon and not embarrass them any further. Maybe the new Fatima is somewhere in the vast wastelands of the Revesby Workers' Club, a halo over the pokie screen that blinks '*BLACKJACK FEVER*'.

Could it be that when all backs are turned, when all faces are focused on the pokie monitors, there is no-one left to witness the moment an old woman levitates as she fills in her Keno form? Maybe we have lost the ability, that sixth sense that allows us to see miracles and have visions and understand that we are something other, larger than what we have been told. Maybe evolution has been going on in reverse longer than I suspect, and we are already sad, dumb fish. Like I say, I am not sure, and the only people I trust, such as Mr Hung and the Conga, aren't sure either.

To be honest, I have come to the conclusion that there is not much in this life that one can be sure about. Despite what may come to seem to you as mounting evidence to the contrary, I value truth, but as William Buelow Gould continued to ask of his fish long after they were dead from his endless futile queries, where is truth to be found?

As for me, they have taken the book and everything away now, and what are books anyway but unreliable fairy tales?

Once upon a time there was a man called Sid Hammet and he discovered he was not who he thought he was.

Once upon a time there were miracles, and the aforementioned Hammet believed he had been swept up in one. Until that day he had lived by his wits, which is another, kinder way of saying that his life was an ongoing act of disillusionment. After that day he was to suffer the cruel malaise of belief.

Once upon a time there was a man called Sid Hammet who saw reflected in the glow of a strange book of fish his story, which began as a fairy tale and ended as a nursery rhyme, riding a cock-horse to Banbury Cross.

Once upon a time terrible things happened, but it was long ago in a far-off place that everyone knows is not here or now or us.

II

UNTIL THAT TIME I had devoted myself to buying old pieces of rotting furniture which I further distressed with every insult conceivable. While I belted the sorry cupboards with hammers to enhance the pathetic patina, as I relieved myself on the old metalwork to promote the putrid verdigris, yelling all manner of vile curses to make myself feel better, I would imagine that such pieces of furniture were the tourists who were their inevitable purchasers, buying what they mistakenly thought to be flotsam of the romantic past, rather than what they were, evidence of a rotten present.

My Great Aunt Maisie said it was a miracle that I had found any work, and I felt she would know, for had she not taken me at the age of seven to the North Hobart oval in the beautiful ruby light of late winter to miraculously assist North Hobart win the football semi-final? She sprinkled Lourdes holy water from a tiny bottle on the muddy sods of the ground. The Great John Devereaux was captain coach and I was wrapped in the Demons' red and blue scarf, like an Egyptian's mummified cat, with only big curious eyes visible. I ran out at three-quarter time to peek through a mighty forest of the players' Deepheat-aromaed thighs and hear the Great John Devereaux deliver a rousing speech.

North Hobart were down a dozen goals and I knew he would say something remarkable to his players, and the Great John Devereaux was not a man to disappoint his followers. 'Get your minds off the fucking sheilas,' he said. 'You, Ronnie, forget that Jody. As for you, Nobby, the sooner you get that Mary out of your mind, the better.' And so on. It was marvellous to hear all those girls' names and know they meant so much to such giants at three-quarter time. When they then won, kicking into the wind, I knew that love and water was a truly unbeatable combination.

But to return to my work with furniture, it was, as

Rennie Conga (this, I hasten to say, lest some of her family read this and take umbrage, was not exactly her name, but no-one could ever remember her full Italian surname and it somehow seemed to fit her sinuous body and the close, dark clothes with which she chose to clad that serpentine form), my then probation officer, put it, a post with prospects, particularly when the cruise ships full of fat old Americans came by. With their protruding bellies, shorts, odd thin legs and odder big white shoes dotting the end of those oversize bodies, the Americans were endearing question marks of human beings.

I say endearing, but what I really mean to say is that they had money.

They also had their tastes, which were peculiar, but where commerce was concerned I was fond enough of them—and they of me. And for a time the Conga and I did a good line in old chairs which she had bought at an auction when yet one more Tasmanian headquarters of a government department had closed down. These I painted in several bright enamel paints, sanded back, lightly shredded with a vegetable grater, pissed on and passed off as Shaker furniture that had come out with whalers from Nantucket last century in, as we would say in answer to the question marks, their ceaseless search of the southern oceans for the great leviathans.

It was the story, really, that the tourists were buying, of the only type that they would ever buy—an American story, a happy, stirring tale of Us Finding Them Alive and Bringing Them Back Home—and for a time it was a good story. So much so that we ran out of stock and the Conga was forced to set up a production side to our venture, securing a deal with a newly arrived Vietnamese family, while I had the story neatly typed up along with some genuine authentication labels by a bogus organisation we called the Van Diemonian Antiquarian Association.

The Vietnamese's story (his name was Lai Phu Hung but the Conga, who believed in respect, always insisted on us calling him Mr Hung) was as interesting as any old whaling tale, his family's flight from Vietnam more perilous, their voyage in an overcrowded and derelict fishing junk to Australia more desperate, and they were better at scrimshaw to boot—a sideline, I should add, in which we also did a respectable trade. As the templates for his bone carving, Mr Hung used the woodcut illustrations out of an old Modern Library edition of *Moby Dick*.

But he and his family had no Melville, no Ishmael or Queequeg or Ahab on the quarterdeck, no romantic past, only their troubles and dreams like the rest of us, and it was all too dirtily, irredeemably human to be worth anything to the voracious question marks. To be fair to them, they were only after something that walled them off from the past and from people in general, not something that offered any connection that might prove painful or human.

They wanted stories, I came to realise, in which they were already imprisoned, not stories in which they appeared along with the storyteller, accomplices in escaping. They wanted you to say, 'Whalers', so they might reply, 'Moby Dick', and summon images from the mini-series of the same name; so you might then say, 'Antique', so they might reply, 'How much?'

Those sort of stories.

The type that pay.

Not like Mr Hung's tales, which no question marks ever wanted to hear, something of which Mr Hung seemed extraordinarily accepting, in part because his true ambition was not to be a steam-crane driver as he had been in Hai-Phong City, but a poet, a dream that allowed him to affect a Romantic resignation to the indifference of a callous world.

For Mr Hung's religion was literature, literally. He belonged to the Cao Dai, a Buddhist sect that regarded Victor Hugo as a god. In addition to worshipping the deity's novels, Mr Hung seemed knowledgeable about (and intimated a certain spiritual communion with) several other greats of nineteenth-century French writing of whom, beyond their names—and sometimes not even that—I knew nothing.

Being in Hobart and not Hai-Phong City, the tourists cared not a jot for the likes of Mr Hung, and they certainly weren't going to give us any money for his tales about steam cranes, or his father's cranes that fished, or his poetry, or, for that matter, his thoughts on the connections between God and Gallic literature. And so instead Mr Hung dug out a small workshop beneath his old Zinc Company house in Lutana and set to work building fake antique chairs and carving ersatz whalebone to complement our more sordid fictions.

And why should Mr Hung or his family or the Conga or I have cared anyway?

The tourists had money and we needed it; they only asked in return to be lied to and deceived and told that single most important thing, that they were safe, that their sense of security—national, individual, spiritual—wasn't a bad joke being played on them by a bored and capricious destiny. To be told that there was no connection between then and now, that they didn't need to wear a black armband or have a bad conscience about their power and their wealth and everybody else's lack of it; to feel rotten that no-one could or would explain why the wealth of a few seemed so curiously dependent on the misery of the many. We kindly pretended that it was about buying and selling chairs, about them asking questions about price and heritage, and us replying in like manner.

But it wasn't about price and heritage, it wasn't about that at all.

The tourists had insistent, unspoken questions and we just had to answer as best we could, with forged furniture. They were really asking, 'Are we safe?' and we were really replying, 'No, but a barricade of useless goods may help block the view.' And because hubris is not just an ancient Greek word but a human sense so deep-seated we might better regard it as an unerring instinct, they were also wanting to know, 'If it is our fault, then will we suffer?' and we were really replying, 'Yes, and slowly, but a fake chair may make us both feel better about it.' I mean it was a living, and if it wasn't that good, nor was it all that bad, and while I would carry as many chairs as we could sell, I wasn't about to carry the weight of the world.

You might think such a venture would have met with the greatest approval, that inevitably it would have

progressed, diversified, grown into a redemptive undertaking of global proportions and national merit. It may
even have won export awards. Certainly in any city
worth its sly salt—Sydney, say—such dreaming fraud-
ulence would have been handsomely rewarded. But
this, after all, was Hobart, where dreams remained a
strictly private matter.

Following the receipt of several lawyers' letters from
local antique dealers and the attendant threat of legal
proceedings, the arse fell out of our noble enterprise of
offering solace to a decrepit empire's retired tribunes.
The Conga felt compelled to go into eco-tourism con-
sultancy with the Vietnamese furniture faker, and I
went looking for some new lines.

III

So it came to be on that winter's morning that was to
prove fateful but at the time merely seemed freezing, I
found myself in the wharf-side area of Salamanca. In an
old sandstone warehouse I came upon what was still a
junk shop, before that space too was appropriated by
tourists and turned into yet another delicately over-
done al-fresco restaurant.

Nestled behind some unfashionable 1940s blackwood wardrobes no tourist would ever be interested
in receiving as absolution, I chanced to notice an old
galvanised-iron meat safe which, with a child's desire
to see into whatever is closed, I opened.

Inside I could only make out a heap of women's
magazines of years gone by, a discovery dusty as it was

disappointing. I was already closing the door when, beneath those fading rumours of love and tawdry tales of sad, lost princesses, my eye caught on some brittle cotton threads cheerily jutting out like Great Aunt Maisie's stubble, without shame and with a certain archaic vigour.

The door scratched a flat note as I pulled it back open and peered more closely inside. I saw that the threads grew out from a somewhat frayed binding, the spine of which had partly fallen away. As carefully as if it were a prize fish hopelessly entangled in my net, I reached in, lifted up the magazines, and from beneath eased out what appeared to be a dilapidated book.

I held it up in front of me.

I put my nose close.

Oddly, it smelt not of the sweet must of old books, but of the briny winds that blow in from the Tasman Sea. I lightly ran an index finger across its cover. Though filthy with a fine black grime, it felt silky to the touch. It was on wiping away that silt of centuries that the first of many remarkable things occurred.

I should have known then that this was no ordinary book, and certainly not one a deadflog like me ought to be getting mixed up with. I know—or at least, I thought I knew—the limits of my criminality, and I believed I had learnt how to say no to any tomfoolery that involved personal risks.

But it was too late. I was—as has been put to me before in the course of legal proceedings—already implicated. For beneath that delicate black powder something highly unusual was happening: the book's marbled cover was giving off a faint, but increasingly bright purple glow.

IV

Outside it was a melancholic winter's day.

Snow mantled the mountain above the town. Mist billowed down the broad river, covering like a slow-falling quilt the valley in which lay the quiet, mostly empty streets of Hobart. Through the chill beauty of the morning, a few figures clad in the motley of cold-day clothes scurried, then vanished. The mountain turned from white to grey then disappeared to brood behind black cloud. The town was passing into gentle sleep. Like lost dreams snow began waltzing through its hushed world.

All of which is not totally beside the point, for what I am really trying to say is that it was cold as a tomb and ten times quieter, that there were on such a day no portents, nothing that might have warned me of what was about to happen. And certainly on such a day no-one else bothered to venture into a dark, unheated Salamanca junk shop. Even the owner stayed huddled over a small bar radiator at the far end of his domain, his back turned to me, surreptitiously slipping off that vile anthem of contemporary retailing, Vivaldi's *Four Seasons*, and putting on the comforting low rubato of the races, a golden slipper of sound.

No-one else in the world was there to notice, to witness along with me that miracle when the world seemed to contract to a gloomy corner of an old junk shop, and eternity to that moment when I first brushed the silt off the front of that bizarre book.

As with the skin of a bastard trumpeter caught at night, the book's cover was now a mass of pulsing purple spots. The more I brushed, the more the spots spread, till most of the cover was brightly glowing. As with the night fisherman who handles the bastard trumpeter, the speckled phosphorescence spread from the book onto my hands until they too were covered in purple freckles, twinkling in splendid disarray, like the lights of an exotic, unknown city glimpsed from a plane. As I held my luminous hands up in front of my face and then slowly turned them around in wonder—hands so familiar yet so alien—it was as if I had already begun a disturbing metamorphosis.

I laid the book on a laminex table that sat next to the meat safe, ran my now sparkling thumb up its soft underbelly of unruly, frail pages, and turned the cover. To my wonder the book fell open to a painting of a pot-bellied seahorse. Gathered around the seahorse, like a flotsam of bull-kelp and sea grass, was a rumpled script. Interspersed every so often would be another water-colour painting of a fish.

It was, I must admit, a dreadful hodgepodge, what with some stories in ink layered higgledy-piggledy over others in pencil, and sometimes vice versa. Upon running out of space at the end of the book, the writer seemed to have simply turned it around and, between the existing lines, resumed writing—in the opposite direction and upside down—more of his tales. If this

13

wasn't confusing enough—and it was—there were numerous addenda and annotations crammed into the margins and sometimes on loose leaves of paper, and once on what looked like dried fish skin. The writer appeared to have press-ganged any material—old sail-cloth, edges ripped out of God knows what books, burlap, even hessian—into use as a surface to cover with a colourful, crabbed handwriting that at the best of times was hard to decipher.

The sum of such chaos was that I seemed to be reading a book that never really started and never quite finished. It was like looking into a charming kaleidoscope of changing views: a peculiar, sometimes frustrating, sometimes entrancing affair, but not at all the sort of open-and-shut thing a good book should be.

Yet before I knew it, I was washed far away by the stories that accompanied these fish—if they can even be described as such, the volume being more in the manner of a journal or diary, sometimes of actual events, immersed in the mud of the mundane, at other times of matters so cracked that at first I thought it must be a chronicle of dreams or nightmares.

This weird record seemed to be that of a convict called William Buelow Gould who in the supposed interest of science was, in 1828, ordered by the surgeon of the penal colony of Sarah Island to paint all fish caught there. But while the duty of painting was obligatory, the duty of writing, which the author carried as an additional burden, was not. The keeping of such journals by convicts was forbidden, and therefore dangerous. Each story was written in a different coloured ink which, as their convict scribe describes, had been made by various ingenious expedients from whatever was at hand: the red ink from kangaroo blood, the blue from crushing a stolen precious stone, and so on.

The author wrote in colours; more precisely, I suspect, he *felt* in colours. I don't mean he would wax on about wine-dark sunsets or the azure glory of a still sea. I do mean to suggest that his world took on hues that overwhelmed him, as if the universe was a consequence of colour, rather than the inverse. Did the wonder of colour, I pondered, redeem the horror of his world?

This clandestine rainbow of tales, in spite of—and to be truthful, perhaps also because of—its crude style, its many inconsistencies, its difficulty to read, its odd beauty, to say nothing of its more ludicrous and sometimes frankly implausible moments, so captivated me that I must have read at least half before I came to my senses.

I found an old rag on the floor with which I rubbed my hands near raw until they were rid of the glowing purple spots, and hid the book back in the meat safe which I then purchased, after some haggling, for the suitably low price that rusting galvanised-iron meat safes commanded before they too, like all other old junk, came into fashion.

Exactly what my intentions were as I walked out into the light snowstorm, struggling with that cumbersome meat safe, I cannot to this day say. While I knew I would be able to spray the meat safe in a heritage colour and then flog it off as an antique sound-system cupboard for double what I paid, and while I was eventually to con a free filling from a dentist in return for the old women's magazines to fill his waiting room, I had no idea what I was going to do with the *Book of Fish*.

To my shame, I must admit that at first I may have had the base impulse to rip out the many paintings of fish and frame them up and sell them to an antiquarian print dealer. But the more I read and reread the *Book of Fish* that cold night, the following night and the many nights thereafter, the less inclination I had to profit from it.

The story enchanted me, and I took to carrying the book with me everywhere, as if it were some powerful talisman, as if it contained some magic that might somehow convey or explain something fundamental to me. But what that fundamental thing was, or why it seemed to matter so much, I was at a loss then—and remain at a loss now—to explain.

All I can say with certainty is that when I took it to historians and bibliophiles and publishers for their opinion of its worth, thinking they might also delight in my discovery, it was sadly to discover that the enchantment was mine alone.

While all agreed that the *Book of Fish* was old, much of it—the story it purports to tell, the fishes it claims to represent, the convicts and guards and penal administrators it seeks to describe—seemed to concur with the known facts only long enough to enter with them into an argument. This bellicose book, it was put to me, was the insignificant if somewhat curious product of a particularly deranged mind of long ago.

When I managed to persuade the museum to run

tests on the parchment and inks and paints, carbon date and even CAT scan the book page by page, they admitted all the materials and techniques seemed authentic to the period. Yet the story discredited itself so completely that, rather than agreeing to attest to the book as a genuine work of great historical interest, the museum's experts instead congratulated me on the quality of my forgery and wished me all the best in my continuing work in tourism.

v

MY LAST PROSPECT lay with the eminent colonial historian Professor Roman de Silva, and my hopes rose for several days after I posted him the *Book of Fish*, then sank for as many weeks after waiting for a reply. Finally, on a drizzly Thursday afternoon, his secretary rang to say the professor would be available to meet for twenty minutes later that day in his university office.

I discovered there a man whose reputation seemed not just at odds, but in complete conflict, with his appearance. Professor Roman de Silva's twitching movements and tiny, pot-gutted frame, his dyed jet-black hair swept up over his pinhead in an improbable teddy boy haircut, suggested an unfortunate cross between an Elvis doll and a nervous leghorn rooster.

It was clear that the *Book of Fish* stood in the dock accused, and the professor opened what was to amount to a withering case for the prosecution, determined never to allow our interview to degenerate into a conversation.

He turned his back to me, fossicked in a drawer and

then—with a sudden movement meant to be dramatic, but which succeeded only in being awkward—he dropped a cast-iron ball and chain onto his desk. There was a tearing noise that sounded like wood fracturing, but Professor de Silva was already well into his act, and, a true pro, he wasn't going to let this or anything else deter him.

'So you see, Mr Hammet,' he said.

I said nothing.

'What do you see, Mr Hammet?'

I said nothing.

'A ball and chain, Mr Hammet, is that what you see? A convict ball and chain, is it not?'

Wishing to be agreeable, I nodded.

'No, Mr Hammet, you see nothing of the sort. A fraud, Mr Hammet, is what you see. A ball and chain made by ex-convicts in the late nineteenth century to sell to tourists visiting the Gothic horror land of the Port Arthur penal settlement is what you gaze upon. A tacky, fraudulent, tourist-souvenir type of fraud is what you see, Mr Hammet. A piece of kitsch that has nothing to do with history.'

He halted, balled the knuckle of a small index finger up into his hirsute nostrils, from which moist black hairs large enough to trap moths protruded, then resumed talking.

'History, Mr Hammet, is what you cannot see. History has power. But a fake has none.'

I was impressed. Coming from where I did, it looked like the past of my own noble art. It also looked sellable. While I stood there wondering what Mr Hung's skills at forging and blacksmithing were like, whether I should call the Conga and advise her of the potentially lucrative new line I had chanced upon, and what euphemisms I might deploy to communicate the erotic charge our American friends would inevitably find in such an item ('Is there *nothing* that doesn't mean sex to them?' the Conga had one day asked, to which Mr Hung had replied, 'People'), Professor Roman de Silva dropped—with what I felt to be an entire lack of respect—Gould's *Book of Fish* next to the ball and chain.

'And this, *this* is no better. An old fake, perhaps, Mr Hammet'—and here he fixed me with a sad, knowing gaze—'though I am not even sure about my choice of adjective.'

He turned, put his hands in his pockets, and stared out of the window onto a carpark some storeys below for what seemed a very long time before speaking again.

'But a fake nevertheless.'

And with his back to me, he continued rabbiting on in a manner, I suspected, honed on generations of suffering students, telling the window and the carpark how the penal colony described in the *Book of Fish* seemed, on the surface at least, the same as that which then existed on that island to which only the worst of all convicts were banished; how its location also accorded with what was known, marooned in a large harbour surrounded by the impenetrable wild lands of the western half of Van Diemen's Land, an uncharted country depicted on maps of the day only as a baleful blankness colonial cartographers termed Transylvania.

Then he turned around to face me, brushing back

his dandruff-confettied quiff for the hundredth time.

'But while it is a matter of historical record that between 1820 and 1832 Sarah Island was the most dreaded place of punishment in the entire British Empire, almost nothing in the *Book of Fish* agrees with the known history of that island hell. Few of the names mentioned in your curious chronicle are to be found in any of the official documents that survive from that time, and those that do take on identities and histories entirely at odds with what is described in this . . . *this* sad pastiche.

'And, if we care to examine the historical records,' continued the professor, but I knew by then he hated the *Book of Fish*, that he looked for truth in facts and not in stories, that history for him was no more than the pretext for a rueful fatalism about the present, that a man with such hair was prone to a shallow nostalgia that would inevitably give way to a sense that life was as mundane as he was himself, 'we discover that Sarah Island did not suffer the depredations of a tyrant ruler, nor for a time did it become a merchant port of such standing and independence that it became a separate trading nation, nor yet was it razed to the ground in an apocalyptic fire as recorded in the cataclysmic chronicle that is your *Book of Fish*.' On and on he blathered, taking refuge in the one thing he felt lent him superiority: words.

He said that the *Book of Fish* might one day find a place in the inglorious, if not insubstantial, history of Australian literary frauds. 'That one area of national letters,' he observed, 'in which Australia can rightly lay some claim to a global eminence.

'It need not be added,' he added, sly smile almost obscured by the limp quiff leaning over his face like a drunk about to vomit, 'that if you were to publish it as a *novel*, the inevitable might happen: it could win literary prizes.'

The *Book of Fish* may have had its shortcomings—even if I wasn't willing to admit to them—but it had never struck me as being sufficiently dull-witted and pompous to be mistaken for national literature. Taking the professor's remark in the spirit of an ill-mannered jest at my expense, I concluded our meeting with a curt goodbye, took back the *Book of Fish*, and left.

VI

AT FIRST, I was partly persuaded by such arguments as I had heard, and agreed that the book must be some elaborate, mad deception. But as one who knows something of the game of deceit, who knows that swindling requires not delivering lies but confirming preconceptions, the book, if it was a fraud, made no sense, because none of it accorded with any expectation of what the past ought to be.

The book had grown into a puzzle I was now determined to solve. I trawled the Archives Office of Tasmania, whose neat, unremarkable urban shopfront belies the complete record of a totalitarian state that it houses. I discovered there little that was helpful, with the exception of the wise and venerable archivist, Mr Kim Pearce, with whom I took to drinking.

Beyond what Professor de Silva had termed 'the undivinable oddities' of the *Book of Fish*, there was the further problem of the identity of the chronicler himself, 'the lacuna of lacunae' as Professor de Silva had called it, a phrase that made as little sense to me as William Buelow Gould had to him.

In the convict records Mr Kim Pearce found several dead William Goulds, while introducing me to a living Willy Gold in the *Hope and Anchor*, an alcoholic watercolour painter of birds with a cleft palate (the painter, not the birds) at the *Ocean Child*; and Pete the publican in the snug—a small and comfy taproom—of the *Crescent*.

Only one of the historical (i.e., dead) William Goulds had a life that seemed to correspond in some ways with the author of the *Book of Fish*, sharing a similar criminal record and the same tattoo above his left breast—a red anchor with blue wings, wrapped around which was the legend: 'LOVE AND LIBERTY'. It was this William Buelow Gould, a recidivist convict artist, who upon arriving in 1828 at the Sarah Island penal settlement, was charged with the specific duty of painting fish for the surgeon.

While such detail tallied with the life described in the *Book of Fish*, the historical Gould's subsequent convict record suggests a life entirely at odds with that which had so captivated me. It sometimes seemed as if the author of the *Book of Fish*, the storyteller William Buelow Gould, had been born with a memory but neither experience nor history to account for it, and had spent forever after seeking to invent what didn't exist in the curious belief that his imagination might become

22

his experience, and thereby both explain and cure his problem of an inconsolable memory.

After such bafflement, imagine then my astonishment upon discovering in the hush of the Allport Library a second *Book of Fish*, attributed to the convict artist William Buelow Gould, which contained wondrous paintings identical to the Salamanca *Book of Fish* in all but one detail, a similarity so remarkable that I felt I was choking for want of air.

I took aside the kindly Mr Pearce, who had been so helpful, and explained why I had so loudly gasped.

I told him how I had discovered that there were clearly not one but *two* books of fish; how these two works that seemed so precisely to mirror each other were at once the same and yet fundamentally different. While one (the Allport Library *Book of Fish*) contained not a single written word, the other (the Salamanca *Book of Fish*) teemed with words as the ocean did fish, and these schools of words formed a chronicle that explained the curious genesis of the pictures. One book spoke with the authority of words and the other with the authority of silence, and it was impossible to tell which was the more mysterious.

'Indeed,' said Mr Kim Pearce, proffering without comment some Mylanta tablets, 'their very mystery is heightened by each book's distorted reflection of the other.'

I rushed home, grabbed my meat-safe edition from its hiding place behind the bathroom mirror, and retired to a nearby hotel once more to indulge myself in drink and fish.

And here, before I go any further, I must make mention of a second unusual attribute of the *Book of Fish* in addition to its self-illuminating cover, a remarkable quality that seemed to mirror life. I have mentioned how the book seemed never to really finish. But that is not the whole truth. Even now I hesitate before I write it down, this trait so peculiar as to be unbelievable—the refusal of its story to end.

Every time I opened the book a scrap of a paper with some revelation I had not hitherto read would fall out, or I would stumble across an annotation that I had somehow missed in my previous readings, or I would come upon two pages stuck together that I hadn't noticed and which, when carefully teased apart, would contain a new element of the story that would force me to rethink the whole in an entirely changed light. In this way, each time I opened the *Book of Fish* what amounted to a new chapter miraculously appeared. That evening, sitting alone at the bar in the *Republic*—once the old *Empire*—was no different, except I knew, even in the decrepitude of my mindless passion, that by the very nature of its content what I was reading with growing horror was the last chapter I would ever read.

As I drew close to its conclusion the pages first grew damp beneath my fingers, then wet, and finally, as I felt my heart pounding, as my breathing sped up and I began to heave and pant, I had the inexplicable sense that I was now reading words written at the very bottom of the ocean.

In a state of utter disbelief I came to what I knew to

be the ending. I realised that no more multi-coloured chapters would ever again so miraculously appear, and gazing in astonishment at the terrible tale of William Buelow Gould and his fish, I asked for an ouzo to steady my shaking hands, threw it down with a single, unsteady gulp and put it down on a Cascade beer towel, and then, still dazed, wandered off to the toilet.

When I returned it was to find the bar top had been cleared.

I felt my throat contracting and found it suddenly hard to breathe.

VII

THERE WAS NO Cascade beer towel.

There was no drained ouzo glass.

There was no . . . no *Book of Fish*!

I was trying to swallow but my mouth had gone dry. I was trying to stand up straight, but I was swaying, beset by a vertiginous fear. I was trying not to panic, but my heartbeat was a deafening roar, monstrous wave after wave of fear crashing on the ocean floor of my soul. Where I had left Gould's *Book of Fish* there now remained nothing—nothing, that is, save a large, brackish puddle being mopped up by the barman with a sponge, which he then wrung into a sink.

Only now I realise that the *Book of Fish* was returning whence it came, that, paradoxically, just as the *Book of Fish* had ended for me, it was also beginning for others.

Only then nothing was clear. Worse still, no-one in

the hotel that night, not the barman nor the several customers, had any recollection of the book ever having been there. A desolate horror, utter and huge as abandonment, gripped me.

Several harrowing, depressing weeks followed in which I pressed the police to no avail to fully investigate this obvious theft. I went back to the Salamanca junk shop in the hopeful, hopeless delusion that by some curious, temporal osmosis the book might have been reabsorbed into its past. I returned again and again to the *Republic*, spending hours searching under the bar, upending garbage bins, ejecting skateboards and their dozing street-kid owners from the skip out the back in my relentless search, confronting customers and staff over and over, until I was forcibly ejected and told never to return. I spent long hours staring at the putrid outfall of sewage drains under the delusion that the book might there metamorphose.

But after some months, I had to face the awful truth.

The *Book of Fish*, with its myriad wonders and its horrific, unfolding and ever-growing tale, was gone. I had lost something fundamental and had acquired in its place a curious infection: the terrible contagion of an unrequited love.

VIII

'TRAVEL? HOBBIES?' ASKED Doctor Bundy in his cotton-wadding voice that I had grown to hate along with everything else about Doctor Bundy in the five minutes since I first entered his surgery. As I sat back up and put my shirt on he told me that he could find no problem with my health, that perhaps all I needed was some new—some other—interest. On and on he went—had I thought about joining a sporting club? A men's support group?

I felt the same sensation of breathlessness that had seized me in the Allport Library and then grabbed me in the pub the fateful evening the *Book of Fish* disappeared. I rushed out of his consulting room. Given that Doctor Bundy refused to countenance the fact of my illness, it seemed not unreasonable for me to refuse to countenance the worth of his remedies. In any case I had no money to travel, no desire to take up a hobby, and a strong aversion to the public humiliations implicit in triathlons or being made to bear-hug sweating New Age dentists in wigwams as they solemnly ran feathers over each other, all the while blubbering about never having known their fathers.

So eating continued to make me nauseous, I spent my nights staring into an ocean of darkness I could never enter, and my waking hours, which were infinite, filled with nightmares of sea creatures, and for a long time I remained inexplicably ill.

In the way they so often do, other tragedies clustered. Great Aunt Maisie died of salmonella poisoning. I spent long hours at her graveside. The book, I came to think, was not unlike those frozen quiches she had once with such gusto produced from her chest freezer with a use-by date stamped for two decades previous, merely waiting for the miracle of the microwave to resurrect. The book was the North

Hobart football ground waiting for a few drops of Lourdes holy water and memories of absent love. The book, I began to suspect, was waiting for me.

Perhaps it was in this way my illness took on the form of a mission. Or perhaps only my joy in the glorious wonder of all that Gould wrote and painted explains my subsequent decision to rewrite the *Book of Fish*, a book in which there is no popular interest nor academic justification nor financial reward, nothing really, save the folly of a sorry passion.

From memories, good and bad, reliable and unreliable; by using bad transcriptions that I had made, some of complete sections, others only brief notes describing lengthy tracts of the book; and by the useful expedient of reproducing the pictures from the wordless Allport *Book of Fish*, I set about my forlorn task.

Maybe Mr Hung with his shrine to Victor Hugo is right: to make a book, even one so inadequate as this wretched copy you now read, is to learn that the only appropriate feeling to those who live within its pages is love. Perhaps reading and writing books is one of the last defences human dignity has left, because in the end they remind us of what God once reminded us before He too evaporated in this age of relentless humiliations—that we are more than ourselves; that we have souls. And more, moreover.

Or perhaps not.

Because it clearly was too big a burden for God, this business about reminding people of being other than hungry dust, and really the only wonder is that He persevered with it for so long before giving up. Not that I am unsympathetic—I've often felt the same weary disgust with my own rude creations—but I neither expect nor wish the book to succeed where He failed. My desire was only ever to make a vessel—however crude—in which all Gould's fish might be returned to the sea.

But I must confess to a growing ache within, for these days I am no longer sure what is memory and what is revelation. How faithful the story you are about to read is to the original is a bone of contention with the few people I had allowed to read the original *Book of Fish*. The Conga—unreliable, granted—maintains there is no difference. Or at least no difference that matters. And certainly, the book you will read is the same as the book I remember reading, and I have tried to be true both to the wonder of that reading and to the extraordinary world that was Gould's.

Though I had hoped he might, Mr Hung doesn't know. On that wet afternoon when we sat down in front of the log fire in the *Hope & Anchor* and I put these troubling questions to him—the only person I know who knew anything about books—thinking he might say something that would quell my ever more unruly heart, Mr Hung quaintly ventured the suggestion that books and their authors are indivisible, and—in what I thought a somewhat obscure explanation—told (between Pernods, another curious legacy of the French) the story of how Flaubert, pestered to declare who was the model for Madame Bovary, finally cried out in what Mr Hung claimed to be both exasperation and elation—'Madame Bovary, *cest moi!*'

After this incomprehensible anecdote which left Mr Hung exultant, and me and the Conga—knowing neither French nor literature, and even after Mr Hung's subsequent translation ('Madame Bovary is me!')—little the wiser, the Conga declared she didn't know either.

'Perhaps,' I venture, 'de Silva is right. It was just a fraud.'

'Fuck de Silva,' says the Conga, her face flushing with drink and anger, '*fuck them all*!'

'Sure,' I say, 'sure.'

But in truth I am unsure.

I had begun with the comforting conclusion that books are the tongue of divine wisdom, and had ended only with the thin hunch that all books are grand follies, destined forever to be misunderstood.

Mr Hung says that a book at its beginning may be a new way of understanding life—an original universe—but it is soon enough no more than a mere footnote in the history of writing, overpraised by the sycophantic, despised by the contemporary, and read by neither. Their fate is hard, their destiny absurd. If readers ignore them they die, and if granted the thumbs-up of posterity they are destined forever to be misconstrued, their authors transformed first into gods and then, inevitably, unless they are Victor Hugo, into devils.

And with that, he drains a final Pernod and leaves.

Afterwards the Conga comes over all amorous, stands close by me, leans on me so we pitch and toss like a single boat in a wild sea, furtively reaches beneath my groin and tugs on my balls like they are the cord to a klaxon horn.

Poop—poop!

We end up in her bed together, faces and bodies crisscrossed by the shadows thrown by stacks of unsold Vietnamese Shaker furniture made by a refugee who suspects God to be Victor Hugo and Emma Bovary to be Gustave Flaubert, and her passion evaporates in an instant.

Her eyes glaze.

Her lips quiver.

'Who are you?' she suddenly cries aloud. 'Who?'

And she is frightened, so terribly frightened, and she is seeing someone else, but who it is I have no way of knowing. For her body is abruptly dead and exists only in the most dreadful state of subjugation, and I, despicably, continue for a short time, before my own feeling of horror overwhelms even my overwhelming animal desire and I withdraw.

'Why are you going?' the Conga cries out, but now her voice is different, and I realise she is back from wherever she has been.

'Don't go, come back here,' the Conga says and she opens her arms to me, and relieved, I remount. And then once more her eyes glaze, her body deadens, and she cries out again and again, 'Who are you? Who are you? Who are you?' and she is crying and this time I simply want to escape this strange circle, and I get up and hastily pull on my clothes, and the Conga all the time saying, as nice as pie, genuinely upset, 'But why? Why are you going?' And I am gone because I have no furniture to offer her that might give solace, no fake chairs or tables to trade for her guilty sadnesses, because I cannot answer either for her or for me who I am or who she is, far less what this *Book of Fish* is about.

How can I tell her that late of a night when melancholia seems to fall with the evening dew, I am taken of the strong fancy that for me alone William Buelow Gould was born: that he made his life for me and me this *Book of Fish* for him; that our destiny was always one?

Because, you see, it sometimes seems so elusive, this book, a series of veils, each of which must be lifted and parted to reveal only another of its kind, to arrive finally at emptiness, a lack of words, at the sound of the sea, of the great Indian Ocean through which I see in my mind's eye Gould now advancing towards Sarah Island, now receding; that sound, that sight, slowly pulsing in and out, in and out.

I fell into an old russet armchair in the Conga's dark lounge room, exhausted from the shameful descent my life had become, and before I knew it, had fallen fast asleep, with a single, insistent question playing like an endless loop deep in my mind.

Who am I . . . ? it was asking. *Who am I . . . ?*

IX

I SOUGHT THE answer to what for me was a growing enigma by taking refuge in the one place left to the dumb and outdated, the ill and aged and unwanted: the old pubs with their new blinking pokies and that dull stuttering sound peculiar to those souls lost within, spinning away to some outer universe that presages death.

In the course of my journeys through this flickering netherworld I asked any who were for the moment not gambling and whose problems seemed not as great as mine, to come drink with me and tell me what they made of my story and my pictures—photographic reproductions of the pictures from the Allport *Book of Fish*, tatty with wear—that I would then lay out on the bar to accompany my tale. And I would ask them questions.

A small number would think the pictures rough but not badly done, and the story—as I paraphrased it—entirely mad. Having acquired from the academics I had met in the course of my enquiries the habit of pointless argument, I would try to persuade my bar colleagues that perhaps in madness lies the truth, or in truth madness.

'Who was your mother and what secrets did she whisper in your infant ear?' I would demand of them. 'Was she a fish?' I would start yelling. '*Was she?*'

'The world was stupid in the first place,' someone said, not in reply but in derision, 'and it's only grown stupider ever since.'

'Travel with me into time,' I would cry out in answer to such, 'you dull mullet-eyed men and gurnard-gilded women! Journey with me far from this land of sodden beer mats and amnesiac entertainments to where your heart may be found! Where is the distant land which your soul wishes to traverse? What is it that beats in your belly and troubles your dreams? What shade of the past is it that torments you so? What manner of sea creature are you?'

But to tell the truth, they really weren't much help at all. They gave me no answer to any of my million and one questions. They took to shunning me even before I opened my mouth, scurrying past to spend the rest of their termination payouts and disability pensions and unemployment cheques, filling their polystyrene Coke cups to the brim with change for the pokies, and then sitting in front of the screens mesmerised at how their hard fates could be so precisely rendered in the perfect image of those spinning wheels.

The few who showed any interest would revile me and laugh at my observation that the meanings of Gould's *Book of Fish* were infinite, while others who knew me would tell me to go back to fooling Americans rather than fooling myself. A stranger jobbed me in the mug so hard that I fell off my chair. Everyone around only laughed as he then poured my beer over me, singing, '*Swim, little fishie! Swim back to the sea!*' all laughing their sad heads off, all, that is, with the exception of Mr Hung, who had just walked in.

Mr Hung put his hands under my arms and dragged me outside. As I lay groaning on the wet bitumen pavement, he felt inside my coat and, finding my wallet, emptied it of cash. He stood up, promised to return, Victor Hugo willing, with enough in winnings to start a fake painting racket. He dissolved into the stuttering neon inside.

To those who continued swimming past my prostrate

form into the gaming bar my pictures of silver dories and stargazers were, I realised, useless; as pointless to them as a row of two lemons and a pineapple, as disappointing as a busted flush. All the fish lacked in their eyes was the sign across their images announcing our mutual destiny in blinking letters—

'*GAME OVER.*'

X

AFTER MR HUNG had lost all my money he came back out, promised he would repay me soon, and took me to his Zinc Company home in Lutana. We entered quietly, as his wife and children were asleep. He disappeared into his kitchen to cook us some soup and left me in his small lounge-cum-dining room.

In a corner was a shrine to Victor Hugo. On a green velvet cloth there was propped a red plastic frame housing a photocopied lithograph of the great man, arrayed around whom were two unlit candles, four burnt incense sticks, several paperback novels, and some puckering apricots.

Next to the shrine sat an aquarium, in which Mr Hung kept a large pot-bellied seahorse and a similar creature, a good foot long, covered in delicate leaf-like fins, which he later told me was a weedy seadragon, both like pictures I had seen in the *Book of Fish*. I gazed on these alien beings that seemed to float so serenely.

Bony-ringed, tube-snouted, the pot-bellied seahorse's small fins fluttered as furiously as a blushing debutante's fan. He had pectoral fins on his cheeks with which he steered himself, a combination of side-burn and steering wheel. Mr Hung appeared next to me with two bowls of steaming soup. As he set these down on the table, he explained to me the seahorse's capacity to transform, how the male gave birth to hundreds of tiny seahorses that it had incubated in a brood pouch.

And then, as if on cue, the seahorse began to give birth. I watched, mesmerised, as before my eyes he jerked back and forth in an anxious pumping move-ment, and every minute or so another one or two black baby seahorses would shoot out of a vent in the centre of his swollen belly as he painfully flexed: tiny little black sticks which would immediately start swimming, with only their large eyes and long tube snouts recognisable, so many rising and falling curlicues. They were like Gould's lost words, and I felt a little like the poor seahorse at the end of his pro-longed labour, his formerly swollen belly now flaccid, was exhausted with all his awkward motions.

My gaze turned to the weedy seadragon, which was, I had to agree with Mr Hung, a magnificent creature. The weedy seadragon swam horizontally like a fish, rather than vertically like the seahorse, but like the sea-horse its movements were beautiful: it hovered up and down, forwards and sideways, like a hovercraft crossed with a helicopter, a jump-jet in rich mufti. Its luminous colouring was exquisite—its trunk pinkish red, purple blacks and silver blues spotted with yellow dots, billow-ing around which were its mauve leaves. Yet there was a serene grace about it that was also the oddest melancholy. As well as wonder, it shimmered sadness.

I was not then a weedy seadragon, and so I could not sense its terrible imprisonment, which was endless. I fancied I understood its horrific calmness; only a lifetime later would I truly comprehend the reason for such: that sense that all good and all evil are equally inescapable. Yet understanding all, the weedy seadragon seemed troubled not at not being understood.

I put my face to the glass, stared closer, trying to fathom its descending mystery. Then I imagined the weedy seadragon's beauty arose out of some evolutionary necessity; to attract mates possibly, or to merge with colourful reefs. Now I know beauty is life's revolt against life, that the seadragon was that most perfect of things, a song of itself.

There was a moment of transition that was abrupt: enlightenment is too smooth a word for the jolt I felt. It was a dream, but only much later was I to realise that there would be no awakening. With that long snout the seadragon was touching the other side of the glass to which my face was pressed. Its astonishing eyes rotated independently of each other, yet both were at different angles focused on me. What was it trying to tell me? Nothing? Something? I felt accused, guilty. I began whispering at the glass, hissing almost angrily. Was it asking of me questions to which I had no answer? Or was the seadragon saying to me in some diaphanous communication beyond words: *I shall be you.*

And shall I, I wondered, be you?

Other than the slightest movements of its leafy fins, I know the seadragon did not move while I muttered away, just stared out and through me in the most awful, knowing way with its unruly peepers.

I stopped talking.

Perhaps I stared too long.

Whatever, there was a momentary sense that was both a sickening vertigo and a wild freedom. I was without weight, support, structure; I was falling, tumbling, passing through glass and through water into that seadragon's eye while that seadragon was passing into me, and then I was looking out at that bedraggled man staring in at me, that man who would, I now had the vanity of hoping, finally tell my story.

THE KELPY

*The invasion of Australia—An unfortunate
misunderstanding—Barrels of black heads—The King
& I—The error of Jean-Babeuf Audubon—Birds as
burghers—Captain Pinchbeck & the French
Revolution—Black War—Clucas the* banditto—*His
perfidy—The Cockchafer—Tragic death of the machine
breaker—Bonfires of words.*

I

MY OWN SMALL part in the great invasion of Van
Diemen's Land as we then knew it—Tasmania, as its
native-born now prefer it, shameful of stories of the type
I tell—has hitherto not been recorded, but I believe my
role one worthy both of record & reflection.

Ever since that moment in 1803 when as a boy I first
leapt off the whale boat with Mr Banks' pistol sticking
in my back, just in case my resolve might falter, & fell
face first into the choppy waters of Risdon Cove, both
me & this country seem to have been in trouble.

I half-swam, half-staggered ashore with what I
thought was the red ensign of the Union, & planted it
most firmly on the beach & claimed the soil of the vast
nation that spread out before me in the name of the
glorious union that the ensign above me signified. But
when I dropped my salute & proudly looked upwards,

41

I saw fluttering what proved to be a yellowed sheet soiled with long clouds from Lieutenant Bowen's languid afternoons with the Samoan princess Lalla-Rookh.

I received seven years for theft of personal property, a further fourteen years for insubordination & twenty-eight years on top of that for mockery of the crown. It wasn't, it is true, the term of my natural life, which would have only been a kindness, but imprisonment forever.

And that's more or less how it's turned out. I did manage to go on the lam & escape the following year on a whaler to the Americas & from there finally back to England—where I lived the life of a rat under different names for the next twenty years, until I once more was apprehended & transported back here. Really the only thing that keeps me battling on now is not the thought that I will one day be released, but that they are finally going to do the decent thing & kill me like they should have done all those years ago.

Lieutenant Bowen, in his fury, took the subsequent arrival of a few hundred blacks out with their families hunting kangaroo as a declaration of war, & immediately ordered our cannons to be opened upon their clustering mob on the seashore, leaving some forty-five dead men, women & children on the sand, & who knows how many more whom their countrymen dragged off with them to die in their distant camps.

Mr Banks was delighted to find most of their black bodies still intact, as well as a good measure of artifacts—spears, fine shell necklaces, reed baskets, skins & the like—& while I was shackled to a tree to await my sentencing, my fellow convicts got on with the severing & pickling of the heads of the blacks. Mr Banks was well pleased with the half-dozen barrels of bobbing heads when they were finally presented to him, feeling, said he, that they could only greatly enhance our understanding of such misbegotten issue of the human race.

When the seawater laps up again at my festering ankles, I think back on those wallowing black heads with their milky eyes curding up in disbelief, & neither they nor I can see then just how much trouble black heads would later get me into. When I once more feel that sharp smarting around the scabby sores that cluster like so many oysters on my ankles beneath my chained iron basils, I know that the tide has turned. Then this cell, built at the base of sandstone cliffs below the high water mark—one of those infamous fish cells you have no doubt read about in those lying street pamphlets that circulate about the bushranger Matt Brady's cruel incarceration & subsequent villainous career—will fill to above my head.

Not that I will drown: I will, as others before me have, hang onto the bars above my head for several hours, holding myself up in the foot of air space that remains at the top of the cell at high tide. Sometimes I let go & allow myself to drift around my small kingdom, hoping I might die as I do so. Sometimes I count my blessings as I float: this twice-daily bath lately seems to have rid me of my lice, & the cell, while damp & prone to a briny, seaweedy odour, is not redolent of the dreadful stench of shit & rancid he-goat that normally prevails.

Two blessings: that's a sufficient challenge for my powers of mental arithmetic. And floating in the cold water, shivering & shuddering as if I were already in rehearsal for the old diddly-back-step off the gallows that awaits me, my mind sometimes breaks loose, & I am back happily painting the fish once more.

Call me what you will: others do, & it is of no matter to me; I am not what I am. A man's story is of little consequence in this life, a pointless carapace which he carries, in which he grows, in which he dies. Or so the porcupine fish said, & he is, as ever, already sticking his bloated head in where it's not wanted. What follows may or may not be my true story: either way it is of no great importance. Nevertheless with the porcupine fish dead & the old Dane now gone, I simply want to tell the tale of my paltry paintings, before I too join them.

It's not because I think the future is like this darkened, wet cell, on the damp sandstone walls of which you might scratch your name alongside so many others before you too disappear like the last tide, vanished; that vanity of thinking such words as these might at least remain as evidence, a flotsam of freedom dashed, that might endear my memory to posterity. I am, in any case, too far gone to place hope in such games. The truth is that at first I had a queer desire to confess something of it, & later it had simply become a bad habit, as inescapable & as wretched as scratching my licy balls.

Not that I would want you to think that I am not well looked after. Far from it. Sometimes they bring me a taj of skilly & rancid pickled pork fat in a cup or a bowl, & they throw it at me. Sometimes I smile back, &

if & when I am feeling especially energetic, I'll lob a turd I've kept especially for the occasion in return. Sometimes after such a happy exchange they give me a good walloping as well, & I thank them for that too, because it shows they still care a little. Thank you very much, dearies, I say, thank you thank you thank you. They laugh about that too, & between the beatings & the turd-tossing I can tell you we really do all get along splendidly. 'That's the good thing about an island prison colony,' I whisper to my cell door, 'we are all in this shit together, all the turnkeys & redcoats & even the Commandant himself. Aren't we? Aren't we?'

'*No!*' yells the turnkey Pobjoy from the other side as he slides the latch, but I won't hear him, because he's not allowed into the story yet, & once he is, like me, I promise you he won't escape either.

I know I ought make it clear from the beginning why I have come to be painting fish, & why the fish paintings came to be of such importance to me, but really, nothing is clear to me any more, & the whole matter seems beyond comprehension, far less explanation. I can tell you that there are no pictures of convicts ever made at this settlement, & that the very making of such pictures is forbidden upon the pain of the severest punishment.

It is, if you ponder it only for a moment, a curious fact that no visual record will survive this time & place, not one single painting of the maimed, of the broken, even of the Commandant. There are, it is true, the written records of the settlement contained in its great Registry—a mysterious archive whose location is kept secret from the convicts lest they try to tamper with their records. In this reputedly labyrinthine repository, it is said the details of every convict & every event of the island's past are meticulously recorded, no detail too insignificant to elude cataloguing & chronicling.

But I won't pretend that my fish are some alternative, upside-down Registry. My ambitions are neither gargantuan nor comprehensive.

At best a picture, a book are only open doors inviting you into an empty house, & once inside you just have to make the rest up as well as you can. All I can show you with any conviction is a little of what happened to me here—the whys & the wherefores, that's so much waffle for the judges with their black caps & powdered wigs, for the criticasters & their like: guilt, sin, motivation, inspiration, what is good, what is bad—who knows? Who cares? All I can say is that between the beatings & the high tides the turnkey Pobjoy has brought me some cheap parchment stolen from the Registry on which he has instructed me to paint Constable-like scenes of bucolick bliss: all happy haymaking & rustick idiots like Pobjoy himself, & wagons crossing sun-dappled English streams, which he can then sell or trade with others.

The gawky Pobjoy stands on the frontier between men & giraffes; he is so tall that when he comes into the cell he has to bend over nearly double, so that it seems it is he prostrating himself to me, rather than—as it must be in our situation—the other way around. I have to bow so low to get beneath Pobjoy that I am almost blowing bubbles in the slimy rock pools at our feet, disturbing my friends that cluster in the darkness there, the crabs & periwinkles & mussels that share this demimonde with me.

'*Thank you thank you thank you*,' I say to all those who like me live in the sea slime, & set to work as quick as buggery before the water rises, because each day I have to complete not one painting but three tasks: first, a painting of pastoral pieties for Pobjoy; second, a painting of a fish for me; & third—the job with which I am always running behind time, & ever failing to say all the things I need & wish—these notes that are to accompany my fish.

II

GIVEN THE KEEPING of any private accounts of the island by a convict is an offence for which even more savage punishment than that meted out for painting is reserved, I have to proceed carefully. Each day Pobjoy takes my paints & paper away with his newly completed Constable fake, checks that not too much paint seems to have disappeared, & that the amount of paper left equates with what I tell him I have wasted on rough cartoons & then used to wipe my bum—a rare privilege Pobjoy in his infinite generosity occasionally affords a craggy-arsed convict such as me, on the grounds that as an Artist my delicate orifices are unaccustomed to indignity.

Each day I purloin a few more sheets for the purposes of my book of fish which I carefully hide, & each day I rearrange prominently in the cell corner where the light hits as the cell door opens the same single crumpled sheet of paper kept specially for the purpose, which I have streaked artfully with some particularly strong greens & browns. In its moist colourings it serves as corroboration of my tale of personal hygiene & is, I believe, consistent with both the facts of my diet & my complaints to Pobjoy of bad gripe in the guts. Mercifully, Pobjoy has not yet been tempted to investigate the matter further.

Having paint but no ink I have to use whatever is at hand to write—today, for example, I have knocked a few scabs off my elbow & am dipping my quill carved from a shark's rib into the blood that oozes slowly forth to write what you are now reading. Blood's thicker than water, as they say, but then so too is porridge, & I don't attach any more symbolic significance to what I am doing than I do to rolled oats. If I had a bottle of good Indian ink, I'd be a hell of a lot happier, & in somewhat less pain. On the other hand, mine is far from a black & white story, so perhaps putting it down in a scarlet fashion is not so inappropriate. Please don't be appalled, compared to most of the vile crap that comes out of my body these days, the mossy mucus & yellow pus & runny shit, my blood really is quite pure & beautiful, & it reminds me that something is always pure & beautiful, if you will just look beneath the scabs & sores.

In any case, colour is a tragedy that should not be taken seriously: 'That God is Colouring Newton does show,' wrote Ackermann's woolly cobber Billy Blake. Even Billy Blake's wife never knew him to wash & his opinions could sometimes be as ripe as his presence. As far as I am concerned, ever since Newton broke white light with his prism into multifarious colours, the rainbow's divided light is for me nothing other than this ridiculous fallen world.

When the water rises to my belly, I hide my fish & these bloody thoughts, then yell at the door until Pobjoy comes to fetch his convict-Constable. And what a splendid spot I have for my book of fish! I hide it in a niche at the top of the cell that opens out from a thin crack behind the first row of sandstone blocks into a space as wide as three loaves of bread. Sometimes when I am floating around my cell at high tide, my pointy honker nearly bumping on the ceiling rafters, I try to imagine I am in that niche with my book of fish, imagine it as a home closed off from the world, a home into which I have escaped. I think Pobjoy knows but chooses not to: it is my one recompense for the convict-Constable he takes from me each day. Or maybe he's just worried about hitting his head if he raises it to look.

But Pobjoy knows I am painting fish, I am sure of it.

III

THE KING, WITH whom I share my cell, betrays nothing to Pobjoy. In truth the King betrays next to nothing about anything, says nothing, is next to nothing, & devotes his time to silent communion with the angels. For which I am grateful.

He is a most remarkable man, the King. His presence is large, inescapable. You can feel him all over you.

Sometimes I think of him only as a creeping slime rising up the walls. At other times I feel an odd fondness & my admiration for his very considerable achievements is unquestioned. He grows daily not only in my estimation, but also, it has to be admitted, in his very being, becoming more & more corpulent, yet remaining in his movements gentle & poetick: the King rolls, the King bobs, the King moves in waves. How he does it, this growth, this dignity, I can't say. The rest of us shrivel & waste like weevil-hollowed husks on what little they feed us, but the King just inflates. As a companion I find him sage-like, inscrutable. I sometimes think his increasingly buoyant dimensions may indicate there is more of the Occidental Divine about him than I have previously suspected.

In argument the King sets an admittedly wide compass, allowing his opponent—me—to play out my own line of reasoning so far it unravels & snags on its own impossibilities & contradictions. It may be objected that he says nothing new, but he communicates it wonderful well.

An example: one day, admittedly as a needle, I put it to him that Scottish Presbyterians had produced numerous works of great theological worth. Typically he was some time replying, but I knew he was thinking, There is not one work of theology worthy of the name produced by those non-conforming oat-eaters. I myself had no idea whatsoever, but by a lucky coincidence I had noticed in one of the Surgeon's catalogues sent him from London bookshops, the title *Aberdeen on the Sumerians*. Armed with this slight, possibly irrelevant knowledge, I stuck the knife full in: 'Perchance you have read Aberdeen's magnificent discourse on the Sumerians?'

He said nothing, admitted nothing. It was an accusation, all the more telling for remaining unspoken. I felt a heat rising & then went full red in the chops, & it was all over, we both knew it, I was exposed as a fraud, yet typically he spoke not a jot more on the subject, & has never raised it since.

There is about him something majestick which produces effects of great regality. I have seen even Pobjoy stunned by the mere sense of the King's presence, though Pobjoy of course fails to see what I do; still he wrenches his nose & lemons his face & I am sure he shrivels his arsehole, as you do only on two occasions: when in the presence of a great power or of a terrible stench.

I would, it is true, like the King more if he were a little more outgoing, more easy with others. He makes no effort with Pobjoy, & though I urge him on about the obvious benefits of a social life, he has no desire to be part of either my turd-tossings or Pobjoy's beatings. Still, such is his choice, & I know he has his reasons. An oak cannot bend like a willow. It is things other than hail-fellow-well-met falsely fawning that mark the King out as remarkable.

Another example: his complexion. Most of us go paler than the Surgeon's white lead in these cells. But the King, manifesting some regal hereditary disorder, some Hapsburgian pigmentation perhaps, grows daily darker, his skin blacker, & more recently, disturbingly greener. But he suffers not to suffer: no word of complaint or distress passes his lips.

As I drift around our wretched cell, I sometimes look back with—well let's just admit it—an *envy* of my life at that time I arrived here. Because I have come to believe that trajectory is everything in this life, & though at the time it felt anything other than promising, the trajectory of my life was that of a cannon ball fired into a sewer—hurtling through shit, but hurtling nevertheless.

In Pobjoy's dull dog-like eyes I can see he knows it's the second time around for me on the fish; he can see that I paint from my memory of my first book of fish that was so cruelly taken from me. But what Pobjoy doesn't know is *why* I paint them. What Pobjoy doesn't know is what I am about to write here, an annal of a life etched in blood.

IV

BEFORE I BEGAN writing, I asked the King:

'How might I commence such a mighty chronicle? By singing a new genesis? By singing of fish & of the man, fated to be an exile, who long since left the land of the English & came to Van Diemen's Land to this island gaol; & how great was his suffering by land & by sea at the hands of gods thought long dead because his crimes demanded that he suffer retribution in the same coin?'

No. I could see the King thought it better to cack your dacks & smear it over the page than to write such rubbish, for who would ever wish to sing this country anew?

The King knows as well as I—indeed better—that this place & its pathetick people will be far happier being eaten up over & over again by the same dreary songs & pictures of the Old World, telling them the same dreary story I have been hearing ever since I went the fall at the Bristol Assizes—you are guilty & you are to blame & you are less—& you will hear all the new singers & all the new painters saying the same nonsense as the black-wigg'd judge. Long after these bars have fallen away, they'll sing & paint the bars anew & imprison you & yours forever after, gleefully singing & painting: *Less! Less! Less!*

'Artists! Ha! Turnkeys of the heart!' I roared at the King. 'Poets! Ha! Dobbing dogs of the soul!—what here I write, & what here I paint are Experiment & Prophecy—do not judge any of it by the shorten'd yard-stick of what they call Literature & Art, those sick & broken compasses.'

To clarify my point a little further, I threatened the King in the manner I had found to be so effective with Pobjoy, & seeing what I had in my hand ready to lob should he say a word in criticism, he ventured no folly of comment. Still, as always, he had a point, so instead of singing a new country & noble race into being, I began with the dirty truth as follows:

I am William Buelow Gould—convicted murderer, painter & numerous other unimportant things. I am compelled by my lack of virtue to tell you that I am the most untrustworthy guide you will ever trust, a man dead before his time, a forger convicted in the gloomy recesses of the Bristol Assizes on that muggy afternoon of 10 July 1825, the judge noting, if nothing, else, my name was good for the Newgate Calendar along with all the other condemned men, before doffing his black cap & sentencing me to death by hanging.

In that courtroom there was a lot of dark wood trying to take itself seriously. In order to lighten all that sorry timber up I should have told it the story I am telling you now, of how life is best appreciated as a joke when you discover all Heaven & all Hell are implicit in the most insignificant: a soiled sheet, a kangaroo hunt, the eyes of a fish. But I said nothing, grossly overestimating the power of silence. The judge, believing me penitent, commuted my sentence to transportation to Van Diemen's Land.

Quarter-flash, half-hopeless, not quite the full bob Billy Gould, who was once pompously ordered to depict the great sea god Proteus who can—as the Surgeon with his dog-Latin was wont to remind me—miraculously assume the form of any aquatic creature. I was to paint fish, you see, all manner of sea life: sharks, crabs, octopuses, squid & penguins. But when I finished this work of my life, I stood back & to my horror saw all those images merge together into the outline of my own face.

Was I Proteus or was Proteus only another mug like me? Was I immortal or merely incompetent?

Because you see I was born not an evil man, but simply the bastard issue of a fair day's passion, a folly, a three-thimble trick like my present name, & beneath whichever one you lift there is . . . nothing!

A fate that leads a French Jewish weaver to an Irish fair is curious, but it is nevertheless Fate that then saw the weaver—'father' seems to me rather too generous a description—struck down with apoplexy at the height of his rude passion in that barn, thinking he was going to ride a cock-horse all day long. But you see there he was, suddenly struck dead in the saddle, beyond life & gone from this tale as soon as he had come. The woman whom he had met no more than half an hour before, laughing in the furmity tent over the rum-laced porridge she had there partaken of liberally, was now too frightened to scream, to curse or cry. She just pushed him off & wiped herself on his fine fustian waistcoat which had first so impressed her, such a dandy-o he had seemed, what with his clothes & long come-hither eyelashes & Frenchie accent, & she ran out to wander morose until she came upon a large crowd in a field.

Being short as a spud (&, or so I was told, of similar demeanour, with a mouth like a spinning jenny) she could not see what it was that had caught the mob's attention, & being suddenly curious, perhaps as some sort of diversion from what she had just experienced, she pushed & shoved until she burst out of the crowd to see the front of a makeshift wooden stage.

The babble of the crowd unexpectedly died away & she turned back around to see what it was—to see whether it was indeed her—that had quietened them so. She saw the gaze of all the people behind her focused not on her at all, but looking over her & up much higher, & she twisted back around & following their line of sight upwards saw that the stage was in fact a temporary gallows.

At that very moment she heard the quick creak of the trap door open & saw a skinny man in a long dirty smock with a noose around his neck & a limp cod in his hands fall from the sky in front of her. As his body reached the bottom of the drop, taut rope conspiring with the sudden weight of the falling body to break his neck, she heard the small but undeniable sound of bone snapping. Afterwards she dreamt the skinny man opened his mouth as he fell, & what came forth was not a cry but a shimmering shaft of blue light. She watched the blue light fly across the field & leap into her mouth, open in astonishment.

The wretched woman became convinced that she had been taken possession of by the condemned man's evil spirit, & gave up on life, surviving only long enough to deliver me into the world & then to the poorhouse, believing that as I was born blue I must needs be the very embodiment of that evil spirit.

I grew up in the poorhouse full of old women, some mad, some loving, some neither, & all as full of tales of the dead & the living as the slops clothing was of lice, for that was all they had in that dark, dank poorhouse — lice & stories, & both left me with a bad itch & scabs that turned into dirty little scars. I grew up with these tales (including their favourite of the weaver dying on the job & the gallows man, his limp cod, the blue light & me) & little else to sustain me.

The old poorhouse priest for a time mistook me for a scholar. He used to read to me from a Calendar of the

Saints, in which for every day there was a saint whose life was an exemplary tale of suffering, torture & original punishments; a fabulous catalogue of virgin martyrs whose voluptuous but eternally pure breasts were smote off by lecherous Roman prefects; medieval monks whose levitating became so annoying they were tied down so as not to disturb the mealtimes of their fellow brothers; anchorites who became famous for flagellating themselves for forty days & nights merely for farting. Really, nothing could have prepared me better for the reality of Van Diemen's Land.

The priest supported me with his teaching like the rope had supported the gallows man. He taught me the 26 letters of the alphabet & would have me read aloud the Bible & Prayer Book as he washed the soles of my feet, my skinny calves, all the while whispering, 'Tell me when your seed is about to spill, tell me, please.'

I would just reply, '*A-B-C-D-E-*' etc, etc, & imagine all God's words were to be had in these letters, & He could just muddle them up into whatever Perfect Prayer & Holy Scripture he wished, if I could just send up those 26 letters each day to Him, *A-B-C-D-E*, etc, etc, but then when the priest ran his chapped hand like broken chalk sticks up the inside of my thigh I kicked him with my washed foot fair in his gummy gob.

The old priest cried out in pain & hissed, 'God may have your letters but the Devil has your tongue—you are no scholar but Beelzebub himself!' & would have not a bar of me or my feet ever after.

One of the old women was so impressed, she hated

that priest so, she showed me her library of a dozen 6-penny pamphlets she was allowed to keep as a special privilege, & she thereafter lent me first one then another.

I began to worry that each night as I slept the letters in the 6-penny pamphlets might rearrange themselves into new shapes & meanings within the blue covers, for in them I discovered that God did indeed mix those 26 letters to mean whatever He wished, & that therefore all books were holy. If God did indeed have a Mystery as the priest had insisted, then perhaps it was in the on-going itch of all those stories.

Such 6-penny books can be had at any market stall, yet I loved them no less, but more for belonging to all. Everything from *Old Widow Hickathrift's Nursery Rhymes* to *Aesop's Fables* did so delight me that long before I knew of the Bard & Pope & Frenchie Enlightenment, they were all Literature & all Art for me. Even now oranges & lemons & the bells of Saint Clements riding a cock-horse to Banbury Cross are to me true poetry that has cast a spell I cannot escape.

Then the priest conspired with the beadle to have me sold off to a stonemason, for whose heavy work my wretched body was unfit, & when I ran away across the water the stonemason must have thought himself well rid of such a clawscrunted rascal, for he made no attempt to get me back.

At first I survived in London by selling myself to those who I thought ought pay to wash my feet & giving myself to those for whom I felt pity. Deciding who should pay & who shouldn't made me feel I had some power, but I had nothing really, nothing but rotten inconsolable itches covering my heart ever more & more dirty little scars that kept multiplying to cover such nameless shame as was mine.

For a time I roamed & robbed, feeling with these ventures that the dirty little scars had been covered over by bigger feelings of excitement & fear & pleasure. Then I was a Villain, you see, a truly haughty Bad Man, most proud of myself. I went hither & thither, at first in search of gold & glory, & then in search of an explanation, & I was greedy for all, but only because the capture of any might prove I lived & was not a nameless man born of a nameless woman in a nameless town whose only sustenance was itchy stories that had to be teased by gummy old women out of oakum & scabby songs stolen from God out of 6-penny pamphlets.

I saw all this & that & much else besides in the morning of my life & many things shocking, near as fabulous, but of an evening there was not one among my new-found world of blue-gin riders & gaberlunzie men & pimps & swing-swang girls & their hanky thieves who could answer my insistent *Why?* which I came to know as the most stupid & pointless & destructive of questions. Deciding that nothing benefits a man other than his own earthly endeavours, I abandoned my uncertain search for an answer to a question that made no sense. I grew Old World-weary & late one evening in a grog shop with some Spitalfields girls with whom I was extolling the virtues of 6-penny pamphlets I found myself agreeing—after a few hard cuffs around the ears & reasonable threats of far worse injury from a press gang, the cream of the English nation—that in truth I had actually all along wanted to join Lieutenant Bowen's mission as a deckhand to assist in civilising Van Diemen's Land. In this way I was persuaded to venture to the New World where Progress & the Future are said to reside.

V

AT FIRST MY painting was an accident & later it came to be the only thing I could do half well. I reckoned it easy work, & by the time I realised it wasn't, it was too late to learn any other trade. It was in the New World, while on my surreptitious return from my successful if misunderstood invasion of Australia, that I met up in the swamps of Louisiana with a Creole who in his own way was responsible for my passion for fish. His name was Jean-Babeuf Audubon & he was a plain-looking man, short, whose most distinctive feature was the large lace cuffs he insisted on wearing everywhere, & which were in consequence always frayed & filthy.

Jean-Babeuf Audubon persuaded me that being in my twenties, I was obviously a man in the prime of his life who would wish to secure his lot against a hostile future by investing the small capital I had brought with me in a business venture he was pursuing with an Englishman called George Keats—running a steamboat in a tiny Kentucky hamlet. His purchase of some very fine frock coats immediately after I handed over my money did nothing to lessen my belief in the dreams of this bedraggled quail of a man, for like all true villains I was credulous in the face of any idea larger than obvious & immediate theft.

Though we all wanted to be Capitalists, it was through Audubon that I was to learn about painting, for Audubon's business was as implausible as his stories of his father—like mine, supposedly French—his purportedly the Dauphin, who under an alias fought with Washington at Valley Forge. We saw ourselves as hardheads & roundly laughed at Keats' story of his dreamy brother John who wished to be a poet in the Old World & who, unlike us, was never going to amount to anything. But no measure of hardheading, of Capitalist Desire, could help when the steamboat's boiler blew up, & the local farmers preferred to use the traditional poled & horse-pulled barges to Audubon & Keats' folly, & the itinerant niggers & backwoodsmen preferred to walk than pay the money we had to charge not to go under.

But the lack of interest in the boat & its consequent lack of movement did at least enable time for other things, mainly outings into the woods where we'd shoot birds & bring them back. I'd watch as Audubon wired their bloodied corpses up to form dramatick shapes of ascent & descent, stretching wings this way & that, & then sketched & painted these bedraggled tormented forms as beautiful birds.

I thought him an exceptional painter & said so, but he was ungracious in the face of compliments & in his heavy Creole accent berated me. He disliked art. It was, said he, the name given to paintings after they had been stolen & sold. He was only a painter of birds.

I learnt also—though more from the birds Jean-Babeuf Audubon failed to shoot than from Jean-Babeuf Audubon himself—the importance of always being a moving target in this life, for there is nothing that people love more than their opposite. Thus in America I learnt the value of being an underworld Englishman, while later, when back in underworld England, I played upon being an American adventurer, & here in Van Diemen's Land they seem to like nothing more than the Artist From Elsewhere—by which, of course, I mean Europe—no matter how mediocre. If I ever get back to Europe I will, I suppose, feel compelled to play the part of the wronged, wide-eyed rustick colonial.

Audubon knew a great deal about birds & their customs & society, & very neat & hard & not fuzzy or soft at all were his bird pictures. As if from under the feathered wings of their mother, Audubon's birds would emerge from beneath his dirty lace cuffs, fully formed, beautiful, sorrowful, alive. From Audubon I learnt to search the animal being painted for its essential humours, its pride or its earnestness or its savagery, its idiocy or its madness. Because to him nothing was ever simply a specimen: all life presented him with an encyclopaedia of subjects, & the only troublesome task—and he conceded it sometimes came less than easy—was to understand the truth that the subject represented & then get it down, as honestly & accurately as possible. To do this—to distil into a single image the spirit of a whole life—he needed stories, & his stroke of genius was to find his stories not in the trees or forests or bayous, but in the new American towns & cities

erupting like a fatal attack of pellagra all over that land,
in the dreams & hopes of those around him.

Audubon painted marriages, courting, all the vain
pretence of polite society, & all of it was birds & all of
his birds sold & it was all up a very clever thing that he
was doing, a natural history of the new burghers. I
could, I suppose, paint the fish in some similar imitation of the schools in which the local free settlers swim.
But the fish come to me in the true condition of this
life: alone, fearful, with no home, nowhere to run &
hide. And if I were to place two of my fish together
would I then have a school? Would I have the appearance of the ocean beneath the waves which only the
native women diving for crayfish see?

No.

I would only have two fish: each alone, fearful,
united solely in the terror of death I see in their eyes.
Audubon painted the dreams of a new country for
which there is always a prospective purchaser; my fish
are the nightmare of the past for which there is no market. What I am painting is not clever like the work of
Jean-Babeuf Audubon, nor will it ever prove popular: it
is a natural history of the dead.

In the end the boat was burnt, we said by angry creditors, they said by us: whatever, we were all ruined, &
the last I saw of Jean-Babeuf Audubon was him waving
a sooty lace cuff out of a slit in the local lockup where he
had been incarcerated as a debtor. But this time no
birds magically appeared. Keats, who was sitting outside, was reading aloud for Audubon's benefit some of
his brother's lamentable verse on the treacherous

promise of the New World—verse I did not think much inclined to cheer Jean-Babeuf Audubon, who in his cell was pleading with his captors, yelling in his deplorable Creole accent: 'I ham Eenglesh caportlist. I ham.'

Outside, Keats paid no heed to such argument, declaiming: 'Their bad flowers have no scent, their birds no sweet song.'

'A men of the on-ore,' the aggrieved Audubon was shouting, 'and shell pay—if cursed.'

'And great unerring Nature,' continued Keats, 'for once seems wrong.'

VI

TWENTY YEARS PASSED.

There ought be a full reckoning of my life through that time, but I have just read to the King what I have so far written. Tellingly, chillingly, he has offered no comment. His natural courtesy forbids open criticism, but I caught his opaque eye & his contempt is transparent, his wisdom—as always—instructive.

I can see he is saving me from the folly of recording what he &, I suspect, you have no interest whatsoever in hearing—what happened to Billy Gould in those years. You may think every moment of Billy Gould's life has equal weight, but the King knows that to be untrue. Most of it passed as in a miserable dream that dissolves upon waking, because it is too immemorable to recall, beyond its ending in arrest for forgery in Bristol in 1825.

I wasn't a forger, & I wasn't happy being accused as

such. I was a Villain on the lam who had once painted, & I was insulted that anyone would accuse me of stooping so low as counterfeiting Bank of Bristol notes. Still, having always maintained that the best way of battling power is to agree, upon being sentenced to be transported to Van Diemen's Land for forgery, I became a forger. After all, what else could I do?

Claiming to be an Artist seemed consistent with the lie of my conviction, & offered the prospect of a better billet than labouring in a chain gang & made me look like something other than the common criminal I was, & that is the only forgery I was until then ever guilty of—forging myself anew as an Artist.

But it didn't begin so well.

My first attempt at a painting, admittedly somewhat derivative of a lithograph of Robespierre I chanced across in a pamphlet illustrating the horrors of the French Terror, was of Captain Pinchbeck, the commander of the convict transport, who had requested his own portrait upon discovering my trade. My picture so angered the captain that he had me clapped back in chains for the rest of the boat's six-month journey to Australia. I tried to make it up by then rendering him as the more manly Danton, but all up it seemed to the captain only a further, & in this case, unforgivable insult.

Too late, as I was being brought up from the stinking hold, did I discover from the mate that the captain had for some time suffered the ignominy of being cuckolded by a French whaler.

I began condemning the pandering ponces of other races to Captain Pinchbeck, only to be told by him to shut up, whilst he lectured me on the horrors of the French—most particularly their dreaded *noyades*. These had taken place at the height of the Terror in the hulks of old slave ships that were filled with rebels from the Vendée & sunk of an evening in the harbour of Nantes, to be each morning ingeniously refloated, emptied of their watery corpses, & refilled with more rebels of whom there was an inexhaustible supply, because, as Captain Pinchbeck put it, tyranny will always bring forth its opponents as the rain does grass.

When finally finished with telling this interminable tale he had me taken to what he called his *petite noyade*, the perforated coffin-like box in which men were locked then dragged behind the boat's wake, so that I could discover what it really felt like to be French.

I would like to say that when I was then dropped for a full minute into the Pacific Ocean inside that bubbling black wet box of slimy oak, I had the first intimation of what the true consequence of Art for my future was going to be. But that would be untrue. I merely resolved to look for templates other than those of Frenchie troublemakers & pants-men, & held my breath until I reckoned I was about to burst.

When I was pulled back out of the water the captain told me that if I ever painted him again he would personally feed me to those he called the sea-lawyers—the sharks that trailed our boat. As I was dragged out of the *petite noyade*, a convict constable gave me a good kicking in full view of the captain. Curling up into a ball, it occurred to me that Captain Pinchbeck might just be wrong on the matter of tyranny, that for every tyrant born, so too are a thousand men willing to be enslaved, & that whoever the rebels of the Vendée were, they deserved to be drowned for entirely misunderstanding this truth of human nature.

I don't want you to think because of this that my reinvention of myself as a painter was a total lie. After all, I had watched Jean-Babeuf Audubon work, & had once even finished off for him a pair of bald eagles that he had to get done in a hurry to honour a pressing debt. There was my time spent with the engraver Shuggy Ackermann, but that didn't seem to count for anything more than the possibility of further criminal charges. As well, I suppose I could mention my half-year of Potteries experience, but I don't feel like going into that just now, because it makes me all sad thinking of how I had once danced the Old Enlightenment with such gusto, & now have only Widow Thumb & her Four Daughters to play with.

Elsewhere there may have been other prospects with both work & women, & frankly I would have welcomed them. But I had to take work as it came, to learn the rules of my art as best I could from such bad experience.

Upon arrival in that grotty modern world of Van Diemen's Land in the stinking late summer heat, all hideous new sandstone warehouses & customs houses & chain gangs & redcoats, I was assigned to Palmer the coachbuilder in Launceston, what passes as the capital of the island's north. For him I painted shiny family crests on coaches, inventing coats of arms for the bastard issue of the New World that wished to dress up in the absurd livery of the Old. Lions rampant & oaks evergreen & red hands & swords ever erect mixed with no good reason & little need for explanation on our coach doors, underlined with absurd Latin mottos provided by an Irish cleric doing time for bestiality: *Quae fuerent vitia, mores sunt* (What were once vices are now manners); *Vedi Hobarti e poi muouri* (See Hobart & die); *Ver non semper viret* (Spring does not always flourish). It was my first great artistick lesson: colonial art is the comic knack of rendering the new as the old, the unknown as the known, the antipodean as the European, the contemptible as the respectable.

VII

I ABSCONDED AFTER six months. I made my way south, heading back to Hobart Town by shanks's pony, with the hope of escaping by boat from there as I had two decades previously. The long weary war with the savages was still far from over, the savages showing such a craftiness in their attacks that many colonists—their dwellings at the edge of great black forests where fear naturally engenders suspicion —believed them sorcerers. The back country was *their* country, but upon it was a plague of escapees & bushranger gangs that shot redcoats & redcoat patrols that shot bushrangers & vigilantes out for the pleasure of shooting up some savages or, failing that, anyone.

The occasional armed compound that passed for a homestead was even more fearful. I approached one in the hope of a night's shelter & was only saved from the wild dogs set on me by the warning musket shots fired from slits in the great outer wall.

I resolved that rather than continue making my way by skirting the highway through the midlands, I would take the longer but far safer route down the coastline of the east. I walked to where green sea broke light into a shrapnel of silver & scattered it over glistening white beaches, along which I often came upon the bleaching bones & skulls of savages slaughtered by sealers in their raids for black women. Such a sight was a peculiar comfort, for it meant the beaches were safe for me to travel, for except in the remote west the savages now tended to avoid the coast. Still of a night I made no fire for fear of the savages finding & killing me, though it was early spring & the frost bitter & hard.

Four days out of Launceston & hopelessly lost I fell in with a man who said his name was Roaring Tom Weaver. He tried to interfere with me on our first night but seemed not put out when I told him to leave me alone, him replying I wasn't really his sort of molly-boy anyway.

Upon being shot at by a whaling party foraging for water the next afternoon, we headed inland. We followed the stars into the night but then it clouded over & we finally halted on a rocky outcrop. It was thick with flies, but we were lost & too tired to continue. We slept like dead men. When the sun rose it was to reveal that the flies had as their home the sloughing corpse of a black woman who lay not a hundred yards down from where we had stopped the night.

She had been staked out on the ground, abused in a

most dreadful fashion & then left to die. Parts of her shimmered white with the light of the sun playing on moving maggots. Roaring Tom began to wail & screech. He was a wild animal & it was a long time before I could have him halt his awful keening.

That night, by a miserable fire we were too afraid to feed with anything other than the smallest of sticks, we said nothing. The following day we hit on open country, a delightful parkland beneath a sky so perfect a china blue—a sky the likes of which I never saw in the Old World—that it seemed brittle, as though it might at any moment break apart & reveal something awful behind all that glorious light.

We smelt the smoke of the burning shepherd's hut long afore we saw that bark & daub hut's smouldering ruins & the charred corpse of its tenant being pulled out of the ash on a long piece of bark by his mate, who could not stop weeping. The weeping man was an emancipist who had a backblock in the next valley & sometimes came over to see his cobber the shepherd, both being Roscommon men. He had arrived too late: the savages had speared his friend in the hut & then set it alight, leaving him there to be burnt alive. Upon him firing on them the savages scattered. The emancipist pointed to a fallen tree, behind which lay a savage he had shot. He had never killed a man before & it was unclear what upset him more, the death of his friend or this killing of the savage.

Seven days out from Launceston we fell in with Clucas, a barbarous man who had been doing work for the free settler Batman, helping round up the savages.

He could, said he, talk their cant from his time sealing & knew something of their ways. We were defenceless, hungry & again lost. Clucas carried a pistol & a musket he could flourish, wallaby meat & flour he was willing to share, & he knew the way to Hobart. He dressed like so many of the Diemenese *banditti*: coarse-cut kangaroo & tiger skins roughly stitched together, a tiger-skin cap on his long-haired head. He happily talked of bursting in on the camp fires of the savages on Batman's instructions & shooting up to a dozen or more & then cooking them on their own fire. He said he was no beast like some sealers he had met on the islands in Bass Strait, such as Munro, who sliced off part of the thigh & the ears of his woman, Jumbo, & made her eat them as punishment for trying to escape. When we told him of the staked woman he was for a moment reflective, & then laughing said some gins were right Amazons & had it coming.

Camping just down from Black Charlie's Opening there was a wild thunderstorm, we could see the plains of Pittwater & beyond Hobart's snowcapped Mount Wellington lit by great lightning strikes. Wet through & miserable we struck out before dawn. A little after sunrise we came upon what was once a great peppermint gum tree, a good two yards in diameter at its base. Broken by the violence of a white lightning strike, the rest of the tree—its trunk & all its branches—were shattered in to a great mess of white & black fragments thrown up to two hundred yards away. Everywhere broken timber, woodchips & sticks, great boughs & tiny shavings. There was no way of telling how big &

wonderful that tree of Van Diemen's Land once was, now broken into a million splinters.

VIII

UPON MAKING IT to Hobart under cover of a chill night, the *banditto* Clucas arranged us a hideout in a sly-grog shop in the wharf area of Wapping run by a Liverpool maroon called Capois Death. He promised to find a place for us both on a departing whaler within the month.

Two days later we were picked up by the wallopers on Clucas' information. Roaring Tom Weaver turned out to be a runaway catamite & was sentenced to fourteen years retransportation to Sarah Island. I was nabbed in the *Shades* taproom painting a mural of bald eagles garlanded with wisteria to pay off a considerable rum tab. I was sentenced to three months on the chain gang at the falsely named Bridgewater, dragging boulders in wooden sleds to create a causeway across the Derwent River. Within a week Lieutenant Perisher, the officer in charge of the causeway, had me taken out of irons & hired me out to paint portraits of officers' & free settlers' wives & other prey freshly killed—weird kangaroos & emus with a pheasant drawn from memory draped scarf-like over tables.

In those days the muddy streets & stinking rookeries of Hobart Town almost seemed something of an artist's colony with more than a few working there under government patronage: there was Bock the abortionist, whose hands had once administered mercury draughts to young fearful women, now painting the colony's complacent rulers; there was Wainewright the murderer, who was as adept at pencilling sketches of virginal maidens as he had once been with poisoning his wife with strychnine-laced laudanum; & Savery the forger, who wrote mannered trash about the colony that flattered its audience with so many imitations of their own stupidity. One day you might see one or another of these artists on a chain gang, breaking rocks with a napping hammer down the Salamanca wharves; the next week they were bustling out of an upper Macquarie Street parlour with pad & paints, trying to look oh-so-very much the Professional Aesthete, but—in rotten old twill trousers & coarse old canary coats, with mangy hair rough-hacked & poxed skin stubbly—inevitably failing.

I, to the contrary, playing the part of the jobbing journeyman, doffed my cap & never pretended to be other than where I was on the Van Diemonian ladder—at the bottom. Competition wasn't so fierce, my manner was not so threatening, & a few holes in the market opened for me.

IX

I BEGAN TO find my services in demand: the painting of portraits of milky-eyed patriarchs on their deathbed; of infant corpses for grieving free-settler families, in which I shared with the undertaker that most hopeless of tasks, trying to discover the shape of a soft smile on those pallid faces; prize stallions, boars & quick sketches of naked women in the manner of melting love pictures —luridly welcoming a young-man-as-bull entering them, trying for a stylised rather than honest line.

The rate of pay was not entirely favourable: Lieutenant Perisher took nine-tenths of every commission. Still, it was easier & warmer work than dragging boulders, barefooted & chained, through the icy mud & hoarfrost & mist of Bridgewater. And, whatever Lieutenant Perisher's sins, he turned a blind eye to my nightly outings.

My subsequent time in Hobart Town I now can recall only as a tedious repetition of lockups & breakouts: sometimes nabbed by the Crown, generally for absconding or some minor misdemeanour, more often by irate publicans & sly-grog shop owners demanding some form of painting work to recompense them for the bill run up by me during one binge or another. It was, in the main, a pattern of drink, debt, imprisonment & incarceration in cellars & barrel sheds where I had to paint in exchange for my liberty, a clean slate, & a fresh opportunity for me to mollynog with some of the ladies—fine or less fine, I was never that fussed—I perchance might meet around the traps. And in the main, it was fine. Did I say tedious? Well yes, that too, but it had the virtue of rhythm & the pleasure of certainty. It was like a child's spinning top that sooner or later cracks.

As my artistick production had to be maintained at an equivalent rate to my drinking, my paintings quickly became as much a feature of Hobart Town taprooms as their tobacco & whale-oil smoke stained walls. At the

Hope & Anchor, for example, I was not let out of the woodshed until I had completed a painting of some dead meat in the Dutch style in payment for my rum tab there. I composed an original picture full of the old rustick favourites—a dead hare strung up by its back legs, a few pheasants, a musket or two, a brown demi-john for domestick effect, & a bald eagle on a perch.

There was if not a certain progress in my art over the next year, then at least a slow alteration, & what began as bricolage ended as a style. At the *Repent & Drink* I painted a mural of flowers in the Potteries manner to recompense that publican, Augusto Traverso, for the supposed passing of a false note. The flowers entwined with some of the patrons, looking admittedly more like a pastoral tribute to the Revolution's Committee of Public Safety—so many elegant, reasoned floralled Marats & Robespierres—than an accurate rendering of dishevelled, unreasonable Hobart Town drunks. Still the old lags—bless their rancid souls—were flattered enough to be happy.

Undoubtedly the high point of my short Hobart Town career was my dramatick canvas for the *Iron Duke* depicting the depravity of circus life after that good publican's woman ran off with the Great Valerio, a Sicilian high-rope walker & seller of aphrodisiac powders. I did a terrifying mural of a soft naked woman being dragged into a Hell of flaming acrobats & tumblers by a rather nasty looking bald eagle, beneath which was inscribed the motto: *Ex Australis semper aliquid novi* (There's always something new out of Australia).

'The only taproom in Hobart without a Gould on

the wall,' remarked the sly-grog shop owner Mr Capois Death, upon seeing this much celebrated marvel, 'is the one with Gould in the gutter.'

He slapped me heartily on the back &, for once being square with me, offered to pay should I do a special job for him. It only took a morning's painting to knock up the sign on a square Huon pine board. It showed an exasperated white woman (model: Mrs Arthur, wife of the Governor of the island colony, Lieutenant George Arthur) scrubbing as hard as she could a black baby in a wooden tub who smiles back at her, below which sat the logo of the establishment this advertised—the *Labour In Vain*, such sign celebrating Mr Capois Death's establishment near the Old Wharf going legal.

Along with the knowledge that I was, after all, only acting on his instructions, I these days console myself with the thought that Mr Capois Death was, one way or another, always destined for disaster. His reputation was as a flash man, gained from his passion for molly-boys, his stable of fast women & slow horses, & a similarly unreliable taste made alcohol in his notorious Larrikin Soup, a violently strong purl-ale flavoured with wormwood, a poor man's absinthe. Then, though, destiny seemed as fresh & promising as the summer sea breeze into which the sign was hoisted & hung flapping above a delighted Mr Capois Death.

It was, if you will allow me the compliment, a grand thing that pub sign, gently rocking back & forth, so light & laughing it brought a smile to the face of one & all who passed beneath it in Barracouta Row. They would have laughed all the more over their pots of purl-ale if they had seen the future it truly signposted, rather than the Larrikin Soup we foolishly thought it adver-tised. It is hard to believe the power such a painting had, that its effect on me & Capois Death was to prove as decisive as if it were not a sign board but Madame Guillotine herself hovering over our heads. But before it destroyed us the *Labour In Vain* was going to bring us together.

We of course saw none of this. Capois Death was himself a man of colour, a maroon from Liverpool, & he found the picture amusing & instructive. He said that I had caught the spirit of the island precisely. I was allowed back into his taproom with a clean slate.

The following day Mr Capois Death was closed down on Governor Arthur's direct orders, on the grounds of promoting subversion. Our splendid sign was burnt & Mr Capois Death & myself were sen-tenced to fourteen days on the treadwheel, he for the inadvertent poisoning of a ship's surgeon, me for absconding without notice from Palmer the coach-builder.

That would have been if not tolerable then at least survivable, if it hadn't been for the unexpected return of Captain Pinchbeck to Hobart Town. He was now working as a whaling skipper, in the hope, it was said, of one day accidentally harpooning his French rival, but his desire for vengeance was, as I was to discover, even larger than the leviathans he pursued through the southern oceans. In the course of a night's carousing he had cause to visit several local establishments, including the *Iron Duke* & the *Repent & Drink*, from whose paintings he deduced that I was pursuing a vendetta through a series of cleverly coded paintings depicting his cuckolding & slow strangulation by Gallic adulterers. This was my second lesson in colonial art: you discover the true nature of your subject at the same time as you discover your audience, but it is an added disappointment.

By chance Captain Pinchbeck had dinner with the Governor & his still aggrieved wife the evening following our arraignment for the *Labour In Vain* clapboard. That much I know—what was said through long candles & over the wombat *consommé* can only be guessed at.

The following morning I was informed that an order signed by Governor Arthur himself had just arrived, in which it was commanded that myself & Mr Death, whose complicity seemed to lie only in his folly of keeping company with me on the treadwheel, were to be transported to Sarah Island for seven years, he upon several new charges of sedition, me—an escapee who had been at large for twenty years—for having conspired to pervert the course of justice through the use of a false name.

Various mentions were made of mutinous & rebellious behaviour, desecration of national flag, etc, etc, at the time of the colony's founding by a person whose name I recognised as one to which I had once answered. But now condemned to Sarah Island, I felt like only answering to myself. When asked if I had anything to say in regard to my sentence, I replied:

'I am William Buelow Gould, & my name is a song that will be sung.'

On the grounds of insolence my sentence was doubled to fourteen years.

X

THE COCKCHAFER WAS a wondrous cruel machine. It left your body feeling as if it were composed of pain rather than flesh. This was not only from the sheer physical fatigue or the rasping effects even a few hours stepping up & down in coarse government slops would have upon one's groin, leaving it a mass of raw red flesh, but from the monstrous brilliance of its utter pointlessness, knowing at the end of the day that your cruel labour was entirely for no other purpose than to propel that monstrous treadwheel.

The Cockchafer took the form of a gigantic, stretched waterwheel suspended slightly above floor level, like some grotesque rolling pin clad in wooden slats that formed steps. It stood the height of two men & was a good two dozen yards long, so that up to thirty men could be punished simultaneously.

We climbed a short stepladder to shoulder height, grasped a fixed handle of sweat & blood-burnished gum wood that ran the length of the treadwheel at elbow height, then stepped onto that rotating waterwheel in which we had to become as water. For the next ten hours we climbed that circle of Hell, never going any higher than the next falling step, trying not to hear the groaning of each other, the thrum of the spindle, the *clock-clock-clocking* of our chains. In the torturous summer heat we ran rivers of sweat, making the steps slimy & slippery & us maddened with thirst.

Near the evening of the second day a machine breaker from Glasgow became beset by terrible cramping & was only able to lift his legs with the greatest agony. Despite his pleas, the guards refused to stand him down. Unable to climb, he finally fell & became stuck between the treadwheel & the stepladder. The slats ground past his jammed body, but still that huge wheel, as if answering to laws other than those of this earth, rolled on as we yelled to the guards to allow us to halt. Even after the order was given to step down, it was not immediately possible to stop the great momentum of the wheel, so it further pounded the poor man until coming to rest jammed.

Some didn't care, were grateful only for the break his suffering gave us, saying if he was lucky he would perish. Others clawed like mad men for a time, trying to roll the wheel back & pull him out. We talked to the machine breaker & he a little to us. In dark words dribbling with bloody gobs from his mouth he admitted that he wished he was a real Villain. We roared our approval & finally managed to drag his broken body, so inexplicably unmarked, onto the dust of the muster floor in front of the wheel.

'My father was a weaver,' he continued, '& I am sorry to have shamed my father, but weaving is no fit business now, in fact it is no business at all.' Then he stopped saying anything for a long time, & we wondered, is he thinking or is he dying?

Then his voice sounded once more, though this time it was much more distant & muffled, as if all the machine-spun cotton in the world was wadding up into his bloody mouth. 'My father was a weaver,' he repeated, 'but it is better for a man in such times to steal silk than weave cotton on the steam . . . ' But he couldn't say the word 'machine', only rucked a further spew of blood onto the floor.

Later he began raving how the kelpy was coming to take him. He was screeching, thin & harsh, like an ungreased treadle no longer used. Another Scot from the wheel said the kelpy was a spirit of the waters in the shape of a horse, & that this kelpy drowned those who travelled too far from their home.

We were ordered back to the wheel & left the weaver where he lay until a doctor could be found. His screeching dimmed to an odd gobby scream, as if he were trying to vomit all those steam spinning machines out of his mouth, & failing.

Capois Death began to talk loudly to the weaver, which was strictly forbidden while one was on the wheel but the guards chose to ignore him for it seemed to calm the weaver & stop him screaming. Capois Death told his mother's tales of her country & of the many fabulous things she had seen & known before the slavers had come & her chiefs had sold her. As we went down & back up on the Cockchafer, I too listened & tried to imagine how it might be possible to fly as Capois Death's ancestors once had; to levitate then fly far from Van Diemen's Land's chains & cockchafers by eating fish eyes & smearing a bird's blood over my arms

& leaping off a certain magic mountain, then diving into the sea & swimming as one with the fish until one was a fish.

Occasionally, as Capois Death talked, he twisted around to grab a glance of the machine breaker now broken by a machine, to see if he was yet dead, but always his eyes were clear, brighter than fire coals, & those eyes were always following us, as if we should not have allowed such a thing as the Cockchafer & our subjugation by it, as though we were somehow culpable for a greater crime than the tawdry offences listed in our convict records.

XI

ON THE FORTNIGHT-LONG journey in a small packet around the uninhabited south coast of Van Diemen's Land to Macquarie Harbour the seas grew so violent that we were forced to take safe anchorage in the expanse of Port Davey.

It transpired that the captain's Cape Town mistress, under the influence of an innumerate Kabbalist to whom she had recourse for divining her future, believed that truth was to be found in threes. As emissaries of his love the captain had thus sent three rings made of gold teeth wrenched with a cruel urgency from several formerly rich convicts' mouths; then three live emus, which had all died in transit; & in a more exotic mood three white-pointer sharks' mouths, though this latter gift was more in memory of the pleasures she had given him than a present to please her. The captain had heard nothing for eighteen months; he worried his gifts needed to be more subtle & enigmatic, & for this reason the presence in his boat of a painter with whose work he was, as a patron of Hobart Town hotelries, passing familiar, suggested to him the idea of a painted triptych of weird Van Diemonian creatures.

I was brought up on deck along with Mr Death, the captain having in former times drunk in his establishments & made use of his women. My first suggestion of three bald eagles he hastily rejected, as he did the idea of three wisteria garlands. He warned me that he wanted nothing provocative in the manner of Mrs Arthur & the black baby, but something that seemed innocent & only of itself yet which could be read in an entirely different manner. Capois Death suggested that the triptych contain an animal, a bird & a fish, & the captain seemed to think this a splendid idea. What truth this added up to, an admonishment or an encouragement, was entirely beyond me, but the subtle messages of my work were, I decided, not for me to decode. 'You are the fish,' said Capois Death, whose opinion I had not solicited, 'not the net.'

The following afternoon I was summoned to the captain's presence & presented with a watercolour set & instructions to paint the outcome of his morning's hunting onshore: an orange-bellied parrot before it was plucked & thrown into the parrot pie the captain was to have for his tea, & a small kangaroo of the type the Van Diemonians call a wallaby, which was also to be cooked into a stew when I had finished with it.

The pictures did not end up the most truthful. The

orange-bellied parrot, a small, rather sweet & colour-ful bird in the flesh, bulked larger on paper than in life. It was unavoidable: half the poor creature's head had been blown apart by the captain's shot & much of its body was matted in dried blood. I drew on experience to fill the hole the captain had made, & the bird took on a regal splendour, its posture one of a brooding aggression, its beak &—well, to be honest—its entire body more bald eagle than Van Diemonian parrot. The kangaroo was worse: this handsome animal on paper evolved a suspicious rodent-face rather than its own gentle physiognomy, to which was coupled a body suffering severe posture problems, the whole absurdity capped off with a long ropy tail more suited to a kite.

My body was, as you might expect after the horrors visited upon it by Captain Pinchbeck when he had been unhappy with my work, a prickly sweat. I couldn't swallow, my tongue rolled around my mouth like a lolling smoked cod. I tried to touch up the pictures, then gave up & started all over again, but the results only worsened each time—the kangaroo ever more some deer with the dropsy & an impossible anatomy; the parrot with each redoubled attempt increasingly a warrior of the wind, an aggressive North American spirit in an ill-fitting, garishly coloured jacket.

When the captain came shortly before dusk to inspect my handiwork, memories of the *petite noyade* flooded my mind as surely as water had that awful box. I was unable to speak, gulped & felt seawater already filling my throat, & meekly placed the pictures before him on the deck without comment. But unlike Captain

Pinchbeck, this captain seemed pleased by the element of the unreal that had accidentally crept in. It suggested, said he, a world at once more fantastick & yet bizarrely more familiar than the one we lived in, & all up he felt it would do him only good with his mistress.

To complete the triptych he had the following day brought me a fish that the sailors liked to catch with hook & line off the reefs of the harbour, & then smoke & eat. The fish was large-scaled & coloured pretty enough; perhaps it was this latter feature that made the captain think it might appeal to his mistress. I was told that in consequence of its favoured food, the great aquatic forests of bull-kelp that occur in the oceans off Van Diemen's Land, the fish was known to the convicts as a kelpy.

XII

IT LOOKED NOTHING like a horse. It looked like a two-pound pretty fish that might, if you were hungry enough, be worth smoking & eating. But that didn't make me feel any better. Was a kelpy a kelpy or just a fish? Was a fish *just* a fish? & then I looked into that damn kelpy's eyes & though I did not wish it they were taking me back, quicker than Mr Banks scalping a blackfella, to the Cockchafer & us sitting around that evening waiting for the machine breaker to die, wondering whether he would last the night, & trying to work out a way of persuading the cook to give us some lard with which we might grease our raw thighs, when Capois Death began once more to talk.

He had an authority about him that is impossible to explain & which was entirely at odds with the bald facts of his physical presence. A portrait would show a short black man with a slightly weak chin, & a twist to his right shoulder that gave him a curious nature, at once intimidatory & suspicious, for he always seemed to be glancing behind himself & would corkscrew his whole body around to listen to you as though he were about to hit you.

Capois Death was originally from San Domingo, his wrinkled prune face as circuitous as his history. Like some other former slaves I had met he carried with him everywhere a spirit bottle. It was a dull, scratched earthenware pitcher & contained, said he, his own invincible memory of himself as a self-liberated man encased for protection in his once-celebrated Larrikin Soup. He had, when taken to Bermuda from Jamaica to be sold there by his master, succeeded in bribing a soldier with fellatio to forge his certificate of freedom & thereupon fled to England where he found work first in the north Atlantic as a harpooner & later in Liverpool as a footman, a position he lost along with his freedom upon being caught stealing silverware from his employer.

He had a crooked mouth constantly in motion, & when night came & we were ordered back to our quarters, taking the machine breaker with us as no doctor had yet arrived, he told us, as we lay on our old damp straw palliasses, in a form so epic & so open as to be never-ending, the story of the great slave revolt of San Domingo in which half a million slaves overthrew in turn the local whites, the soldiers of the French monarchy, a Spanish invasion, an English expedition of sixty thousand men, & a second French expedition led by Bonaparte's brother-in-law.

And he told it just like that, like he was an infantryman firing, loading, & refiring his musket, brickfaced without pause & without emphasis, & the horror & the glory & the wonder of it all were in the accumulation of endless detail, of how as a child he had witnessed the ferocity of the revolt; of Bonaparte's brother-in-law's attempt to quell it; of seeing Negroes being publicly fed to dogs & being burnt alive; of their leader, Toussaint L'Ouverture, the black Napoleon, betrayed by the white Napoleon; of L'Ouverture's cultured black general Maurepas, having to watch his wife & children being drowned before his eyes as the French soldiers nailed a pair of wooden epaulettes into his naked shoulders, taunting him, laughing as they hammered so: *A real Bonaparte now!* And yet it was also another Frenchman, the sea-captain Mazard, to whom he owed his life, who had refused to drown the one hundred & fifty slaves given him for that express purpose & instead took them to Jamaica. There he sold them to the English planters, something for which the captain was reviled by both white & black for the former wanted the blacks' death as punishment for their rebellion, & the latter would rather die in any manner than continue to live as slaves, because to die as a free man meant the revolt never ended.

Capois Death fell silent. For a moment it seemed that we were back on the wheel & there was only the sound of our irons as we stepped, *clock-clock-clocking*, the slow rolling thrum of the wheel, as though there was no escape except in stories. Then the Glasgow machine breaker once more spoke, but his voice was now a wretched rasping croak, & he asked us to kill him.

At first we dismissed his pleadings, reassuring him that at some point the doctor would arrive & he would be treated.

But he was gasping repeatedly, as if he was bound to a new wheel & could only reprise its rhythm:

'*I am dying!*'

Over & over & over, *clock-clock-clocking*.

As though we doubted it.

XIII

CAPOIS DEATH PICKED up his palliasse & walked over to where the machine breaker lay. He knelt down & looked away from the man's eyes. He seemed to be looking at his thick black hair, which he pushed into a side part with gentle sweeps of his hand. He ran the side of his hand down onto the machine breaker's cheek, holding it there for a moment. Then he stood up, dropped the palliasse over the machine breaker's head & kneeling, straddled the man's covered head, stretching the palliasse taut between his knees.

In this manner he held the machine breaker tight & began to sing in a soft voice the songs he had learnt from his mother. The smothered man's body bolted & bucked, but his thrashing seemed to all too quickly grow subdued & then halt altogether. Capois Death stayed sitting on the man for a good minute more, then stopped his singing & stood up & dragged his palliasse off.

No-one moved. All eyes were fixed on the machine breaker for a sign of life. There was none. Capois Death rifled his pockets & finding half a garnet ring, dropped it in his spirit bottle. Then he lay back down on his palliasse, closed his eyes, & on the deck of the convict ship I opened mine & saw around me the low rolling wildlands of Port Davey, & knew that was all now behind me, that the most frightful task before me was only to paint the fish the captain had given me as the subject of the third part of his lover's triptych.

The kelpy which he had presented to me to paint was not one that seemed to be cognisant of its fate as an ambassador of romance. Curled in a bucket of seawater, it was still alive &, it seemed, somehow faintly contemptuous of its new role. I took the kelpy out of the bucket for half a minute or so, arranging it on the table in front of me, working quickly, then placing it back in the water so it might breathe & not yet die. This dry table, I realised, was the kelpy's *petite noyade*, & I his Captain Pinchbeck. Like me, the kelpy was guilty. Like me, it had no idea why.

I found it not so hard to paint a reasonably accurate picture, but the kelpy's eyes followed me as if it knew all our true crimes, just like the machine breaker's eyes had followed me until the moment of his death, but that was not exactly how I painted the fish—as an accusing, horrified eye in a dying body. No, emboldened by the oddities the captain had so unexpectedly sanctioned with the first two paintings, I must confess I began taking liberties with that fish's face, so it was both the fish's knowing eye & the horror of the machine breaker's eye watching us on the treadwheel; so it was both that & so many other things. It was Capois Death's stare & buck teeth & his half-horrified, half-fascinated look forever backwards over his shoulder at his own past as the machine breaker bucked beneath him. It was all that blood—of fish eyes & revolting slaves being torn apart & Maurepas' nailed shoulders haemorrhaging & the blood in the machine breaker's eyes after we drew the palliasse away—and it was my own fear at this cracked world in which I & they & everything was trapped. It was a funny thing but then it didn't seem so funny that all these things were bound together for a moment & all existed as a single dying kelpy.

They were stupid thoughts, & I was glad when the captain took the picture away for his mistress & gave the sailors the kelpy to smoke & eat.

XIV

How could I then—as I was painting my first fish—have known I was setting out on a venture as quixotic as it was infinite? I have read the lives of the artists &, like the lives of the saints, greatness seems imprinted upon them from the beginning. At birth their fingers are recorded making painterly flourishes, merely waiting for a loaded brush & a canvas to fill with the images they seem to have been born with, so many immaculate conceptions.

But art is a punitive sentence, not a birthright, & there is nothing in my early life that suggests artistick aptitude or even interest, my pastimes & fascinations nearly all being what may—& were—deemed the merely villainous. And though I am, of course, the hero of this, my own tale, if only because I can't really imagine anyone else wanting to be, my story is no remade myth of Orpheus, but the story of a sewer rat made worse.

I am William Buelow Gould, sloe-souled, green-eyed, gap-toothed, shaggy-haired & grizzle-gutted, & though my pictures will be even poorer than my looks, my paintings lacking the majesty of a Girtin, the command of a Turner, believe me when I tell you that I will try to show you everything, mad & cracked & bad as it was.

I'll make the mark my way, be buggered if I won't & I know I'll be damned if I do, for it may not be Lake poetry or Ovid or that damned dwarf Pope but it will be the best I can do & like no other has. Rough work with a soul will always be open to all, including condemnation & reviling, while fine work housing emptiness is closed to all insults & is easily ivied over with paid praises. They say the storyteller is the man who would let the wick of his life be consumed by the flame of his story. But like good Trim Shandy I shall confine myself to no man's rule. Next to my paintings I intend to make a bonfire of words, say anything if it illuminates a paltry moment of truth in my poor pictures.

I am William Buelow Gould & I mean to paint for you as best I can, which is but poorly, which is but a rude man's art, the sound of water on stone, the fool's dream of the hard giving way to the soft, & I hope you will come to see reflected in my translucent watercolours not patches of the white cartridge paper beneath, but the very opacity of the souls themselves.

And is that not enough for a struggling deckhand to have from a wild sea hauled into his boat? Answer me—is it not? Or do you desire evidence of the sublime? Of the Artist in control—indeed at the peak—of his powers?

You'll get none of that poppycock from me. For I am out of control here, badly & I hope dangerously so, & when my brush starts to attack Pobjoy's paper in small stipples—*rat-a-ta-tat—rat-a-ta-tat-tat*—I am shooting for freedom, nothing less, liberty, & my aim is untrue & my weapons a sorry paintbox I'd be ashamed to hock, a few poor brushes, some pots of poorer paint & a bruised talent for nothing more than reproduction. But my sight is level & I will make the best of it I can.

What?

Where, I hear the criticasters ask, is the *fineness* of approach? The evidence of anything other than a poor *provincial* mind relentlessly on the make?

They diminish me with their definitions, but I am William Buelow Gould, not a small or mean man. I am not bound to any idea of who I will be. I am not contained between my toes & my turf but am infinite as sand.

Come closer, listen: I will tell you why I crawl close to the ground: because I choose to. Because I care not to live above it like they may fancy is the way to live, the place to be, so that they in their eyries & guard towers might look down on the earth & us & judge it all as wanting.

I care not to paint pretend pictures of long views which blur the particular & insult the living, those *landscapes* so beloved of the Pobjoys, those *landscapes* that trash the truth as they reach ever upwards into the sky, as though we only know somewhere or somebody from a distance—that's the lie of the land while the truth is never far away but up close in the dirt, in the vile details of slime & scale & filth along with the Devil, along with the angels, & all snared within the earth & us, all embodied in a single pulse of a heart—mine, yours, ours—& all my subject as I take aim & make of the fish flesh incarnate.

The criticasters will say I am this small thing & my pictures that irrelevant thing. They will beat a bedlam outside & inside my poor head & then I cannot keep time with the drum of my stippling. They will waken me screaming from my necessary dream. They will try to define me like the Surgeon does his sorry species, those cursed Linnaeans of the soul, trying to trap me in some new tribe of their own invention & definition.

But I am William Buelow Gould, party of one, undefinable, & my fish will free me & I shall flee with them.

And you?

—well mark the great Shelley—

Ye were injured, & that means memory.

And you are just going to have to begin as I did: by looking long enough into the fish's eye to see what I must now describe, to commence that long dive down,

down into the world of the ocean where the only bars are those of descending light.

Hush!

Pobjoy is coming, the sea is rising, my wound is clotting, so just sit back & agree with the Russian convict that it's all better in a book, that life is better observed than lived. Nod like the lucky bastards you are, like nobby Hobart Town clerks who breakfast on the upper storey of the Colonial Secretary's office watching early morning public executions, fat arses flapping on padded seats, enjoying in comfort & company with the jolly pissy taste of fried kidneys still sweet in their gob the spectacle directly across Murray Street at the gaol entrance of a good gibbet.

In that brief moment before the gallows' trap door opens its own gaping, insatiable mouth, let me continue now—like all good confessions of a condemned man—with the immediate events that have led me to such a sorry pass as this.

THE PORCUPINE FISH

*Sarah Island—Several forms of
torture—The Commandant founds a nation—
Mr Lempriere—Sharing the joys of Voltaire—Dancing the
Enlightenment—A death & a new name—
Bedswerving—Castlereagh the Pig—Dr Bowdler-Sharpe
on eggs—How I came to paint my second fish.*

I

AT THE END of that strangest of voyages, we slowly
approached our new prison in the late evening on an
early autumn sea so still that we were frequently
becalmed. In this age of abominations, in a time when,
as we are so often told, everything that is sacred is pro-
faned, nothing is more abominable, more without
precedent in the annals of degradation, than this island
on which my story was now to unfold. In the entire
unknown, unmapped western half of Van Diemen's
Land only savages roamed & no white settlement was
to be found, save for this one gaol for the recalcitrant.

Yet in the pale curd-coloured moonlight in which
we first saw it, Sarah Island appeared not as we
expected. The captain had granted several convicts—including myself & Capois Death—a special
dispensation & allowed us up from the sweating, fetid
hold onto the deck. Like a silvered sea monster of

fable rearing its terrible head, the island loomed over our boat still far away.

It was as if a giant octopus had spread itself over the island & eaten up every last vestige of vegetation, every last tree & plant & fern, leaving only its upturned tentacles of log fences, fifty feet or more in height, running up & down the settlement. Soaring above these were the island's great buildings, so many quicksilver kraken heads: the Commandant's pink marble palace at the foot of which we would later feel as though we were in some man-made gorge where wild winds played & whose shadow reached over the rest of the settlement; the magnificent stone Commissariat which would have not been out of place in a great port; the Penitentiary in the centre of which was a Cyclopean lintel, emblazoned with the settlement's odd coat of arms, a smiling mask.

Then I looked away from the island & down at the sea. I saw something I had never seen before, a very remarkable thing that I wished I might have words to describe but for which I knew there were no words: the stars reflected in the water, shining as bright as in the sky, as though we were journeying through the very southern heavens to arrive at this place of wonder; as though there were a thousand candles burning just beneath the surface of the still dark water, one light for each soul of every dead convict buried on the small isle of the dead to our right. When several of these lights were extinguished by the head & afterwards the body of a dead man as it so very slowly swept around our becalmed bow & floated into view, face down, I wondered if at last the machine breaker was one with his dream of freedom.

The corpse was later identified as that of an escaped convict who had failed to make it to the mainland in a raft made of a door. Whether the captain meant the convict's fate or the island he could only escape through death, his comment as he watched the convict's body being heaved up with gaff hooks still chilled me.

'A full stop,' said the captain, 'to the end of Empire.'

II

WHEN LATER THAT evening the wind finally rose & we came closer in to berth we were able to see the bold streets running along & across the island's natural contours, the extensive landfill & unfinished wharves & shoreside streets of looming stone warehouses that would shame Liverpool—collectively a prophecy of a nation that might be summoned into existence simply by the night-time will of its leader, a man we were to rightly come to regard as extraordinary.

You may well say: How lucky the colonies were to have such a man!

But when you saw his vast shipyards—I say 'his' advisedly—it quickly became apparent that we had passed from one dominion, that of the English, to another, much more remarkable, that of His Bulkiness, the Napoleon of Sarah Island, the Great Doge of the South Seas: the Commandant himself. Even then his shipyards were the busiest in the southern colonies; far, far larger than the colonial authorities knew, because for every brig or sloop built by the convict shipwrights out of the Huon pine felled by shoeless chain gangs of felons up the Gordon River & sent as a form of tribute to the Van Diemonian governor in Hobart Town, a dozen more were built & reserved for the growing trading fleet of the island, through whose agency the Commandant had established links, at first commercial & then political, with Javanese traders & several newly independent South American countries.

Under the influence of mercury, which he administered to himself daily as a salve for his syphilis, & laudanum, which he drank each evening in imprecisely measured amounts to enable him to sleep, because of all things, this brave man feared only his dreams, opiate-enhanced nightmares that gave him no respite & which always ended in flames from which he rose phoenix-like just before dawn each morning, to recommence building what was already ash.

You may well wonder: How on earth did he expect this to end?

But his ambition was as enormous as his appetites, both dietary & carnal, & it was no less than the creation of a nation that would have as its heart the city-state he was already building the foundations for, with him for its Father.

You may well ask: How was any of this possible?

But it was only necessary to hear him speak of his dreams, his visions, & the rough hewn planks beneath your feet would begin to sway & roll, the flaking split-sandstone walls of the room around you would fall away, & the world of that dull, desperate prison would transform in front of your eyes. Before we were in any way aware of the transformation, we would be flying through the southern heavens to a distant land of fable, a tyranny perhaps, but one enchanted by his stories of his hopes & despairs, a world that with his every word & every gesture was becoming more & more real to us.

After berthing we were made strip, & whilst shivering naked on deck, convict constables stuck their fingers up our arses & grouted around our mouths for tobacco wads or precious stones. We were then allowed to dress & waited for the Commandant to arrive.

Shortly before dawn he came aboard to address us. His appearance was unusual: it was not that he was short, but that his small body tapered away from his very large head, & in consequence he seemed to have no neck. His black hair, which was dense & wavy, was his best feature, yet its extravagance only highlighted his other physical shortcomings. On any other, such exotic dress as was his—the blue uniform, the gold mask—would have been his most distinctive features. But that early morning it was the way he spoke: directly, simply, occasionally even lapsing into *dementung*, the pidgin issue of blackfella language & convict fly talk, & there was something mesmerising about his words, his passion.

Before we knew it the ship had transformed into a moving cloud, & as the cracked pastels of sunrise began to escape into the early morning sky behind him, he was pointing out the future as we flew over it; the small island that had become a noble trading giant, revered & feared in equal measure around the world, for its wealth, its power, the beauty & majesty of its civic arrangements. We saw how traders & artists & all manner of other courtesans made the long trek from distant provinces in their youth, abandoning their pasts, their accents, disavowing their families, their friends, their lovers, & carrying with them only the flaming desire to identify their own ambition & wild dreams with those of the rising island of the south.

He imagined—and we with him—himself being painted in a Roman toga, himself the subject of epic odes, himself founding a dynasty that would war in the name of his disputed memory, himself revered as Himself, & he saw no conflict between his despotick & dynastick desires, his official duties as an English officer in charge of an Imperial penal settlement, & the high regard he held for Renaissance city-states such as Florence & Venice, about which he had gained certain misleading conceptions from blue chapbooks on Italy. These he was sent by the woman we came to know as his sister, Miss Anne—a Romantic watercolourist whose minor distinction lay not in her art, but in once having had a short, illicit affair with Thomas De Quincey during the opium-eating writer's single term entombed within the decrepit, dull cloisters of Worcester College—accompanying her letters from Oxford.

The Commandant suffered from a strange variant of Saint Vitus's dance, nourished himself on a stuttering deference to the mirages & ghosts of the new age, & declared to us that man's highest creative urges would henceforth be realised through engineering. We were swept up in his great never-ending romance of construction—his plans for rebuilding the market as a colossal glassed-in arcade; for the crooked, muddy track that led up from the water to be reconstructed as an immense, straight Boulevard of Destiny at the far end of which would be a massive iron arch, down which lovers might promenade if the weather proved pleasant, & up which troops would rush if the convicts were not.

Yet he never saw what it was that dazzled us all so about such a city: his words.

When he spoke anything & everything became possible, & though we knew our part in it all was not to benefit from these dreams, but to give our lives over to transforming them into brick & mortar, into glass panes & iron lace, our decrepitude was so great that we felt—for at least as long as he kept talking anyway, & that was long enough—this offered us a purpose, a meaning, something that meant we weren't convicts, something beyond the Cradle & the Tube Gag, & that's what we all craved. Some alternate idea of ourselves, some steam machine by which we could remake ourselves & our world, for to escape being a convict, we had to escape who we were, escape our past & the future decreed by the Convict System.

It was a world that demanded reality imitate fiction, demanded that of us all. For a forger the possibilities momentarily seemed endless, and, to be frank, who then could have honestly foretold both my fabulous future & the horrific destiny that was to consume us all? In the end, of course, the Commandant was to suck the sea dry, then explode with an oceanic excess of pride & maroon the island & its few survivors once more in their desolate isolation. The easiest path with authority is inevitably acquiescence: the stupider they are, the stupider you need to be. It was then inevitable, I suppose, that I would on Sarah Island become what I had hitherto only ever feigned being—that most despicable of creatures—an Artist.

III

ON DISEMBARKING, WE were to discover all the requisite brutality & squalid circumstances you might expect of such a place. But even before alighting, even before we saw anything up close, our noses were assailed by the effluvium of death. Death was in that heightened smell of raddled bodies & chancre-encrusted souls. Death arose in a miasma from gangrenous limbs & bloody rags of consumptive lungs. Death hid in the rancorous odour of beatings, in the new buildings already falling apart with the insidious damp that invaded everything, was seeping out of sphincters rotting from repeated rapes. Death was rising in the overripe smell of mud fermenting, enmities petrifying, waiting in wet brick walls leaning, in the steam of flesh sloughing with the cat falling, so many fetid exhalations of unheard screams, murders, mixed with the brine of a certain wordless horror; collectively those scents of fearful sweat that sour clothes & impregnate whole places & which are said to be impervious to the passage of time, a perfume of spilling blood which no amount of washing or admission was ever to rid me. And perhaps because everywhere was death, life has perversely never seemed so sweet as what it did when I first came to Sarah Island.

As we stumbled in our chains up the hill towards the Penitentiary, perched precarious on a small cliff abutting the sea, as our eyes found sordid images to unhappily marry all those horrific smells, we saw that the island was both something more & something less than the marvel we had first supposed it to be, as if it was unsure whether it was to be the Commandant's dream or the convicts' nightmare.

Jammed next to magnificent stone buildings, some completed but empty, others as yet half-built, were dilapidated sod huts & broken-down timber sheds leaning at so many odd angles it seemed as if they were drunk. While the wharf area & the road leading into it were cobbled, the rest of the island's thoroughfares were stinking mud-churned paths in which you might disappear up to your waist. Swarms of fleas that rose in small clouds wherever people sat & immense quantities of flies infested the island, along with rats that were so bold they would be seen scurrying in packs around buildings of a day.

As I bob about my cell now & think back on it, we were not surprised when we felt upon us as an implacable hatred the malignant stare of that unholy army of the persecuted—filthy little clawscrunts & half-starved wretches, their pus-filled eyes poking like buttercups out of scaled scabby faces, their misshapen backs hacked & harrowed out of any natural form by endless applications of the Lash; brawn-fallen, belly-pinched wrecks of men bent & broken long before their time, the one I thought the oldest only thirty-two years of age.

Nor were we at all shocked by how here all Nature was

inverted—from the molly-boys to the nancy-men, one such blowsabella even getting about with a blind-tam hidden beneath his slops, a bundle of filthy rags he claimed was his baby that he would make to feed from his bloke's bub; how here Nature herself was to be feared—the harbour, so we were told, full of sharks, the unknown wild lands beyond full of murderous savages. In an odd way it was a relief finally to see it & begin to learn how best it all might be endured, & if at all possible evaded.

But in truth there was no way to make a cosy push of the several forms of torture unique to the island. You might succeed in tipping the blacksmith to give you lighter chains, but there was no cure for the agony of three months, day & night, wearing thirty-pound leg irons the inside basils of which were deliberately jagged to lacerate the flesh.

There was, I knew even then, long before having their intimate acquaintance as I do now, no way of copping sweet the saltwater cells where one might spend months or even years bobbing up & down with the tides. Nor the Tube Gag—that ingenious instrument which taught silence at the price of agony, a hardwood tube thrust into the mouth like a large horse's bit, often with such force that teeth were knocked out. With a leather strap fixed to each end, the tube was then fastened at the back of the head & winched tight until a low spasmodic whistle & a froth of blood indicated that the gag was working. Nor the Spread Eagle, where a man's arms would be chained to two ring bolts six feet apart & six feet high, his feet to a bolt on the floor, his head facing the wall, with the Tube Gag applied if any screams were forthcoming when he was bludgeoned around the head & body.

There were several other exotic tortures with names redolent of perverse humiliation—the Scavenger's Daughter, the Witch's Broom, the Mistress's Scald. Most feared of all, also the most passive, the Cradle, an iron rack to which men were strapped down on their back, often after a flogging, for weeks on end entirely immobile, their scarified backs sloughing into maggot-ridden putrescence beneath their stilled, rotting bodies, as their minds dissolved into an even worse mush.

One or several of these punishments could be incurred for the crimes of being found with tobacco, some fat, a tamed bird, or sharing food, singing, not walking fast enough on the way to work, talking (insolence), not talking (dumb insolence), laughing, scowling—though really the only true crime was running foul of a convict constable, or a dog who dobbed. You fell or rose on the Ladder of Sarah Island not according to your behaviour, your reformatory zeal or your recurrent villainy, but only because of luck, good or bad.

For all of which I was ready.

But for the porcupine fish nothing could have prepared me.

IV

ALL THAT I have recounted about new nations & the remaking of Europe as a stunted island of misconceptions beneath the southern heavens still lay before us to discover, while before me that following chill morning after we had landed & been incarcerated in the miserable brick-nogged barracks reserved for new arrivals, stood a big, bowl-headed steaming pudding of a man, floury & treacly by turns, who was about to alter my life forever.

'TOBIAS ACHILLES LEMPRIERE—*MISTER*,' the pudding said, 'SETTLEMENT SURGEON—DEMANDING—AS AM *I*,' hot-breakfast breath pouring turbid clouds of mist into my cell. Even if his mode of speaking was largely incomprehensible, his tone was portentous, which is perhaps why he inevitably spoke in capital letters. Words existed in his speech as currants in a badly made bread-and-butter pudding—clusters of stodgy darkness.

His appearance was so dreadful that on first sight it made me shudder. He was so rotund he looked as if he had been coopered rather than conceived. His black swallow-tail coat, too small & more tatty than natty, his tight breeches, his tiny silver-buckled shoes, all suggested a sufferer of the dropsy unsuccessfully masquerading as a Regency rake of yesteryear.

What was most distinctive about him was also what was most terrifying—the utter whiteness of his great bald head, so striking that at first I thought it was the shade of the machine breaker returned to haunt me. Contrasting with the white desert of the rest of his face were flaps & folds of fat in which darkness ran in scheming rills. Later I discovered his face was naturally sallow rather than spectral, that he used glistening white lead powder to make himself look as if he had been freshly floured. Perhaps as they say of the crazed hatters of London, it is this too close association with that metal that explains something of his later erratic behaviour. Even so, my first impression of his grotesque unhuman visage is what has most strongly endured of him in my memory.

His eyes were large & dewy and, if I may permit myself the word, *moony*, but what in a different body might have suggested a poetic or even mystical disposition, here suggested only a certain callous lack of interest with others. Still, in that ghostly moonscape of a face, they were the only things that hinted at life & drew you into their gaze, &, as I was to discover, into the obsessions upon which they so relentlessly focused.

I dimly apprehended that Mr Tobias Achilles Lempriere, as surgeon, occupied a position of considerable power over us, who were, it was already obvious to me, no better than slaves. It was Mr Tobias Achilles Lempriere who would determine whether a man was too sick to be sent out working on some back-breaking task or other on one of the gangs, or whether the man deserved to be charged & flogged for such malingering. It was Mr Tobias Achilles Lempriere who would determine if a flogging should cease, & it was Mr Tobias Achilles Lempriere who would say whether the stroke of the cat was too light & needed to be heavier & more forceful.

I hiked myself up from the damp earthen floor to try to look a man of some dignity rather than the miserable felon I was, but as I rose my body felt the weight of my chains being taken up, felt the lice itch with the sudden movement, felt the scratch & rasp of the filthy convict slops upon my skin. My oppression heavy upon me, I longed simply to fall back to the ground, but I stood as tall & erect & still as I could make myself in such squalid circumstances.

I was preparing to be all suitably meek & mild, to fawn & feign, when to my surprise Mr Tobias Achilles Lempriere produced a tiny shoeing stool from behind his back, placed it on the slimy floor, & then sat his own considerable bulk down on it, looking for all the world in his tight black coat like a burnt jam roly-poly resting on a bent dinner fork that might any moment disappear up his great lardy arse.

'STUDY OF THE KELP FISH—FINE WORK—MOST FINE,' said he, settling himself on the stool. 'CONCEPTION—EXECUTION—SPLENDID—SCIENTIFICK.' I thought that he must want his portrait painted; he looked a little like Marat gone to fat, & I felt I might just be able to swing a passing copy when the Surgeon sighed once more, & continued. 'MOST APPLICABLE —DINED LAST NIGHT—GOOD CAPTAIN,' said he, a little irritated, thinking perhaps that my lack of reply indicated some imbecile incomprehension on my part.

'VIEWED TRIPTYCH L'AMORE—FISH GREAT WORK —EAGLE, NOT SO; CRIPPLED RAT, HARDLY—YET THOUGHT I—AN ABILITY TO PAINT, IF NOTHING ELSE—FISH—YOU—ME—DESTINY—MY DESIRE TO SERVE SCIENCE.' Then he asked—with what I felt to be some humility, & the unprecedented deployment of a full sentence—'YOU ARE AN ARTIST OF SOME EXPERIENCE?'

I hastily fashioned several stories that seemed agreeable to him, each new tale built upon his own conceits as to what art should be & what it should not be. It

required me to be halfway between haughty & humble,
a little above my fellow felons, a little below such masters as he, a highwire act from which I nearly once or
twice fell, but recovered at each stumble by making an
oblique reference to Shuggy Ackermann—of whom
he, of course, had heard not a sausage—who was, after
all, an engraver. I celebrated him in my asides as the
amazing Ackermann, the genius Ackermann, the thick-
accented Hanoverian emperor of London engravers,
Ackermann, & bathed in the glory I hoped the Pudding
might find reflected in me.

'ACKERMANN—YES? NO? YES,' Mr Tobias Achilles
Lempriere finally sighed, knowingly tapping his nose
with a podgy index finger revealing varnished scarlet
flesh beneath the powder. 'NOW THAT WAS ENGRAVING.'

But beyond saying I had served valuable time with
Ackermann—which indeed it was—I avoided saying it
was time more spent on his petty schemes of fraud &
theft than on engraving, & much more time than either
simply drinking at the dear old *Man of War* in Spitalfields.

Nor did I bother the Surgeon with tedious details
now flooding my memory of the publican's offensive
behaviour there, pressuring Ackermann & me incessantly like some Eightways harpy about our tick, *him*
would you believe with all his money planted away!

Then the publican with his throat cut, the money
gone, & Ackermann for once looking a quarter-
flash, dandruff spilling over the yoke of his new
pig-skin jacket, a look less than fortunate continued
in his brown buck teeth flecked white with potted
eel, his favourite dish, as he flashed a grin that went

from Wapping to Tyburn, & Ackermann not realising that he was soon to follow his grin there, dancing
the diddly-back-step from the gibbet as a wretched
murderer.

My past, which until then had not really existed for
me, was now exploding like a jumping-jack firecracker
all over my mind. It was as though I needed the truth of
these memories I didn't mention as a necessary ballast
for all the lies I was sprouting.

For as I was telling the Surgeon of my passion to
pursue a higher calling with my art, I was filling with
the same terror that I had had when the peelers were
out searching for me in the grizzled shadows of my old
haunts, that terror that seized me & threw me down a
shivering root outside of myself, huddling in the stinking dirt & filth behind barrels in dark rookery laneways,
the terror I may actually *be* someone else, that everything around me was beginning to whirl, that all my life
was only a dream dreamt by another, that everything
around me was only a simulacrum of a world, & I was
crying, lost, I really was somewhere else, somebody
else, seeing all this.

v

BUT THEN I was already long gone, out of London
like a musket ball leaving everything behind, including
my old name, my terrible fears, all that whirling &
hurtling & nonsense at last dying down, & as I walked
north, my humours picked up. Said I to myself, I am
indeed now an Artist, the well-known Portrait Painter

Billy Bellow—it had a definite ring to it—though after further thought that seemed too common, & I became Billie Buelow—it sounded all Frenchie & fancy-like & made me feel some connection with my father, as though I now had an ancestry that meant something rather than nothing—but then thought I, No, Frenchies are not flavoursome with the People, but when I found work for a time in the Potteries, I there answered to the cry of William Buelow because I could think of nothing better.

I had the good fortune to meet up with a master potter known only as Old Gould. Coupled to the old man's endless chattering—and upon reflection, perhaps its cause—was his fear of being trampled to death beneath a passing cart or coach. So great was his sense of this inexorable & cruel fate, that he would stand for up to an hour at the side of a street summoning the courage to cross it. Our first meeting was accidental & providential. I had staggered out of the *Bird in the Hand* in Birmingham with nothing left in my pockets & walked straight into his trembling figure on the corner. Feeling well disposed to humanity, I agreed to his stammered request to escort him across the street. Then, sensing that his need for help in this regard would not be ended until he reached his destination—a pub where he was staying the night a mile & a half away in the old town—I walked him there, & by the third crossing the tall, stork-like figure was bowing over me, full of such heartfelt gratitude for saving his life that he there & then offered me work in his workshop.

The Surgeon interrupted my reveries by asking me

in his stilted fashion what my opinion of still lifes as a form might be?

I told him in no uncertain terms how my work was strongly influenced by the great Dutch masters of the last century—van Aelst, de Heem & van Huysum—but did not mention that my entire knowledge of them, along with my standard design for a wisteria garland, came from those six months that I had then spent in the Potteries, working for Old Gould on his fine china, painting that same tedious floral arrangement over & over, & every night in the tap-room, Old Gould drearily & endlessly eulogising some dull Dutch hacks of yesteryawn—he loved them so, you see. One night his only daughter, said she, '*Come*,' she with the hair long & red gorgeous & face fern-tickled with freckles, said she, '*Come with me*.' We sneaked out & we drank so much I could hardly find the way back to Old Gould's darkened workshop where we fell onto a canvas on the floor in front of all the paintings that he had collected, & on that canvas we danced the old Dutch still life, rolling waxen pears & bursting pome-granates & me a dead limp hare at the end of it all.

In this & other ways Old Gould was a greater educa-tion than he ever realised. Scattered among his brushes & tools would be copies of Grotius & Condorcet & he would sometimes have his daughter stand up in front of the workshop with a small bust of Voltaire's sitting on the bench above her with his inscrutable smile, & she would read to us from the great man's work as we painted our intricate designs over & over.

So taken with Candide & Dr Pangloss were we that

me & my beauty forsook the Dutch still life & began dancing the Enlightenment instead, & she would take such joy from Voltaire's smile of reason entering her, advancing & receding like a slow wave waiting to break, thinking all the time to herself how lovely it was to have one's own garden attended to so.

As you can see, it was then a tragedy when Old Gould on his way back from the market with some onions was pounded to death beneath a stagecoach bound for Liverpool. The workshop was sold by his executors, his daughter unexpectedly gained a small sum of money & larger pretensions, & she, armed with both & abandoning the joys of reason that had meant so much to her as well as me, made a suitably advantageous marriage with an ironmonger from Salford with a face like an anvil & a soul like slag, & so I never saw her freckles fade, her auburn hair dull, never had to watch our love turn to that non-colour, white.

I, meanwhile, was forced once more to make my way in the wider world, taking with me three things that have served me tolerable well since: a knowledge of the joys Voltaire can bestow, which went somewhat beyond what Reason can ever know; Old Gould's book of engravings of his beloved Dutchies' still lifes; & his last name, for which neither he nor his daughter any longer had use.

When asked my handle in the first pothouse I stopped to pass the following evening, I tried it on for size, & cried out, 'I am William Buelow Gould!'

I really did think it sounded a whole lot better than before, those splendid three words pulling the mouth *out-in-out* &, proper pleased with my new self,

I winked at a woman I later came to know as the publican's wife while sounding my new middle name. And what do you know?—the publican's wife smiled back! Before said she aught a word I knew that she was a bedswerver, aiming to sweep out from her hubby's cot into mine, which poor as it was that night—a damp straw palliasse with a mouldy scent in the stables—was still more than welcoming enough for us.

'And my name,' whispered I close to her ear, 'is a song that will be sung.'

Later that night I learnt that a stranger with a ludicrous name always fares better than a familiar with a normal moniker when dancing the old Enlightenment.

'You know what I like about you?' said she. 'You're different from the others around here.' Then she told me how she had walked to London the previous year to watch Lord Byron's coffin go past, & because everyone has to be a poet now & few are, she liked me all the more when I told her how she had breasts like wax fruit, which really wasn't a compliment at all but the first thing that came into my mind when I saw them, & when said she, 'What else do I remind you of?' said I, 'Well, that just depends on what else you might care to show me.' Said she, 'The Devil you are indeed! Perhaps you aren't that different after all.' Said I, 'You'll just have to see,' & so it went, until she felt the full Flemish painter & agreed that it really wasn't that different, & nor was I, that we men were all the same, & then she grew angry . . .

Yet again the Surgeon interrupts, & yet again I am compelled to agree, this time with his assertion that the role of Art will diminish as that of Science grows. And why not?—when it is after all the Surgeon's very own fine idea & my mind is in any case filled only with thoughts of what art might mean to me, which as you can see really wasn't that high & pure at all but lovely nevertheless, a vision glorious of the publican's wife's splendid white thighs & buttocks rising & falling as we danced the dear old Enlightenment, & it all seems a dim, lost thing—

'SCIENCE—INEVITABLE ASCENT—ART—SERVANT—' & he is off again. I myself have no real thoughts whatsoever on this matter of Science & Art but only a few sweet memories to which I cleave, for I am nothing more than a falsely accused forger & take each job as it comes & do it as well or as badly as money demands. For some reason I remembered being told by Old Gould, who prided himself on such matters, that the Frenchie philosopher Descartes thought all matter consisted of whirlpools, but somehow I didn't think the Surgeon would want to hear that everything from foetuses to hangovers to death circles, so instead said I nothing more.

Finally the Surgeon stood up, picked up the shoeing stool, turned, rapped twice on the cell door with the stool, & light & a burst of fresh air briefly filled my dark, fetid cell as the turnkey opened the door to let the Surgeon out.

At this point I knew it was time to intervene.

'A man such as you, sir,' began I appropriately deferential, 'being, if I may be so bold, somewhere in his forties, obviously a man in his prime who desires to secure his lot against a hostile future by inviting posterity to share in your wonderful achievements as a scientist . . . '

'PRECISELY,' said the Surgeon. 'THOUGH—ESTIMATE OF AGE—FLATTERING—FORTIES?—YES? NO?—YES—POSSIBLY.'

'Being such a man,' said I, tongue sliding into the easy rut of well-worn words, 'you know that such things cannot be bought cheaply or easily, but arise out of the estimation of one's peers.'

'ABSOLUTELY,' said the Surgeon, & he swallowed somewhat embarrassed, 'ADVANCEMENT OF SCIENCE THOUGH, NOT SELF—DESIRE?'

'Science,' said I, feigning both comprehension & agreement, 'desires only science.' I began lowering my head. 'But to record that on canvas, one needs the scientist as well as the science, to paint you with your achievements, to . . . ' The Surgeon swallowed some more, as if his dreams of scientifick immortality demanded proofs other than those I was offering. I could feel my tongue slipping out of its rut, losing its way. 'If you would allow me the honour of painting your portrait. I—'

The Surgeon cut me short with a fierce uplift of his beetle brow—and for a dreadful moment I feared two of the many marsupial mice in my cell had leapt up onto his face, mistaking it for a pumpkin, & were hanging off his forehead over his warty eyes.

'FISH, GOULD!—THAT FISH—THE EYE—MOST SCIENTIFICK.' I must have been still so bedazzled by his eyebrows that he thought I had not heard him properly. 'CAPTAIN'S FISH,' he continued, a little irritated. The mice arched up in emphasis over his nose. 'MAN MUST FIND HIS MÉTIER—YOURS I BELIEVE —YOU HAVE FOUND—*EN UN MOT*?—FISH?' He paused, looked at the ceiling & back at me, 'IN FISH, YES?—NO? YES—IN MR TOBIAS ACHILLES LEMPRIERE, A MAN WHO RESPECTS TALENT, A SCIENTIST—YOUR PATRON, YES YOU MAY HAVE ALSO FOUND JUST THAT—TO YOU, SIR, GOOD DAY.'

And with that he was gone, & with him, reckoned I, any chance of my evading the chain gang.

VI

OUR SECOND MEETING took place immediately after my entirely unexpected release, when I was trooped straight from my cell to Mr Lempriere's quarters, a small, somewhat ramshackle whitewashed earth cottage. On the way we passed a flogging taking place in the muster yard. The flagellator was pausing between each stroke of the cat, running the tails between his fingers to squeeze out the excess blood, then dipping the cat's tips in a small bucket of sand kept for the purpose at his side, so that they might have extra gravelly bite on each new stroke.

After a short walk we arrived at a roly-poly building near the boatyards. I was ushered without ceremony into a dark, odorous &, in spite of the darkness, what appeared to be a messy room. I almost failed to notice the Surgeon reposed like a sea lion on a chaise longue.

About him I began to make out his proudly arranged

possessions—overbaked, crusty & craggy to the touch, doughy & soft in their centre, be it the rough worm-riddled table, or the portraits that oozed over his walls, all of which seemed to wish to shout, 'We too are Lempriere.' Being of a polite disposition I had no desire to express how much sorrow I accordingly felt. Most striking were the innumerable oddities arrayed around him like the sun around Egyptian kings in the pyramids: more bones than a knacker's vat—racks of marsupial skulls, rib cages, thigh bones & entire skeletons of various animals—as well as assortments of feathers, shells, dried flowers, rocks; framed collections of butterflies, moths & beetles; & trays of bird eggs.

Before I had even sat down the Surgeon was launching into a subject about which I was devoid of either interest or curiosity.

'AS YOU KNOW—WOULD WELL SO—IN SCIENCE FEW NAMES HIGHER,' Mr Lempriere told me, 'THAN CARL VON LINNAEUS—YES? NO? YES—GREAT SWEDISH NATURAL HISTORIAN.'

Bewildered, I nodded knowingly. Mr Lempriere gestured for me to sit down on a stool opposite him, & pointed toward a decanter of the best French Martinique rum (no watery Bengal rum was this, that tasted of burnt sugar & a damp fire, to which I was accustomed), indicating I was to help myself. He then—to use one of his more favoured words—*discoursed* upon the revolution in the affairs of man that the Linnaean system of classification of plants & animals was beginning.

For every plant, a species; for every species, a genus; for every genus, a phylum. No more vulgar folk names

for plants based on old witches' tales & widows' remedies, no more ragwort & nightelder & foxglove, but a
scientifick Latin name for every living thing, based on a
thorough scientifick study of its physical features. No
more thinking that the natural & human worlds are
entwined, but a scientifick basis for separation of the
two, & human advancement on the basis of that scientifick difference forever after.

He seemed all index learned, & I wondered if he had
ever listened to a book in its whole as I had to the old
Frenchie's tales of dear Dr Pangloss & Candide. He was
full of inkhorn words going so far as to call grog shops
zythepsaries, which seemed several syllables too long to
be uttered by any I had ever met within such places, &
never used a straight word when a long bastard Latin one
could be awkwardly jammed in its place, so that his sentences became like the room in which we sat,
overcrowded & awful confused.

If in his appearance he harked back to the past, in his
ideas & ambitions he wished to be seen as a man of the
future. But this was clearly not a conversation—much as
I tried to make it one by occasionally repeating the last
phrase he had spoken, as if by echoing him he might be
alerted to the notion of another person in the room—but
a manifesto in which he managed to spectacularly meld
scientifick & domestick opinion into a single sentence
that made no sense whatsoever.

'ERASMUS DARWIN—WISE MAN,' said he at one
point, 'BUT WHY LEMON IN GREEN TEA?'

Again I found myself understanding nothing of
what he talked about but I nodded sagely, occasionally

uttering a slightly sceptical 'Well' or an uninterested 'Oh,' & pushing my closed rum-moistened lips out & up to my nose, to convey the sense of comprehending what he was heating up about, & to indicate an active, critical interest when he showed me his most prized possession, the celebrated—he told me in no uncertain terms—tenth edition of Linnaeus's *Systema Naturae* for animals.

The Surgeon was now rising to his fullness: 'INDEED,' he continued, & to ensure no abatement of my interest he poured me another French Martinique rum, 'TIME IS RAPIDLY COMING—PROPERLY CLASSIFY NOT JUST ANIMALS—ALL LIVING THINGS—*EN UN MOT*?—PEOPLE—YES? NO? YES.'

I nodded, skolled, & held out my empty glass this time without even being asked, & the Surgeon—wonderful, generous Mr Lempriere—filled it yet again.

'DON'T BELIEVE ME—DON'T?—BUT YOU WILL, YES, YOU WILL—FIRST SUCCESSFULLY CLASSIFY ALL CONVICTS IN A CLASS FROM I TO 26—THEN ON SUCH BASIS MAKE SOCIETY ANEW.'

'Science?' asked I.

'APPLIED,' confirmed he.

He then went off into several byways of conversation, about how gonorrhoea could be successfully treated with mercury ointment. 'A NIGHT WITH VENUS,' he sighed at one point. 'A LIFE WITH MERCURY.' He shook his head. 'HOT RUM—YOUNG GIRL—OLD DOCTOR—CRUEL—CRUEL.' He rattled on about a French botanist called Lamarck whose seven-volume *Histoire naturelle des animaux sans vertébrés* he described as a taxonomic *tour de force*, & the infinite perfectibility of pigs through breeding.

At this point he indicated with the wave of a fat finger that we were to make our way outside. After showing me the beauty of his one sash window at the rear of his cottage, the only such window on the island, which he had brought with him from Hobart Town to be fitted in his new residence, Mr Lempriere led me around to the back of his cottage where he kept a pig, a large boar he called Castlereagh after the Prime Minister, because, as a Whig, Mr Lempriere saw himself as a man of advanced opinions who held no truck with simpering Tories.

It was difficult to get a bearing on where this was all going, & I gave up trying & simply followed. The hog was of indeterminate breed & lived in a pen that adjoined the cottage. Even by the squalid standards of the island, Castlereagh's home was a festering, stinking horror of churned mud in which the Surgeon daily threw his slops & leftovers any convict would have happily scrabbled for. The hog—a black & white mottled porker—was consequently the only life form that seemed to prosper on the island & had reached a gigantic size, a great stench & an ugly disposition.

It may be thought that the hog, being an intelligent animal as pigs are known to be, would have tried to curry favour with the Surgeon, who insisted on feeding it himself in order to ensure that all food went to the animal & not the servants. But to the contrary, Castlereagh's anger with the world & all who lived in it seemed only to grow with his bulk, & it would as readily charge the Surgeon as anyone else.

The Surgeon's purposes in keeping the pig seemed confused. Sometimes he declared that it was to be for a banquet for the officers of the establishment, at others for a Christmas dinner, or the arrival of the new pilot, & sometimes just for the perverse pleasure of drawing a knife across its throat, so that the pig's end might mirror that of his contemptible namesake. Sometimes he talked of selling it to the Commissary for money, & at other times of bartering pieces of a slaughtered Castlereagh with the other officers for the substantial items fresh meat commands among those who have tasted only rancid pickled pork for years.

In truth, I suppose he kept it because it made him feel powerful to have so much food in his control, to know that no-one could look at him without enviously dreaming of an unbroken banquet of pig—pea&ham soupbrawnbaconbakedtrottersblackpuddingporkknuck lesroastporkcracklingpig'sfootjelly. So a day of reckoning for Castlereagh was constantly postponed, with the effect that the hog continued to grow ever more gigantic & with a temper fouler than its breath.

But at that time I knew little of this because the Surgeon was off talking again, as he guided me back inside his roly-poly cottage. He continued on about how he believed that we had a valuable role to play in breaking the world into a million classifiable elements that would lead to a whole new society. I understood none of it, except that feigned interest was returned with more French Martinique rum, which I had initially thought was very good & now was inclining to believe excellent.

'I AM,' said he, leaning back & raising his obelisk of a white head & pulling back his slobbery walrus lips, so that I might understand that the next few words were to be underlined, 'IN CONTACT—VERY IMPORTANT—COSMO WHEELER?—WITH *THE* MR COSMO WHEELER —NOTED ENGLISH NATURAL HISTORIAN,' something which was clearly of great import, if only I knew what that import was.

I didn't.

But I wasn't so stupid as to betray my ignorance & let it be known that the repute of the aforementioned Mr Cosmo Wheeler was not yet completely universal.

'Famous,' suggested I.

'EXACTLY,' agreed he.

Whoever he was, the mysterious Mr Wheeler had impressed upon the Surgeon the majesty & centrality of the Surgeon's work in collecting & cataloguing specimens & sending them all back to him in England. This work, Mr Wheeler had written, was to be the Surgeon's 'Historical Destiny'. Reading between the lines, underlined or otherwise, it seemed to me that if this English natural historian was noted, it may well have been because he was building a fair old career out of the various bits & pieces the Surgeon & his other colonial collectors were shipping back to him.

For his part, the Surgeon appeared blind to the uses to which he was being put, & pathetickally grateful for the slightest association with such an eminence as he deemed Mr Cosmo Wheeler to be. It sometimes seemed that the Surgeon believed that if he could only smash the mystery of the world up into enough fragments & ship them all back to Mr Wheeler to catalogue, then the mystery would disappear & all would be knowable, & with all knowable, everything would be solvable & improvable, all matters of good & evil explicable & remediable on some Linnaean ladder of creation.

Our own part in this gargantuan act of vandalism was to record as fully & as clearly as possible what the Surgeon, quoting Cosmo Wheeler, referred to as 'THE SMALL WORLD OF MACQUARIE HARBOUR ICHTHYOLOGY', & then send our records off to Mr Wheeler for him to categorise & systematise.

As always when I didn't understand a word he had said, I nodded & the pitcher was brought once more to my glass & levelled but not poured. The good Surgeon held the pitcher poised, fixed me with his watery stare, to indicate that his system of thought was now about to reveal its genius in a revelatory statement of the greatest profundity.

'WHAT I AM SAYING, GOULD,' said the Surgeon, leaning close, placing one small fat hand on my knee & at the same time smiling—two physically repulsive gestures to which I may well have had a very adverse response had not at that moment the glorious rum of French Martinique once more begun to flow—'IS FISH.'

VII

IT WAS CLEAR to me even then that the Surgeon was entirely mad. We were to start making pictures not of ferns or birds or kangaroos or platypi but fish, to record in paint pilchards & pike, monkfish & boarfish, or whatever their antipodean equivalents or opposites might be. For fish being fish, specimens of a useful nature could not easily be preserved, &, more to the point, Mr Cosmo Wheeler had been very specifick in writing the Surgeon that the reputation of a scientist grew not simply out of Industry & Genius, but, as the great Swedish naturalist - collector Count Linnaeus had himself shown through the example of his life, by being as strategic as Wellington in making choices as to what to collect & what not to collect.

I could not then have known how such madness, this job of painting fish to further another man's reputation in another country, would come to overwhelm my life to such an extent that it would *become* my life—that I would, as I am now, be seeking to tell a story of fish using fish to tell it in every which way, even down to the sharkbone quill & the very sepia ink with which I write these words, made from a cuttlefish that squirted me only a few hours ago.

It had drifted in to the cell with the tide last night & I managed to spear it with my paintbrush as the tide went out this morning. A poor creature swept up in something greater than itself, it spewed its dark ink up at me with as much fearful fury as it could muster. Though I copped some in the eye & a bit in the gob, I managed to catch a good third of it in my skilly bowl, & with this dark ink that dries to the shitty colour of this shitty settlement, I put all these memories down.

'Fish were what were crying out to be next

Systematised & thereby Understood,' Mr Cosmo Wheeler had written the Surgeon, '& someone in as privileged a position as you, my dear Lempriere, as to be able to collect & record a whole new Exotic World of Fish!'

I recall that I did not feel the rum in either my mouth or throat as I drained the glass in a single gulp, my eyes still focused on his milky peepers as the Surgeon went on detailing the contents of Mr Cosmo Wheeler's most recent correspondence with him.

'And,' added Mr Cosmo Wheeler in a rhetorical query, 'is it not out of such happy coincidences of Place (Macquarie Harbour—Transylvania—Van Diemen's Land) & Genius (Tobias Achilles Lempriere) that History is so often made?'

Because he valued his amateur collector - naturalist so highly, continued Mr Cosmo Wheeler, he would be willing—if the specimens proved sufficiently novel, the pictures of a proper standard—to reproduce the fish in his next work, tentatively titled *Systema Naturae Australis*.

The Surgeon had talked so long & so hard that he had allowed me the privilege of not having to say anything that might expose my story of being an Artist for the lie it was. He had so cleverly convinced himself of my own worth that even I briefly succumbed to the vanity of believing it might just be possible for me to paint accurate pictures of fish of the highest scientifick standard.

Not that I said so, or said anything.

To tell the entire truth, I wasn't able to get a word in.

The Surgeon interpreted my inability to interrupt as only the necessary & praiseworthy servility I now owed him as my new patron, an acknowledgment of the supremacy of power that was as necessary to the Artist as the ability to draft. He grew drunker, & his conversation became more intimate & confessional.

'SEE ME,' he at one point confided, 'LATTER-DAY MEDICI—YOU BOTTICELLI!'

I briefly smiled, but then I noticed he did not, that his dull eyes seemed to have become incandescent, that this was not a joke, that he was only talking all the more, saying:

'BUT OUR TASK—GREATER—NOT INTERPRETING NATURE FOR DECORATION—SEEKING TO CLASSIFY—TO ORDER NATURE—THEN ONLY RIDDLE REMAINING WILL BE GOD—BUT MAN?—MAN'S DOMINION WILL BE ENTIRELY KNOWN & KNOWABLE, & MAN'S MASTERY COMPLETE—HIS FINAL EMPIRE NATURE—DO YOU UNDERSTAND?—YES? NO? YES—DO YOU?'

I didn't. It sounded suspiciously like an attempt by the Surgeon & Mr Cosmo Wheeler to recreate the natural world as a penal colony, with me, the gaoled, now to play the part of turnkey. Still, I had had worse offers.

'Hierarchy?' offered I.

'ELYSIUM,' said he.

As Ackermann's china plate Billy Blake used say, only by contraries do we advance. But guessing this wasn't what the Surgeon meant, I was trying to think of something else to say about the Nobility of Science when the Surgeon saved me from answering by pouring me yet another French Martinique rum.

Brandishing the decanter in front of him like a torch he told me how our work was to begin with my painting one by one all the fish to be found in the inland sea of Macquarie Harbour, all the sea creatures that floated dead along the poisoned waters of the King & Gordon rivers. He had talked to the Commandant, & henceforth I was being taken off all other duties in order to become the Surgeon's servant.

My duties would divide into spending half a day cleaning & washing as the Surgeon's house servant, & the other half-day I was to be absolutely free to concern myself solely with fish, and, more precisely, their painting.

The Surgeon, now well-primed, stood up & wavered back & forth, a tubby metronome beating a slow sweep between his need for dignity & his desire to present me with a gift. He stumbled & then half-fell, half-collapsed into my lap, bearing as if in offering a wooden box, the size of a large cigar case, inside which were arrayed numerous pots of watercolour paint, some used, a few not—all the colours of a worn-out rainbow—& six brushes, all of them old & tatty.

Then he slid to the ground, still talking, & I resumed daydreaming of new names & old loves. At some point later in the evening I realised he had been asleep on the floor for at least half an hour & I hadn't noticed.

VIII

IN A BATTERED portmanteau made of dark morocco stowed beneath his bed, the Surgeon kept his several books of natural history, along with a short letter he had received from Jeremy Bentham in answer to a long discourse the Surgeon had written to the great man on how Bentham's principle of the panopticon—a model prison in which all men could be constantly watched—might profitably be extended to natural history.

This letter was his most prized possession, talisman of his prospective status as a future fellow of the Royal Society, which, he assured me, was the ultimate imprimatur that could be given a Gentleman & Scientist, & marked one out as a Man of History.

To tell the whole truth, I must admit at first Billy Gould had no great interest in the fish, & if he could have escaped them, he most surely would have. Searching through the Pudding's portmanteau he came upon Linnaeus's *Systema Naturae* as well as an abridged chapbook edition of Pliny's *Natural History,* which the Surgeon dismissed as superstitious claptrap written by an ignorant Roman.

But I discovered in its pages something more than a mythical bestiary of manticores & basilisks. In Pliny's observations I discovered that man, far from being central in this life, lived in a parlous world beyond his knowledge, where a pregnant woman might lose her child when a lamp was snuffed in her presence, a world in which man is lost & less but lost & less amidst the marvellous, the extraordinary, the gorgeously inexplicable wonder of a universe only limited by one's own imagining of it.

Dr Bowdler-Sharpe's *Book of Eggs* on the other hand, nesting at the bottom of the case, was a different matter, altogether more in the spirit of the panopticon. It listed 14,917 different types of eggs produced by 620 different species of bird. Dr Bowdler-Sharpe's style was economical to the point of brutal obviousness.

Viz—
The eggs of the *Orthonyx temmincki* (Spine-tailed log-runner) are of an elliptical form, moderately glossy, & of a plain white colour. Three eggs measure respectively: 1.07 by .76; 1.13 by .8; 1.17 by .8.

The Pudding's tastes, I was coming to realise, could never—no matter how hard I tried—be mine. He was a cracked system lacking only a subject, Dr Bowdler-Sharpe in search of yet one more egg to measure. He wanted to be the ichthyologist, but I would rather have been the fish. His dreams were of capture, mine of escape.

I would prefer to see a thrush, as I had as a child, feeding in a hard winter on snails, than read such rot as Dr Bowdler-Sharpe; rather watch the thrush smashing the snails against a rock in the midst of a litter of other similarly shattered shells until it can free the meal inside. Much better that than an illustrated inventory of thrush types, defined by claw similarities, by beak differences. Much better to hear the plaintive *toot-toot* of the nightingale when it is alarmed & see its young chicks freeze stock-still in response, than analyse a collection of stuffed birds in a glass case by radius of head & distance of extended wing tip. Such collecting &

classification is all up, as my cobber the madman Clare once remarked, a sort of ambitious fame, & not one worthy of any praise.

Let me confess at this point, that never have I been so ill-prepared for a task as that of painting the Surgeon's fish. I felt a momentary & rather dreadful sense of panic. There was, I reasoned to myself in an attempt to calm my nerves, my past as an engraver upon which I could draw. But all I had really got out of that was one more warrant for my arrest under my old name, and—for a short time anyway—a blemish-free new name. There was my experience as a colonial painter—a decorator of taprooms & pub signs & occasional portraits—but I knew my limits. My drafting skills, such as they were, were restricted to a crude copying of the details of bank & promissory notes or caricaturing the whims of the lowly & the vanities of the free settlers, all flat objects that can be part traced, part graphed & reproduced through a system of squares, part easily guessed at.

A fish, on the other hand, is not an easy item to forge.

A fish is a slippery & three-dimensional monster that exists in all manner of curves, whose colouring & surfaces & translucent fins suggest the very reason & riddle of life. When forging money, I had always salved my conscience by concluding that I was merely extending the lie of commerce.

But a fish is a truth, & having no idea how to tell a truth, far less paint it, for several days I entirely avoided the issue by burying myself in enormous industry in &

around what passed for the Surgeon's home. As I cleaned & washed & then rebuilt the rotting & decaying parts of the Surgeon's cottage, as I tidied up his many & varied collections, I returned to my fantasy of becoming a portrait painter for Hobart Town society—a contradiction, I know, I heard the joke a dozen times before I even arrived there—but I fancied faces as rough as theirs with pasts as dirty as theirs deserved someone with as little talent as me to paint them. This wasn't work for the Academy or the Prado or the Louvre, but for the bastard & idiot issue of the Old World who through theft & terror thought they had a right to rule the New.

Which, I ought add, they did.

It's the only way anyone ever got to rule & I for one didn't seek to argue with it, only to derive a small living on its fringes. For as Capois Death said, if shit ever becomes valuable, the poor will be born without arseholes. That was our fate, & I didn't pretend I could alter it, I only wished to survive as best I could, & what else was I to do? I had no desire to become a sawyer or shepherd or whaling deckhand. I didn't have the hands or back for it, far less the necessary practical skills.

At the beginning I only wanted to rub along with the whole rotten system, & if that meant making copies of whatever got me through the day—be it bank notes or burghers' bumfaces—rendered in a way that didn't draw undue attention to themselves or to me, well so be it.

My immediate problem was that while my painting skills may have been adequate to misrepresent the gentry, they were not so sufficiently developed that I was convinced I could turn out acceptable paintings like the kelpy at the standard that was obviously expected, & I worried that if I was found to be not what the Pudding had persuaded himself I was, then I might yet end up on the gibbet. And even if I did manage to rise to the job, I was no longer sure I wanted it. I had been seductively promised the position of Botticelli, but in the cold light of a new day it was starting to look suspiciously like taking up the burden of Bowdler-Sharpe.

If I could have found a more comfortable & less dangerous billet I would have gladly taken it. But there were no other options & I had no choice but to concentrate my mind on the matter of how I might come up with a passable rendering of a fish.

When the Surgeon went out to supervise a flogging, or to the muster to deny all the sick & dying on the chain gangs time off or entry to the hospital, & I was sure I was safe, I would fetch the portmanteau & carefully examine the method & style used in the various volumes to illustrate plants & animals. The best of them showed a certain spontaneity that I knew I could never approach, but the worst of them were as flat & dead as their subjects must have been when studied, & I flattered myself I could do no worse.

But then I would go down to the fishermen's jetty & look at the fish that had been netted that day, along with the occasional bloated convict drowned trying to escape, & my heart would again fill with dread, for the flopping, flapping masses of fins & scales seemed entirely beyond me.

The one talent I fancied I had in art—of capturing a certain crude likeness of character in cartoons of people's faces—I indulged myself in of an evening with charcoal on the sandstone wall of the Penitentiary. Here we all slept in lice-flecked hammocks up & down a long dreary barrack.

And here, on the evening of my seventh day as the Surgeon's servant, when, for the amusement of my fellow villains, I was sketching a crude caricature of the Surgeon naked, the most astonishing thing happened.

The Surgeon grew a dorsal fin.

I halted for a moment, a little shocked.

Someone smirked.

Capois Death laughed.

I resumed my task momentarily, resketching his eyes as big mournful orbs behind which a gill began sprouting. Then a bulbous scaled body grew outwards from behind the eyes, the over-inflated entirety of which I covered in wild slash strokes to resemble small spikes, & at the end of this prickly football a tail could be seen protruding.

IX

THE NEXT MORNING I collected a live specimen from the fishing gang, spent only a cursory time cleaning the cottage, & then moved the small round mahogany table to take advantage of what morning light made it through the single window, took out the paintbox & set to work.

The day passed fitfully, the sun swung around, & in

the afternoon the early winter rain began, scratchy & volatile, but I was much too absorbed to pay it any heed. I made several preliminary sketches, all on the same piece of paper, then wasted two perfectly fresh pieces on paintings that I botched at one point or another, the first by accident when I knocked a small bottle of Indian ink over the table, the second when I simply failed to get the proportion of the tail right because of my desire to make the picture as lifelike as possible.

But my third attempt pleased me—oh, it was no work of genius, I'll grant you—but in the slightly fearful, slightly bellicose uplift of the eye's large pupil I could feel the sudden excitement of being the angler & him being unexpectedly hooked. In the exaggerated prominence of the forehead in which he took such pride (the reservoir of genius, he had the day before confided to me, tapping at the top of his scone) I could feel his thrashing weight seeking to escape, & so I let my line run out a little in the downturned fleshy mouth, speaking of a certain unconcealable bitterness & a sensuality that was transformed into a surly, oppressive physical presence. But then I pulled back & oh! oh!—Oh I knew I now had him, yes, that was most surely him, & oh the bloated body & oh the ridiculous display of prickles & oh the ludicrously small tail at the end of the balloon of the flesh as he finally broke water & became visible. A current of joy passed through me because now I really had him, finally caught for all to see.

That evening, when the Surgeon returned, I presented him with my first picture.

The Surgeon held the painting out at full arm's length, looked out of his absurd large doe-dark eyes & down his flat fat nose at it, &, in the manner to which I had now grown accustomed, began a lengthy discourse on the defensive nature of the porcupine fish, how it blew itself up to triple its size, spikes bristling, to intimidate other fish. All the while he talked, he kept fiddling with the picture, holding it out, bringing it in close, laying it on the table, picking it back up & staring at it yet again with his arms fully extended.

Finally he declared it passably well done.

And then he was called away to attend a hanging, leaving me & the porcupine fish alone together in the late evening light.

I took a knife down from where it hung on the side of the fireplace, & placed the sharp tip against the taut body of the porcupine fish. Then I pushed.

The flesh compressed but little, then with a sudden rush of air its skin tore, & the fish deflated with the abrupt hiss of a burst bladder.

On the table there now lay a fish entirely different from the prickly monstrous form I had painted, a tiny minnow with large eyes that accused me of not understanding its need for posture, a minnow with flaccid skin & a large knife stuck through it.

I knew there would be no instruction to paint it again, that even the chain gang would not barter for such poisonous flesh. I threw it on the fire, where it draped around a slow smouldering log like one more collapsed soul.

The Stargazer

On the pus of whelks—Moonbirds, their returning—Premonitions of doom—Rise of the Commandant—His seizure of power—The question of nations—Miss Anne, her subtle influence—The invention of Europe—The sale of Australia—Rolo Palma, treating of his talking with angels—Musha Pug—His hatred of catamites—Railway fever.

I

POBJOY, WELL PLEASED with his last Constable, has returned with some sea urchins for me to eat. It is a small reward, & not much of a meal, but one more important to me than Pobjoy can imagine. I scoop the roe out with my fingers, although in truth it is not for this small salty pleasure that I covet the sea urchin, but for the bright purple spikes with which its shell is armoured like a lurid aquatic echidna. On a low-tide early evening I snap the spikes off their shell, take two of the many small beach stones that form the floor of the cell and, grinding the spikes between the stones, make a purple powder.

Next, I swirl this powder with spittle & fat, saved from the occasional rancid gob of pickled pork, in the smooth grooved palm of the scallop shell that serves as my ink pot. In this way I make my ink, watching the purple whirling in the white shell, while thinking of how purple, the colour of emperors, seems appropriate for the next part of my tale, which is of how my fortunes became inextricably entangled with those of a Caesar of the south seas, whom none will remember & who was tormented by premonitions of the ravages he knew time would inflict upon his achievements.

The King, I suspect, deems it strange that I will spend some pages talking about the Commandant, but his story is mine & mine his, for his dreams determined my destiny. I tell the King that he cannot begin to understand the perversity of my fate if he does not fully appreciate how the Commandant finally created not one but *two* alternate hells. The second, which I was only to discover much later—too late as it transpired—was the one that truly terrified me in its immortal aspirations. But the utter perversity of his achievement can only be understood by those who know the full, true & terrible story of the Commandant. Our destinies were soon to meld, however much neither of us would have wished it.

The ink with which I seek to tell this tale is not, it is true, the majestick Tyrian purple of which Old Gould would wax lyrical, that dye the ancients obtained from shellfish, squeezing the pus that purpled in sunlight from a small cyst behind the whelk's head, a dye so precious that only the richest & most powerful could afford robes of this colour, but rather an urchin purple—and that seems right for one who, far from being born in the purple, fought & kicked & killed for the sake of a colour that fades far too quickly. I make no apologies for what is then both obvious & necessary: that the prose which follows is also of a similar hue.

II

HIS TRAJECTORY WAS as silent & dark as his countenance, which he was later to take to hiding behind a gold mask, though whether out of shame or modesty or embarrassment none seemed to know; no more than they knew about his family or his military background. He was, like the bushranger Matt Brady who came to haunt him ever more, an enigma, though of a different kind, for where Brady was forever invisible, elusive both in life & dreams, the Commandant was everywhere to be seen. Yet none claimed intimacy or understanding, for that would have been to invite death.

There were stories, whispered and, much later, after his purported demise, shouted, that the Commandant had never been popular but was regarded as an idiot. It was undeniable that his precisely parted & oiled hair, his parrot's beak of a nose that he inexplicably allowed to protrude through a hole in his gold mask, the slightly ovine set of his eyes, & a mouth that even when giltedged appeared weak & crooked, conspired to give an appearance which in power was callous & formidable, but outside of power seemed merely simpering.

The strangest of all the stories was also the most persistent: that he—like us—was a crawler, a man transported for unspeakable felonies, a lag who worked on the Parramatta gangs, who had been reconvicted &

sent to Norfolk Island where he had become a fly man, beyond fear of God or indeed of any man.

When that settlement sacred to the genius of torture had been finally closed & its miserable inhabitants sent to Van Diemen's Land, his ship had met with a great storm leading to its wrecking on a Bass Strait island. The only survivor was him, now representing himself as Lieutenant Horace, whose corpse—its white face pocked with a hundred holes eaten by sea lice—had washed up alongside him on the beach that early evening as the sky above his terrified eyes had darkened, not with dusk, but with a thrumming river of moonbirds.

Such a sight he had never seen! Hundreds of thousands of moonbirds, perhaps millions, eclipsing the falling ball of sun, all swiftly gliding in one direction on long wings that seemed but rarely to lazily flap, returning to their sand-dune burrows in what was for him always a dreadful presage of night.

Trees, shelter & comfort were, on the other hand, strangers to the island. In addition to him & the moonbirds, its principal inhabitants were fleas, flies, rats, snakes & penguins whose relentless screeching of an evening combined with the cold howl of the westerly gales to render his nights an unceasing horror.

He survived for several months upon the moonbirds' fatty mutton-like meat & the solace provided by the one book washed up with him, Huntington's *History of the Napoleonic Wars*, until rescued by two Quaker missionaries who were scouring the distant wild islands of the strait for native women either purchased or abducted from their tribes by sealers. They in turn would purchase or abduct the women, & then interrogate them in order to write a fulsome report on such abuses for the London Society of Friends, which was sponsoring their mission. He had, by the time the two Quakers rowed their small whale boat into the rocky, wind-swept crag that had been his home for so long, succeeded in metamorphosing into something else, having acquired the greasy odour of minor authority, & beneath the moonbird down that lightly fluttered over his face & clothes he had even then begun convincing himself of the inevitability of invention.

With the Quakers, a black woman, & three children of another black woman who had died, for whom the Quakers had bartered some axes & sugar with a sealer, they headed southwest. They sailed for a week across the rest of the strait, then down the west coast of Van Diemen's Land until they came to the notorious penal settlement of Sarah Island, the subject of another of the Quakers' investigations.

Here the rescuers & the rescued parted ways, the latter armed with a high-pitched rhetoric of penology acquired from the earnest, thoughtful Quakers, & his own, older & lower knowledge of the animality of men, two strings which when stroked by the violin bow of his growing ambition created a powerful dissembling chord. The then Commandant, Major de Groot, welcomed one more soldier to join with the undermanned military guard of the penal settlement, while Lieutenant Horace welcomed the opportunity to augment his own invention with some actual record of service.

After Major de Groot's funeral, the Surgeon & the

Commissary had quarrelled as to who was the senior official, & ought assume command. When they proved unable to resolve the impasse themselves, Lieutenant Horace stepped into the breach. Declaring himself the only man capable of maintaining order amongst the soldiers & discipline amongst the convicts, he made himself the new Commandant. In a fashion peculiar to himself, he took advantage of his own limitations by declaring that while he had no knowledge of civil law, he understood well enough the law of men under arms, & he had the pompous old Danish clerk, Jorgen Jorgensen (until his death I never saw him without the most preposterous of affectations, a lapis lazuli necklace which he claimed to have won off General Blucher in a game of skat whilst sojourning in Dresden), prepare a declaration of martial law, the first document of what I later discovered was to be a long & remarkably fecund collaboration.

Even by the ugly standards of that ugly island, Jorgen Jorgensen—in spite of his affectations—was a miserable looking piece of pelican shit, all elongated & sharp angles, a coat hanger of a body trying to remember the coat that years before had fallen off. Invariably he wore an overly long & rusting sword that trailed in the dust & mud behind him, with his principal companion—a mangy three-legged dog he called Elsinore—hopping along in its rutted wake. As he walked he often mumbled to himself, & sometimes he sang for the dog, which could stand on its two good hind legs & whistle in response. Like his dog, Jorgen Jorgensen possessed the trick of whistling the same tune as his master. At some point, this minor clerk decided that his master would no longer be Major de Groot, but Lieutenant Horace.

No-one thought overly much of Lieutenant Horace taking command, viewing it as a formality that had to be observed until Governor Arthur in distant Hobart Town appointed someone fit & proper for the post, neither attribute being in evidence with Lieutenant Horace, who merely shrugged aside the disrespectable oddities of his own behaviour, such as the retention of the black woman the Quakers had left in his care in exchange for a solemn promise of moral & spiritual enlightenment. The convicts called her Twopenny Sal, but the Commandant—as he soon insisted on being called—with whom she first found work as a domestick, then later favour as a mistress, insisted on calling her the Mulatto. In his mind perhaps such miscegenation with someone of mixed race origins was somehow more acceptable than that with a woman so obviously a Van Diemonian native. In this, as in so many other things—such as his own unfitness for the post—he at first laughed along with everyone else, saying, 'Touch me, see, I am just like you, you can touch me.' But even as he spoke the moonbird down was falling away from his face & something else, like rock, was being revealed.

III

IN THE BEGINNING, as at the end, it was as the Commandant had long suspected: he was immortal. It was said by the handful who knew where the penal colony's Registry was that even there no precise records were to be found of the boat on which he arrived, or, for that matter, of his military history, for Jorgen Jorgensen had many years before, on the order of Major de Groot, checked through all the shipping registers & found no mention of a Lieutenant Horace.

After the Major's untimely demise, rumoured to have been the consequence of poison, official documents were found (though, admittedly, these were loose inserts in Major de Groot's letter books) that referred to letters signed by Major de Groot appointing Lieutenant Horace as his successor. Subsequently, according to an addendum in the margins, these letters had been unfortunately lost in a small fire that had taken hold of the Registry immediately after Lieutenant Horace assumed control of the settlement.

At first the new Commandant was a model of obsequiousness to his distant superiors. He had Jorgen Jorgensen pen long reports on his various improvements to the machinery of penal administration—his dietary reforms that made less food go further in ways guaranteed only to enhance the health & vigour of his convict charges; his new individual sleeping cages the length of a man & the height of a forearm intended to prevent unspeakable sin amongst the convicts; his rocking chamber pot with its elliptical bottom that needed two hands to successfully operate, thereby rendering impossible the crime of Onan, who needlessly spilled his seed in the sand.

No replies ever came.

No word of praise, of encouragement, or even, for that matter, of approbation or admonishment.

The tone of the letters the Commandant had Jorgen Jorgensen write began to alter. He began listing the problems of trying to run a settlement composed of the worst types of convicts engaging in unspeakable sin with soldiers of almost equally bad character—the latter only distinguishable from the former by the dull pink of their faded red uniforms; the dilemma of trying to ensure the settlement's survival, much less—as he was expected—making it pay its way, when he was given so few tools, no skilled labourers to make boats or to build houses, no cash & no spare food that might be bartered with passing traders. He begged for a little more in the way of rations. A few more soldiers. Some officers of some calibre, rather than as they routinely were, in disgrace for having defrauded regimental funds or having slept with the commanding officer's wife on Mauritius, or, worse yet, the commanding officer himself in Cape Town.

No replies & no supplies & no reinforcements were forthcoming.

His letters grew petulant, & then angry, & finally insulting. A short, curt memorandum arrived in reply. It was signed by an underling of the Colonial Secretary. It repeated the terms of his commission as an officer & reminded him of the sacred duty of his role until such time as the governor appointed a successor to Major de Groot.

It became clear to the Commandant that his letters, for all the good they seemed to do, might as well have been thrown into the ocean & eaten by the huge whales out beyond the heads, whose almost hourly passing in large pods was signalled by distant small rainbows of whale spout. It was at this point that the Commandant entered a slough of despond lasting several months, during which he neither shaved nor changed clothes.

When he emerged from the winter of his solitude he was wearing a gold mask that perennially smiled & other evidence of the profound effect his long isolation following his shipwreck had had upon his mind—a magnificent new blue uniform, reminiscent of that worn by Marshall Ney at the battle of Waterloo, featuring oversized feathered epaulettes startlingly similar in form to outstretched moonbird wings. Whether he adopted the mask simply to hide who he had been & prevent the possibility of exposure as an impostor, or whether he wore it to invent himself as someone who was neither Lieutenant Horace nor yet whoever it was he had been before the shipwreck, but as a new creature altogether, the Commandant, I know not.

All I can report was that the smiling mask was soon everywhere, glinting, gleeful, reflecting to us our own greed & desires, so omnipresent that no-one seemed to notice when it quietly & quickly usurped the broad arrow as the symbol of government property, stencilled on barrels & tools alike, later branded on our forearms, in a spectacular fusion of state & self & concealment so characteristick of the great man.

The Commandant had the first of innumerable long conversations with Jorgen Jorgensen after which the Dane took to penning stolid reports for the Colonial Office of steady, if unspectacular growth. In his reports progress was hampered, but never halted

nor overly impeded, by the inevitable problems of isolation, of indolent & incompetent convict workers, of
shortages of skilled workmen & tools. It was a picture
of a well-led, respectable establishment achieving small
profits & some reclamation of both land & criminal
souls. But only Jorgen Jorgensen noticed that the saliva
that glistened in the recesses of the Commandant's
gilded lips was black from the mercury he was already
taking to treat his syphilis.

The Commandant then ordered the commissariat
store to be opened up for trade. He ordered that the settlement's entire stock of barrels of salted pork be traded
with a Nantucket whaling merchant for two old whalers,
which he sent out with new convict crews in search of
the great fish of Jonah. One sank with all hands lost just
out of Hells Gates, but the other returned to a starving
settlement living on rationed flour & fish, with two
humpback whales in its hold, & the Commandant
began a trade in whale oil.

With his profits he bought more boats, & had others
go back to the island upon which he had been
marooned & hunt the moonbird for its flesh & the
seals for their skins. He formed those convicts he
trusted into an elite guard, had them shoot dead half
his soldiers, & by not informing the colonial authorities, kept receiving their wages as dead-pay. He
doubled the rate of felling of Huon pine, & halved the
amount he sent back to the colonial authorities, then
as trade grew brisk, quadrupled his felling & quartered
the amount he sent now only as a forlorn tribute to
Hobart Town, along with letters speaking of the

almost insurmountable problems of poor tools, sawyers of no experience, epidemics of unspeakable sin, & weather so awful the rivers were frozen for six months of the year.

His trading grew exuberant & exotic: a score of barrels of whale oil for the decadent scent of a single overripe guava, shipwrights' tools for iguana eggs, a whale boat for a large cargo of green bananas, much prized redcoat uniforms for silk turbans.

In spite of what the Portuguese traders told their Brazilian sailors under their breath as they emptied their ship holds of Moluccan feathers, & contrary to what the barefoot convicts grunted to each other during their cruel, unending ardour of hauling huge Huon pine logs through trackless rainforest to the frozen river's edge, not all his trade was complete madness.

For the pine, the oil of which he claimed could be used as an aphrodisiac & a cure for the clap, making it a doubly virtuous wonder that both promoted & protected its adherents in the torrents of love, he extracted the finest silk cloth from India. For a horde of sulphur-crested cockatoos he had painted to resemble baby macaws & trained to recite melancholic verse in the manner of Pope & several songs of passion in the earthier argot of their convict trainers, he gained fourteen Brazilian caravels & seven cannons, which he promptly exchanged for a principality in Sarawak that a Levantine merchant had won in a game of tarok on his way south to the fabled kingdom of Sarah Island, the subsequent sale of which financed his palace & the new wharf.

For the continent of Australia over which he had recently claimed sovereignty by having Musha Pug row over to the mainland & there plant the new flag of the Principality of Sarah Island upon an abandoned beach, he obtained a fleet of Siamese girls. At the beginning they set up their trade in groves lined with manfern fronds, but when the evening light grew thin & their groves grew damp, the Siamese girls took to gathering with their manfern fronds along the protected northern wall of the Penitentiary. There they touted for trade & called upon the crawlers to show that they were real men, & drank their semen in the belief that it cured the consumption that had become a plague among so many of them.

His reputation grew, his name began to be spoken far & wide, & boats began appearing with all manner of traders, merchants, beggars & charlatans. The Commandant welcomed them all, & what started off as furtive trading along the southern stockade wall, administered but not controlled by the felons of a Saturday afternoon, grew into a market & the market into a bazaar & the bazaar into the idea of a nation. 'For what is a nation?' asked the Commandant of the Surgeon, his high voice weird & bowing as the old saw he was repeating, 'but a people with a trading fleet? A language but a dialect with an army? A literature but words sold as provenance?'

IV

THE COMMANDANT'S IMPERSONATION of Lieutenant Horace had one great & unforeseen consequence:

the receipt of the dead man's mail. This was unremarkable & sporadic, save for a relentless river of letters from
the dead lieutenant's sister, Miss Anne. From certain
asides in her writings, the Commandant gathered the
impression that Miss Anne's original brother, before
being bored in his death by sea lice, was bored in his life
by Miss Anne's letters. He rarely, if ever, had responded.
But Miss Anne's surrogate brother, the Commandant,
proved more dedicated a correspondent. He wrote
regularly & enthusiastically, sometimes sending two or
even three letters to her every one.

Perhaps at the beginning he was intending to use the
letters as a small library of relevant personal information to help in his impersonation of Miss Anne's dead
brother. Instead of himself, he filled his letters—
copies of which I many years after came across in a letter book—with questions seeking to tease out details of
her family, her world, her interests & passions &
enthusiasms.

But the correspondence rapidly took on a life of
its own. Whether it was directly implied by her writing, or simply inferred by the Commandant in his
reading, he came to believe that his newly found sister was an utterly remarkable being. Miss Anne,
delighting in her brother's fresh interest & growing
appreciation of her, wrote more, & wrote more
closely to her heart. So changed was Miss Anne's
tone, that it almost seemed to the Commandant
that they were being written by an entirely different
person, one he now recognised as his true sibling.
And as her letters altered, the Commandant no

longer found them a necessary task of research, but rather a passion demanding demonstration. For as his confidence in the impregnability of his own position as the leader of the island had grown, so had his sense of isolation from others. Only in Miss Anne's letters was he able to find both a source of intimacy & inspiration that demanded, he increasingly felt, some requital in kind.

I have used the image of a relentless river to describe Miss Anne's letters, but this is imprecise. Certainly her enchanting tales seemed to be written in this fashion, twice, sometimes thrice weekly; but they were delivered & thus received only once or twice a year—and therefore their effect on the Commandant's mind was not so much the gentle erosion of a stream upon its banks, but more that of a tidal wave, obliterating everything in its path.

When later I came to paint several of these letters, I found their tone inevitably exuberant, the form overrunning, sentences tumbling over each other, phrases leapfrogging ideas, the writer panting to tell the one she believed to be her younger brother of all the new wonders of the age, made all the more remarkable by some personal association—high tea with George Stephenson's sister who thought her idea of calling the locomotive 'The Ebullient Thunderer' excellent, a risqué evening watching bear baiting at the Five Courts where she was introduced to the poet John Keats, with whom she had compared notes, wrote she, on wayward brothers lost in the New World.

These letters tormented the Commandant, who

had become profoundly afflicted by the pathos of distance. They distorted his perspective of the Old World, diminishing the everyday, the banal, the chicanery & the mediocrity of Europe; exaggerating the marvellous, the sublime, the astounding of that distant world half a year's voyage away.

In the Commandant's mind events in Europe came to seem epochal, & connected in unexpected ways. Thus the steam locomotive & Byron's *Don Juan* & Baron Rumford's splendid scientifick fireplaces—all of which arose from some delightful personal association with Miss Anne—leapt into the Commandant's imagination simultaneously as one, creating an idea of smokeless Romantic travel & the pleasures of the flesh that he was later to pursue with a certain mad ardour.

One night, when behind his gold mask his eyes had finally wearied from rereading her wondrous letters & closed in a dully pleasant anticipation of nearing sleep, he realised that all the new technological miracles in Europe had either been invented by Miss Anne or directly come into being from her good works, wise advice or kindly intervention: be these the locomotive, the steam ship, the steam press or the generation of the supernatural force of electricity—all were the creation of Miss Anne!

And then, after a further time, he had to concede to himself that not only matters technological, but also the very marvel of modern nineteenth-century Europe were clearly a direct consequence of his sister's imaginings. With the force of profound revelation he realised that his sister was inventing Europe, & his body shuddered in a single, violent clutch.

The next morning, as he had the old Dane calculate on a large abacus their monthly takings for spermaceti, he found himself beginning to wonder if he might not do the same. As the black & white beads clacked back & forth something else was tallying in his mind, the sum of which was that he might make the penal colony of Sarah Island the product of his imaginative will as surely as Miss Anne had Europe.

He cried out so loud that the old Dane in shock dropped the abacus, which broke upon the flagged flooring of the Commandant's cell. As the black & white beads rolled in every direction, the old Dane scrabbling after them, the Commandant shook his head in revelation. He would reinvent Europe on Sarah Island, only this time it would be even more extraordinary than any of his sister's descriptions.

And that day the old Dane's calculations were shown to be only so many black & white balls dribbling away in the dust, the Commandant found his monochrome dreams of a man inspired by the nightly return of moonbirds exploding into a kaleidoscope of colourful desires. Through a sea of convict blood he would later claim to have only ever spilt in furtherance of his people's destiny, Miss Anne's letters would henceforth be to him as a crazed lodestone by which he would navigate his strange journey, with us his unwilling passengers.

V

AT THAT TIME my life had settled into a routine that was if not pleasant then, compared to most of my fellow felons, at least tolerably comfy. Though I continued to sleep with the other convicts in the Penitentiary, between the morning & evening muster I was largely free to do whatever took my fancy & go where I liked on the island. I received extra food, a rum ration & was allowed to keep a small vegetable garden for my own use next to Castlereagh's pen. I even had a woman, which in a colony full of men, was no small matter.

She was the Commandant's mistress, Twopenny Sal. My assignations with her were accordingly risky & thus furtive affairs hidden from all view, normally undertaken in that one place no-one else ventured, the small piece of bush between Castlereagh's pen & the steep bank behind it.

Here, protected by a copse of dense tea-trees & the rising miasma of pig shit, we stored in terracotta pitchers our contraband supply of a rough grog we fermented out of stolen currants & sugar, flavoured & coloured green with sassafras leaves in memory of Capois Death's Larrikin Soup. Though I would claim I was elsewhere painting fish, inevitably I was in the tea-tree fishing for Twopenny Sal's delights.

Hidden from the world, here we passed day after day. It was early winter. While over us brutal westerly winds cut across the island, in the tea-tree we had us our snug, warm & protected, close & holy as the night. Here we traded words.

My favourite: Moinee.

Her favourite: Cobber.

Twopenny Sal thrilled to stories of London, was at once terrified & excited by descriptions of crowds larger than the largest mob of kangaroos & buildings so tall & densely arrayed they made their own valleys & gorges & ravines without a tree in sight. She would in turn tell tales of how Van Diemen's Land was made, by the god Moinee striking the land & creating the rivers, by puffing away & blowing the earth up into mountains.

'And how was Macquarie Harbour made?' one day asked I. 'By *Moinee?*'

'Macquarie Harbour?' said she. 'Moinee's piss pot—*cobber.*'

She would smell of pickled herring & I would pass her my pipe & with the pipe clenched firmly in her teeth she would quiver like a fish, then smell of something altogether different & even better & then we were rooting swimming flying mollynogging most marvellous. She had small breasts & a large waist & skinny shanks & was at first voracious in her lovemaking. She would make a great deal of noise, somewhere between a Van Diemonian devil screeching at night & a stampede, which was both pleasing & frightening because it meant we ran the risk of being caught, even with Castlereagh carolling away in the background. No matter how much I implored her to enjoy her passion in muted delight, she ignored me. She had little knowledge of shame & when passion was upon her, which at the beginning, as I have said, was more than frequently, she would have as happily taken me in front of the Surgeon or the Commandant or a chain gang.

But I would be less than honest if I said all was well with me & my routine which was—though I did not know it—about to end. Looking back, it is true to say that things were even then beginning to fall apart. After a time Twopenny Sal did learn the necessary proprieties, but by then she had lost pretty well all interest in me & was spending time with Musha Pug, a dog who by dobbing had been rewarded with the cosy billet of assisting the storemaster in the Commissariat, & was a far better source of food & grog & tobacco than I had been. And I, who had taken her so for granted, missed her much more than I thought possible.

My style in my paintings of the fish was mercifully improving, & with it the prospects of my survival. My pictures were becoming pared down, as useful as a good boot, as solid as a well-fitted mizzen mast for the Pudding's ship of glorious Science.

In any case—or whatever parallel—the Pudding was well pleased, sometimes to the point of glee, as his daydreams filled with images of the Glorious Return of the Great Natural Historian & Noted Ichthyologist Lempriere to the Capital London, as he mouthed silently his rejoinders to those Ladies of Society who at the Grand Soirees of Science fell at his feet & asked how did he survive Savages & Jungles & the Hungry Hottentots, & he, with the greatest humility, replying:

'Because I believed in Science, Madam, & my own small part in its Sacred Mission.'

VI

IN DIFFERENT WAYS does the Devil present & never one easily reducible to illustration. My work was becoming increasingly frustrating & it seemed only appropriate that the evocative & luminous name 'stargazer' would suggest to my mind a fish entirely different from that which the fishing gang one morning presented me to paint. I imagined a fish possessed of some ethereal quality, as if it were some meditative virtue incarnated as fish-flesh. Such a fish would, reckoned I, be ideal for the medium of watercolour, which I found difficult in capturing density, but which had a certain ability to render the passage of light.

But the stargazer the convict fishermen had given me was a far from easy fish to paint. I don't know why I found it to be so, though in the darkness of its being, in its fiercesome looks, in its satanic horns on the edges of its terrible bull head, its vertical mouth locked in a perpetual scowl, its slimy skin, the strangeness of its eyes that sat on top of its head rather than on the side—as if it were always looking upwards at the heavens, hence its enchanting, celestial name—in all of this was contained the suggestion of something I found not alien but familiar. Yet I could not say what the nature of that familiarity was, nor why it at first disturbed me so.

A stargazer is a frightening fish by any stretch of the imagination, but not until the day I first saw one in its own world did I understand its true nature. I had gone to the fishing jetty to marvel at the netting gang's latest catch—a giant cod, with a large ball inside its belly. Beneath the sloughs of milky skin the ball was still recognisable as Doughy Proctor's head—the only thing left of him after attempting escape strapped to an old pickled-pork barrel. The chief of the netting gang, a

Vlach from the Levant by the name of Rolo Palma, gestured me to come over to where he was standing at the end of the jetty & look into the sea.

In a way that was as much a defining characterstick of the lands he came from as it was of him, Rolo Palma's destiny was to be bound up in other countries. Having ended up in England & finding English friendship manifesting itself typically as a lack of conversation, Rolo Palma—in the manner of his hero Swedenborg—instead took up speaking with angels. He had a fertile imagination & a keen interest in the natural world, & every prospect—if his acting on the angels' orders had not interposed, forcing his compulsory migration to Van Diemen's Land as a convicted murderer—of inventing a natural history system even madder than that admired by the Surgeon. But he had to make do with speculating on the existence of mythical creatures such as the minotaur & gryphon in the Van Diemonian interior & pointing out to me, perhaps five feet underwater, two devil eyes protruding from the sea floor. The fish to which the eyes belonged lay submerged in the sand—its huge head, its satanic horns, its tapering circus strongman body—still, tensed, hidden, waiting for the moment when a baby flounder drifted by overhead.

Then, an explosion of sand out of which the stargazer's great body appeared, as if forming out of the very disorder it had created. That huge mouth opening & closing all at once & all together. A body flexing & leaping, propelling the stargazer up & sharking down the hitherto unsuspecting baby flounder, leaving only the Vlach cheering & sandy water swirling suggesting a life leaving.

The lines of my first painting were weak & untrue to this capacity to manifest menace. They failed to render the monstrous proportion, the oversized head that dominated the subordinate tapering body, & my colouring was inadequate to reproducing the tension that is implicit in the musculature of all fish, but most particularly that of the stargazer.

At such times, when the fish remained only a miserable scientifick illustration, there would enter my mind like an uninvited guest the wretched image of Mr Cosmo Wheeler reinventing the World as a Great Steam Engine like those the machine breaker had tried to smash, cogs within crushing cogs, & me & all the fish being pulped to a mass meal in between their grinding teeth of taxa & systemae.

I worked & reworked my sketches & my paintings until they overflowed with redundant crisscrossed lines & colours, all of which were a net in search of a fish, but still the fish escaped me. Finally I made a painting that was still mediocre, but which I hoped might prove passable for the Surgeon. By then the fish had gone off, & though it was still boiled & eaten as soup, the netting gang were not happy with my request for a second stargazer, which they thought would be similarly spoilt.

As it transpired they never had to give the fish to me, for my fortunes were about to take one last turn for the better before everything went to Hell, & Hell came to us.

VII

THAT A BOOK should never digress is something with which I have never held. Nor does God, who makes whatever He wishes of the 26 letters & His stories work just as well *Q-E-D* as *A-B-C*.

The only people who believe in straight roads are generals & mail coach drivers. I believe the King is with me on this one. He is, I have no doubt, all for bends & diversions & sightseeing, which, while ever only the ongoing art of disappointment, still make a journey the memorable thing a journey ought be.

Warming to my idea, I put it to the King that this question of roads marks the fundamental divide between the ancient Greek & Roman civilisations. You make a straight road like the Romans & you are lucky to get three words: *Veni, vidi, vici.* You have a crooked goat path like the Greeks all over the Acropolis & what do you get? The entire damn *Odyssey* & *Oedipus Rex*, that's what. The King, something of a Classicist, stares at the ceiling, his mind filling with gryphons & centaurs &, of course, Pliny.

How could I forget Pliny?

Once more, the sagacious King had won, showing that to generalise is to be an idiot, for Pliny may have been a Roman, but he made a book more crooked & bent than Capois Death's face the day he came back to implicate me in yet one more inevitable digression. Oh, how the black publican seemed to resurface in my life at regular intervals with promises of infinite hope, & depart it leaving my world in complete despair. He was

Adventure & I was Envy, he was Trouble & I was Excitement, he was talking & I was already not hearing thinking dreaming wishing that somehow escape might now be possible.

Capois Death was as bright & breezy as if he had just been freed from the Cockchafer, smiling as though Brady himself were his closest cobber, laughing like he was the top swell of Hobart Town, quarter-flash, half-cut, fully primed Capois Death strolling through the Surgeon's door, crying, 'Damn fish, Billy boy!' & before I can say a word he's thrown my painting of the stargazer into the dull ashes of Lempriere's fire, & is off brightly yabbering again, saying, 'We've got better work on our hands.'

Even in his government slops he still cut a dash, or at least to my mind. And, as ever, he had managed to rise back up the ladder of Sarah Island. He was now, said he, an official of the National Sarah Island Railway Station, Commissary with Special Responsibilities for Travel.

Under the influence of Miss Anne's stories of the new steam locomotives that had become the rage in Europe, the Commandant, increasingly frustrated in his desire to be seen as a man of destiny, intoxicated by his sister's long descriptions of the exhilaration of a New Age coming into being, riding the railway from Manchester to Liverpool, had three years before decreed that a great train station be built.

It was a huge undertaking, requiring sandstone be quarried & shipped from far up the coast, the purchase & assembly of all the machinery needed for the work-shops & smiths & factories associated with a great train station. All this in face of those who quietly expressed the timid doubt that a train station on an island in the middle of a wilderness far off the coast of a nowhere land so blighted it existed only as a gaol was unlikely ever to be either the terminus or point of departure for any traveller. Such arguments were calmly refuted by the implacable conviction of the Commandant that railway lines grew out to train stations as willow roots to a lake, & that therefore before long it would be the busiest train station in the antipodes; that soon Manchurians & Liverpudlians would enviously & covetously talk of the National Sarah Island Railway Station. In this way, said he—and some even claimed that the gold mask was seen to smile—we will have traded our tyranny of isolation for the liberty of commerce.

Two hundred yards of line were laid to the round-house, around which ran a loop of line, such that locomotives—when they finally steamed out of the rainforest—could be turned around either on a large wooden turntable powered by a spindle pushed by two dozen convicts who had been reconsigned from the caterpillar, or by traversing the loop & then back to the station. When after several months there was still not the slightest sign of willow-like tendrils of lines snaking their way across the adjacent wilderness towards us, no evidence of iron bridges arising between the island & the mainland, the Commandant announced that he had ordered a steam train from an American whaler, using the last of the gold he had gained in selling the Gordon River & the Great Barrier Reef.

VIII

BILLY GOULD HAD not been without his problems on Sarah Island. But compared to Capois Death he had been lucky. Soon after arriving at Sarah Island Capois Death had met back up with Roaring Tom Weaver who had managed to find an easy billet for his old landlord with the shellfish gathering gang. There Capois Death incurred the malignant enmity of the convict constable Musha Pug, the gang's supervisor, who had been transported to Sarah Island because of an unsavoury interlude with a sheep. At his trial Pug, committed for bestiality, had wrongly thought himself accused of sodomy. When asked by the judge what he had to say in his defence, he felt obliged to point out that it was not a ram but a ewe with which he had been caught. Forever after his hatred of catamites—with whom he presumed he had been so criminally confused—was for him a guiding passion that fortunately found numerous outlets for expression on Sarah Island.

After having been dobbed in by Musha Pug for selling ship's silk to the Siamese girls of the manfern fronds, Capois Death was given a hundred lashes, strapped to the Cradle for a week, & then sent up the Gordon River to work as a sawyer. One evening, beneath the mottling shadows thrown in the firelight by the myrtles looming over them, he recalled the tragic history of the machine breaker of Glasgow to his fellow sawyers, speaking in such evocative language of the murderous power of steam machines, that it was mistakenly assumed he had some familiarity with mechanickal matters.

When the huge wooden crates of forged iron pieces marked 'Locomotive' arrived at Sarah Island the following month, the accompanying complex assembly instructions defeated even the ingenuity of the best shipwrights. The Commandant's despair was complete until misinformed by Musha Pug, through his extensive network of spies, that a maroon working on the felling gang up the Gordon had been boasting of how he had once built steam engines.

Upon being summoned, Capois Death offered the Commandant confident reassurances, & gave the shipwrights erratic instructions based only on an indistinct memory of a street pamphlet he had read about George Stephenson's new marvel. But it was only after the Commandant told Capois Death that he would have both him & the shipwrights feast on their own balls after having had them sliced off & grilled on a fire made up of faggots of their useless arms, that Capois Death was able to persuade the shipwrights to make sense of what seemed utterly without order, & manufacture out of a confusion of cast-iron a locomotive, with the unique feature of a small mast from which cantilevered cables held up a double smokestack that stuck horizontally out of both sides of the boiler, like a waxed moustache.

With the steam machine finally assembled, the Commandant took to taking his leave of the island with great ceremony & two Siamese girls every evening, band playing, cannons booming, soldiers parading. After which he would travel two hundred yards in the train from the station to the roundhouse. Here the train would spend the rest of the evening travelling around in circles until the engineer was vomiting & the outward wheels grew so worn from the extra weight thrown by centrifugal force that the train developed a wearying outward tilt. Inside the melancholic Commandant had fallen asleep, head on the lap of one or the other Siamese girls.

When after another year there was still no sign of any incoming rail traffic, the Commandant had four search parties sent into the interior to discover exactly from which direction the new railway lines must be inevitably advancing. No-one returned. In their absence the Commandant had all those who were in those search parties lost somewhere in Transylvania summarily tried & convicted, having by the application of hot brands to the belly of a returned escapee secured the true story of their disappearance, that they had all boarded an express locomotive bound for Ambleside in the English Lake District at a wayside stop near Frenchman's Cap—from which, incidentally, Brady & his Army of Light had alighted—with the declared intention of never returning.

When it was determinedly but respectfully put to the Commandant that a train station on an island in the middle of a wilderness was unlikely to attract any other traffic that might bring in income to offset its enormous cost, the Commandant placidly & unexpectedly agreed. He then revealed that he had for the last several months not been asleep at all in the revolving locomotive cabin, but in deep discussion with a Japanese trader called Magamasa Yamada, a man in whose land there was a great demand for wood & with whom the Commandant had entered into an arrangement to sell the entire Transylvanian wilderness in exchange for more rolling stock which the pirate had come in possession of while on a trading trip to South America. These mechanickal carts would allow the Nation to reap the inevitable boom that would accompany the abolition of the wilderness & subsequent opening up of the cleared land for settlement. No-one was willing to say to His Gold Mask that the endless circling in the railway carriage had tipped the already disturbed equilibrium of his mind into complete lunacy.

The only one not surprised the following summer when the junks of Japanese sawyers arrived was the Commandant himself. He watched as they unloaded the promised rolling stock. The cabins were riddled with woodworm & rot, but as the Commandant would always sit only in the improvised coal truck that had been designated the Regal Cabin, this seemed to be of no real matter.

IX

As I STARED at the stargazer ascending into the chimney, now so many pieces of charred paper, Capois Death, with his cack-headed leer, began telling me all about his new position, how following his success in redesigning the locomotive, his role was to foster a notion of travel that might encourage use of the national railway station, the national locomotive & accompanying rolling stock.

I knew better than to be talking when I needed to be

listening, but still I felt the need to venture the observation that on an island approximately one square mile in area, there was nowhere to go.

'Precisely,' said the old publican seeking—I felt—to affect an air of mystery which to my shame I must say succeeded in making me feel intrigued, 'but there *will* be.'

He told me I was to present myself at the train station immediately prior to that night's departure of the Sarah Island Express. That misty evening, as the boiler was slowly brought to pressure in preparation for departure, as the air became a fiery-coloured scrim of cinders & ash, as I stood barefoot & ankle-deep in the mud below the siding staring upwards, the Commandant, from behind a drawn sooty curtain in the Regal Cabin, explained at length to me his conviction that Commerce—for which, it seemed, he mistook the endless circling velocity of his locomotive—was now entering not only new territory for Trade, but also for Art. He then explained why he felt it entirely necessary to have me strapped to the front of the locomotive so that I might better experience the new aesthetick of movement.

He drew the curtain back a little, but from where I stood all I could make out was a little of his gold mask & two small eyes reflecting the disturbing glowing yellow of the mask. Though I demurred—politely— the Commandant insisted—gently—and had me immediately seized by Musha Pug. Without further talk, I was firmly bound with several belts & leather thongs to the locomotive's front railing.

To the growing roar of the steam engine & the

rhythmic clatter of iron wheels on iron rails, I circled endlessly. Within a few minutes I was vomiting, & a few minutes after that I had nothing left to retch save a foul green bile that spread like the vomit before over my clothes. On & on, round & round, & no attempt to lose myself in sleep or daydreaming or focusing on thoughts of food or women helped in any way. My only sensations were a nausea that bordered on a violent assault of the senses, a stench of coal smoke that filled my lungs, a feeling that my entire body was being violated & crippled, a knowledge that I was utterly alone. If this was the future, thought I in one of the few moments of lucidity granted me that long evening, it was not a future that seemed worthy of the name.

After the locomotive slowly screeched to a halt, I was unstrapped & dragged senseless & sick to an easel set up especially for the purpose with a magnificent view of the roundhouse.

For some time I struggled merely to stand upright. The world rolled in waves around me; the roundhouse rose & fell like a forest of bull-kelp, Siamese girls floated past, Musha Pug & his henchmen darted hither & thither, a school of alien aquatic creatures. Somewhat unsteadily I picked up a paintbrush, my light body stumbling in the heavy mud, recovered my balance, & set to work, fully intending despite the fug of nausea that overwhelmed me, to paint the Commandant a picture of Revelation & Profound Discovery that remade the world anew as Commerce.

But then I finished.

In every way I knew I had failed.

Billy Gould had always felt if something was worth doing, it was worth doing badly. Worry about doing it too well, he believed, & you may well be crippled by your ambition. In this regard, if in no other, he suspected he may have succeeded.

For what I had painted was not a warm thing or a happy thing, but a cold thing, a frightful, frightening, frightened thing. They had wanted of me consolation, & this was desolation. The latent violence, the manic vision: I had got none of it. They had wanted Hope & Progress, & to my horror I saw sullenly staring back at me—a *stargazer*! They had wanted a New God & in my monstrous confusion I had given them a fish!

It was no good. A fate worse than Captain Pinchbeck's *petite noyade*, crueller than Governor Arthur's Cockchafer awaited, the Tube Gag & the Cradle & the Scavenger's Daughter all bound up together & me dying the most terrible death in the middle.

Feeling ever iller, I stepped backwards, gulping, slightly stumbling, terrified of what my failure might augur. As I sought to regain my balance, to my horror the Commandant, who I had not known had been standing behind me all that time watching, stepped forward.

Unlike the Surgeon, who could fill days examining a single image for flaws, the Commandant spent only a few seconds surveying the picture as I surveyed him for the first time since he had spoken to us on the day of our arrival. From behind, it was clear what the gold mask was intended to obscure: the great size of his head, the disproportionate smallness of the body beneath, that subordination of the body to the spirit.

Then he turned around, but all I could see were those jaundiced eyes highlighted by the eye sockets of the gold mask, & behind that mask's smiling slit the suggestion of a cavernous black mouth opening ever wider. The incongruous small squawks issuing out of that dark emptiness pronounced the Commandant as pleased as I was appalled, as if I had done a fine portrait of him as one of Napoleon's marshals he had once so admired, rather than a painting of a lousy fish.

Here, I realised, was a man clearly in the prime of his life. I smiled and, with the flourish I also remembered of Audubon, bowed.

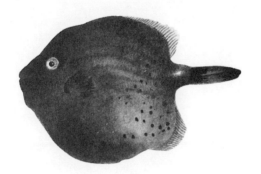

THE LEATHERJACKET

Which treats of how a Flemish painter came to see Reason—Sublime possibilities of modern travel—The Great Mah-Jong Hall—On the colonising force of fish—Underlining Europe—Goethe's passion for Miss Anne—Paganini—Cockatoos—Culture, so much guano—The dream of a silent city—A surfeit of love.

I

THE NEXT DAY I was summoned to meet the Commandant in his cell. The weather was full Van Diemonian. The wind beat brutal. Loose shingles were torn off roofs & hurtled through the air with great & unintentional ferocity, wounding the unwary & unlucky. The great Huon pine log walls were to be heard cracking & groaning in the ongoing agony of continuing upright, as the wind beat into them & at them again & again. The rain fell & fell. The soldiers' second mess was buried in a mud slide. Spume & mist rose & ran fifty or a hundred yards a time, to rest for a moment or a minute before the wind hurtled them on again. And beyond the sea beat into a white fury hammering at the island. Part of the new wharf caved in & then washed away. No boats had been out for three days after a party returning from the Gordon made a dash for it across the harbour & lost all hands. Rushing between

Lempriere's cottage & the Commandant's quarters in one of the few breaks in the rain, my eyes smarted with the salt mist & the grit & ash thrown around in the air like loose shot.

Wet & cold I waited for several hours in a dark narrow corridor with the redcoat who had brought me. When in early evening I was finally admitted it was to an unspeakably small, unusually scented room—no wider than a single arm span, at the most just slightly over a man's height long.

Rats as large & bold as anywhere else on the island occasionally scuttled in & out of the dull light given off by a guttering candle impaled on a wall hook, their size accentuated by the very smallness of the cell & the weird shadows they threw in the jumping light. It seemed impossible that two people could be together in such a confined space & still not see each other, yet such was the case, for he remained behind a drawn curtain that divided the cell, as if it were some papist confessional.

The cell was largely unadorned, save for a small glass bust of Voltaire, half-full of some amber fluid that I suspected to be whisky. In form & size, if not material, it looked identical to the bust which Gould's daughter had once dansey-headed known the blessings of the old Enlightenment. Its uses for a man trying to win back the passion of Twopenny Sal were to me, if no-one else, obvious.

I did not then know—how could I?—how strong was the Commandant's desire for smells. I did not know from Twopenny Sal how he once begged her not to wash for a month so that he might savour the full universe of her natural odours. I did not realise he had his favourite cologne shipped from Naples; I was not aware when I felt its slight weight in my hand & slipped it down the front of my government blouse that the Commandant's most precious perfume of all—a special scent made for him by Napoleon's very own perfumer, Chardin—came in *that* small glass bottle shaped as none other than a bust of Voltaire smiling, now down my dacks staring at the sorry sight of a jobless Flemish painter.

The Commandant told me, his voice muffled by the curtains, that given the wonderful painting of Progress that I had completed the evening before, I was to be given a new task that would—if executed with both diligence & creativity as well as a certain discretion—see my living conditions improve considerably, & perhaps reconsideration of the severity of my original sentence. He understood that I did illustrative work of some technical description or another for the Surgeon, but what he was proposing was only an interruption, not a cessation of such scientifick work, & I would, when I had completed this task, return to my duties for the Surgeon.

My relief, that porous day when the Commandant told me of my new mission, was immeasurable. I would—at least for a time—escape my horror of the fish without losing any of my valuable privileges. The Commandant was offering me a path away from the pitiless corrosion of my soul that was beginning to affect me so badly that I was unable to sleep of a night lest I awake in the ocean. I wished to sigh, to smile, to throw an arm over His Bulkiness's back. But said I nothing &—save continue listening—did nothing, as the Commandant went on to outline his vision for the railway line in the absence of movement.

He wanted me to paint a series of theatrical drop screens Capois Death had devised depicting different views & sublime scenes that would form an outer walled circle lining the circular railway track at the roundhouse. These would, he believed, anticipate a new trend in travel whereby people would never have to move in order to have their desire for exotic spectacles gratified, occasionally looking outside as they circled around endlessly to see that they were rushing past Tintern Abbey or Windermere or, as a poetic touch, the new rookeries of Salford—just to add that sense of movement from Industrial to Natural, from Modern to Pastoral, that sense of contrast in which Capois Death, who had once read the Lake poets, had told him all true appreciation of Romantic scenery to be so deeply & indelibly rooted.

These proposed paintings did not sound uncertain slimeballs of trouble like fish. To the contrary; they sounded the fine sort of paintings with which I could quickly find myself happily familiar, splendid vistas in which bald eagles might be sighted, perhaps, thought I wistfully, sporting splendid garlands of wisteria.

As I took my leave that day from the Commandant's cell & headed alone down that dreary, whale oil-lit damp stone corridor, Voltaire bumping away at my ball-bag, I heard the rain carolling as ever outside & for the first time in such a long time I felt that it did not sound like an infinity of chain links softly drumming on stone. It sounded like hope, serenity, a drizzle of security. It sounded like things were looking up at last for Billy Gould.

You may wonder what the Commandant's motives were in all this. Why such paintings? Why me?

But I didn't. I never questioned the peculiarities of power, only sought to serve it, be it Captain Pinchbeck or the Commandant or that great goose, Pobjoy. If they were to say, 'Kiss my arse, Billy Gould,' I would only ever reply, 'How many times? And will you be wanting my tongue up there as well?'

II

THE BACKDROPS PROVED no great Garrett-drama to paint, all big gestures that tended to run into dreary & dismal washes when it rained, but this was turned to our advantage by Capois Death. He invented a schedule that saw the drop screens replaced every week with a fresh set; one of the Swiss alps, the next of the great Russian taiga (which was just the alps with the rain-dissolved mountains presented as sky), the next of the marvellous African veldt (the further distressed taiga) then the sublime Lake district (the veldt with daffodils) & so on, round & round.

As the Commandant circled endlessly in the Regal Cabin past the aching emptiness of the Oriental plains, the soot-smutting sadness of the satanic mills of Yorkshire, the white invitation of the Arctic Circle, the

Japanese sawyers made camp on the edge of the swamp at Liberty Point. Dividing the surrounding forests up into squares, they set to work in a thorough & systematick way which over the next few months turned the surrounding blue & green wild lands into an unruly chequerboard of stubbly bare brown squares where they had felled & cleared the forest, & the verdant, as yet, uncut & uncleared squares. Then the Japanese left for winter, the rains came, & while the Commandant gasped in astonishment as the crowded chaos of the isle of Manhattan ceded to the trackless glory of the recently discovered American Rockies, first the soil, then several mountains washed away, so that when the Japanese sawyers returned the following summer they were confronted with an immense & entirely disorientating boulder desert to the north.

On & on the Commandant circled, flying past my many paintings of bald eagles in every exotic location known to man, & the more he advanced in his belief in his manifest destiny, the more he declined in the practice of sense. His talk became of impossibilities—of building a temple of odours; of lifting the Penitentiary into the air by the power of levitation, so escape would be impossible except in balloons; of developing mesmerism as an offensive weapon for his army by raising a regiment of spiritualists who would stand in the front row of great battles willing the other side to lose.

In spite of his epic nation-building projects, the Commandant grew depressed at the way trade seemed to have dropped off to next to nothing, the insolent manner his creditors pressed ever more urgently for repayment, & his own inability to find a solution to his growing debt.

Not long after the Japanese sawyers, unperturbed, had set off in the direction of Frenchman's Cap never to return, but some time before the boulder desert turned to button grass & the forest drifted back, stories began to surface of how the Commandant had conceived of a remarkable project for which there was no precedent on any continent. Though rumours of the Japanese sawyers succumbing to an incurable melancholia & then floating away continued for some years after, what quickly came to dominate nearly all talk—other than that of Matt Brady—was the Commandant's grandest idea of all, that of the Great Mah-Jong Hall.

III

AFTER THE FAILURE of the National Sarah Island Railway Station to attract any travelling locomotives, the Commandant became convinced that this building would finally generate the money he needed to become a truly great power. It would attract Javanese & Chinese traders, Moluccan pirates & Dutch merchants, English sailors & French scientists, all searching for a place in the South Seas to gamble their hard-won fortunes. Wrote he lengthy letters to Miss Anne asking questions as to the numerous forms the gaming tables of London took, the latest fashions in architecture & interior decoration.

Then he called for Capois Death.

The publican was ordered to design a building

combining the wonder of Versailles with the cruder pleasures afforded by the Five Courts bear-baiting pit. Inspired though he was only by what he had seen—seashells & silk sails & the parabolic etching of the night sky glimpsed whilst lying with the Siamese girls beneath the manfern fronds—Capois Death was in terror of the normal sort of parasites he had found around the Commandant. Ever ready to do their master a favour & their rivals a disservice, all of them professed a love of the Commandant's stated ambition to outdo Europe by rebuilding it. They praised the plaster busts of Cicero that began to arrive even before the plans were complete, wrote sonnets in imitation of styles long dead & succeeded in creating Art that was a death mask of fashions buried everywhere else.

Accordingly Capois Death went to great pains to describe his first set of plans as being in the Egyptian revival style with some rococo elements. To the Commandant they looked suspiciously like six iron-ribbed, glass-paned domes above which sat a giant gilded scallop shell held up by some ornate columns from which flew silk sails tied down to a great bowsprit.

Whatever doubts the Commandant may have had were, however, suppressed by his acolytes' polite applause for the plans & his own delight in seeing the way even a building as ambitious & large as this would in turn be dwarfed by a statue of himself, so high that his head would always be in the clouds, so massive that just his single finger—forever pointing north towards Miss Anne's Europe—was to be ten yards long. He heard no derisory comments about the big scallop, recognised only the admiration & necessary backing & loans of the Javanese traders & the Chinese merchants, as long as various sureties were made & signed for.

The Commandant's predilection was for strict symmetry followed by adornment, both of which suffered in consequence of his desire to have the building the embodiment of his desire. No plan could proceed without his signature, & when Capois Death later submitted three alternative drawings for the design of the six domes, the Commandant in a moment of inattentive weariness appended his signature to all three, & in consequence eighteen domes, all of varying shapes & materials, were built by his fearful underlings.

The scale of such a building was staggering, its construction a nightmare of suffering for all who worked upon it, the hundreds who died in its construction, the thousands who were maimed & crippled in the forging of the iron, the cutting & carrying of the timber, the quarrying of the stone, the masonry, the carpentry. Yet it was a nightmare of such stupendous proportions that it was impossible not to feel a perverse astonishment at what was being raised in the middle of that wilderness.

Long after he had forgotten why they were to him so important, his endless believing in Miss Anne's missives led the Commandant to call for Capois Death.

'I have in mind,' the Commandant told the publican - architect, 'the most magnificent decoration conceivable: the replication of Miss Anne's letters in huge gilt script around the walls of the Great Mah-Jong Hall.' Capois Death twisted his head so his gaze would be directed at the ceiling & not at the Commandant. 'The painting of these Sacred Words,' continued the Commandant, his high voice rising to the point of near inaudibility as it sought to capitalise important words—'was the Greatest Honour Conceivable, demanding a religious belief in the sanctity of the Nation's Noble Mission.'

As Capois Death listened to the Commandant's forceful, forgettable, falsetto words, he was reminded of the sound of a stream of piss hitting sand. He lowered his eyes to meet those of the Commandant's. He assured him he knew just the man for the job.

IV

MY BOWELS ARE buggered now, & have in a moment of great need betrayed me. Back then my bowels still voided rather than irrigated, before me I had a fine future as a National Artist & beneath me I had sturdy stools to deploy defensively as necessary. Now my guts clench tighter than the dying machine breaker's gob, I fear the lousy fish I paint, I have been shitting through the eye of a needle for the last four days, & today I did not have a single solid turd to toss at Pobjoy when he visited.

On & on he went, all about his new passion, Art, in which he sees me as something of a guide & something of a rival & something of an impostor, & me defenceless. He seemed impervious to the acrid stench of my quarters, my groans, far less the watery arguments I was cheerfully contriving out of every orifice in the forlorn hope he might leave.

As Pobjoy took some pleasure in pointing out to me, definitions belonged to the definer, not the defined. Now I realise it is an idea that would appeal greatly to the King in his dialogue with Heaven, but when I mention it the King rolls his body slightly which is his way of showing utter contempt for an opinion other than his own.

Look at Lycett, continued Pobjoy, his lithographs of Van Diemen's Land were made without ever feeling the burden of having to visit the island & proved such a success in London, they show that the less Art can have to do with the real world, the more successful it will be.

I can offer no argument—after all, what, other than Pobjoy's pottage, have my fish ever won me? I just tried to get him to leave as quickly as possible so that I might get back to my work. From his alpine heights Pobjoy produced a chart of the island of Van Diemen's Land to further prove his argument, & asked what its shape reminds me of?

Pobjoy was a man who could not look at a knot of wood without getting overexcited & undoubtedly he wanted me to say its triangular form resembled that of a woman's wonder, & said I so. Pobjoy reacted like it was a turd not a word I had thrown, leapt upon me & began thrashing me. I thanked him for that also, as it meant he would shortly be leaving. 'You idiot!' yelled Pobjoy as he dropped me to the floor with a sledgehammer right. 'It's a mask Van Diemen's Land looks like, a damn mask!'

As I curled up like a dying fish beneath his flailing boots, I managed to stay his assault long enough to tell

him that I had only ever seen myself as his most loyal
servant & had no desire to displease him. I further put
it that those above should never underestimate the
desire of those below to do the right thing. I recounted
how when I worked at Palmer the coachbuilders, Old
Man Palmer—who was given to strong expression—made it clear in his home that he had no truck
with the savages.

One of his trusted convict servants used borrow
his horse to go out shooting kangaroo. Old Man
Palmer complained to the servant that he was using
an excessive amount of powder & shot just for hunting. The servant objected that he needed that much
to kill blackfellows. Old Man Palmer dismissed this
as vainglorious nonsense & boasting. Some time
later Old Man Palmer had to take his horse as soon as
the servant returned from one of his hunting forays.
Upon halting at a creek, he reached into his saddle-
bag for his pannikin to fetch a drink, but instead
pulled out a black child's head & three flyblown black
hands. On returning home, he fronted his servant
about this grisly discovery. The servant replied, 'Now,
Master, understand that I only ever seek to please
you & that I do not tell lies.'

Pobjoy had collapsed in a corner shaking his head in
complete dejection, looking like Saint Aloysius who on
hearing a man break wind burst into tears & sought solace in prayers.

'So you see,' I told Pobjoy, 'servants are to be trusted
in the sincerity of what they say.' And with that Pobjoy
arose in a complete fury & gave me a hiding the likes of

which I had not experienced for some long time. 'Are you a complete moron, Gould?' Pobjoy was shouting. 'Yes, absolutely,' I replied, though it was less than easy to get all the words out with Pobjoy's fist & boot clattering around my teeth. 'I would most respectfully have to say that I am.'

As my body slid along the cell floor with his kicks, as his heaving boot snapped my head back & forth like I was disagreeing with him when all the time I was only trying to tell him for both our sakes what he wanted to hear, I felt my mind unhinging & floating back to when I once spent my days serenely painting Miss Anne's stories of Europe on the walls of the Great Mah-Jong Hall.

V

AT FIRST, IN the misty, damp confines of the rising building, I pencilled in the letters on the already painted walls. Then, with the Commandant's aide-de-camp, Lieutenant Lethborg—who supplied me with the carefully selected gobbets of Miss Anne's letters —supervising to ensure no theft took place, I gilded the words with the finest gold leaf.

Later, when the hall began to run into problems of finance, I painted Miss Anne's words straight onto the wet plaster, unsupervised & ungilded, all her descriptions of the new miracles of mechanickal steam & unfettered poesy. It was as if the Commandant wished both to extol these wonders & yet prove by their very capture in the Great Mah-Jong Hall that he had escaped them by imprisoning all those words between the papier-mâché elephants of Hannibal & the authentic plaster-of-Paris busts of Cicero & Homer & Virgil—as if honour was the cruellest & subtlest form of mockery.

When Miss Anne's letters proved thin material, Lieutenant Lethborg ordered Jorgen Jorgensen to invent more grandiose tales. For the first—though not the last—time, I began to have a glimmer of Jorgensen's capacity for invention. He invented conversations between Miss Anne & the greatest minds of Europe: with Goethe & Mickiewicz & Pushkin, the latter supposedly penning the following ode in honour of Miss Anne's brother's achievements:

Here we are destined by nature
To cut a window into Europe;
And to gain a foothold by the sea.

I put that in large red letters in the banquet room, just in case anyone was unsure as to its meaning, for unlike the fish the whole affair seemed in desperate need of underlining.

The Commandant, who noticed this verse on an inspection tour the following day, was said to be so moved that a tear erupted out of an eye socket of the gold mask & trickled amber down its glowing side.

Goethe's verse, on the other hand, apparently written in the heat of what we all knew to be a passion conceived whilst on a short vacation in London, a passion that we knew could never be consummated with the ever-chaste Miss Anne, I painted in a purple italic across the mirror that spanned the far wall of the ladies' washroom, above a long teak vanity table that had been a gift of the Javanese traders:

> *All transient things*
> *Are only a parable;*
> *The inaccessible*
> *Here becomes reality*
> *Here the ineffable is achieved;*
> *The Eternal Feminine*
> *Draws us on.*

The less esoteric sentiments & stories of how an aside by Miss Anne upon the power of mists had inspired Nasmyth's steam hammer I put in the corridors, along with her European anecdotes about the violinist Paganini rethinking his practice of fingering after an evening in her divine company, of how when flying over Strasbourg in a balloon with the Montgolfier brothers, the earthbound Malus glimpsed her through his telescope & was struck with his great revelation about the polarisation of light.

It was hard work, more physical than you might suspect, but the days never seemed as long as they had with those stinking fish. The months divided into so many letters, the days into so many words, & Billy Gould's mind was free, unlike with the fish who he already sensed had designs on him. In so far as one could be happy imprisoned on an island, he ought to have been. But his mind kept returning to Twopenny Sal.

He made friends, impressed others with his thoughtful industry. He brought to his lettering both his brief experience painting livery for Palmer the coachbuilder & a modest but genuine creative deftness: some he did in block Roman, others in a looping Italianate; great descriptions he gave a quality almost sculptural, while intriguing maxims were surrounded by expanses of space into which their meaning might grow. He showed appropriate deference, saying that his work was easy when given material as magnificent as Miss Anne's writings. But in truth when he painted a word or a sentence particularly beautifully, it was not in honour of Miss Anne, but another.

When there were no more walls to paint, all this industry & toadying paid off. Through Lieutenant Lethborg I was told that the Commandant, delighted with my work, had ordered that I was now to paint a series of portraits of him in various historical poses. In the meantime, if I didn't mind, I was to knock up a few copies of Rubens from a book of etchings.

During this time the fortunes of the island changed. The endless river of money that had once flooded into the settlement dried up. The Commandant was forced to sell whatever he could, including a priceless collection of Rubens, to meet his ever greater debts with the Chinese pirates & Javanese usurers who had financed the hall's construction.

When finally the Great Mah-Jong Hall opened the island rejoiced, but no-one came to pay to play mah-jong. Though it was incomprehensible to everyone on Sarah Island that people might not wish to travel halfway across the globe to lose money in this wonder of the New World, still no-one came. A chill wind blew through its reception halls, stately rooms & ornate gaming rooms with ceilings so high that clouds gathered there, & there was nobody to marvel with us at how so much could mean so little.

The Great Mah-Jong Hall sat empty. The black children for whom Twopenny Sal cared were left to run through its echoing ballrooms & banqueting halls, chasing birds & playing games of hide and seek in its growing decrepitude.

In the encroaching rising damp & descending mists that now pervaded its interior, Miss Anne's letters grew bedraggled & her words began washing away. Within a short time those wet tales of the wonder & glory of Europe with which I had adorned so many walls were flecked, then covered with the refuse of rainbow-hued rosellas & harsh crying yellow-tailed black cockatoos that took to flying in flocks through the vast emptiness.

In the rain that now fell inside, Miss Anne's observations on the illumination of Pall Mall by gas light & her pivotal role in Count von Rumford's treatise on communal kitchens began running into her descriptions of the steam press & mesmeric healing, & all were soon encased in a hardening shell of more bird dung. As sea eagles spiralled far above, swifts began nesting above Miss Anne's lyrical reports on macadamised roads. While bats blurred her observations on the invention of the electric telegraph, a mob of sulphur-crested cockatoos took roost above her inspiration of Wordsworth's latest rewriting of *The*

Prelude (done in best Grasmere blue), & in the
manured waste that gathered below a small rainforest
began growing. In such a fecund catastrophe of decay
everything became muddled & then one & all of it was
covered in more & more stinking, encrusting lice &
maggot-crawling crap.

Down all those inscriptions sacred to European
ingenuity & European thought & the European genius
of progress, stalactites of white & green droppings grew
daily longer. Then the shit mounting on the floor
began ascending like the wondrous voices of a choir of
castrati into the exquisite European cornices, & shit
was to be seen tumbling like eloquent Augustinian arguments out of the charming European gargoyles. Shit
erupted like Vesuvius out of the great European windows, shit flowed like the mighty Danube out the grand
European doors, & in the end the Commandant sold
the whole sorry mess of shit-encrusted Europe as
guano to the Peruvians who paid for it with several
crates of bad pisco—a sweet, savage liquor popular with
the whalers—& had it shipped back to their own country to there grow corn from.

VI

THE COMMANDANT CEASED his travels around the
Great Sarah Island Railway Line, rarely went to his
palace, & now spent not only most of his days but all of
his nights in his solitary confinement cell. He would
sometimes imprison one or another of his close advis-
ers in the cell next to him for a few days, so that they

might better understand the Commandant's ultimate goal of a city where every man could be trusted to be his own gaoler, living in perfect isolation from every other man.

The old Dane—with whom the Commandant now spent much of his time, dictating reports, letters & what we thought was the necessary administrative minutiae of running a rising nation—once told Capois Death that the Commandant in the course of a long game of cribbage had sighed that a great city is a great solitude. I long suspected that embedded in this comment was his true motivation for first turning the prison island into a city, & then, later, the city into a larger, more complete gaol.

The Commandant's dreams, as ever, transcended our abilities. He wanted the city to be silent. He wanted the people no longer to talk but to communicate through an elaborate system of written messages. These would be rolled up & placed in small wooden cylinders, that would be propelled with compressed air along pipes, shooting the message off to wherever & whomever it was meant.

Apart from the sheer mechanickal impossibility of such a scheme, it was respectfully pointed out to the Commandant, as he sat alone on the bare flagstone floor of his darkened cell, that it was not likely that people in the future would want to live in a world where they could only communicate through such sterile means, never to see or meet each other.

'Speech was given to man to conceal thought,' the Commandant said, his own speech now almost entirely reduced to the poverty of such endless aphorisms, & some said his mask was seen to smile in the dim light of his prison cell, his feathered epaulettes to flap as he spoke.

The Commandant went on to argue that this—at which he held out his arms as if to wrap them around the cell—*this* was our future, a claim so patently ludicrous, so demonstrably untrue that no-one took any further issue with it or the Commandant for the rest of the day. He was left alone in the dull catarrh of his cell to invent further impracticalities & the pointed maxims that justified such excesses of uselessness.

VII

AS THE SHADOW thrown by the Great Mah-Jong Hall slowly diminished as it was dismantled, the Commandant could feel another growing, until it covered not only Sarah Island but all of Van Diemen's Land, a shadow to which no definite body could be attached but whose corporeal presence was everywhere rumoured.

The name of the shadow was Matt Brady.

'Mutt Braddy,' some unknown convict etches into the soft sandstone of the prison wall, '—THE LIBERATOR!' The lustrous legend that is the bushranger Brady, a convict who with fourteen others escaped by stolen whale boat from Sarah Island, & with the Pilot Lucas & an armed guard in hot pursuit sailed it under full sheet round half Van Diemen's Land to Hobart Town, where they abandoned the boat

& quickly established themselves as the most feared, the most admired bushranging gang in the land.

Like fish in the sea the bushrangers swam through the uncultivated backblocks of the east, peopled by ex-convicts & convict stock-keepers & shepherds & savages who sheltered & fed, hid & kept informed the most powerful, the most admired of the Tasmanian *banditti*.

Reports & rumours reached us of how the rest of Van Diemen's Land was seething; how more & more convicts were escaping to join bushranging gangs growing in both size & ferocity. Some, hopelessly ineffectual, others pointlessly cruel. But the sum of their ventures was that the rule of English law was collapsing.

Van Diemen's Land—intended by the authorities to be a transplanted England—is mutating into a bastard world turned upside down, & increasingly the convict & ex-convict population of this topsy-turvy land look to Brady as the leader of that new world.

The island waits.

For a final confrontation, a reckoning.

In the face of Brady's growing power, the increasingly unsettled, unruly nature of the convict population in consequence, & the unceasing black war, the settlers begin abandoning their farms & retreating into the larger towns.

Brady, relentless, growing in his power like his nemesis Governor Arthur, also a master of public gesture, pursues them.

A short, dapper man rides a splendid roan into the

centre of Hobart Town & posts a notice offering a reward for Governor Arthur's head. *Sgd Matt Brady, King of the Woods.* The short man in splendid dress pulls the roan around, smiles, takes his hat off & sweeps it low to those running to form around him a crowd, jetsam bobbing in an eddy at the side of a rapid.

And then the rapid is gone.

Larger rewards are posted. More money for any information on Brady. Freedom to any convict who betrays Brady. And everywhere Governor Arthur's ever-growing network of informers, & with the information he gathers from them, Arthur's minions threaten, blackmail & start to build a web from which none can escape. The muddy streets of Hobart run with the blood of Arthur's Terror. Up to fourteen pairs of legs dance the diddly-back-step a day, up to fourteen pairs of pants putrid with the shit of dying men are buried with their finally stilled owners each evening in nameless graves.

Meanwhile Brady wins ladies' hearts by never taking advantage of them, plays their heavy husbands & fathers for the inflated fools they are, renders the women complicit with his smiles, his grace, his flash clothes—the mulberry waistcoat, the fancy brocaded breeches, the emu feather in his hat, the gold chain with diamond-studded cross hanging from his neck. He caresses their wrists with bindings of silk, leaves them with closeted desires they will take to their graves as the most vivid moments of their lives. His total lack of weapons—in a society where every free man wears arms & vies for the honour to shoot Brady down like a

dog—only reinforces his aura of invulnerability &
destiny.

As if filling the void that seemed to arise between
our dreams & our daily life, the word was rising that
Matt Brady had vowed that when the winter blizzards
had abated he would force a passage through the
uncharted western wilderness of mountain & rainforest that coming summer, bringing his forces westwards,
intending to free his former prison, Sarah Island, &
recruit the liberated felons into a new army.

It was so implausible, so impossible, it was hard
not to believe. Various elements were added in gossip
—that he was seeking to free the island from its
wretched subjugation by making common cause with
the warring savages of the island & that he even slept
with one, Black Mary; that she was to show him the way
west over the uncharted mountains; that he was intending to use us as a basis for an army which would
proclaim a republic in which everything solid would
dissolve into air & no man would remain enslaved.

The Commandant wrote to the Governor begging
for more soldiers to keep order on the island, to prevent a mass outbreak, & to repel Brady when he
inevitably attacked.

For Brady was invading the Commandant's drugged
dreams as surely as he continued to conquer our feverish imaginings; Brady who could take on a dozen
redcoats at once; Brady who outwitted the Governor;
ethereal Brady of our most sacred desires; lascivious
Brady of our most depraved thoughts; strong-armed
immortal Brady who struck down the government

men, the rich, the dobbers & deadflogs—fearless Brady, great Brady, astonishing Brady, a rummy, canny coot the equal of ten men, Bradyo! & everyone waiting for his triumphant entry, his declaration of the Republic, for we all now knew the day of liberation was approaching.

Then I wake & before properly waking I am making dreaming praying painting a fish before muster, before fear reason hope thought a small leatherjacket begins appearing on the paper, not bristling with spikes, but lovely after its own truth, fish that lives not on other fish but only seaweed & kelp, with inquisitive eyes, the dandyish bright yellow fins, its gentle soft sandpaper skin glowing purple below its gills. Gentle leatherjacket, beautiful leatherjacket of my dreams of impending release, a touch of such softness after so much horror.

VIII

AND WHEN I finished the painting & looked at that poor leatherjacket which now lay dead on the table I began to wonder whether, as each fish died, the world was reduced in the amount of love that you might know for such a creature. Whether there was that much less wonder & beauty left to go around as each fish was hauled up in the net. And if we kept on taking & plundering & killing, if the world kept on becoming ever more impoverished of love & wonder & beauty in consequence, what, in the end, would be left?

It began to worry me, you see, this destruction of fish, this attrition of love that we were blindly bringing about, & I imagined a world of the future as a barren sameness in which everyone had gorged so much fish that no more remained, & where Science knew absolutely every species & phylum & genus, but no-one knew love because it had disappeared along with the fish.

Life is a mystery, Old Gould used say, quoting yet another Dutch painter, & love the mystery within the mystery.

But with the fish gone, what joyful leap & splash would signal where these circles now began?

IX

WITH ALL THE rising vapours & damp earth the building of the Great Mah-Jong Hall had entailed, the Commandant's consumption—caught amongst the manfern fronds from the Siamese women—worsened to the extent that no amount of bleeding seemed to do any good.

Both the Commandant & the Surgeon came to fear that they would fill the entire harbour with his blood without any cure being affected. Nor did the consumption respond to any of the Surgeon's other invariably successful treatments—not the nightly drinking of chamber-lye, which the Surgeon fermented from his own urine; nor the daily swallowing of album nigrum, the excrement of rats, which at least had the virtue of being the most readily available medicine on the island; unlike the tobacco, which the Surgeon used as a final desperate expedient in the practice of insufflation, which saw him injecting tobacco smoke into the Commandant's rectum after every voiding of the bowels.

Then to grant the Commandant the illusion that something was being done for his body—beyond enabling it to fart smoke—the Surgeon came up with a new treatment that was apparently meeting with some success in England. At first the Commandant was unwilling to eat large amounts of butter several times a day, on the foolish grounds that it made him nauseous, but the thinking behind this treatment was scientifick, incomprehensible, & for both these reasons, undeniable.

That the Commandant was now malnourished as well as consumptive did not help his humours, which daily grew more vaporous & even less easily divined than before. He was troubled by nightmares in which he was revealed not as a Roman emperor but as a Lakes poet, given to long dreamings at the edges of Grasmere on the Sublime & Majestick, as if his very dreams were capitalised to drive home the idea so strong he felt suffocated by it, because a father of the nation ought be born to the role, not have to fight for it every day.

He knew for him none of it came easy, not even the cruelty, & it only made him even angrier that in his dog days when a little understanding from others would not have gone amiss, that so many mistakenly thought harshness his second nature, for even his malevolence he had to struggle for & with.

'You understand me, O'Riordan?' he cried, leaping from his infantryman's palliasse & seizing a musket from his aide & smashing the butt into the aide's face, again & again, all the while the lieutenant protesting that his name was not O'Riordan but Lethborg. This only antagonised the Commandant all the more, because he knew all his soldiers to be feckless, cowardly Irish peasants, & it was evident O'Riordan was even worse, being a feckless, cowardly, *lying* Irish peasant.

The Commandant took to kicking him in the nuts & head, hissing, 'Brady-brady-brady' with an unrestrained vigour that might have been mistaken for glee had it not been obvious that both men were weeping, one blood from his mouth & nose, the other only tears from his masked eyes, because he was the Commandant & a certain dignity became him, because his way was so hard & why was he not composing *Tintern Abbey* at Rydal Lake?

Because his anger was so misunderstood, that's why the Commandant had the lieutenant & the platoon of perfidious papists he commanded arrested, bound & gagged; because the Commandant could stand the sighing of O'Riordan's wounds no longer, that's why he had no choice but to have the whole mass of bound & gagged green treachery thrown into the sea to join the fish.

His symptoms grow daily worse, wrote the Surgeon to Sir Isaiah Newton, a distinguished colleague in Liverpool with whom he had trained, & from whom he now solicited professional advice on what was to be done for his Commandant, *for his chest grows noisome & flutters like a prisoned moth.* Given the great beyond gobbing distance of the globe that separated them it would be months, perhaps years before a reply came, & meanwhile the prisoned moth grew into a slopping mullet caught in the collapsing creel of the Commandant's ribcage.

'You understand, Commandant,' stammered the Surgeon, 'these things take time.'

'But time!' roared the Commandant, 'time! dear Surgeon is what our Nation does not have!' because now in his mind His Destiny & that of His Nation were one & the same, that's why the Commandant could not ignore the quietness that beset the island in the wake of the respective failures of the National Railway & the Great Mah-Jong Hall, & a hundred & one other monumental disasters.

Of a night he was unable to sleep for want of the sound of a nation. All he could hear echoing up & down the lonely market aisles that were supposed to be full of the noise of bartering, of trade, of people, was that hollow sound of the waves ominously slapping the shore.

Lying awake, terror mounting, he began to wonder whether that one sound was the sea or was it his lungs or was it his destiny calling slap-slap-slap even then, calling him back, was it his own breath rasping brady-brady-brady or was it the convicts with their ceaseless perfidious gossip of how Brady would liberate them, no matter how many old lags he made stand behind the bare stalls & feign commerce, how Brady would avenge them, no matter how many fine new stone buildings he put between him & his night-time visions, no matter how much of Europe he erected between him & the silence, it was the same nightmare of the sea rising & rising & rising, & Brady coming ever closer & closer & the flames of Hell ever hotter . . .

The Serpent Eel

*Which is not so long as some chapters—Uncontrollable
urges—Making of a nation—Gelding of
Mr Lempriere—A bowsprit of suffering—Barrels of
talking black heads—Rise of Cosmo Wheeler & other
misfortunes—Sorry demise of
Mr Lempriere—Castlereagh the homicide.*

I

So THERE HE is, this Gould, this pathetick forger, this drunkard trying his best to be on the make rather than back in chains on the Triangle & the Cradle. He is, if you will—& as he would most certainly like—trying to rise up the ladder of convict society, & what is happening?

Having been made paint fish & then having been freed of those little balls of leprous slime & scale, having copped the best billet of them all, painting that ponce of a Commandant in a hundred & one different historical poses, what do we now see—

A man who is going to use this newly found position of influence with the Commandant to get ahead?

No.

Who is to begin to transform from the status of lackey to adviser, insider, confidant, with all its requisite perquisites?

No, you see nothing of the sort. Granted this Gould wants merely to abuse his position to his own advantage, but he is troubled by Thoughts. Though he desires only an easy cop of it all, the truth is that he feels ever more imprisoned in growing Notions & Fancies.

What you see—& here I am afraid I just have to come out with it—what you see is an idiot who feels *an unbearable desire* to once more paint fish.

And why? Because it is passion?

No.

Because he thinks he has a role to play in the furtherance of Science?

No.

Of Art?

Heaven help us, no, no & no! Because, Jesus wept, because of all things, he is starting to feel uncontrollable urges toward fish!

But before I can get to all that I have to sharpen my sharkbone quill, dip it again in this green laudanum, & make a necessary detour if we are to reach our destination of our man's growing weakness of mind, this saltwater cell of an inescapable & putrid destiny, & swerve back to one of the Commandant's nightly binges with Mr Lempriere in the latter's cottage.

Mr Lempriere is by now, as you might have expected, more than a little morose that his Grand Scientifick Mission of Transylvanian fish-finding has been temporarily, perhaps permanently, halted by the Commandant's need to put Art to National rather than simply Scientifick purposes. So permit me to change tack, swoop back down into Sarah Island, over the Commandant's Moluccan guards, & tumble down Mr Lempriere's sooty chimney into the smoky living room where the Commandant in his cups is admitting to the outrage of his ambition.

'To make a nation, my God yes, a nation that's what we can & must become,' he is telling Mr Lempriere, '& no, sir, I am not ashamed of it. No, sir, how can I be when I have been anointed by Destiny for this role? A nation & me its founder & it a Nation not some god-forsaken dreg of a Prison Island. A nation of which I will be the father, the father whom they will honour & revere & write epic poems & paint atop glorious white stallions rearing against a tempestuous night. You hear me, Lempriere? And none will know that it was work, our hard work, our sweat & sacrifice that raised this island from a prison into a nation.'

'PISS,' muttered the drunk Surgeon, 'GOT TO.' Heaving with some might, he managed to lift his much vaunted sash window open & bowed outward, sighing slowly, '*G-O-U-T-T-E À G-O-U-T-T-E,*' as he began relieving himself.

Mr Lempriere dressed in the style of thirty years previous, with knee breeches & large buckles on his shoes which he had once made me polish each evening. They were made of some poor man's pewter which Mr Lempriere insisted to be silver, despite them being duller than dishwater. He leant up & forward on these shoes to better his trajectory out of the window.

At the moment of his relief one of the buckles finally gave up its long & unequal struggle with the contortions of Mr Lempriere's oversize body. The buckle snapped. Mr Lempriere's foot shot forward. At the same moment, he lost his grip on the window & he lurched first backward, then forward. With a great & abrupt crash the window slammed down onto the sill across which lay like a lost caterpillar Mr Lempriere's protruding member.

You might think from all I have said that the Surgeon at this point would have bellowed like a Brahman bull, or screamed in some terrible high pitch, but no, beyond his white lead-powdered face blushing an exquisite shade of coral pink, there was for a moment nothing to indicate the full horror of what had just passed.

Perhaps in that moment of agony he knew no amount of yelling or screaming was going to alter the undeniable fact of his sex having been awful mangled by the accident. He felt a vertiginous horror, both at the pain & at the apprehension at what it might mean for his future. He felt his legs bowing, falling, failing him, & then at the same moment, everything passed to black.

II

UPON BEING REAWAKENED from his faint with salts, Mr Lempriere refused outright his own cure-all for every blight, arguing that bleeding the sex was an affront to a man of his dignity. He cited Sir Isaiah Newton, mentioning several instances of brewers' droop becoming a permanent condition after such precipitate & unscientifick treatment, & so instead of slicing himself he swallowed large amounts of laudanum, tinted green from the copper pot where it was kept for the Commandant. Beyond granting him a vision splendid of the Commandant as a rutting elephant, the opiate did nothing to alter the steady progress of his sex over the next few weeks from a sorry red worm to a large black slug, which he rested upon a small Huon pine platform he had built for the purpose. This he would daily fasten to his body by the expedient of looping a turquoise silk ribbon around the upper rim of his voluminous love handles & tying it in a large, ostentatious bow on the boil-contoured & hair-forested flab of his back.

He wandered the settlement, shirt flaps splayed out like sails over his pine promontory, a bowsprit of suffering that he constantly inspected whenever alone, witnessing the transforming wonder as bruising turned septic, as flesh turned putrid, as red turned black turned green. In the end the stench was so unbearable that it enraged even the odourphilic Commandant, & he ordered Mr Lempriere to be tied down, a funnel inserted into his protesting gabbling gob & several pints of pisco poured down. Through the ensuing procedure the Commandant cradled his dear friend's head as if it were that of a newborn, blubbering all the while that it was his love for his friend that demanded this of him. After a wait of a quarter of an hour the Commandant had wearied of his own compassion. He nodded to a convict cook who had been standing in a shadowed corner, slowly running a long filleting knife back & forth on a steel. The cook stepped forward &, before Mr Lempriere could protest in either French or English, had with a single slice severed the suppurating penis.

After the sorry loss of his member, Mr Lempriere was at first even more bellicose & obnoxious than he had been in the past. But then his choleric manner underwent a change autumnal, slowly altering into a melancholy so deep that he seemed to have lost all interest in life, even his passion for collecting & cataloguing.

He grew solitary & acquired the odd habit of spending long periods of time talking to Castlereagh, one sad monologue after another about the Hard Hand of Fate & what might have been if he had only specialised in lichens or liverworts. The pig, accustomed to roaming its hellish sty alone, unbothered, seemed to grow ever angrier with Mr Lempriere's commentaries, headbutting the sty's fences every time the Surgeon appeared, shaking them with so much force the island trembled with each blow. The Surgeon was oblivious to his companion's antipathy, not noticing that the more he talked the more the pig grew in size & savagery until it blocked the sun, until it was accused of causing lunar eclipses & interfering with celestial navigation of a night. The enraged animal would sometimes squeal as if the endless torrent of talk was drowning it, a shriek so high-pitched & grating that it drove men far out to sea wild with aural pain, yet such pitiful displays only seemed to fuel Mr Lempriere's tales of loss & failure & personal oblivion.

Lost, depressed, gelded, his most intimate companion a monstrous pig—it scarce need be added that Mr Lempriere had by now lost all interest in getting me back from the Commandant to paint fish.

I had tried painting a few fish in the oils with which I was so liberally provided by the Commissariat for the paintings of the Commandant. But oils are a medium of the earth, too loaded with gravity, too opaque to serve for a fish. I needed the Surgeon's watercolours.

I determined I would visit Mr Lempriere in the hope of reigniting his interest in the project of the book of fish. I intended to ask if I might borrow his watercolour set, to seek to continue with the fish in what little spare time I could find.

I told myself it was only about survival, to ensure if my billet with the Commandant ever ended I had some alternative to the chain gang. But that was a lie, & though I tried to veil my heart from my mind, the truth was that no longer being compelled to paint for Science, my feelings for the fish were for a second time changing, & what I had formerly hated I now missed. For the oddest of reasons I now found myself needing the fish.

The fish were at the beginning only a job, but to do that job well & keep the undoubted benefits that flowed from it, I had to learn about them. I had to study the manner in which fins passed from the realm of opaque flesh to diaphanous wonder, the sprung firmness of bodies, the way mouths related to oversized heads, heads to expanding bodies, the way scale dewlapped with scale to create a dancing sheen. On one fish I would seek to perfect those inexplicably sensuous mouths, on another the translucence of fins. And I would have to admit that all this painting & repainting began to affect me.

Perhaps because I spent so long with them, because I had to try to know something of them, they began to interest me, & then to anger me, which was worse, because they were beginning to enter me & I didn't even know that they were colonising me as surely as Lieutenant Bowen had colonised Van Diemen's Land all those years ago.

They were boring into me, seeping through my pores by some dreadful osmosis. And when within me glimmered the unexpected, somewhat terrifying knowledge that they were taking possession of my daytime thoughts, my night-time dreams, I grew frightened & longed to repel them, to fight back as the blackfellas had. But how do you attack a dying gurnard? A mullet in its death throes?

It was as if it was not possible to spend so long in the company of fish without something of their cold eye & quivering flesh passing across the air into your soul.

I use the word 'across' advisedly.

It was as if their spirit was seeking another watery medium, & at a certain point when death was imminent this spirit to ensure its own survival would leap across the deadly medium of air, a leap so sudden & so quick as to be invisible to the naked eye. In the way the blue flame had leapt from the condemned man's mouth at the fair into my mother, I wondered if all spirits seek another eye to enter at the dreadful mortal moment, to avoid being consigned to some nether world of lost shades.

It was just my idiocy, like when I went back to Old Gould's daughter after she announced her betrothal to the ironmonger from Salford & I asked her to elope with me & she laughed in my face, I just had to go back for more fish & why?—for as long as I was charged with the task of painting ever more of these cruel new settlers of my soul, first by an insane Surgeon & then more insanely by myself, there seemed no escape from their insidious invasion, no respite as they commenced swimming toward the backblocks of my heart, of my mind, preparing to take total control of me.

And how could I have known that day I went to see him, that within that huge head of Mr Lempriere's was being born one final tawdry passion, that was to forge fish & me into one forever?

III

On my way to Mr Lempriere's cottage that still, blue winter morning two convicts in dirty smocks crossed my path, sweating & cursing as they dragged a sled on which long heavy hessian sacks rolled around.

'More dead niggers,' one said without looking back at either me or the sacks.

The savages had arrived the previous week with the white conciliator Guster Robinson on a cold, blustery day. They were a motley, emaciated party, some covered in a skin disorder, many coughing & spluttering incessantly; slashing their afflicted chests & throats with broken bottles & sharp rocks. When their sickness turned to fever, they lacerated their foreheads similarly & blood streamed down their faces so that they might, as they put it, 'let the pain out'. They began to die as soon as they had arrived.

Yet such doomed savages regarded us convicts as slaves below themselves. By their own account they were a free & noble people who had given up their nation for exile & who in return would be looked after by the government & did not have to work like we did. Of a night some convicts in the Penitentiary pissed through the boards on the savages housed on the floor below us to prove the superiority of an imprisoned white man over an exiled black man.

To his quixotic, government-sponsored venture with the savages—in the service of which he had travelled the length & breadth of the dark, wild woods of Transylvania—Robinson had given the grand title of the Conciliation, a white man's mission to round up all the savages who had for so long waged war against them & who still remained at large in the wilds.

In the paintings of him I had seen back in Hobart Town—large canvases trying, & failing, to create a noble & tragic history of saviours & damned for the antipodes—Guster Robinson appeared as a podgy presence in bright relief against the dull background of assembled savages, his fingers pointing portentously to some unseen future, a Renaissance prophet centre-stage in Regency motley, all enlightened & billowing blues & whites, Beau Brummell as an improbable & foppish Moses of the South Seas.

But when I was summoned to meet with Guster Robinson, he cut no such dash.

The savages called him their word for eel, which I cannot recall with any accuracy. He was, it must be admitted, a short string of a man, wasted worse than his black charges. Hunched over in ragged slops as filthy & lice-ridden as ours, a lost apostrophe in search of a word to which he might belong, he radiated little beyond the superior air of his self-appointed task that he claimed to be sacred.

Robinson treated the savages as though they were his entourage, & the savages treated him like he was one of the many stray dogs they picked up on their travels. Neither seemed to notice the earth falling away beneath them as a breaking wave.

Robinson thought convicts scum, & was the type who would happily walk naked in front of you, so little opinion did he have of those he felt below him, as though you were a dog to be kicked or a chamber pot to be pissed in. When I arrived he was talking with Musha Pug—who as a convict constable he must have regarded as a little higher on the ladder than an ordinary lag—& rather than making any attempt to acknowledge my presence, he kept on, telling Musha Pug how the black women stolen by the sealers & taken to the islands claimed that the Devil comes to them when they are hunting seals & has connection with them, that they are often with child by this spirit & they killed the evil issue in the bush. They said that they sang to please the Devil, that the Devil told them to sing plenty.

The Commandant's maid, the Mulatto, said he, was known on the islands as Cleopatra. Before being brought to Christian enlightenment by the Quakers she was infamous for inventing the Devil dance. The Devil dances were, said he, the most obscene that could be imagined & were known only to the sealers' women on the islands & not the mainland.

She had been seized by the sealer Clucas whose conduct was notorious throughout the strait. Clucas, in company with some other sealers, had been on a raiding mission. They had rushed a mob of blacks on a beach, but only managed to seize a baby boy before being beaten back to their boat by the natives. The sealers made it clear that the child was now theirs, & if their mother wanted the boy she would have to come with them. The mother was Twopenny Sal.

She came to the boat & offered herself to them if the child could go back with the tribe. The sealers grabbed her. Clucas, taking hold of the boy by his legs, swung him against the rocks & beat his brains out. Then they rowed off with Twopenny Sal. One native man swam after them & succeeded in gaining hold of their stern post. Clucas chopped off his hands with a tomahawk. On Clucas's island, where she was condemned to live as a slave, Twopenny Sal was reputed to have had two children to Clucas, & killed both by stuffing grass in their mouths.

Having finished his tale, Robinson turned to me & informed me that the Commandant had agreed that I might paint some of 'his sable brethren', beginning with the one he called Romeo.

A tall elegant man, with something of the look of a Hasidic Jew of the east, Romeo in his own language was called Towtereh. I discovered that he was a chief of the Port Davey people &, it transpired, the father of Twopenny Sal. I witnessed their reunion. Both wept much & seemed greatly moved to be together again.

Talking with Towtereh, I found my own opinions of the savages changing, & I could no longer think of them as I formerly had. Towtereh was a fine wit, fond of making puns across the black & white languages. Moreover he was a true patriot, whose profound love of his country seemed undeniable. I painted Towtereh as a man of dignity, a portrait which for a single, very obvious reason, has no place in a book of fish.

Among the blacks' number to whom Towtereh introduced me was a flash man known as Tracker Marks. In stark contrast to us convicts he dressed like an Eightways dandy. He was meticulously clean, & in the filth of the settlement was fastidious about daily washing his clothes. He wore a white shirt with long lapels that he spread outwards over—instead of under—his collar, & a stiff round hat that was somewhere between a fez & a stocking cap, in the fashion of the American whalers with whom he had once roamed the southern oceans. He was quiet unless challenged, but his fierce eyes & the angry stretch of his mouth suggested that challenge would be unwise.

Tracker Marks was a mainland native who had for a time worked for the Van Diemonian troopers tracking down bushrangers, & had then, for no clear reason, fallen in with Robinson's mission to bring in

the warring tribes from the wilderness. He seemed
not reconciled to what he did, nor yet was he hostile.
In his words, Robinson's party was simply a mob to
travel with, but it was not his land through which he
travelled, & though he was a black, they were not his
people. Unlike Barrabas, the other New South Wales
black, he did not deride the Van Diemonian savages
as rock apes, as if by denigrating them, he might
advance a little further up the Europeans' ladder of
creation. He seemed to have no feeling for anyone,
only an immense & knowing weariness.

For a time Tracker Marks was often to be seen in
the company of Capois Death. The two would talk
incessantly in a queer, jumpy argot of their own invention: a blend of English-influenced Creole &
Aborigine-influenced English. Tracker Marks would
tell Capois Death of his people & their world, of their
land & their place in it. Capois Death, who had only
ever known rupture as his heritage, would listen
intently. Each seemed to be searching in the other for
what they had never known: Capois Death for where a
black man came from & where he would go & what it
meant, but he could not in the end overcome his own
sense, beaten into him on the San Domingo planta-
tion, that the white man's ways, if not the white man,
were better than the blacks'. For Capois Death hated
the white man, but loved his civilisation.

Tracker Marks was of a different opinion. Though
he seemed more white than a white man, he had no
time for their ways. For him his dress, his deportment
was no different than staying downwind in the shadows

of trees when hunting, blending into the world of those he hunted, rather than standing out from it. Once he had excelled at the emu dance & the kangaroo dance; then his talent led him to the whitefella dance, only now no-one was left of his tribe to stand around the fire & laugh & praise his talent for observation & stealthy imitation.

The whites have no law, he told Capois Death, no dreaming. Their way of life made no sense whatsoever. Still, he did not hate them or despise them. They were stupid beyond belief, but they had a power, & somehow their stupidity & their power were, in Tracker Marks's mind, inextricably connected. But how? he asked Capois Death. How can power & ignorance sleep together? Questions to which Capois Death had no answer.

Then more blacks began to cough & splutter & enough snot flowed from their noses to fill the harbour, enough blood ran down their lacerated heads to dye the island pink, & within two days seven more of them were dead.

Tracker Marks disappeared from Sarah Island not long after. Maybe he worried how much longer he was going to survive Guster Robinson's oft-professed deep respect & love for his sable brethren. His last words to Capois Death before his flight were incomprehensible to the former slave from San Domingo, who constantly told & embroidered his own personal history in the belief it explained & meant something.

'Hide your life,' said Tracker Marks to Capois Death. 'Completely.'

When that morning on the way to Mr Lempriere's, I watched the two convicts empty their sacks into a large pit just off the side of the track, I noticed with a shock that those dead black bodies were headless. The convicts quickly covered the decapitated corpses with a shallow layer of soil, leaving the rest of the pit unfilled, & ready, I presumed, for more dead.

'That's right,' I heard the other convict say, without looking back at either him or the pit as I scurried away down the hill to Lempriere, 'dead niggers. One's Romeo, but there's no way any of the others is a Juliet.'

IV

MR LEMPRIERE'S COTTAGE was empty, but from out the back I heard the muddled sounds of exertion & wood occasionally cracking, like a giant eucalypt dropping boughs. I headed down the side lane & then saw, outlined against the umber tones of the muddy yard that flanked Castlereagh's pen, the ivory profile of Mr Lempriere's great wen of a head.

In that way peculiar to a Van Diemonian winter, the sun was an intense egg-yolk & the sky a vivid ultramarine, yet the day was chill. Still, Mr Lempriere did not have to exert his mighty bulk greatly to raise a torrid sweat, & he clearly had been busy that morning for large beads of sweat rolled like pearls down his white-leaded face. He stood at the centre of a ring of half a dozen or so wooden barrels, one of which a convict cooper was fitting a lid onto, another of which Mr Lempriere himself was hammering away at the side of with his fists, while yelling all sorts of vile things in argument with somebody I could not see.

On noticing me, he raised a hand & flicked it away from his face, as if to say the argument was of no concern to him.

'PAY NO HEED—HAPPENS ALL THE TIME,' he assured me. 'BUT!—BARREL SEALED—THEY QUIETEN DOWN.'

I stepped over to him & peered more closely at the barrel with which Mr Lempriere was busying himself. It appeared to be full of brine—though I cannot vouch for this being the exact nature of the pickling solution. I glimpsed a dark glint, & at first I guessed he was potting eels, of which the harbour had that year an abundance. Then thought I, no, my eyes are playing tricks on me, that some effect of the southern light is making me see men as fish everywhere.

And then so slowly & so awfully that I still felt a fool about it for several days after, it dawned on me that bobbing up & down in the barrels, rolling around like apples at a fair, curing like so many cabbages, *they* were not eels: *they* were the severed heads of several blackfellas. Multiplied by the half-dozen barrels, I guessed there must be somewhere between forty & seventy black heads pickling that fine midwinter's morning in Mr Lempriere's backblock.

It also became apparent that Mr Lempriere believed these heads of dead blacks were yelling at him & mocking him. He tried to feign an oblivious air to their imagined derision, but would every so often crack & start yelling back. Then he would look weary with the demands scientifick respectability was placing upon him & would glance fondly, almost coquettishly across at the pig yard where Castlereagh was asleep in the muddiest corner. He allowed himself a small indulgent smile at the sight of such bucolic bliss, a slight curving rip in his glowing globe, took a sip of rum from a chipped earthenware pitcher at his side, & wiped his white-leaded brow with a filthy spotted silk handkerchief.

Mr Lempriere explained that he was annoyed with the heads as they would not sink, but kept bobbing up to break the surface of the pickling solution & then would talk back at him. He worried that these faces might decompose if exposed to air on the lengthy ocean voyage to Britain. But in death, as in life, the black heads remained a force with which to be reckoned & their open eyes seemed to follow Mr Lempriere wherever he went, much to Mr Lempriere's discomfort. He asked the cooper if it might be possible to weight the heads down with stones. The cooper stifled a sigh & went away to search for some string.

Mr Lempriere had many qualities, not least what he referred to as his *common sense*. I admired how he in no way regarded a severed head talking as if it were still connected to its body & alive as abnormal or paranormal, but only as a practical nuisance. There was something so tremendously & stoutly English about this that I was for a moment overcome with yearning for the dear Old World that produced such giants as this moonfaced servant of Science who several times told the silent heads to shut up while he & the cooper tried to figure out a solution to the problem of weighing their heads down.

In the middle of that circle of heads he believed to be jeering him & his work, he welcomed me as some sort of long lost friend. He leant up against a closed barrel & launched into a tale of exasperation that centred on one of whom I had only ever heard him speak with the reverence normally accorded a sage: Cosmo Wheeler.

'AT FIRST—MERELY—COLLECTING—FLOWERS— FEW LEAVES—*THINGS*,' began Mr Lempriere, mopping his brow yet again with his grubby handkerchief, rubbing the powder off & leaving a sorry purple skin with the sheen of varnish in the wake of his wipe. 'SUCH WORK, SAID WHEELER—EARN ME MEMBERSHIP OF SOCIETY, THE ROYAL—BUT THEN—A LETTER, THAT'S ALL—OFFICIAL THANKS FROM THE EMINENT BODY—TOUCHING I'M SURE—SINGLED OUT—PRESER-VATION & PACKING EXEMPLARY—ENSURED CONTENTS SUITABLE FOR SCIENTIFICK STUDY—THAT'S ALL!—IT! A LETTER!

'THEN MR COSMO BECOMES *SIR* COSMO WHEELER—RECOGNITION OF *HIS* GREAT WORK ON ANTIPODEAN FLORA—NEXT HE'S WANTING—*EN UN MOT*—MOLLUSC SHELLS—SHELLING SHORT? NO! LONG TIME, VERY LONG—EVERY FREE DAY SCOURING THIS WRETCHED COAST—MOST INCLEMENT & MISER-ABLE CIRCUMSTANCES OBTAINING—YEARS OF WRETCHED WORK—SECOND OFFICIAL LETTER FROM THE ROYAL SOCIETY—EVEN MORE LAUDATORY THAN FIRST—BUT WHAT MENTION OF MY MEMBERSHIP OF THE SOCIETY?'

'No,' said I.

'YES,' said he, 'NONE.'

At this point he momentarily broke off to take issue with what he believed to be some lewd commentary emanating from the barrels, before returning to his story.

'SO YOU SEE,' continued Mr Lempriere, 'I RAISED THIS—RESPECTFULLY—WITH *SIR* COSMO—NOW SEC-RETARY OF THE SOCIETY IN CONSEQUENCE OF *HIS* PATHBREAKING RESEARCHES ON INVERTEBRATES OF THE SOUTH SEAS, WITH SPECIAL REFERENCES TO ANTIPODEAN MOLLUSCS.

'SIR COSMO ASSURED ME IN A SEPARATE & PRIVATE CORRESPONDENCE THAT MY FEARS OF BEING IGNORED &—I HAD NEVER DARED IN MY LETTERS EVEN WRITE IT, FAR LESS THINK IT!—*USED*—MIS-PLACED ENTIRELY—MATTER WELL & TRULY IN HAND—ASSURED ME—SAW ME—HE DID, THE SOCI-ETY DID—MOST EMINENT & DESERVING OF ITS COLONIAL COLLECTORS—MOST PRACTICAL SCIEN-TIST—REPUTATION SUCH THAT IT MERELY NEEDED SOME GREAT, FINAL WORK TO CAP ALL OTHER UNDOUBTED INDUSTRY OFF—THEN I COULD RETURN TO ENGLAND IN TRIUMPH.

'SO—WHOLE FISH THING—MEANT TO BE MY GREAT WORK—MY TICKET TO SOCIETY, SARDINES & SQUIDS, TO THE *SOCIETY*—BUT NOW WRITES HE:

'"No, fish have been done by Hooker, between you & me it's a poor work that Hooker has done, but never-theless fish are finished, done for, & don't bother me with sending your pictures, it's all too late."'

'UP-&-COMING FIELD NOW—WRITES HE—NEW SCIENCE—NEW SOCIETY—NEW AGE—PHRENOLOGY, PARTICULARLY IN REGARD TO VANQUISHED & INFERIOR RACES—SCIENCE POISED TO MAKE GREAT ADVANCES IN ITS UNDERSTANDING OF HUMANITY IN ITS SUPERIOR & INFERIOR FORMS FROM SUCH STUDY OF SKULLS BUT FOR WANT OF GOOD SPECIMENS.'

I then gathered—as much as one could gather anything from such a cavalcade of clauses—that Sir Henry Hooker, who in spite of Sir Cosmo Wheeler's dismissal of him as a mediocre mountebank, seemed nevertheless to be his chief scientifick rival, had chanced upon six barrels chock-a-block full of black heads belonging to his friend, Sir Joseph Banks, that many years before Banks had collected in Van Diemen's Land. Hooker's subsequent monograph upon Banks' black heads—proclaiming their *innocence* of white civilisation, their *nobility* of black physiognomy—had excited much interest.

'SO MUCH ROUSSEAU-AN NONSENSE,' continued the Surgeon, 'SENT LADIES INTO A FAINT—HA!—BUT SIR COSMO BELIEVES HOOKER'S WORK FOUNDED UPON FLAWS FUNDAMENTAL—FASHIONABLE FRENCHIE ROT—INTELLECTUAL ONANISM!

'IF HE, SIR COSMO, HAD, MORE UP-TO-DATE BLACK HEADS—ONCE & FOR ALL WILL PROVE HOOKER'S WORK—NOT SCIENCE—JUST SO MUCH VAINGLORIOUS TOMFOOLERY.

'SO NOW INSTEAD OF FLOWERS OR MUSSELS OR FISH—BLACK HEADS!—IF I AM TO BE ACCEPTED INTO THE ROYAL SOCIETY—BLACK HEADS!—BUT IT'S NOT SO

EASY—WHERE?—& HOW?—CAN'T NET BLACK HEADS—CAN'T PRISE BLACK HEADS OFF SHORE ROCKS—NO!—CAN'T SNIP A BLACK HEAD AS YOU MIGHT A WILD FLOWER, CAN'T PRESS & DRY A BLACK HEAD—CAN'T SHOOT THEM LIKE SNIPE, THOUGH SOME DO—WHAT WAS I TO DO?

'FORCED INTO MOST UNSAVOURY TRADE—LOWEST TYPES—CONVICT GRAVE DIGGERS—MORTUARY ATTEN-DANTS—SYDNEY SOLICITORS—RESULTS? ENTIRELY PREDICTABLE: LOST BEST PART OF SAVINGS—PROCURED SERIES OF SLIMY, STINKING HEADS—MANY THINGS BUT NEVER A BLACK MAN—CONVICTS' HEAD VAR-NISHED WITH JAPAN BLACK—PAUPER SKULLS' RADDLED MEAT BLOTCHED WITH TAR—ALL MANNER OF OTHER HEADS MOST PATHETICKALLY DISGUISED AS BLACK MAN'S HEAD—INEVITABLY MOST DISGUSTING CONDITION—SELL YOU ANYTHING—WHALER TRIED TO PASS OFF TWO SHRIVELLED MAORI HEADS CARRIED IN A DILLY BAG AROUND WAIST AS VAN DIEMONIAN NATIVES—NO BETTER THAN SHRIVELLED APPLES COVERED IN INDIAN INK STENCILS—THEN—'

'Guster Robinson?' suggested I.

'*VOTEZ-VOUS*,' said he.

'Tragic,' said I.

'*EN UN MOT*—BUT WHERE OTHERS SAW TRAGEDY—I SAW—WHAT?—I SAW AN OPENING.' He leant forward in the manner I had learnt was that which he used when wishing to impart knowledge he regarded as revelatory.

'Science?' guessed I.

'BLACK HEADS,' nodded he sagely.

I ran my fingers over the still sappy wood of the barrels.

'POSTHUMOUS REDEMPTION,' said he, '—OTHER-WISE TRAGIC UN-CHRISTIAN LIVES.'

'Salvation,' ventured I.

'HOPEFULLY,' said Mr Lempriere, '& NOT ONLY FOR THEM.'

Mr Lempriere wiped his face again, told the cooper to go & bring out some tea & more rum from the cottage. We sat down. 'IGNORE THEM,' said Mr Lempriere quietly, as though he could once more hear muffled protests emanating from inside the barrel & would not acknowledge them. 'NEVER ANSWER INGRATITUDE.' The cooper returned & put the teapot & rum pitcher on top of a sealed barrel.

The cooper went back to nailing more lids down, oblivious to whether the heads were floating or sunken, sullen or shouting. It was probably not the best time to say what I then did, but nevertheless I launched into a speech about how the fish were still a project of the highest scientifick significance & that perhaps if Sir Cosmo Wheeler were not interested, Mr Lempriere might consider publishing them himself with the printer Bent in Hobart Town.

A London imprint with the attachment of Sir Cosmo Wheeler's name—that meant glory, recognition, a path back into the world Mr Lempriere had so long stood outside of, the key to which Mr Lempriere had desired above all else: membership of the Royal Society. But a Hobart Town book . . .

'*EST-CE QUE JE SUIS SI MALADE?*' bellowed the

Surgeon. 'A HOBART TOWN BOOK—A CONTRADICTION, SIR!—A VERITABLE INSULT TO SCIENCE!—TO CULTURE!'

Then he drank some more rum & tea, & went round beating each barrel in turn with the hammer, yelling at them to desist & to be grateful for the fact that they would finally be of some practical use to Civilisation.

He came back & sat down & told me how the most temperate climes lie between the 40th & 50th degrees of latitude & how it is from this climate that correct ideas of the genuine colours of mankind & of various degrees of beauty ought to be derived.

'FOR NEVER WAS THERE A CIVILISED NATION—ALL WHITE—WHAT INGENIOUS MANUFACTORIES—WHAT ARTS OR SCIENCES—HAVE ARISEN ELSEWHERE?—THE NOBLE GAIT & BEARING OF THE WHITE!—AND WHERE EXCEPT ON THE BOSOM OF THE EUROPEAN MAIDEN?—WHERE POSSIBLE TO FIND TWO SUCH?— SUCH!—PLUMP & SNOWY WHITE HEMISPHERES— TIPPED WITH VERMILION?'

My poor mind filled with a parade of white hemispheres not plump, & hemispheres less than hemispherical, & of black hemispheres dipped in a darker dye with their lush plum-purple triggers, & not one pair of that happy procession that I had at some time or other been fortunate enough to be on more or less intimate terms with had I found without its attractions & compensations.

My attempts at hiding the shock I felt at all this—at the unwelcome supremacy of snowy white hemispheres; of the black heads who Mr Lempriere was convinced would not cease babbling & who still had not woken up to the fact that their hemispheres were on the wrong side of the globe; at the sad lack of goodwill in this world & its pitiful consequences; at my own fate now any hope of a future cosy billet of painting fish seemed about to disappear—must have been obvious.

'I WILL HAVE SCIENCE, GOULD—NOT A RUDDY CIRCUS.'

Then Mr Lempriere swung around wildly, as if he had heard some jeering or mockery. His back turned to me, he roared at the barrels.

'I'LL NOT DON GRIEVING BLACK FOR YOU—I AM A PATRIOT NATURALIST, &, LIKE ME, YOU WILL MAKE SACRIFICES FOR SCIENCE—FOR THE NATION.'

In his mind the general outburst from the barrels must have grown louder, for he picked a heavy stick up from his firewood heap, & went about with it whacking the lids again & again, telling them how no-one could have done more for them than he. He yelled, how the past was the past, but his interest was the future & how overjoyed they ought be at the prospect of working together on such a mighty project of Science & finally be of some use to Civilisation. At this last word the pig Castlereagh awoke startled, & began trotting around its pen squealing. This contributed to a general cacophony of noise: Mr Lempriere beating the barrels with a stick, Mr Lempriere yelling abuse of the most vile kind as he ran round, his pig screeching.

'I LOVE YOU—DON'T YOU UNDERSTAND?' he was now blubbering. 'OUT OF LOVE—ONLY LOVE—DO I DO THIS FOR YOU.'

Finally Mr Lempriere seemed to give up as though defeated, throwing his stick away with such force that it sailed out onto the Commandant's as yet unbuilt Boulevard of Destiny. He sighed, flicked some tears out of his eyes & slump-shouldered went & stood over near the pigpen, striving to bring the squealing Castlereagh into the conversation.

'THEY,'—& here, so that the pig might see, he pointed an accusing finger at the recalcitrant barrels —'THEY FAIL TO *APPRECIATE*—SHAPE—SIZE— RELATIONSHIP OF PARTS OF CRANIUM—ALL SURE INDI- CATORS OF BOTH CHARACTER & INTELLECT—&—AM WORKING ON A PAPER ON THIS VERY MATTER—*THE SOUL ITSELF*—STUDY OF SKULLS WILL REVEAL THE FUNDAMENTAL DIFFERENCES BETWEEN—PRECISE NATURE OF—EXACT REASONS FOR HIERARCHY IN RACES OF MAN.'

He turned, shook his head, & walked back to me.

'YOU SEE,' Mr Lempriere continued, refilling his pitcher of rum & tea, 'SCIENCE IS PRESENTED— *HERE*—WITH ITS GREATEST CHALLENGE—WHEELER IS DETERMINED TO SOLVE—OUR SABLE BRETHREN LIKE DOGS—FLEAS—ARE NOT DESCENDED FROM ADAM—GOD CREATED THEM—SEPARATE BUT INFERIOR SPECIES, AS HE CREATED MULLET OR SPARROWS AS SEPARATE BUT INFERIOR—AS STURDY ENGLISHMEN —WE APPREHEND THIS—STOUT COMMON SENSE —BUT WITHOUT SCIENTIFICK CLASSIFICATION

& CATEGORISATION WE DO NOT KNOW IT AS
SCIENCE—*YET*.

'SIR COSMO HAS CRANIOLOGICAL TREASURES—
UNRIVALLED FOR PROFUNDITY OF ANATOMICAL
VIEWS—BUT—THEY ARE *WHITE* SKULLS.'

Mr Lempriere leaned forward, dropped his great
sweating bald head low, swivelled it this way & then
that, like it was a hog's head on a spit, then when he
seemed satisfied no-one else was about & listening,
continued in a conspiratorial voice.

'HERE'S THE RUB—FOR HIM TO COMPLETE GREAT
WORK TO PROVE ALL THIS AS SCIENCE—WHEELER
MUST HAVE—WHEELER *NEEDS*—BLACK SKULLS TO
EVALUATE & STUDY.'

Mr Lempriere rolled his head back on his shoulders, a boiled egg wobbling in its cup, & hissed—

'*HE NEEDS ME.*'

V

SEVERAL DAYS AFTER I left Mr Lempriere & his barrels
without the watercolour set, I received a message that I
was to meet him first thing that morning to discuss my
future role as his assigned servant. My mind filled with
worry that this was the end of both the fish & of me. I
resolved that I must do everything in my power to
argue the worth of continuing with the project, & as I
walked to his cottage through the cold, slapping my
hands to warm them up, I tried to think of all the scientifick arguments I could invent, the only arguments
that ever cut any mustard with Mr Lempriere.

In the week since I had seen him, Mr Lempriere had been busy with his black heads, which he had given up trying to transport whole in casks & had instead decided to render down into skulls, which were being prepared by a mute convict assistant for cataloguing & transporting to England.

Oddly, there was no-one at his cottage. Odder yet, there was no violent shuddering & squealing coming from the pigpen. I went for a walk round the back just in case the Surgeon was involved in some uncharacteristically silent meditation with Castlereagh. I found the pig, seeming for once sated, asleep on its side in what appeared a deep & happy repose. But there was no sign of his master & confidant, Mr Lempriere.

Only later did I notice the giveaway white shadowing around the pig's snout, like an old man's stubble. But at the time I was overwhelmed by an unusually large cloud of vapour—so dense that it obscured much of the pigpen from which it was billowing forth—& the treacly, sour aroma with which the mist was so strongly redolent. I closed my eyes with the childlike instinct that this would somehow erase reality. But the smell only grew till it was an oppressive presence, so heavy it felt as a weight upon my head, so wet I could feel it as a dewy acid on my face, so pungent that my nostrils felt as if they were on fire.

And when finally I reopened my eyes & saw that the acrid mist had parted like a theatre curtain, there was no way of mistaking what now rose up in the muddy horror of that stage before me.

VI

IT WAS A TURD.

It was enormous.

It might even be, reckoned I in awe, the largest pig turd on the planet that morning. Perhaps ever. It was most certainly an astounding sight, not easy to immediately reconcile with the idea of pig dung. How in that ruddy early winter morning light that steaming obelisk of crap glowed. It might just have been possible to mistake it for a sublime & infinitely valuable gold nugget were it not for the somewhat tarnished, yet unmistakable form of a once-mended, now mangled cheap pewter shoe buckle protruding from the pyramid's base.

I climbed up on the fence & peered more closely. In the churned-up earth around the pile of glinting pig shit, looking as if they had been discarded after some bacchanalian excess, I saw shreds of a shirt (bloodied), a tail of a black swallow-tailed coat (torn), a blue silk sleeve (shredded), & half a spotted silk handkerchief (slobbery).

Then I noticed what looked uncomfortably like a human thigh bone. Other gory, muddied bones. Ribs. Femurs. And yet more & more—shin bones. Forearm bones. Vertebrae. Then I saw the great wen itself, a huge bloodied skull lying on its side like some fallen Pacific Island idol.

Castlereagh farted, an odour at once sweetly acrid & horrendously overpowering, & at that moment I, who stood immediately downwind, knew that familiar stench to be no other than the atomised essence of Mr Lempriere.

I noticed some smashed pottery at the far end of the pen, & recognised it as the remnants of the pitchers in which Twopenny Sal & I had been fermenting our Larrikin Soup. Castlereagh had somehow managed to roll them under the fence & into his pen with his front trotters, whereupon he had smashed them open & drunk their potent contents. I looked at the pig. The pig opened its eyes & looked at me.

I swear to God he smirked.

I staggered back in revulsion, hand over my mouth.

Like a dull daydream, I saw how Mr Lempriere must have met his end, sitting on the fence, drinking, drunk, talking to Castlereagh, the choleric boar his final audience, about Science, Civilisation, Kabbalist tracts & snowy hemispheres that were little more than a corrupted, corrupting memory. I saw Castlereagh drunk on our rough rum, ever angrier, trotting up & down, up & down, wondering, in as far as drunk pigs may be said to be capable of active thought, when this maddening racket would halt. I saw Castlereagh finally breaking into a deafening squeal & charging the fence with all his might.

And then, losing what little balance remained to him, Mr Lempriere had fallen into the void.

There he must have seen many things he had avoided seeing for a very long time. He must have heard the sound of slobber approaching at a trot. And then, I suppose, at a certain point, he must have known there would be no avoiding anything now.

THE SAWTOOTH SHARK

*Christ, Kabbalists, & pig turds—On what befell the love
shovel—Hallucinations of History—A bare
escape—Classification of the wen—Jorgen
Jorgensen—On his becoming the King of
Iceland—Reports of Waterloo—Jorgensen's new
mission—Discovery of Voltaire's head—Framing of
Gould—A second Book of Fish.*

I

RATHER THAN MR Lempriere's puerile, ultimately
fatal belief in the perfectibility of pigs, I chose to
remember his intense—if shortlived—passion for fish
that was so powerful it took on in his mind an unfortunate religious dimension. He was confirmed in this
delusion when, in an old Kabbalist tract lent him by
Jorgen Jorgensen, he discovered that the initial letters
of the Greek words for Jesus Christ, Son of God,
Saviour—ich-th-ys—were the same as the Greek word
for fish—*ichthys*.

'ALL THAT LIVES IS HOLY, GOULD, BUT FISH ARE
HOLIEST OF ALL,' he had once told me, before his
cracked passion became my belief, 'WHICH IS WHY THE
FISH WAS USED BY THE EARLY CHRISTIANS AS A SYMBOL
OF CHRIST.'

Lamentably, God remained in His Heaven & the

239

great scientist in a pyramid of pig turd & a cloud of vile methane, & now the fish were with me—but I was no Father or Son or Holy Ghost & I had no idea what to do with the fish, or with Mr Lempriere's remains, or what they might all end up doing to me.

I tried to see the fiasco as a blessing—possibly divine intervention on the part of old Ichthys. The *Book of Fish* would now never be published, annotated & falsely authored by Sir Cosmo Wheeler. It seemed as though the Surgeon's death had delivered the fish to me, unencumbered by the demands of Science or Mr Lempriere's social ambitions, which had amounted to much the same thing. The compass of the fish, formerly so limited, seemed suddenly infinite. I should have felt elation, but my immediate dilemma was too pressing to feel anything other than terror. Because it was known I was today visiting Mr Lempriere, because his death would inevitably be discovered, & because a death on a convict island is invariably viewed as murder, I knew that if something was not done with his bones, something would be done with me.

I am not saying what I then did was the smartest thing I have ever done, or for that matter the wisest. But for a time it did at least solve the problem of his remains. I fetched what was left of my grog supply & threw it into the pen with the homicide Castlereagh, who had awoken from the sleep brought on by his splendid repast. The pig lapped & slurped the rum with a vigour that within a quarter of an hour had transformed into a cathartic backflip. Castlereagh rolled over & fell back asleep, trotters like four empty bottles rising into the air.

After checking that the pig's slumber was sufficiently deep by throwing stones & watching them bounce off his stubbly hide without reaction, I eased myself down into the pen & undertook the awful job of sorting through the shit for Mr Lempriere's remains. In a frenzy his clothes I threw on the fire in the cottage, his belt & shoe buckles I buried nearby, & his bones I tossed into an old water barrel at the back of the cottage. Then I stood back, drew breath, & wondered how—& on a crowded island *where*—I might hide a barrel of reeking human bones.

II

TWOPENNY SAL HAD no more idea than Billy Gould as to what to do with the bones. Her tiny & dark room—little better than a cell with its ceiling so low, its walls so damp, its cot bed so cramped with its wretched straw palliasse & its only other piece of furniture, a broken wicker chair—he filled with his problems. He started with the dilemma of surreptitiously disposing of the past & ended up on the verge of the Enlightenment, when the bedroom door awkwardly creaked open.

Billy Gould had just time enough to hide his naked body under Twopenny Sal's cot, when he heard the heavy, unmistakable wheeze followed by a creak as the Commandant sat down in the broken wicker chair, uncomfortable as Billy Gould's panicked state of mind at that moment. Only then, too late, I realised that part of me was protruding from beneath the blanket.

In the dark & in his stupor the Commandant mistook the two buttocks blossoming out from beneath the bed for a dilapidated footstool. With the back of his heel he gave them a few kicks to puff the age-flattened cheeks up into some semblance of comfort, then wriggled his boots back & forth along the line of my crack. It's far from easy for a man to stay silent & still naked on his knees, with the old love shovel being biffed back & forth. It was an awful thing, a torment not eased by the long monologue that the Commandant then commenced, though not before taking, I later gathered, some drops of laudanum.

In a growing delirium he spoke of how history, far from being past, was ever present. All those who had over the centuries deliberately or inadavertently discovered Van Diemen's Land, he now believed all to be here, now, sailing into Twopenny Sal's bedroom. He saw twelfth-century Arab traders in their triangular-sailed dhows, fourteenth-century Japanese pirates ill & wasted from their long voyage, soon dying of an inexplicable melancholia, their gummy bald corpses so light they floated in the air & had to be tied down with stones in order to keep them in their graves. He saw scurvy ridden fifteenth-century Portuguese adventurers in three caravels seeking gold & converts for Christianity, trying to reconcile their Ptolemaic charts at the bottom of which was a vagueness marked as *Terra Incognita*—the land unknown—with the certainty of naked black inhabitants so uninterested in trade they threw back at the Portuguese all gifts offered, keeping only red handkerchiefs to tie around their fuzzy heads.

The Commandant shook his head at the sadness of such innocence. The Portuguese left the bedroom, turning their caravels southwards where, on moving mountains of ice, their leader, Amado the Reckless had heard there lived a race of more commercially inclined people who had no noses but only snake-like slits & lived solely on odours for which they were willing to trade gold.

I felt a flea bite my crutch & inadvertently wriggled my arse. The Commandant gave a hefty kick to right what he presumably felt to be a toppling foot stool, & resumed talking about those who the Commandant seemed to think were also with us in the by now very crowded bedroom of history.

Then the Commandant began yelling out at the Dutch—shining a boot on my cods in his excitement —who sailed over the crest of Twopenny Sal's cot in their stumpy fluyts looking for trade, followed by Javanese in their long & narrow proas blown far down from their fishing grounds in the distant northwest, & a French expedition of naturalists, astronomers, artists, philosophers, encyclopaedists, & savants, led by the gallant Monsieur Peron who, upon landing on a long beach in what he thought was Van Diemen's Land in Year Six of the Republic but was rather here & now, drew off his glove while bowing to a black woman, at which she screamed, thinking he had peeled off his skin. Her fears could not be allayed until, to her great amuse-ment, he sang the *Marseillaise* & she was able to take off his trousers in order to ascertain if he were a man like real men.

And then the Commandant was beset by the most terrible fear:

'What if time never passed?' shrilled he. It was as though the Arabs, Japanese, Portuguese, Dutch, Javanese & French were always all there discovering Van Diemen's Land in Twopenny Sal's bedroom along with Major de Groot, face smiling and talking in spite of the poison, along with all those who died on the Cradle with their minds more maggoty than their backs, once more alive along with a thousand and one others in a long procession now streaming in through Twopenny Sal's door, ending with Lieutenant Lethborg and his platoon, their water-bloated and rad-dled bodies marching in like balloons trying to keep martial order. Abruptly the Commandant swung his legs off my bum, stood up, & without a word more stag-gered out.

Later Capois Death told me that he had heard the Commandant's opiate-induced hallucinations always took this form. Yet many years before, when the Commandant had first taken laudanum the effect was said to have been profound. Now in Twopenny Sal's squalid room, it had, like all events of spiritual signifi-cance when degraded through intimacy & repetition, been reduced to the sadly diminished realm of art, even entertainment.

Now he would whoop when the Javanese disap-peared, hiss the French & laugh at the dying Japanese. But back then history became a nightmare from which the Commandant could not awake. Beneath his gold mask his face erupted in a plague of chancres from the worry of it all. He began to see everywhere unsettling evidence that the Past is as much a Chaos as the Present, that there is no straight line only infinite circles, like rings proceeding ever outward from a stone sinking in the water of Now. He took more & more green laudanum. He doubled, & then doubled again his dosage of mercury to treat his clap, which seemed to be eating both his body & mind away. He feared above all else that he was mad, & that he was now imprisoned in his imaginings.

The convicts could always bolt, but no such release, even one as wretched as perishing in the wilderness, awaited him. Once he had searched out the Mulatto in order to assert his existence, in order to lose the sense of his life, in order to forget the confusion that daily crowded him more & more. It did no good whatsoever. The Mulatto would bend over & throw her skirt onto her back, exposing the splendid rump that so excited him, & merely ask that he be quick, as she had matters to attend to. The Commandant would plough a lonely furrow, curse her, & withdraw feigning a triumph they both knew to be illusory.

It may be asked as to why & how Twopenny Sal—and by obvious implication, Billy Gould—had avoided the clap with which the Commandant was riddled. But his disease had been with him a very long time & in the nature of that curse it was now his alone; like his thoughts no longer communicable.

The day many years before, after he first saw the

horror of a past that was inescapable, the Commandant interrogated Jorgen Jorgensen at some length, then issued an unequivocal command while making water in the corner of his cell.

'I charge you,' the Commandant had said, 'with keeping all the records of the island.'

The Commandant turned toward the old Dane, flipping his pustulant penis back inside his breeches without shame or care but with the slightest tremor of an intense pain.

'If I cannot control the past now,' he continued, wiping his wet fingers on a moonbird epaulette, his mask shining so bright the old Dane had to shield his eyes with a cupped hand, 'I will at least control it in the future.'

In comparison to such ambitions of temporal tyranny, Billy Gould's problems were small fry indeed. No doubt, in the future people may wish to view his subsequent actions as an *inner rebellion* or a *fierce declaration of humanity*. But the King & I know otherwise: Billy Gould was in more shit than Lempriere's bones & needed to get out of it as quickly as he could.

III

I DRESSED & left Twopenny Sal's quarters. Her only suggestion seemed not the best, but it did have the virtue of at least being an *idea*, unlike the one fear of being caught which was all that was rattling around my terrified head, lonely as a piece of meat in convict soup.

I carried the barrel of bones back down the Boulevard of Destiny, feigning to one & all I met along the way that it was rancid pickled pork being returned by the Surgeon, making my way to the same room in the commissary where were stored the Aboriginal skulls Mr Lempriere had collected.

In that dim, windowless room lit only by the slippery light of three whale-oil lamps & smelling of the mournful screams of dying cetaceans, Mr Lempriere had with patience & occasional violence trained the convict mute Heslop in the cleaning, cataloguing & correct packaging of the skulls in preparation for shipment to Sir Cosmo Wheeler in England.

'A CALLING,' he had told the mute convict, 'GLORIOUS & SACRED—WHAT I HAVE GIVEN YOU—WHAT SAY YOU, EH, HESLOP?' to which the mute, was, of course, unable to say anything.

When I presented Heslop with the latest set of bones for cataloguing, he was annoyed. By gesture he made it clear that he thought he had finished with the bones of the dead blacks & would be able to return to the more congenial cataloguing of plants & flowers. He took a look inside the old barrel I had with difficulty carried in on my back—unaccountably redolent of the smell of pig—in which he discovered, in a muddy, muddled pile, yet another fresh human skull streaked with particularly nasty looking peat. He shook his head, & grunted angrily.

No doubt the mute was peeved with Mr Lempriere for dumping yet more bones upon him. I sympathised. There was a cutter returning to Hobart Town that night, & Mr Lempriere had been insistent that the complete set of Aborigine bones be on it, bound for London.

So, it had to be done, & to avoid Mr Lempriere's wrath, Heslop there & then set about the cleaning, preserving & cataloguing of the skull that had been so badly damaged in its exhumation as to appear as though gnawed by a wild animal. He took the brown-streaked pink skull &, temper abating, gestured that he was relieved that unlike the other heads, it didn't mouth silent rebukes as he set about scraping, boiling & cleaning it. I helped as best I could, carefully registering a description of cranial measurements in the catalogue that was to accompany the skulls.

There was in all this a symmetry & beauty that did not escape me—the way the Great Scientist in death had become part of his own Immortal System. I felt teary as I wrote on the damp page of the catalogue what was to be both the skull's identification number & Mr Lempriere's epitaph, as concise as it was appropriate, reminiscent of the deflated porcupine fish thrown into the fire. As the thirty-sixth skull of the Macquarie Harbour collection, it was according to Mr Lempriere's own method to be called MH-36. I lifted my quill & threw sand across the page. Beneath the speckling I watched as those four fluid letters dried into reality.

When that evening the cutter was loaded with the specially constructed crates, each containing several individual compartments, one for each Aboriginal skull carefully padded in aromatic Huon pine shavings, with their destination—

The Sawtooth Shark

Sir Cosmo Wheeler,
Royal Society,
London

—marked on each box as Mr Lempriere had instructed, there were oddly no accompanying comments to be found from the noted colonial surgeon - collector entered next to the skull designated MH-36 in the enclosed register of descriptions. It was a rum thing, thought the mute, but he had no desire to have his hide whaled for asking why.

I slapped Heslop on the back, thanked him for a job well done, but should have known that the disappearance of Mr Lempriere would not so easily be allowed.

Several days passed. It had been raining without cease for most of that time, & I was working in a room in the Commandant's palace, painting a new portrait of the Commandant swimming the harbour surrounded by loving multitudes. With the noise of the rain I never heard him, only smelt his odorous presence behind me. When I turned there stood a three-legged dog & a wet, bedraggled figure I knew instantly, lapis lazuli necklace flashing in the late afternoon light.

'*Who loves longer?*' hissed Jorgen Jorgensen, '*a man or a woman?*'

I swallowed.

The mangy dog stood up on its hind legs & whistled. Jorgen Jorgensen gave it a hearty kick. Applause wasn't what he sought from his audience, but their complicity in making up the story. Gifted as Elsinore was, her limitations in this regard sometimes irritated him immensely.

In his outstretched hand he held a perfume bottle in the shape of Voltaire's head, half full, half empty. It was, I noticed for the first time, the colour of turquoise.

IV

TURQUOISE'S VERY NAME is suggestive of the exotic other, the Occident. It is derived, the Surgeon once told me—no doubt inaccurately—from the French *pierre turqueise* meaning Turkish stone. Equally redolent of mystery as the green ink with which I now write this sentence was the one I would come to forever associate with this colour, the one who now held out before me the treacherous attraction of Voltaire's head: Jorgen Jorgensen.

When he stood before me that wet afternoon, reading out a charge of murder that I had not committed, I realised the awful truth about Sarah Island: that this was not a colony of men at all, but a colony of fish masquerading as men. When he pronounced with such savagery upon my future, I recognised not Jorgen Jorgensen but saw a sawtooth shark, thrusting & cutting me into pieces with his long mouth.

If I were to contrive some motivation for what Jorgen Jorgensen did—his jealousy of a supposed influence with the Commandant, say, or his clerk's desire for obvious cause & effect—this would be merely literature, rather than life, where there is no explanation or motivation for people's actions. It was, I suppose, simply his nature, as it is that of a sawtooth shark's.

I was later to discover—too late—that like the Commandant, Jorgen Jorgensen suffered a sense of slippage. He had read too many books, & at the age of sixteen, inspired by their tales of romance & adventure, had one day in 1798 ventured out from his hometown of Copenhagen only to discover that the world did not correspond to anything he had read.

Things were rupturing & nothing held. Books were solid, yet time was molten. Books were consistent, yet people were not. Books dealt in cause & effect, yet life was inexplicable disorder. Nothing was as it was in a book, something about which he forever after harboured a dull resentment that finally found expression as vengeance.

Nothing held on the storm-tossed English collier to which he was indentured & where he shared his lice-ridden hammock with a fellow sailor who in the heat of passion & the rolling darkness of the crowded low space where they slept turned out in his trembling, descending hand to be a woman. Nothing held in the hands of cards he was dealt on the rare occasions ashore, which invariably left him both with no money & a desperate need for money that could be answered only by invention: of stories—lies if you like—that he traded for credit to play the gaming tables again the following evening. He began by using gossip to ingratiate himself, & ended up as a spy telling the agents of various governments whatever fears they needed to know.

He discovered his capacity for reinventing the

world was matched only by the world's capacity for destroying itself. He was, said he, with Erasmus of Rotterdam. '*The reality of things*,' he would say, quoting the peregrinatory Dutchman, '*depends solely on opinion.*' It was a maxim that the example of his life, he believed, amply bore out. When the world's belief in him seemed low, his fortunes went sour, he was beaten up, incarcerated & finally transported all because of the erroneous idea that he had no intention of honouring his debts. '*There are words*,' he would say from the box of the accused, hoping to win the court if not by his history then with his philosophy, '*& things, & ne'er the twain shall meet.*' But it was untrue, & he knew it. He made words things—that was his gift, & that had been his downfall.

He suffered badly from the nostalgia of realism, &, imbued with the great Romance of the Age, he made his own revolution as best he could, overthrowing at the age of twenty-six the defenceless Danish governor of Iceland with the aid of an English privateer & by sending six armed men to the back of the governor's house in Reykjavik, & six to the front, then marching in, waking the poor man from his afternoon slumbers on his sofa, & arresting him. He next hoisted the ancient flag of a free Iceland, issued a proclamation declaring that the people of Iceland, being tired of submission to the Danish yoke, had unanimously called upon him to head their new government. Forever after he insisted on titling himself the King of Iceland, though the English usurped his sovereignty within a week.

He arrived at Waterloo a day after the great battle for the future had ended with the past ascendant, invoking his own particular genius for arriving too late at the wrong place, something which he rightly felt qualified him to be a journalist, though his report (largely cribbed from newspapers) from the field of battle was not a great success with the street pamphlet sellers of London in the hungry winter of 1816. He was, in any case, promptly arrested as an escaping French soldier in disguise, & was only able to escape after bribing a guard on duty with a field spyglass he had stolen from an English soldier's corpse.

Jorgen Jorgensen was a man given to telling stories—true or untrue it didn't really bother him or matter to others—for they were his trade & he was a journeyman of tales, a traveller through the republic of fictions. In his stories he tended to present himself & his ventures as though he were the narrator of one of the picaresque novels that had in the last century been so in fashion with scullery maids & skulking servants, & of which he was himself such an avid reader, so much so that behind his back Mr Lempriere was to call him Joseph Josephson.

His complexion was sallow, his white hair bedraggled, his nose long & pointy, & he wore a droopy moustache of the type that hangs in pointy strands over the lips & holds soup fat at the tips in small congealed pearls.

In times long before the arrival of Lieutenant Horace, Jorgen Jorgensen had been posted to the settlement as the Commissary, purportedly to head up the government's stores, but in truth as an agent of Governor Arthur, ready to report on whatever intrigue may have arisen in such a far-flung post of the Van Diemonian despot's then small empire. But with Lieutenant Horace he recognised the limitations of his perfidy.

Later, when their work was to bind them together in a bond as sacred as that of murder, it was said that it was his conspiratorial complicities that brought Jorgen Jorgensen to the Commandant's attention, that capacity to be ever ready to invent whatever story he fancied the Commandant might want to hear. It may well be that Jorgen Jorgensen saw the necessity of ingratiating himself with the new Commandant with his tales, but perhaps also—that day long ago he was commissioned to keep the records of the island—he found in the Commandant a mirror to his own long repressed desires to betray the world in a more fundamental way, as he felt the world had once betrayed him by not being a book. In the Commandant he sensed the creative mania of a true audience, an absolute desire to believe at any cost.

Continuing to hold Voltaire's head in front of him like Yorick's skull, Jorgen Jorgensen told me in his unusual voice—as affected, as I was to discover, as his overly decorative Italianite handwriting—how it was no longer possible to present Mr Lempriere's demise as death by misadventure. Circumstances demanded that the animality of man occasionally be shown, & when shown, punished. The Surgeon's family would settle for nothing less, & the Commandant had no need of an enquiry being launched from Hobart Town, given the extent of his commercial ventures & political ambitions. The Commandant would have me killed in a particularly slow & barbaric fashion for stealing his favourite perfume if told of my theft. On the other hand, he, Jorgen Jorgensen, was willing to allow me the opportunity to do some final good for the Nation as well as myself. At this point he paused, somewhat obscenely raked his tongue along the sorry sawteeth of his moustache, then continued. He would, said he, ease my passage to the other side with a relatively quick death on the gibbet if I would just sign a statement confessing to the murder of Mr Lempriere.

With as much conviction as I could muster, I told him that Constable Musha Pug, while assistant to the storemaster in the Commissariat, had sold me the perfume bottle—which he had boasted he had stolen in order to advance himself in his pursuit of the Mulatto, the Commandant's housemaid—& that therefore I couldn't sign.

V

I SIGNED. IT was the next morning, it was still raining, & Jorgen Jorgensen had presented me with a florid statement detailing my lurid boasts to others of how I had drowned Mr Lempriere, then fed his body to the sharks. All of the aforegoing corroborated by a lengthy confession written & signed by the Commandant's black housemaid.

There were no sharks in Macquarie Harbour. But

there seemed no reason to point out either this, or that Twopenny Sal could not write. To be frank, it seemed unreasonable not to sign after it was mentioned in passing how Constable Musha Pug had been woken in the middle of the preceding night & had his groin pounded with a hammer, ending up with a ball bag the size of a sugar sack in which the gritty remnants of his manhood swam in a ragout of pendulous horror.

When I was fairly tried for Mr Lempriere's murder—along with Roaring Tom Weaver for dressing in a maid's petticoats—there was placed next to us as we sat in the condemned pew, in revival of the old practice, a pointed reminder of our soon to be fates, as if they were our cat & dog, two coffins.

Roaring Tom Weaver laughed as he stepped up onto the scaffold the following day &, with a broad grin, pulled a ribbon out of his hair & let his blond braids fall, reached down & taking his laceless boots off, threw them to Old Bob Muff who had first looked after him when he had arrived at Sarah full of plans of escape & liberty. *Walk with me, Bob!* he yelled, then began his famous roaring & wailing. It was clear he was drunk, full as a fat girl's blouse, & we all cheered & laughed, & his roars & wails rose with us, through us, beyond us.

The executioner, outraged at such a performance mocking the solemn power of capital punishment, rushed his work. The trap door fell open with a dull thump, Roaring Tom dropped, shook & shuddered, his roaring blowing up inside him one last time, & it became apparent that the hangman had botched the noose & failed to snap Roaring Tom's neck. Rather than rapidly dying, Roaring Tom thrashed around slowly choking, his roaring now a shrill gurgle. The hangman walked around to the front of the gibbet, shaking his head, leapt up, grabbed Roaring Tom's thrashing legs, & hanging on, swung with him, bringing his additional weight to bear in order to kill him quicker. It was an awful thing: even Capois Death, to my surprise, gave a choked scream.

The following morning in the Penitentiary, the convicts were awoken for morning muster. Hammocks were furled & neatly hung, each from a hook on the wall, from one of which now hung Old Bob Muff. The hooks were only at elbow height, but it doesn't take height to hang, only some rope & a strong will. They worried I might do the same & cheat the gallows, & so had me brought to this saltwater cell & put under the regime of Pobjoy.

In the court I was asked for an explanation—but what was there to say? That at first I saw people in fish? That then, the more I looked at those sad creatures, still dying, the occasional mortal flap of the tail or desperate heave of the gills signalling their silent horror was not yet ended, the more I looked into the endless recesses of their eyes, the more something of them began to pass into me?

And how then could I confess to something even more peculiar, more shocking: how lately some small part of me, without me willing it, was beginning a long, fateful journey into them! Some small part of me & then more & more of me was tumbling downwards, was falling inwards through their accusing eyes into that spiralling tunnel that was to end only with the sudden awareness that I was no longer falling but rolling ever slower in the sea, not knowing whether I was finally safe or whether I was finally dead, & at a certain point in my fall I realised with horror that I was looking up at a saw-tooth shark pretending to be Jorgen Jorgensen, & I was seeing fish in people!

I would get all prickly & sweaty just thinking about such terrifying things, far less saying them publicly, because I knew in order to survive & prosper it was important to feel nothing for anyone or anything, & I knew I wanted to survive & prosper. But because of my newfound proximity to what hitherto had been little more than stench wrapped in slime & scale, I began to dream that there was nothing in the extraordinary universe opening up in front of me, not a man or woman, not a plant or tree, not a bird or fish, to which I might be allowed to continue remaining indifferent.

The ostensible crime with which I was charged, & later to be tried &, inevitably, found guilty was of murder. But my real crime . . . ?

My real crime was seeing the world for what it is & painting it as fish. For that reason alone, I was happy to sign a confession of guilt with no need for the Cradle or the Tube Gag, however inaccurate the details of my crime may have read.

I have been in this saltwater cell now for the best part of a year and a half waiting for my execution, which Pobjoy through various subterfuges succeeds in constantly postponing. At first this suited me well enough. My original fish paintings were collected & bound together by Pobjoy, who then sold them off to a Doctor Allport in Hobart Town. It was no matter to me, for I was never satisfied with any of that work for Mr Lempriere's book of fish. Oddly, not until now, painting only from a shoddy memory in the bad light of this saltwater cell, have I felt my fish finally worthy of the name.

Pobjoy sensed that since being incarcerated in the saltwater cell my belief was renewed, that here my talent was unfolding like a fern frond into the shade. Pobjoy, who formerly only saw me as an object to beat & kick, was impressed by the way I now cared about—& only about—painting, & even more impressed by the sum the Hobart Town doctor was willing to pay for Mr Lempriere's book of fish.

Pobjoy came to see that paintings were a currency more useful than tobacco or rum when parlayed in the right quarters. But for me to paint, for Pobjoy to make money, I needed materials, which he, in his careful way, has provided.

In my saltwater cell, under the cover of the convict-Constables, I determined I would repaint all the fish from memory, this time around adding to them these notes. Pobjoy provided me with oils & canvas for my Constables, as well as the paper I insisted I needed for my preliminary sketches. But to complete my second book of fish I needed watercolour paints.

The last time I saw Twopenny Sal was when she came to the cell ostensibly bearing some food. My life in the cell was fabulously monotonous & apart from Pobjoy, I was blessed with being spared the problem of people. Heaven is other people, the old priest, who would rub my feet in the hope of rubbing other things, used say, but then, I suppose, so too is Hell. So I didn't want to see Twopenny Sal—to tell the truth I never wanted to see her again. But there she was, dressed as the domestick she sometimes pretended to be.

I could see from her heavy belly that she was far gone with child. But we didn't really talk of that or, for that matter, of her father's death. Though said she nothing I knew she would soon be bolting back into the bush, leaving the Commandant broken-hearted & me in possession not only of Mr Lempriere's watercolours that she that day smuggled in, but Mr Lempriere's copper pot of green laudanum in which, after her leaving, I must confess to having resorted to for solace.

Green—fertility, birth, immortality, the resurrection of the just. In Art denoting hope, joy. Among the Greeks & Moors, victory. In church, God's bounty, mirth, the resurrection. In planets, Venus. But the smell of pig shit, the malevolent power of jealousy & the visage of hallucinations are for me forever turquoise.

Eyes fixed on her belly & wondering which devil was responsible, I said only one word as she turned to leave.

'Moinee?' asked I.

'Cobber,' said she.

VI

Do you think I was only gaoled? I wished to cry out as she turned to leave & rapped thrice on the door for Pobjoy to come & open—for I too was the gaoler. Do you think to keep my own hide unflogged I never lied? Never stole off a mate? I have a weakness for blue gin, old women, white rum, young girls, porter, pisco, human company & the Commandant's laudanum. I have a great fear of pain. I am beyond shame. Do you think I never informed on a mate? I was both cobber & dobber, I liked them & wept for them when they took them off to be flogged on my false information. I survived. It was bad & wrong & I may as well be the cat-o'-nine-tails stripping bark off their backs when I traded souls for some scraps of food or paint. I gave away all I needed. I was a vile piece of cell-shit. I smelt the breath of my fellows. I tasted the sour stench of their rotten lives. I was the stinking cockroach. I was the filthy lice that didn't stop itching. I was Australia. I was dying before I was born. I was a rat eating its young. I was Mary Magdalene. I was Jesus. I was sinner. I was saint. I was flesh & flesh's appetite & flesh's union & death & love were all equally rank & all equally beautiful in my eyes. I cradled their broken bodies dying. I kissed their suppurating boils. I washed their skinny shanks filled with ulcers, rotting craters of pus; I was that pus & I was spirit & I was God & I was untranslatable & unknowable even to myself. How I hated myself for it. How I wished to essay the universe I loved which was me also & how I wanted to know why it was that in my dreams I flew through oceans & why when I awoke I was the earth smelling of freshly turned peat. No man could answer me my angry lamentations nor could they hear my jokes why I had to suffer this life. I was God & I was pus & whatever was me was You & You were Holy,

Your feet, Your bowels, Your mound, Your armpits, Your smell & Your sound & taste, Your fallen Beauty, I was Divine in Your image & I was You & I was no longer long for this grand earth & why is it no words would tell how I was so much hurting aching bidding farewell?

THE STRIPED COWFISH

Mrs Gottliebsen's areolae—Other surprising phenomena recounted—Twopenny Sal & her circles—On why the striped cowfish quivered—A mysterious calamity—Discovery of the Registry—The old Dane's invention—A fatal confrontation—Literature of murder—Surgeon's head multiplies ceaselessly—A cocoon unravelling.

I

I CAN SEE I have put the cart before the horse in my telling of this tale, while all the time Mrs Gottliebsen was waiting, ready & harnessed at all points to speed me on to my fateful destination.

If the reader should have the fancy that Billy Gould—back before being found out as the Murderer of the Enlightenment & while still a painter of fish for the Surgeon—having been with Twopenny Sal remained faithful to her, the reader would be at once entirely right & entirely wrong. She was having her way with Musha Pug, & Billy Gould was being introduced to Mrs Gottliebsen, wife of Pastor Gottliebsen, visitors on a sloop bound for Sydney that had stopped over at Sarah Island.

They were suffering the hospitality of Mr Lempriere, who had given them use of his cottage while he was away doing a tour of the settlement's out-posts up the Gordon River. I had been instructed to act as their manservant & to suspend all painting until their visit was ended.

Pastor Gottliebsen was a gaunt & pursed individual. He was not without that particular confidence that arrives unencumbered by the need for thought, & for that alone I disliked him. He had a mind as narrow as the neck of a vinegar cruet, & saw himself as something of an aesthete, a veritable Lakes poet, & the idea of the artist - criminal interested him; it interested him, he told me as I served dinner that evening, that these two polarities can exist—perhaps *must* exist?—under the umbrella of one soul.

If you ask me, it's a pretty tatty & leaky umbrella & only someone very foolish would seek shelter under it; but Pastor Gottliebsen was not asking & I was not say-ing, only assuring him as a man obviously in the prime of his life that he could look at worse investments than Art.

'Why do you paint?' asked he, & before I could point out that it beats being gang-buggered behind a black-wood, but only just, answered he his own question: 'Because you must find beauty in the most adverse of worlds. Because even in the heart of the most depraved,' reflected he, so that I might confirm his trite observation, 'is the hope of Divine Redemption through Nature, which is Art.'

'You wouldn't happen to have a taj of nigger-twist on you?' asked I.

Pastor Gottliebsen halted, turned his head sideways

in wonder at his own revelatory insight. He shook his head in exaltation at the glory of man, his infinite desire to ascend to the ethereal realm.

'For my pipe,' continued I, 'Mr Lempriere won't object.'

But he didn't seem to hear, relaxed after a time & offered me some snuff which I took as an acceptable alternative, along with his considered opinion that criminality arises precisely from an imbalance of bodily fluids that he believes could be rectified if, as children, cases such as mine were suspended upside down for several hours a day over a period of some years as a curative treatment.

Maybe if I had been hung upside down as a child I would have ended up different, maybe it would have improved me. But I suffered more than my share of humiliations back then & it didn't seem to improve me at all, & a lot of what I suffered was a good deal worse than just being trussed up & left to hang by the ankles, let me tell you.

On the second evening of their stay, after I had brought in the decanter of finest Martinique rum—watered down as per the Surgeon's instructions—Mrs Gottliebsen placed her hand over mine. She told me how her husband had seen some of my work & regarded me as a sensualist, no doubt because of my imbalanced bodily fluids. She took my hand up to her lips & kissed it, caressed my arm, then asked me if I might take her while Pastor Gottliebsen watched at a discreet distance. She offered 6 oz of the best nigger-twist tobacco. For 6 oz, said I, Pastor Gottliebsen can come as close as he wants, but Mrs Gottliebsen seemed not so keen on this.

She asked that I blindfold her & bind her wrists with cord to the bedposts. For 6 oz I felt obliged to show her all my best steps, & so we danced the old Dutch still life & we jigged along to the Enlightenment, & she cried out over & over in her blind pleasure, which was all very fine for her but it was hopeless for me, for the Flemish painter just wasn't loading from the palette.

Poor Mrs Gottliebsen! She was a bold woman, & her body bolder yet: big alabaster thighs & rolly belly & heavy breasts with particularly large areolae. Face damasked with florid effort, she was yelling now, 'Ravish me! Ravish me!' But all I could do was put my nose to her thighs, run my fingers over her nipples, tongue those splendidly generous areolae, & begin to feel ever more desperate for all was to no avail.

Poor bugger Billy Gould! Once was the time he'd root a pair of drawers on a rat trap. Now where were his imbalanced body fluids when he most needed them? I felt bewildered. She was damning me as a depraved monster. I was lost. She was thrashing around worse than a trumpeter just caught. 'You beast!' cried she. In response I bellowed. 'You awful beast!' cried she in delight. I brayed. Mrs Gottliebsen began to moan. It was awful. I neighed & snorted & mooed & baaed. I was a menagerie of loud lust. But no matter how many ludicrous noises I made that might keep the fiction of my passion alive a little longer, I was but an echo searching for its lost caller. Neither Mrs Gottliebsen's wild, earthy cries nor my own inward exhortations or outward displays were going to make any impression upon my flaccid loins. The Gottliebsens had desired a leviathan & I had transformed into a sardine.

It is difficult, looking back on it, to believe that Billy Gould could be privileged to know so much flesh & still remain unmoved. I would not insult Mrs Gottliebsen who was in so many ways a nice woman & most attractive, apart from her face, but then who looks at the mantelpiece when they are stoking the fire? Except I couldn't have lit a candle, far less got a fire up & racing. I thought maybe it was the blindfold & then I tried to imagine Mrs Gottliebsen's eyes but I couldn't remember them, & then I felt put off by Pastor Gottliebsen behaving unspeakably in the sofa behind me, & I tried to imagine he wasn't there.

Then I was angry that they were making me play the priest with his chalky fingers. I tried to imagine every wicked thing in the world & my mind was filled with more imaginings than it is possible to imagine but still I was a child before her. In terror I prayed to Saint Guignole, patron of the impotent, in the hope of imitating his celebrated statue in Brest, famous for its erect member which—in spite of being constantly whittled away by desperate lovers—miraculously continues to maintain the same remarkable length & orientation.

But the truth was that Twopenny Sal had somehow got into my head & pray as I did, try as I liked, want as I wished, she wouldn't leave & let me rise to the occasion. Mrs Gottliebsen spread out in front of me larger & whiter than all Europe, & all I had to do was conquer her like Alexander & weep thereafter. But all I could see was the frail sisal ropes of Twopenny Sal's dark biceps & forearms, the ribs coopering the small firkin of her chest beneath her slight, slightly sagging breasts, the stretchmarked glory of her puckering belly, the lips like moist mussels urging me inwards . . .

I didn't feel loyal to Twopenny Sal—after all she was hardly a vestal virgin—but it was something between us getting between me & the writhing Mrs Gottliebsen, who was now saying any manner of foul things about me being an animal. Would that we be so lucky. It made me feel all angry because it wasn't rational & I wanted to please myself as well as Mrs Gottliebsen & I knew it just wasn't going to happen & none of it stood up to Reason—at which thought I thankfully recalled the Great Philosopher.

I grabbed Voltaire & pressed him into service & Mrs Gottliebsen began to squeal worse than Castlereagh & Pastor Gottliebsen to groan & his eyes were rolling in the back of his head, & I am not sure if he ever really saw what was going on with all his moaning, for the following day when I bad them farewell at the dock I kept on catching them stealing glances at my crutch which they obviously believed to be a valley of hidden giants rather than the desert of desire I knew it to be.

The 6 oz nigger-twist I calculated would last me four months if carefully rationed. I smoked half in two days, & then sent word to Twopenny Sal that I had some tobacco if she was interested. Her reply came the following day.

She was.

II

ON THE BACK of her black calves Twopenny Sal had
showed me two circles that had been cut into her flesh
& then scarred to form raised cicatrix, steel blue in
colour, strangely soft in feel. One circle she touched &
said 'Sun,' the other, bisected but not broken by a single
line, she touched &, again in English, said 'Moon.'

Then she found a Y-shaped stick amongst the
Surgeon's firewood, & after sharpening two of its
points with the kitchen knife, had me pull my shirt up
& lie on my belly. I felt her pushing the stick into the
small of my back & using it in the manner of a compass,
cutting a circle on each side of my backbone. The pain
as she slowly scribed the stick around made me shiver &
I momentarily bucked when she began bisecting the
second circle with a line across its middle.

As she rubbed ashes from Mr Lempriere's fire into
the wound to create the finished cicatrix, she again
touched the first circle & said, 'Palawa,' her word for
her own people; then when rubbing ash into the second
circle that she had bisected, said she one word over &
over, 'Numminer,' like I was some foolish child, said
she, laughing, 'Numminer, numminer.'

'I am no numminer,' said I after a time, rolling over,
knowing numminer was their word both for ghosts &
white men, that they believed England was where their
spirits went after death to be reborn as English men &
women, that the white men were their ancestors
returned.

To prove it, I then had her lie down. I studied the

circular fish & the circular canvas in front of me. I studied the various raised scars in the shape of circles on Twopenny Sal's body. The sun, the moon. Black woman, white man. But for me the most wondrous of her circles was that on which I then began to paint.

The variety of breasts is infinite & every breast brings forth an image at once ludicrous & beautiful: breasts that barely hint at being, slight mound & all areolae & nipple as if concentrating all their beauty in this coned essence; large breasts that seem to long to be rolled & cupped; dog-like tits & cow-like udders each with their own undeniable erotic charge; breasts to run your tongue over & breasts to hold your cock between; breasts that look away from each other like a rancorous couple that can never be parted but will never speak to each other; blue-veined mother's breasts with the close smell of sour milk; taut breasts & flaccid breasts; breasts with nipples like revolver barrels & breasts with inverted nipples that have to be sucked till they pop out into your mouth as if standing to attention. But the image that Twopenny Sal's breasts brought forth that day as she lay on Mr Lempriere's dusty floor was of a small round fish that darts around reefs like a curious spinning plate, most sumptuously decorated in velvety stripes.

I pointed the tip of my brush on her tongue, then ran it slowly over her cheek & the red ochre there that she used to rouge herself. With my tongue I moistened her brown breast in preparation & then began working the red ochre over as a foundation, at first with my brush that puckered & caught her flesh, & then with my fingers, tracing them slowly round & round, leaving the lower crescent of her breast as it was.

To the right of her nipple I got up a bluey hue from some ultramarine pigment. The little white horns I made out of Mr Lempriere's white lead powder, & for the fish's distinctive yellow iris I used a little gilt long-ago pilfered from the Great Mah-Jong Hall. I rubbed so gently her charcoal-tipped eyelashes between two fingers, & on a palette I improvised on her belly I worked up that black residue into a small dark paste with spittle. With this I striped the contours of her breast. Finally, over her off-centre nipple, long & dark with wonder, I ran light traces of lines to give it the appearance of the fish's pert pectoral fin. The result was at once not completely satisfactory & yet entirely vivid. Twopenny Sal eased herself up on her elbows, but I had eyes only for the striped cowfish as it slowly moved.

I laid my brush aside.

When, leaning down, I with my tongue tip touched the cowfish's pectoral fin, it quivered as if in anticipation of life.

I hoped she did not dislike me, but I was under no illusions that she might remember me in any way fondly; that is, if she remembered me at all. I was but one of a procession; I provided extra food, drink, that day some tobacco, beyond that I did not exist for her. When I thought of the way money & dirt & the frenzy of human desire & the bitter aftertaste of life all come together when you buy a woman in whatever way, I felt dizzy like I was peering into an infinite black hole & losing my balance. I thought: it is not dishonest; it is

the most honest expression of the whole infinite sadness of us all. I had willingly passed like quicksilver
through too many women's hands, but there was a reckoning. There was no absolution of love; no redemption
in the idea that the world had shrunk down to just two
people. For in her that day I knew myself to be
absolutely nothing.

I looked up & stared at the intricate arabesques
large huntsman spiders formed with the webs they
spun, silken shoulders linking the crumbling walls &
ceiling of Mr Lempriere's squalid cottage. When I
looked back down I thought I saw in her face an impression of absence; it was perhaps this more than anything
else that lent her—at least to me—a certain serene
profundity. Her eyes seemed so full of wisdom, but
when she spoke it was only to ask for more pisco, &
then she danced.

That autumnal day in Mr Lempriere's cottage as a
chill wind was rising into a gale outside, that one &
only day she came back to me, lured I thought by my
promises of tobacco & pisco, she stood up naked, with
that roaring fire of cracking wet myrtle logs behind
her, & danced as though she were evading musket
shots: feinting as if to go one way, then twisting & leaping in the other direction. Her dance had nothing of
the feminine about it; nothing that we might know by
the words woman & womanly. It was by turns violent,
shameless, devoid of grace, & seemed to aspire not to
beauty but only to tell a story that I had the vanity of
thinking might be intended for me. She seemed to be
seeking to exist in defiance of weight, of gravity. The

striped cowfish leapt & cavorted & flitted through the ocean of her dance.

After the dance she was sweaty & cold. I did not dare & she did not desire coupling on Mr Lempriere's mouldy cot so we used the filthy floor instead. I started kissing her back then she rolled over & I began sucking & licking. As we started dancing the old Enlightenment & Voltaire's smile of reason began building in her a slow wave waiting to break, I saw these things: on one wrist a large silver bangle, on the other a large unlanced boil. A cowfish staring. Lice crawling up her arm & onto a cowfished breast; this sight of one body ceding to others, of the inevitable advance of death & at the same time its transformation into new life, struck me as terrible & wonderful. Nothing was reconciled: everything was beautiful.

There was a bitter tang in the taste of her, a little salt, a little fruit, a little sour, a little cinnamon, & all of it a very large, strong, sweet thing. As I lay with her on Mr Lempriere's filthy floor & saw her dark arms & thighs & torso mingling with the dust & the dirt & the dead flies, the blue of her cicatrix, the dark hue of her skin seemed to me all the more brilliant, more beautiful for lying in such filth.

That day, the more I loved her, the more mysterious she became to me. I began with certainty; that she was black, that she was for me pleasure, & that I could make love to her without consequence. I ended in doubt, both as to who she was &, even more shockingly, as to who I was.

I rolled the ball of her head in the palm of my hands,

held the short curly shanks of her hair in my fingers &
pulled her head back with them knotted so, so hard I
worried I might be hurting her, yet the harder I held
her head, the more her insistent rump seemed to
respond in rising & falling pleasure, pushing &
demanding more & more of my straining loins, & the
more I stared into her face, the more I knew it had
nothing to do with her face or my own empty, barren
conceits of what beauty was & where I had foolishly
supposed it resided; the more I searched her close eyes,
the more I knew she was far, far away, drifting ever further from me, demanding of me only that I continue
rolling her head & pulling her hair & answering with
whatever strength left me the rising, rolling heave of
her velvet loins, roiling over me like the most exquisite
storm that was about to shipwreck me forever, while
beneath us the striped cowfish slowly dissolved into
sweaty smudges of lost, dusty colours.

III

THE WATERCOLOURS WERE almost all used up.
Twopenny Sal was gone. The Surgeon a foul miasma.
My laudanum pot empty. Pobjoy only ever taller.
Capois Death disappeared—some say escaped, others
murdered, on the express orders of the Commandant
following the unfortunate razing of the frozen wastes
of the Northwest Passage, after it caught fire from the
steam engine cinders & burnt down in the middle of
the Commandant's nightly train journey. There was at
that time no King with whom I might discuss my

increasingly forlorn plight, for what I am about to relate occurred before he came to join me in this cell.

There was, in short, nothing left for my chronicle to interpret. My work, my life, was achieving a correspondence to which I was not completely blind, for one was ending & the other lagged not far behind.

I know it was Christmas Eve, for with my death approaching rapidly I was highly conscious of passing time. The day had been uncommon hot, & when the tide began to rise that evening I welcomed the water's serene enveloping. The water rose & me with it, until I was floating around my pitch-black cell, nose bobbing into the ceiling. For no good reason, I took to poking one of those very large flagstones above my nose, which, supported by heavy beams, formed the ceiling of my cell.

I had been playing in this absent-minded fashion with the ceiling for an indeterminate time, listening to the slow percussion of the sea lapping at the cell wall outside & drawing an inexplicable comfort from the sound, running the backs of my wave-wrinkled hands along the ceiling's soft harshness, pushing it & prodding it with no purpose or desire, when the most terrifying thing happened.

I suddenly found myself being violently thrust deep down into the chill, lamp-black water. Though I fought & thrashed, still I continued sinking. My thoughts were galloping far away, transforming into bubbles racing upwards, so many confused questions that could never be answered. Was Brady's Army of Light laying siege & demolishing the building in which I was held with cannon fire? Had one of Pobjoy's clients come under cover of night with the aim of drowning me because he had become an admirer of Titian & my convict-Constables now seemed limp works unworthy of his passion?

Just as I was wondering how much longer before the pain in my chest, the pounding in my head, the constriction of my throat would transform into death, I felt the large weight that had been driving me down slide off my chest, rasping my flesh as it did so. My body stopped sinking & began to rise.

Only after I bobbed back up to the surface & had spent several moments spluttering & gulping air like a starving man bread, filling his mouth but unable to sate his craving, did it begin to dawn on me what had happened. Reaching upwards with an arm, it was to find myself not just at the top of my cell but in a cavity somewhat larger than the one I had so recently left. I gingerly raised my arm a second time & with my hand felt some edges of broken flagstone ceiling above me, upon which it was possible to get some purchase.

Sand, damp & salty, fell in heavy crumbs wherever I touched, onto my face & into my half-open mouth. And then I realised—the local sandstone, soft at the best of times, was succumbing to the daily exposure to salt water. With my pulling & prodding it was now falling apart, causing a large piece of flagging to drop from the ceiling, pushing me with it to the bottom of my flooded cell.

Possibilities I had for too long repressed began to resurface. With an excitement animating my body I would not a minute before have felt capable of, I groped around as a blind man, small pieces of sandstone scattering all over my face as I did so. I searched for a small crevice in which I might insert my hand & use as a point of leverage. As if in a fever I pushed & shoved so much that the water-softened skin of my hands began to slough off, & I began to know the sandstone as the undeniable gritty sharpness of a thousand needles.

I had no plan, no clear thoughts as to what I might do. I didn't even know what the dim void above me was, whether it was open air or just another cell. I raised my arms into that unknown dark, finally found a hold, & taking firm grip, began to pull.

IV

NOT WITHOUT DIFFICULTY, I half-hauled, half-clambered up past dangling broken beams & through the broken flagstone into the brave new world that I could see opening above me. For a man who has always prided himself on his absence of physical strength & who had moreover been confined in a cell only an arm-span wide for several months surviving on slops thrown him by Pobjoy, this was no mean feat.

I found myself lying on a damp flagstone floor, panting, breathing in a confusion of rich odours: dust, dried hops, damp leather, smoked tobacco, &, over-riding them all, that particular must I would later discover to be that of parchment when combined with the imminence of death.

I went to stand up, hit my head on what I realised

was some sort of table, fell back down, crawled out, & this time stood up, daring all, only to discover myself in a large room bathed in a bright, coldly luminous moon-light that lent it an ultramarine mystery. The room appeared entirely empty—except, that is, of books.

Books were everywhere and everywhere I looked there were more books, & all those books neatly stacked & arrayed on rough-hewn, heavy blackwood shelves in great bookcases that rose from floor to ceiling, all radiating out like the spokes of a wheel from a hub where sat a large, circular desk from beneath which I had emerged like a moth from its cocoon, stiff & awkward.

Circling all round me were so many books it made me dizzy just to look at them, to realise that not only might there be this many books in the world, but that there could be this many books in a single room. There were tall vellum-bound volumes above me & huge dusty tomes below me. Behind me there were string-tied manuscripts of varied sizes & at my front, newer, smaller ornate registers covered in dark Morocco leather.

I would like to say that in the full moon light that shone from windows high above, that the room took on the colour of dark honey & the amber charm of old libraries. But that would be to lie. It is the sort of non-sense Pobjoy would like me to paint, or that Miss Anne might write. The truth was that the room was a shifting labyrinth of grey & blue shades, ugly & sinister.

On the circular desk there lay open a plain folio volume clad in abortive, that dainty vellum made from cow foetuses. I looked down at its blue-inked columns, the slipping Italianate hand, its ornate, archaic loops & whorls throwing long shadows of monstrous links, as though all the words were manacled & subjugated.

What I then read confused me: it purported to be a list of convict activity for the previous six months, but seemed wrong in almost every detail. Still it cleared up one puzzle: that of the room's purpose. It was, I realised, the settlement's mysterious Registry, the bookcases the repository of all the island's records; the circular desk at its centre presumably where the old Danish clerk, Jorgen Jorgensen, had daily disappeared to work compiling the only enduring memory of our strange world for longer than anyone could remember.

Dawn came & the light grew stronger. My eager eyes no longer had to strain but reluctantly I closed the volume I had only partly read, & prepared to return to the underworld.

I concentrated on trying to render my break-in as invisible as it was possible. Fortunately the part of the Registry floor I had destroyed under the circular desk was a dank, dark place where it was hard to imagine anyone ever looking. I took a large & what seemed little used volume from near the top of one bookcase, & splayed it over the hole. It was a desperate expedient, but I could think of none better.

Then, with my primitive trapdoor in place above me, I returned to my cell. As best I could I shored up the broken beams in a way I hoped not obvious & covered the fallen flagstone with the sea pebbles & gravel that formed my cell floor, so that Pobjoy might not discover anything untoward. That he might look up & notice something amiss with the ceiling worried me less; given his need to stoop such was unlikely, & the ceiling was in any case heavily shadowed.

You might well ask why Billy Gould didn't just bolt there & then, seeking to escape via the unlocked door of the Registry he had earlier chanced upon. He had—showing that singular boldness that was entirely in character—resolved to postpone his escape until he had made proper preparations. In truth I think he was like a bird when taken out of its cage—his first response was fear, then a desire for familiarity; his initial thought simply to retreat back into the world he knew, that of his saltwater cell.

And then there was the further matter of what he had read that first night in that opened volume—things so inexplicable & shocking in their effrontery, yet at the same time so compelling in their lucid madness, that they demanded further investigation so he might better plumb &, he hoped, divine their mystery.

V

FOR THE NEXT seven nights I could not wait for the tide to rise quick enough, so slowly did it seem to lap my mussel-bound ankles, my lice-crawling crutch, my scabby guts, & it seemed as long as one of Miss Anne's interminable letters until at last I was floating, rising, & finally able to touch the rough split sandstone & then lever myself into the Registry above.

For seven nights, lest my light betray my presence, I would sit on the floor next to the round desk in a small puddle of light thrown by a Registry candle & the larger dull illumination of the moon, & continue with my reading of those great volumes so heavy that some took all my strength simply to lift from the bookcase.

What I discovered between their clapboards was no chronicle of the penal colony I knew, the Commandant's nation of Nova Venezia. As I leafed through memorandum register after letter book after convict indent, I searched for records, drawings, mason's plans of the wonder of the Great Mah-Jong Hall.

There were none.

For seven nights I scoured the commissariat records for accounts, invoices, receipts, that might prove the Commandant's purchase of South American locomotives; tried to find paper trails that would definitively establish his sale of the Transylvanian wilderness, or, for that matter, his even more audacious bartering of the mainland of Australia & the purchase of Moluccan jewellery, Chinese medicines, sea cucumber, Javanese furniture & boatloads of Siamese girls.

There were none.

For seven nights I gleaned personal letters & diaries for the smallest details that might hint of the Commandant's nightmares of a past that never left, of Arab traders & immortal Japanese pirates & naked French rationalists.

There were none.

As I made my way through the old Dane's writings my feelings passed from bewilderment to wonder as to why he might have written such so much with so little foundation in life.

The necessity to lie to Governor Arthur in Hobart Town & to the Colonial Office in London was clear enough: I had come upon letters dated several years earlier from the Colonial Office requesting full acquittals, reports, inventories & audits, all of which demanded an untruthful response, the portrayal of a penal colony as they might imagine it & not as we knew it to be.

At what point—& why—this necessary clerical invention had been extended to the much grander project of reimagining the penal colony, I know not. All that was clear was that it was the old Dane who was selected by the Commandant to work upon the entire records of the settlement, in a way that would accord with expectation & not reality.

But at a certain moment Jorgen Jorgensen's work began to outstrip even his master's ambition in its deranged achievement. Though at first he had allowed his works to be guided by the desires of the Commandant, a seeming cipher of another's whims & inventions, he had slowly drifted into his own extraordinary conceit of an alternative world.

As night succeeded night, as I read on & on, the magnitude of his audacity became clear, & my wonder changed to simple awe.

The world, as described by Jorgen Jorgensen in those blue-inked pages, was at war with the reality in which we lived. The bad news was that reality was losing. It was unrecognisable. It was insufferable. It was, in the end, inhuman. It was also impossible to stop reading.

I tried to imagine the old Dane at first compelled to reinvent all that barbarity & horror of our settlement as order & progress, material, moral & spiritual, recording it by slipping whale-oil light in his elegant Italianate hand in the official papers of the settlement. It was for him, I suppose, a necessary burden, & at the beginning he probably saw it as trading his life for an incredible & entirely untrue story as he once had traded lies for credit to play the gaming tables of Europe.

And then after some time—one year? several years?—perhaps there was a moment so exhilarating that he was forever after imprisoned in its mad liberation, a moment when he first transcended his own consciousness, dipping his quill in demons, & discovering to his fear & astonishment that contained within himself was all men & all women: all good, all evil, all love, all hate, & all time that single moment when his soul exploded into a million beads of vapour through which the light of his imaginings began pouring, refracting into a rainbow of stories made concrete as reports, standing orders, convict indents, letter books & memoranda.

For in the old Dane's account everything was different. Every life, every action, every motive, every consequence. Time, which the Commandant understood to be something of which we were all inexorably composed, our essential substance & lifeforce, was in these accounts something separate from us—so many equally weighted bricks that together made the wall of the present that denied us any connection with the past, & thus any knowledge of our self.

Where waking & dreaming & nightmares under the Commandant had been one, with the old Dane's records they became hopelessly divided & opposed. Nightmares were banned, & no collusion between living & dreaming was admitted to. It was the greatest piece of card sharping in history, & how proud I thought dear old Marshal Blucher would have felt of his one-time skat partner.

VI

I TOO, LET me add, felt a growing glow toward Jorgensen, a feeling only heightened by the discovery on the seventh night of a stash of Danish schnapps hidden behind a pile of unused Commissariat requisition forms. As I read on in the waxing summer moonlight beneath the circular desk, pausing only to squash a mosquito or pour another finger of schnapps or take a quick piss in the hole that opened into my cell, I came to appreciate how the old Dane's invention was as subtle as it was infinite: in the universe he had spent so many years creating for his master every detail—no matter how trivial—was augmented & qualified & tabulated.

I could only marvel at all that Jorgensen had created: for example, the long ordered columns in which he had tabulated statisticks showing a declining use of the lash over several years, the books of handwritten sermons, the drawings of new cells, etc etc, collectively depicting a regime of necessary corporal punishment battling the convicts' inherent brutality slowly ceding to more enlightened practices, the use of solitary confinement & Wesleyan missionaries.

It was no doubt slow & often tedious work for Jorgensen, but by obeying the laws of pattern & succession, of cause & effect—which never characterise life but are necessary for words on paper—he had created an image of the settlement that would persuade posterity of both the convicts' animality & the administrator's sagacity, a model of the power of unremitting, tempered discipline to transform pickpockets into cobblers & catamites into Christians.

There were buried in these volumes—entwined like so many fibrous roots of twitch—individual stories one could tease out, mainly of convicts but also of their gaolers, such as the mundane, but successful career of Lieutenant Horace, latterly the Commandant, as implausible as the life of any saint. He had come from the humblest of backgrounds, born in a cottage he had built with his own hands, rising in the army from an ensign in the 91st Regiment with displays of gallantry in various administrative postings, his successful work as a staff officer in the British Honduras, dealing humanely & in an enlightened fashion with the native Indians prior to their mass execution & his transfer to Sarah Island, a record of humanity underlined by copies of several letters to his dear friend William Wilberforce on the evils of the slavery system.

I toasted such a benign prison so marvellous you'd happily pay to leave England just to come & live here, & I toasted the way he even permitted us convicts a random agency. I raised my glass repeatedly to all the artful forgeries of smuggled convict letters that backed up details to be found in the official reports & standing orders of felons dropping tools & refusing to work until certain conditions were allowed, or grievances addressed. On one high shelf there were even bottles containing the skin of hanged men on which particular tattoos were emblazoned, which tallied with lives of crime & punishment to be found in the many volumes of letter books, so that these real pieces of dead flesh were given correspondence, nay, the very breath of life, by the old Dane's tales, & I drank to every last bobbing anchor & angel & blue-inked maxim.

On & on, round & round, went more stories & down & down went more schnapps. I toasted Jorgensen again & again & each time Jorgensen's glass was empty how it seemed only right & proper to fill it once more to toast the wonderful world Jorgensen had made: a penal system as some enlightened mass-migration scheme created by beneficent elders, in which horror was only very occasional but always deserved, & in which men made good rather than bad. This world was not an act of creation, for good or bad, in which people constantly reinvented themselves, but a system in which one was accorded an ignoble but necessary part, like a piston head or belt in the steam engines the Scot weaver had once so futilely smashed.

I guzzled to the greater glory of machines & systems & then my head was spinning with the brazen audacity of all those forged reports & letters & standing orders that suggested none of the monstrosity or derangement with which I had become familiar—of which I was part.

I toasted the total absence of such things, & I toasted the inclusion of all the new gorgeous lies. And then I ran out of things to toast so I just finished drinking straight from the bottle, & at its end I found myself feeling queasy & guilty, & I began to worry that Jorgensen's world might be the Hell that had filled the machine breaker's eyes & mouth before Capois Death sat on him.

Then—& my shame is such that I can only refer to myself in this regard in the third person—Billy Gould felt the urge to throw up. Not that Billy Gould thought vomiting a bad thing, for the Surgeon had told him it rid the body of unwanted fluids & humours, & prevented the continuing horrors of crapulence & flatulence the following day.

Indeed, to hasten this therapeutic cleansing of the body of which I am sure Pastor Gottliebsen would have approved, Billy Gould even stuck two fingers down the back of his throat & waggled them back & forth, until he felt rising up his chest, filling his throat & then issuing as a broken stream from his mouth, amidst the tomatoes & carrots he had never eaten, the dreadful awareness that all he had read was simply the Commandant's image of rational society as a prison of which even Miss Anne in Europe did not dare dream,

& this final creation, perhaps in many ways his most monstrous—if unintended—achievement, outdid the Great Mah-Jong Hall & the National Railway Line in its unknowing yet grotesque reverence of the Old World.

It was a lot to be aware of & have sprinkle your feet & splash your dacks at the same time—too much if one is to be absolute frank—& Billy Gould would have started trying to clean up all that mess of partly-digested Europe there & then if he had not suffered a second realisation even worse than the first.

It came upon him like the heaviest, the most intolerable of burdens pounding away at the front of his head as he wiped his mouth with the back of his hand: that in this universal history, all he had seen & known, all he had witnessed & suffered, was now as lost & meaningless as a dream that dissolves upon waking. If freedom, as Capois Death carrying his spirits of the past in a bottle of purl-ale had maintained, exists only in the space of memory, then he & everybody he knew were being condemned to an eternity of imprisonment.

VII

MY MIND FELT a sickening horror that is beyond words to describe. Gargoylish faces seemed to cluster at the windows far above & plead for something to appease their endless suffering that went unremembered & unrecounted. I felt as if those awful flayed skulls were advancing & receding—with their red bone sticking through as though they had been gnawed by dogs—as if they wished me to make the past right, something that was totally beyond my powers.

I had read & I had read, & still the past went unavenged & unnoticed, & how was it possible for me to remake it as anything else? Out of the staring, accusing sockets of the skulls of the Scottish weaver & Roaring Tom Weaver, out of Towtereh's stolen skull & his grandson's smashed skull crawled cockroaches. Fleas flew out from their jagged nose bones. The skulls began dripping putrescent tears of pus & blood that passed through the glass & spread all over me. In terror I brushed fiercely at my shoulders, my arms, my head as if I could so wipe them away; *No!* cried I, & *No! Please leave me alone!* But those fearsome shades would not leave & were begging of me what was impossible. I, who was covered in sloughing rotten flesh, who felt all the maggots that once had crawled over the staked dead black woman now crawling over me, who stank of all decay & of all sickness & of all return, saw the incarnation of the world passing me by in all its horror & all its beauty, & how could I say that both were inescapable?

I am but the reader, I tried to plead with them. But they did not listen, could not listen, would never listen, & seemed intent only on making me the instrument of their vengeance.

And then Billy Gould found himself being not just a little sick, but most violently ill.

For the world no longer existed to become a book. A book now existed with the obscene ambition of becoming the world.

VIII

I SLUMPED TO the floor. I lay there for a time like a Chinese lantern emptied of light, crumpled & flat, my head sunk in disbelief & bewilderment. Was *this* what people would one day remember as their past?

It was then I heard a bizarre shrill whistling. With a terrified jerk, I swung around, at the same time throwing my arms over my head in protection.

In front of me was a small, mangy dog, standing on its two hind legs in the moonlight, whistling. Then the dog ceased, fell down on to its one other good leg, & looked up over my shoulder. Before I could turn back around, before I even heard him speaking I knew who it was behind me.

'*You are a counterfeiter, Gould,*' said he, his words slipping & sliding like his handwriting.

I slowly turned & saw smiling down at me, of all people, Jorgen Jorgensen. For a moment I thought he was standing on a chair or a bookcase, he seemed so high up. He leant over me, throwing me into shadow, looking like a bookcase waiting to fall. Very slowly, my eyes never daring leave his, I stood up.

Jorgen Jorgensen was, like everything else in the Registry, monochrome & chill. Criss-crossing his grey skin were white lines taking many different forms: a line of white foam creasing that crooked mouth, long wisps of his white hair hanging at odd angles across his lolling head like broken spider webs.

'*Doomed,*' continued he, savouring the word, '*to suffer torment for all eternity.*'

Jorgen Jorgensen didn't make a good God: for one

thing he didn't have the beard, only that wretched moustache with half last night's skilly hanging off it in congealed dew drops. For another he smelt of rotting offal, & God who is everything isn't really, because otherwise He would be every bad smell in the world as well as Daffodils, Love, Sunrises etc, etc. But God seemed a role Jorgensen wished to play, for having created the world anew, he now seemed determined to do some pearly gate pronouncements, the first of which was that I had to die.

Ever since the poorhouse priest told me it was only God's Love that made him wish to rub my feet so, I have been of the opinion that even if you accept that something is God's Will it doesn't mean you have to agree with it. You can, for example, accept that it is God's Will that it is raining, but that doesn't mean you continue standing in the rain. And so on. And while I accepted Jorgensen's argument that my miserable skin really didn't deserve anything other than the most miserable death, I didn't agree that I ought die there & then. And so, when he suddenly leapt at me with a strength & agility out of all proportion to his wretched body & age, rusty sword unsheathed & aiming straight at my heart, I jumped out of his way, knocking over my candle on the floor as I did so.

The candle extinguished, I ran to hide behind a bookcase, but the old Dane knew his maze of books better than a rat its nest. Before I even smelt that odour of decomposing liver, I felt the cold flat of his sword upon my neck.

'*Like Dante's Adamo de Brescia who forged the Florentine florin,*' hissed he, '*your body will balloon like a mandolin with the dropsical torment, in the dark, stench pit of the circle of Malebolge in Hades!'*

As his language grew more purple, his gummy mouth filled with foamy spittle as if all his adjectives were aerating the froth collecting about his lips. He pressed the flat of his sword harder against my neck & I began to choke. I was shaking so uncontrollably that the bookcase against which I leant also began to tremble. On the uneven floor the rough-made cabinet rocked awkwardly, its balance, I could feel through my body, at best precarious.

The old Dane shoved up against me, communicating his vision of my future Hell not only with mere words but in the dribbly froth which accompanied them & blew in a spume over my face.

'*You will be afflicted by thirst & loathsome diseases,*' sprayed he. '*You will be but one of an infinite parade of the broken dead, another mutilated shade, condemned to live amidst the sickening stench of putrid flesh, all you falsifiers covered in loathsome scabs & each other's sloughing flesh.*'

With these words he gave the flat of the sword a good shove. Its corroded edge drew a thin, broken line of blood across my neck. As he pushed the sword harder yet, one of my vomit-slimed feet slipped backwards. Unable to keep balance, I slid with it, my lower back whacking into that unsteady bookcase, its dead weight giving way to the momentary possibility of a pivot. I thought of Twopenny Sal's circles, of her rump rising, but it would be wrong to credit what I then did with the dignity of the word idea.

With all the might left me, I shoved my arse as hard as buggery into that wobbling edifice of a bookcase.

The book-scorpion must have heard something—perhaps a sharp creak of timber or a dull thump of one volume falling back domino fashion onto another—for suddenly he looked upwards. I don't know if he saw the bookcase staggering but, in such quick succession that it was almost a single movement rather than three, he glanced upwards, took a short step backwards, then tripped on his own feet. Losing his balance, he fell just as the first books began dropping earthwards.

My last sight was of him uselessly trying to parry with his sword those huge tomes that now were falling upon him heavy as boulders, ubiquitous as rain, dreadful as an avalanche. As those volumes now bore down on Jorgen Jorgensen I heard him shrieking how nothing held, not even books.

But then I could hear no more for I was far back in a cavern of collapsing books, arse up & head down, concentrating all of what little strength I had in levering the bookcase further up my back. Being close to its base should have meant that the falling books & shelves, having no great distance to fall, would only hurt rather than severely injure me. But then a shelf from higher up was arcing out crazily & swinging wildly toward me.

I never felt it hit.

For I was bracing failing falling not knowing if I could any longer live under the great weight of so many words.

IX

I HEARD THE noises of morning: muster-call, chickens scuffling, the distant, happy cries of the homicide Castlereagh. Yet everything around me remained in darkness. How long I had been in that darkness I had no idea. My mind felt fogged, & so heavy that for a moment I panicked, thinking my head, severed but still conscious, was lolling in a barrel bound for England.

When I felt a book splayed over my face, the heavy corners of other books sticking in my ribs & belly, my chest enshrouded in the formidable weight of unopened books I knew my head & I must still be one. I smelt parchment, vellum, sour sweat, the decaying kidney scent of Jorgensen. There was a dull heavy pain in my lower back that I took to be a corner of the bookcase resting on my body. Beyond, names were being yelled & answered. I heard the dull chip & chuck of the chain gangs' fetlers as they set off for work. The curses of the sawyers, the bark of constables.

But no-one seemed to hear or notice me when I sneezed several times from the insufferable amount of dust in the paper which wrapped around me.

I took stock of my situation.

I heard. I smelt. But I saw nothing.

This immense weight of inanimate matter that seemed to be so important to Jorgensen was for me a smothering blindfold I needed to be freed of. I feared it, the way it would kill me if I did not find a way to escape it. I felt I might at any moment start screaming uncontrollably from the wretched closeness of it all.

Worse than any jagged basils, these books followed my every movement, mocking me, seeking to smother me even more effectively as I writhed first this way & then that. Less than easily, I slid & pushed, until I dragged myself backwards out of that darkness.

I felt sick, light-headed. Above the fallen bookcase that sweet peculiar scent of the oil of fresh blackwood rose from broken & shattered shelves. I managed to stand up.

And then at the far end of the bookcase I saw a black puddle. I staggered toward it, clambering over the rubble of fallen books & smashed timbers. The puddle was congealing blood, dust-scummed & creased with strands of hair that led down beneath a large book.

I pulled the book back.

One eye of the old Dane's dangled from its bloodied socket, forced out by some blow of a book corner or a shelf edge. His sword had partly skewered a raggedy old volume which, on closer inspection, turned out to be Pliny's *Natural History*. I wondered if he were really dead, or just in a state of grace like Saint Christina the Astonishing who, after a fit, appeared dead only to then fly from her coffin to the rafters in the middle of a Requiem mass. But there was nothing of grace about what I could see. I shoved the old Dane's body & then his head with my foot, kicked it a few times, but it was already stiffening.

I looked at him a long time.

I don't know how long.

After a great time or a short time, an infinity or a few seconds, I went through his pockets. What began as a dim inventory of rubbish did produce a few useful items—two broken quills, one pen knife, some black bread of the good quality that was baked for the officers & was thus unadulterated with sawdust & mud, spectacles (one lens broken), & a gold ring. Sewn into his coat's collar I found a dozen Bengal dollars that were later to prove invaluable.

An intense blue light seemed to pulse within the wrinkled folds of his neck. Old Gould had taught me blue was the feminine colour, the most expensive of pigments with which the great painters of the Renaissance had decorated the Virgin Mary's mantle, how ultramarine was so called because it had to be imported from the Middle East—from beyond the sea.

But the distance I had to travel was far less. I only had to reach down, wrench that lapis lazuli necklace from the chook-flaps of his neck, & that very day grind that bright blue stone with rocks to make the powder for the ultramarine ink with which I now rightly write this tale of cold death. Blue speaks of the morning, of the sky & of the sea. Yet as the fish with their cross-weaving of colour had taught me, contained in every colour is its opposite, & blue is also the colour of sorrow & anguish & lewdness. And in front of me that hot summer morning slowly turning that same cursed colour, covered in a growing number of flies, was a corpse which, if I didn't do something about it, would see me implicated with a second murder.

Death is such a simple matter, yet as Castlereagh's turd taught me, it can have unforeseen consequences, all of which I was keen to avoid. I dragged the once-King of

Iceland's body over to the circular desk, kicked aside an empty schnapps bottle, pulled back my makeshift trap door, & pushing the corpse through a puddle of vomited Europe let it fall into my world below.

It was a stupid thing to do, but having done it, there was no turning back. Now, at low tide I hide the corpse behind the cell door along with the broken timber & debris from the partial collapse of my ceiling. At high tide we simply drift around together.

In so many ways a corpse is the negative image of the living man; in so many ways I have discovered it is preferable to the man who once inhabited that collapsing stretch of flesh. Where Jorgen Jorgensen tried to make this world conform to his desires, his corpse the King—freed from the subordination of the brand of the Commandant's mask that fell away along with the rest of his skin—is the very model of Occidental acceptance. While Jorgen Jorgensen wished to tell posterity what he thought, the King is content to ponder the thin soup of my ramblings.

There is much about the King's subsequent company which, as I have detailed, has come to help fill my emptiness here & which I have come to admire. Without him & his encouragement, I would, for example, never have made such progress with this *Book of Fish*. He never criticised my efforts, belittled my ambitions, attacked the poverty of style. It was an attitude of benign neglect, & I firmly believe my writing has prospered in consequence.

But at first, with his milky eye & drawn cheeks & beard & nails still growing, Jorgen Jorgensen's corpse was—I must admit—disturbing. Later, as he bloated with death gas, as his body grew black, then green & slimy, as his flesh began to slough off his now elephantine form in greasy, putrid rags, his stinking balloon corpse would bump into me as we floated around.

In disgust I would with shuddering hands seek to push him away, only for my hands, as if by magic, to pass through his grossly swollen, rotting flesh until hitting the last firm thing left of the King: his bone—the bone of his arms or legs, the bone of his rib cage or skull. I recalled the King's final words to me that night in the Registry, about the dropsical sufferings I as a counterfeiter would suffer in my Dantesque inferno, & yet here swimming about me was the bloating corpse of the true counterfeiter, his last kingdom my cell, now his circle of Hell.

X

THE NEXT NIGHT I returned to the Registry. The day had passed exceedingly hot & even late in the evening the room was clammy, its air thick & close. Everything was as I had left it: the fallen bookcase, the smashed shelves, the books scattered & splayed in odd positions & raggedy heaps. The Registry—being the domain of the old Dane—had not been visited, no-one daring enter during the day, nor would they, I realised, until his absence was noticed, which might be several days. I picked up the book that had lain across the old Dane's face—its corner darkly bloodied from where it had gored his eyeball out—to see what, if anything, it might have to say on the matter of unmeditated murder.

It was a large & elegant folio, only very recently published. Embossed across the front, in gold Gothic lettering, was the title—

CRANIA TASMANIAE
Sir Cosmo Wheeler

I opened the book, & read inside the inscription:

To Toby Lempriere
From your Fellow Foot-soldier in Science—
Cosmo Wheeler K. C. B.

There were several cuttings of reviews inside the cover taken from learned journals, all effusive, one praising *Crania Tasmaniae* as Wheeler's *magnum opus*, another hailing Wheeler as the British Blumenbach, noting—

> . . . *that while that great Prussian craniometrist,*
> *Johann Friedrich Blumenbach, has established beyond*
> *doubt the existence of a European race he terms*
> *'Caucasian' separate from the other four human races,*
> *his theory of Caucasian superiority to the other races*
> *has—until the seminal publication of* Crania
> Tasmaniae—*been more bold Teutonic assertion than*
> *proven scientifick fact.*
> *The corollary of Blumenbach's skull from the*
> *Caucasus region, which he considers displays in its shape*
> *and form the finest features of the human race, and has*
> *led him to give the European race the appellation*

'Caucasian' in its honour, is Sir Cosmo Wheeler's Negroid
skull from Van Diemen's Land, known only as MH-36,
in which the degenerate and . . .

In my astonishment I had let the cutting fall out of
my sweating fingers to the floor. Beneath where it had
lain was a review which declared—

A propensity to undue and excessive animal passion of
the sexual variety, amativeness is most readily apparent
by the way this decadent energy over a lifetime voids a
space larger than normal on either side of the skull (to the
retardation of all other cerebral growth) between the
mastoids, immediately betwixt the ear and the base of
the occipital bone. Sir Cosmo Wheeler rightly describes
MH-36 as possessing 'the Great Southern Land of
amative cavities, a dark lacuna of monumental proportions
awaiting further scientifick exploration'.

Which seemed cruel irony when I pondered the
sorry fate of the Surgeon's penis. The last review I read
before throwing the rest away was definite in its opinion that—

. . . one only has to look at the hideous depravity, the
ovine set, and the generally regressive shape of skull MH-
36 to understand why Crania Tasmaniae *is one of the*
great scientifick achievements of our age.

Wheeler proves beyond doubt the Tasmanian negro is of
an entirely separate species, one possibly even more barbarous
than the New Hollanders, approaching the mere animal.

*The marks of mental inferiority and racial degeneration
are everywhere evident in the corrupted cranial features
so splendidly illustrated in the book, and generally lends
weight to the growing body of scientifick knowledge that
such a wretched, if fascinating, species must have been
created separately from European man. Its origins are
therefore not in the Garden of Eden, but outside of it, with
all the spiritual, moral and utilitarian consequences this
therefore brings into modern human affairs.*

I leafed through the book, tearing its uncut pages
with my index finger as I went. There were many intricate etchings of the Van Diemonian native skulls,
wonderful well done. None though were more finely
realised than the several pages devoted specifickally to
different, detailed views of that seminal skull, MH-36,
in which the skull multiplied endlessly in top-down,
bottom-up & side-on images. Such reverential devotion
put me in mind of Saint Agapitus, no fewer than five
perfectly preserved skulls of whom are venerated
through the Italian peninsula.

Accompanying the book were two letters, both
addressed to Mr Lempriere. The first, bearing the
intact seal of the Royal Society, informed Mr
Lempriere that in recognition of his assiduity & perseverance in his collection of natural history specimens,
the society had decided to award him a Commendation.

The second was a personal letter from Sir Cosmo
Wheeler in which the great phrenologist of our age
assured his dear friend that he had fought hard within
the Society for membership to be given Lempriere. He

had told his colleagues how critically important his disciple's collection of skulls had been; of how, in particular, the skull marked MH-36 had proved conclusively what Sir Cosmo had long believed. More clearly than any other skull he had ever examined, this particular cranium demonstrated the moral deficiency, the reduced cranial capacity, & the regressive nature of the Tasmanian negro race that would ultimately assure its destruction, irrespective of the arrival of the civilised & advanced European.

Yet, sadly he had to report that fine work, like fine words, butter no parsnips, & his proposal for Lempriere's admission had been defeated by the more general will of the Society. Nevertheless, continued Sir Cosmo, a commendation from a body of such prestige was not to be sniffed at, & would, no doubt, serve as a vital stepping stone to his ultimate goal of membership.

In the meantime had he considered collecting eggs? Bowdler-Sharpe was hopelessly inadequate, & Sir Cosmo was contemplating a comparative study of eggs of the Old & New World, & wondered if Toby might be interested in being part of this great collective endeavour?

XI

I FELT MYSELF slowly suffocating, as though pages as large as houses were falling upon me, pressing in upon me as if I were only a flower to be desiccated & preserved through flattening; as though a book as vast as the sky were wrapping around my humbled form, soon to close forever.

Men's lives are not progressions, as conventionally rendered in history paintings, nor are they a series of facts that may be enumerated & in their proper order understood. Rather they are a series of transformations, some immediate & shocking, some so slow as to be imperceptible, yet so complete & horrifying that at the end of his life a man may search his memory in vain for a moment of correspondence between his self in his dotage & him in his youth.

I cannot say when I first realised that all that long time on Sarah Island had really been an infinitely slow process of metamorphosis. As I tentatively began seeking to break out of the darkness of *Crania Tasmaniae* & the letters contained within, how could I have guessed I was soon to be reborn new & different? That the process of painting the fish had been so painful & arduous not because the fish were dying & I was unequal to their form, but because in order that my own form might begin to change I also had to die? How could I have known that all that long time my paintings had been transforming me, that I was with my brush creating not so many pictures, but spinning out of the innumerable threads of my paintings a single cocoon?

And how was I to know as I tossed that letter to the ground, seeking finally to leave my chrysalis, that my desperate mission of escape was about to begin?

THE CRESTED WEEDFISH

In which is recounted a most bold & audacious
escape—The sled of thwarted memory—Brady, an
avenging angel—Return of Capois Death—Attacked by
blacks—A murder—The funeral pyre.

I

IN THE BEGINNING was the Word, & the Word was
with God, & the Word was God. The same was in the
beginning with the old Dane as it was with God, all
things were made by him; & without him was not anything made that was made.

But then the Word was made flesh & dwelt among
us as part of *our* darkness, & it comprehended not our
darkness; for its flesh was putrid & slimy green bloated
rotted rags floating flotsam-like around my cell. As I
tried to keep my head above this slime that nightly rose
around me, to avoid the sensation of sinking forever
into the primeval Word, it became my life's most
sacred desire to expose that the Word & the World
were no longer what they seemed, that they were no
longer One.

It was New Year's Day, 1831, & I was determined to
keep my newly made resolution to leave—but with an
ambition far greater than escape: the intention of
once & for all destroying the Convict System. The

weapon with which I would achieve this end was the large selection of records that I had stolen from the Registry.

These, along with me, Rolo Palma's fish-netting gang agreed to ferry across the harbour under the cover of night. In return I gave them an assurance that neither they nor any authorities would ever again see their convict records, six Bengal dollars & a copy of the highly esteemed, if somewhat tatty & partly mutilated 1628 Rotterdam edition of Philemon Holland's first English translation of Pliny the Elder's *Natural History*, with all its tales of strange races—the Thybians with two pupils in one eye & the image of a horse in the other; the Monocoli who on their single leg hop with amazing speed & who, to shade themselves on hot days, lie down & raise their leg like a parasol; the Astomi, who having neither mouths nor noses, but only holes for nostrils like a snake, lived on smells.

The settlement was in an uproar: the inexplicable disappearance of the old Dane, the rumoured imminent arrival of Matt Brady & the Army of Light, the Commandant's reclusion—all had people rushing back & forth for no clear reason. In such tumultuous disorder, to flee was not so difficult & I shall not bother here with the tedious story of my escape. It would demand of me an explanation of details—the initial night-time meeting with Rolo Palma, the quarter moon allowing enough but not too much light, the tide running our way & the flour & pickled pork, the axe & pot, the boots & sled & the way I bought all this, along with my freedom—& details have never interested me. It was, in any case, not an affair of courage & daring, but—as these matters tend to be—bribery & timing.

Recalling their last sight of me as madness made paper, the fish-netting gang later spoke of convict registers, letter books, the miscellaneous marble-endpapered records, papers & manuscripts all shaping together out of the grey light of dawn into a single hut-like mound upon a sassafras sled.

Rolo Palma's men pulled on their rough-hewn oars & felt the whale boat beneath them slowly come to life with their rhythm, at first little more than a quiver, & then an undeniable glide along the water, black & silent, heading back for Sarah Island.

As in that chill summer dawn the men sought warmth in their work, I heard their voices whisking with tufts of mist over that still water to where I was attempting to draw the sled into the wilderness, still dark & dewy, a tatterdemalion man bound to his burden by a harness of kangaroo leather.

'He looks all the world,' I heard Rolo Palma say, 'like a praying mantis trying to drag a brick.'

Then the sun was up & they must have realised that the hut, like their whale boat, had come to life & was also moving for I heard them cry in astonishment that it was gone—swallowed in that green immensity that went east for hundreds of miles with only blacks & wild animals & wilder rivers & God-only-knew-what other monstrous races & creatures—& with it an escaping lunatic destined for oblivion.

II

IT HAS TO be understood that Billy Gould attributed to the records a power only those immersed in paper too long can appreciate, if even then not fully comprehend. I worried that unless I did something, the lies I now dragged behind me would one day be all that remained of the settlement, & posterity would seek to judge those who had gone before—to judge Capois Death, Mr Lempriere, the Commandant, even poor Castlereagh, to judge them, to judge me—to judge us all through the machine of the Commandant's monstrous fictions! As though they were the truth! As though history & the written word were friends, rather than adversaries!

There was, I knew, only one man who would know what to do.

Matt Brady was for us all an enigma, but in the darkness of my stinking cell, as the old Danish scribe slowly disintegrated around me, Brady had for me become a beacon. No-one I knew had ever seen him: stories of his physical nature varied greatly in consequence. Yet I was convinced that the moment we met I would recognise Brady. Some said he was tall & swarthy with a Maori-like tattoo down one cheek; others that he was half-Samoan & that this explained his warlike propensity; others yet that he was short, freckled & wore his red hair in two long ponytails. For the Scots he was William Wallace, for the Irish he was Cú Cucalain; for all, a hero.

But only for me was Brady the one who might avenge History.

My desires, you will by now have gathered, were manifold; I should have known they were also unrealisable. I intended first to paralyse the settlement by removing its basis of administration, the paper records of its invented history, the necessary fiction by which the reality of the prison-island was maintained. I had then determined I would find Brady & deliver these records to him. For I was labouring under an illusion even more monstrous than my sassafras sled of crudely hewn hopes—the belief that once Brady had both the official, fictitious records & my own true testimony as their corrective corollary, the bushranger would be in a position to organise his vengeance when he came to liberate Sarah Island.

Brady would bring to a divine justice the rats who dobbed, the convict constables who sold their mates out for a cosy billet, for all were depicted in the old Dane's records as heroes, as worthy & respected convicts. Brady would free the rest, & a convict without a record would remain a free man, for it was clear to me now that it was these false words which enslaved us. Without them, who was to say which man was free & which man not? Upon being liberated the convicts would be able to travel anywhere & call themselves free, & with no records, no longer living within the prison of paper, none could prove they were not. And after, Brady would circulate a truthful account that exposed the horror of the settlement for what it truly was, which showed the lie of the official record, of all official records, & in so doing inculcate through the length & breadth of Van Diemen's Land a spirit of revolt.

So, at last the instrument of glorious purpose, I slowly made my way further into the unknown with my strange burden, always with the vision of Brady my redeemer before me.

Yet even without my sled of such outrageous ambition, my journey was preposterous. The violent land was uncharted, the whereabouts of Brady within that wildness the size of England unknown. The terrain was densely, at times even impenetrably, forested by primeval trees & ferns. It rose in great wild waves of mountains, it fell in the harshest cataracts, glistening white as granite.

The journey became a torment beyond imagining. But as I dragged my sled of a thwarted memory through snow, through driving sleet, up yet one more gully or over yet another button grass plain, across several mountain ranges & through as many swollen rivers, never in my most despairing of moments, in my greatest of physical agonies, would I ever, ever countenance the thought that I would not find Brady, because Brady, when I found him, would understand it all. Brady would know what it was that I did not. Brady would tell me how this world might be turned upside down & once again made right, the way it once was, & the way it should be.

III

He came into the flaring circle of my fire early in the evening. His scabby & sored body withered & miserable, he was as good as naked apart from a grass hat on his head, a dull & scratched earthenware pitcher in his right hand, & a brand 'S' big on his arse like two puckering horseshoes raised & entwined.

I was nestled up under a flaky shale rock shelf & was as astonished by his desperate audacity as I was first mystified by his identity. My hand gripped my axe. But when he made his bold proposal there was no doubting who else with so little would seek to turn such weakness to his advantage.

'If you will share your food,' said Capois Death, 'I will share shouldering your burden.'

I gave him some pickled pork. I watched as he chewed it on one side of his mouth like a dog, the rest of his teeth I guessed having fallen out. I asked why he had escaped—after all his billet was a privileged & far better one than most on the island.

Still chewing, Capois Death took off his grass hat & removed from the top of his head a wretched & filthy scrap of paper. It had been folded & refolded so often that the creases were now largely tears, & it was four almost separate pieces of paper.

'*Dear cap,*' it read:

> *you was always my one & only you was everything*
> *how sweet how good how I will never forget how I*
> *loved your crooked smile your kinky hair how I*
> *always loved you*
> > *your darling forever*
> > *Tommy*

I handed the letter back to Capois Death.

Following Roaring Tom Weaver's hanging last winter, said he, his own heart broke. At first he was going to kill himself, after a time he instead resolved to escape the following summer. He had fled with a party of six several weeks before; they had split when the last of their food ran out. One mate had drowned fording a river, the other gone back to the lime burners' camp to give himself up. Capois Death had fought a devil off for the carrion of a wombat a week before; since that time, nothing.

'Yes,' said he, though in answer to what I don't know, & he uncorked the pitcher he carried, still full of some piss-stained fluid that was once Larrikin Soup, & a history, said he—his mind I realised now well addled—that had once been his. He extracted a slimy thread of grass & told of how, not long after arriving on Sarah Island, he had witnessed the interrogation of a recaptured convict.

The convict—a pieman from Birmingham—had spent several weeks on the run with three still missing escapees. For want of food in that harsh world, he was believed to have eaten his colleagues in the course of unsuccessfully trying to find a passage through the wild mountains of the west to the settled east, before finally, a starving wretch, returning to the settlement & giving himself up.

Declaring he was tired of this life, confessed he to his cannibalism, but he was not believed until taking off & flourishing his moccasins made of human skin. More interested in what the pieman had learnt of the unknown Transylvanian wilderness than in confessions of depravity, Musha Pug pressed him to describe the exact nature of the country through which he had travelled.

Exasperated, the pieman leant forward, &, asking

316

permission of the Commandant, took a sheet from Jorgen Jorgensen who was making a record of the interrogation. With a violent gesture he crushed the page into an ugly ball.

'Sir,' calmly said he, 'Transylvania looks like that,'—& he dropped the crumpled page to his feet.

For the sake of what little food I had left, Capois Death now joined me journeying through that crumpled labyrinth of cascades & rainforest & ravines & limestone tiers that was unfolding before our eyes into something beyond words.

We were bound for Frenchman's Cap, the great massif of Transylvania. Visible for up to a hundred miles in any direction, its distinct broken crescent shape, when viewed so far away by those in bondage at Sarah Island, vividly—& to us convicts, ironically—suggested the Frenchman's cap of liberty, where I had reason to believe (based both on the constancy of endless rumours & certain secret letters I had found from the Governor addressed to the Commandant) that Brady was camped.

We were bound for Frenchman's Cap, but we were not the first. We came upon camp fires with the occasional thigh or forearm bones. We came upon myrtle roots entwined with the manacled skeleton of a nameless escapee.

We stood still, listening for something, I don't know what.

'What do you want to do?' asked Capois Death, scratching at a large, angry looking scab that had formed over the smiling mask brand on his forearm.

We hobbled on. Our pickled pork ran out. The books grew damp, collected moss, sprouted lichen, acquired insect & small plant life. The scab on Capois Death's arm grew septic, his movements slow, his mind feverish. Our tea ran out. Somehow we lost the axe, though I think Capois Death may have thrown it away, lest one of us was tempted to use it in the manner of the pieman. Our flour ran out. In a deep river valley we came upon the dead white stag of a blue gum, as wide as a score of men in its girth. Upon its trunk were nailed in a straight line what looked at a distance like pieces of bark. In his fever, Capois Death believed them to be the multiple issue of the machine breaker's eyes peering into him, determined upon vengeance, & would not come near. But they were nothing of the sort: on examination I found the pieces of bark to be a dozen pairs of shrivelled black ears.

Later limping down from a high rocky outcrop we came upon a great plain of button grass, sags up to chest high, copper hued with small flowers & fresh growth. We saw an irregular shimmer moving through that plain towards us, that after a time we came to recognise as two blackfellas.

Neither was frightened off when we played the old trick of picking up sticks & raising them to our shoulders in pretence of muskets. There was no point running, we even hoped they might prove friendly & offer us some of the kangaroo we could see hanging over one man's shoulder.

But upon them walking up to us, it was clear they were not going to share anything. One was a tall man, &

somewhat scabby. The other was of a shorter, stouter build. We could see they were angry. We never saw the spears they dragged along the ground, clenched between their toes.

'Numminer? Numminer?' queried they, & I, a stupid white man thinking by numminer they meant white man allied to all the horrors inflicted by white men upon blackfellas, said, 'No, me no numminer.' Capois Death, a smart black man thinking by numminer they meant ghost & that he might be able to play the bogy man to such simple souls, straightened his body & with all his will kept from violently shuddering so that they would not know how ill & weak he truly was.

In as strong a voice as remained to him, said he:

'Yes, me numminer, me bloody big numminer.'

IV

CAPOIS DEATH'S LAST sight before his own pitiful death was to be that of his whole sorrowful history being played in reverse. All his vicissitudes on Sarah Island, the machine breaker, the Cockchafer, his successes as a Hobart Town publican, his times in Liverpool, he was seeing running backwards through the spilling of a pitcher of purl-ale.

He looked up & he saw himself as he swam back up into the slave ship & delivered himself into servitude after a humiliating act with a white man, gazed with ever-growing sadness as he gradually abandoned all his fierce desire for freedom, while Frenchmen laughingly drew nails out of the wooden epaulettes that were so peculiarly attached to the black general Maurepas's shoulders.

Maurepas gazed up at the jolly Frenchmen in shivering incomprehension, as his wife & children returned from the sea, as dogs vomited forth pieces of human beings that reformed into whole people, as the brutal repression of the slave revolt turned into a brief liberty then finally, once more, an infinite servitude.

Capois Death felt his unquenchable rage & determination to not remain enslaved diminish like a guttering candle flame & as he lost the strength of manhood & descended into an ever weakening childlike body, he simply came to accept the world of endless labour, ceaseless brutality & pointless violence from both his masters & his fellows as the way all life was here, there & everywhere. Only the taste of a guava stolen from his mouth & grafted back onto a tree redeemed that long time that ended, finally, when the black overseer dragged a weeping black woman forward.

With great force a white woman insisted on pushing Capois Death, now a baby, on to the screaming woman, whose screams quickly subsided & after holding the still wet & bloody child at her breast for a short time, got off the stool & squatted in a dusty courtyard under a guava tree & allowed Capois Death finally to return to the one time of serenity he had never known & to enter feet first into the immensity of her through the wild, torn, bloody cave of her opening.

Just at that last moment before darkness encompassed him forever, Capois Death turned & saw himself reflected in the mirror of an emptying purl-ale bottle in which time had halted wheeling backwards & was now rapidly spinning forwards, but he was unmoved by his future, was indifferent to the revelation of his destiny that revealed him & me leaping out of the sled harness & seeking to run away from the blacks, & two spears passing into & through his fevered torso.

Capois Death turned away, took a deep breath, slowly stood back up & had taken only three slow steps from the bottle that moved backwards & forwards in time, when he felt the first spear like the blow of a sledgehammer; felt himself staggering, then a second blow even more powerful than the first. He spun like a skewered blackbird & fell clumsily to his knees. As he tried to crawl away, he felt their waddies begin to drum his body & he felt language starting to drift

away,

words tendingto fall intooneanother an dlittlemade sen se & thenthes centof aguavareturned &tommytalk- ingwalking   withme&   farfarfaraway&tommy! tommy!cold&cold &

As I ran I glanced over my shoulder & saw the black- fellas beating Capois Death hard with their waddies, & they seemed to be trying to break the bones in each of his limbs. I saw him raise one arm slowly, an odd & insuffi- cient gesture. Perhaps he was farewelling somebody or something. They were beating him around the head, lay- ing into him with all their force. From the dense cover of a band of tea-tree I watched them then leave him to die.

When with much care I returned the following morning to retrieve the sled, it was to find it untouched, unlike Capois Death's corpse, already with viscera trailing from his sunken belly in rich sausage & offal forms & the colours of clotting blood from where the devils & tigers had started feeding in the night.

To the side of his head, milky eyes still fixed firmly upon it, was his broken, emptied spirit bottle. Scattered around its fragments were its stories: half a garnet ring; some pebbles & dull weeds & three small seashells—a periwinkle, a baby mussel, & a broken scallop shell. He was Larrikin Soup robbed of its wormwood. He was bird's blood with no body to smear over & make fly. He was history.

With my poor painter's hands & with rotten sticks that kept snapping I started to dig a grave in the sour gravel that forms a damp desert beneath the button grass. After a time I gave up in exhaustion, having only made the shallowest of depressions. I dragged Capois Death's body into it, & then left, not-turning fleeing wishing wanting life to be otherwise.

Time passed.

I grew delirious.

Time did not pass. My visions & vision became one. Time circled. I was hauling a sled of lies called history through a wilderness. Time laughed. I was awaiting a death that would never happen in a cell in the Sarah Island penal colony. Time mocked! Hurt! Wounded! Broke! I was writing a book in another time trying to understand why there were no words for what had taken place.

None.

Nothing.

Semi-naked, emaciated, I began the conclusion of my march, the ascent of Frenchman's Cap. Each day I cut one more strip off my kangaroo-skin jerkin, & chewed it for sustenance. Calculating the vest was good for twenty strips, the slow disappearance of my clothing served as my calendar, as my teeth first grew wobbly & sore in my inflamed gums, & then began falling out.

It was in the relatively calm lee of some large granite tors halfway along a westerly ridge some long time later that I found huddled around a small fire battling in the rain the most unexpected group of familiar faces. I had eaten the last strip of vest two days before.

V

THERE WERE THREE small girls & a young boy with next to nothing on their frail bodies; several ravenous, mangy dogs; & a shoeless woman I recognised as the one the Commandant called the Mulatto, Robinson named Cleopatra & the convicts & I knew as Twopenny Sal, breaking boughs to put on the fire. For some—no, for almost anybody—they would not have been a prepossessing sight, but for me, who had not seen a fellow human for what seemed an eternity, they were beautiful beyond compare.

Twopenny Sal was clad in an old black cotton skirt, a coarse woollen yellow convict jacket, & red woollen stocking cap. She carried on her back in a sling made of wallaby skin a baby, who I came to understand was the twin of the child whose tiny skull Twopenny Sal, in the fashion of her people when grieving, carried tied to her dress. The child was of a lighter hue than her other children; her eyes blue. She might, I realised, be my child. Or if there was a child that was mine, perhaps Twopenny Sal had killed it. A black man with his back turned to me was putting three potaroos on the fire to cook. At first he did not even bother looking up when I called his name.

But when Tracker Marks did finally raise his head, it came as a shock to me. No longer the elegant, strong man I had met on Sarah Island several months before, he was now a figure not so much emaciated as shrivelled, his once elegant maroon waistcoat transformed to a greasy black, hanging as heavy around him as iron basils had once upon me, his fine blue striped shirt dull & torn, his dark moleskin trousers hanging in long shreds from his skinny shanks.

His appearance was grotesque. His face was mutilated, & when he came up close to me, it was clear that at some point his ears & nose had been cut off, & only fleshy, still partly raw lumps, red & angry, remained where these organs had once been. All over his mangled face, like so many cruel carnivorous beetles, I saw the telltale pustules of the pox. Tracker Marks, whom I had always wished to paint as the dandyish crested weedfish, now resembled only the curling, flaccid & stinking stretch of flesh fish became after a few days sitting in Mr Lempriere's cottage.

I could not help staring. Then Tracker Marks did something that had I journeyed a thousand miles through a hundred wildernesses to find this one place, I would never have anticipated.

He was extending his arm.

He was reaching toward me.

With the back of his fingers, on my cheek & lips, he was touching me.

VI

His hand fell from my face, & I sat down on the earth with them around their fire. As the potaroos' fur began to singe & hiss, Tracker Marks, through signs & the Van Diemonian patois they called *dementung*, that bastardised dialect that was part-blackfella, part-whitefelon, told me they had been expecting me for some time, having sighted & tracked the smoke of my fires for several days as I slowly wound my way up the flanks of the mountain.

Twopenny Sal lit a pipe & after a few puffs offered it to me. It was some sort of native tobacco, strong & greasy & refreshing. I passed it to Tracker Marks, who inhaled once, sneezed & coughed a great deal—a very bad deep cough it sounded—then told me how he had decided to leave Sarah Island to hunt for kangaroo. After some days travel he had come to the river mouth the whites called Pieman Heads. There he had run into a party of redcoats who had been sent to find the Tracker & ask him to help them find the notorious bushranger Matthew Brady.

At this point Tracker Marks interrupted his story to take the singed potaroos off the fire & deftly gut them with a sharp stone. After returning them to the fire, he coughed some more, then continued with his tale.

The redcoats offered gold, as well as land near

Jericho where the Tracker might establish his own farm. For the next several weeks they criss-crossed Transylvania. The Tracker showed them rocks that were Brady, tarns that were Brady, fish that were Brady, made them swim rapids in deep mountain rivers that were Brady, made them stand in the chill wind that was Brady, & then they showed the Tracker the boot, sliced off his nose & ears, one ear so close that they took part of a cheek, then gave him a good hiding & told him that if they came across him again they would shoot him up for the cocky coon he was, for having led them away from their prey for so long.

I felt a stirring of excitement at this story. My soul had warmed at such unexpected company & my mind felt oddly lucid from the tobacco. With the force of revelation, I realised that my journey was coming to its fabulous conclusion. Clearly, though Tracker knew where Brady's camp was, he had skilfully avoided showing the redcoats. Now he would lead me there.

VII

THE WORLD GREW grey as great clouds, immense & black, came over & obscured nearly all light, hastening the onset of nightfall. Almost immediately, with a perversity entirely consistent with the Van Diemonian summer, it started to sleet.

As sloppy snow hissed contempt into the fire, Tracker Marks took the cooked animals off and cut them into pieces, sharing them around. He himself ate nothing, not even when Twopenny Sal cracked open the thigh bones of the cooked potaroos & held them close to his mouth, imploring him to suck the marrow for strength, then, when he refused, rubbing the marrow on his cheeks & forehead as though this might similarly impart strength.

When after the meal I then asked Tracker Marks where Brady was, replied he that the rocks were Brady, that the tarns were Brady, that the fish were Brady . . .

I might have mourned that not only Tracker Marks's body, but his mind seemed to be in such decline. But to tell the truth I felt little other than a great weariness consequent on the sudden & unexpected meal of marsupials, slightly sick but also strangely sated. I drew closer to the fire until Twopenny Sal bad me join them in a small cave-like recess in the rocks into which they had all retreated.

Once under the overhang Tracker Marks had me sleep with them, the fire in front of us, dogs curled at our head & feet, his children cuddled up to me on one side, Twopenny Sal on the other, with Tracker Marks on the far side of her.

I found the proximity unexpected, &—to be frank—a little inappropriate, but as no-one else seemed to find it the least bit odd, I rolled over on my side & found my nose nestling into the back of the one the Commandant called the Mulatto, Robinson named Cleopatra & the convicts knew as Twopenny Sal, & whose Aboriginal name, I realised with a sudden sense of shame, I had never bothered finding out.

I felt childlike, & with a dim sense that my knowing so little was a vague but real sin, terrible & unspeakable, which had yet been forgiven, I fell asleep. As I slept I felt my muscles & bones slowly warm & then relax, & I felt, for the first time in many, many days, that I was safe.

VIII

WHEN I AWOKE it was night, dark save for the fire—which had earlier looked doomed to die in the cold & wet—now roaring & driving, a huge wild red presence three yards high & at least the same in radius filling our cave with a yellow leaping light.

Tracker Marks, Twopenny Sal, the children & dogs—all were gone. A smoky yet somehow familiar scent came to my nostrils, which reminded me of that particular must I had smelt on my first entry to the Registry.

On the far side of the blaze I saw Twopenny Sal dancing with the children. She had abandoned her European clothes & apart from a red ochre smeared necklace made of sinew & a strip of roo skin wrapped several times around her waist to which the tiny skull was now attached, she wore nothing other than red ochre smeared on her face & through her pubic hair, the latter looking like rusty iron shavings attracted by the magnet of her pudenda. Her hair had been remade with a thick pomade of red ochre & grease, fashioned into overlapping scales like those of a fish. The children were similarly naked & similarly decorated.

As I made my way toward them around the fire, I felt something fall upon the side of my shoulder, then drop away. I stopped, turned, & looked down. Lying on the ground beside me, terminating in the smoking stump of a forearm, was a smouldering black hand.

THE FRESHWATER CRAYFISH

*King Canute—An antipodean auto-da-fé—The
leaving of Twopenny Sal—Metamorphosis—Firesite
of skulls—Song of Solomon—Beehive hut—The
wages of reading—Eating Brady's journal— Universe
of horror, infinity of love—Clucas ahead—His
perfidy rewarded.*

I

WITH A SENSE of impending horror, I stopped,
turned & looked up. At first I refused to believe what it
was that I was witnessing. That it was a confusion of the
eye & brain, that I was mistaking the endlessly liquid
form of flames for other things. But the longer I stared,
the more I knew it could be no mistake.

For high in the middle of the fire, sitting bolt
upright seven feet above, was a shrivelling, flaming dark
log supported by burning branches piled up on all sides.
The dark log was a black King Canute enthroned happy-
as-you-please while a yellow & blue tide of flame rose
ever higher around him. I blinked—once, twice—but
there could be no mistake: King Canute was Tracker
Marks, now dead, & this was his cremation.

The black dandy, his hacking cough now forever
stilled at the dancing fire's heart, was charring into
something unrecognisable. Red flames were wrapping

like slavering hands around a waist, caressing a chest, desiring a chin. There was an arm ending in an elbow spluttering fire. An earhole burning with a soft yellow flame like a tallow lamp.

I heard a yelp & looked down to see one of the wretched dogs attempting to race off with the hand that had dropped from Tracker's corpse onto me & from there to the ground. A foot fell on the hand, a foot I recognised as thankfully unlit & alive & belonging to Twopenny Sal, who bent down, wrenched the still smoking hand free from the dog's jaws, gave the dog a kick, & with a casual lob threw the hand back on the fire.

If the reader should suppose that at this point Billy Gould screamed or screeched they would be greatly mistaken. If they think Billy Gould boldly leapt up, wrested the Tracker's body from the flames & thereafter gave him a good Christian burial they would be even more mistaken.

For one thing, it was all I could do to continue standing. For another, I've never been one for telling people how they ought live their lives &, given my own experience, it seemed a not unreasonable principle to now extend to death. I had already interfered with two corpses, & one had transformed from a turd into a scientifick system, while the other had become a slimy sage. It had become clear to me that no good, scientifick or spiritual, comes from messing with the dead. And besides, I felt the Tracker looked rather happy up there at the top of his bonfire, like the glowing star of Bethlehem atop a Christmas tree. It wasn't beautiful, & it wasn't ugly. It wasn't right & it wasn't wrong. It did smell similar to what I hoped Castlereagh would one day smell.

I realised that Twopenny Sal was looking up at me. I could feel the heat of the fire on my face, & I could see the flames painting their cavorting leaves of red light & black shadow over her body, her face, her black eyes wet with tears. From a small kangaroo-skin basket hanging by a belt of sinew from her waist she took a clump of red ochre which she crushed to a powder in the palm of my hand, then mixed to a paste with spittle, saying all the time the words, *Ballewinny—ballewinny—ballewinny*, & all the time crying & her face twitching & shaking in that leaping light, & she kept looking at me & I only looked down occasionally at her work with the spittle-greased red ochre, too embarrassed to do anything else, even when she brought a red daubed finger up to my cheek & began to smear markings on my face.

As she rubbed the ochre in she stared at me, as though I were some long lost friend, as if I were her man, her brother, her father, her sons, all the other people who had preceded Tracker Marks, for whom she had rubbed ochre on her face & charcoal onto her body to mourn as one by one they had perished of colds & smallpox & the clap & musket shot, as if we shared something that transcended our bodies & our histories & our futures, & as if by marking me so with red ochre I might somehow also know something about all this.

But in the twisting light & shadow of the fire with the daubings of death & life on my face & the secret mysteries of which they spoke, I only sensed that I knew none of it.

The black woman turned away, took a large bough, & beating it hard down against Tracker Marks's flaming head broke open his skull & exposed his brains in a perfect state to the fire. She then worked her way around the body with the bough, poking & lifting & prodding, seeming determined to ensure that Tracker was all properly burnt to ash.

After she began singing, & the children joined her, the children singing together, & she singing an octave above them, forming a concord of such exactness, that I, though I understood none of the words, felt greatly moved.

It was at this moment, when I was trying to rid myself of my frustration at not understanding a word she sang but possessed of the terrifying suspicion I actually understood everything too well, that this woman of many names whom I no longer knew how to address turned back around & began tearing pages out of a book & throwing them on the fire.

I looked up & realised that Tracker's head, pointed north, was shrouded by sheets of the convict registers, the letter books, the records of reports & standing orders, all now reduced to the purpose of fuelling a funeral pyre, bursting into flame & then rising & floating off past Tracker's cheerily charring face, their flapping pages momentarily illuminated by the light of Tracker's ear before they disappeared into the night as leaves of disintegrating carbon.

As she came around to the side of the fire closest to me, I saw that while dancing Twopenny Sal had been all the time feeding the fire with pages she was ripping with a great frenzy from the registers.

The registers!

The registers I had dragged for so many days with so great a sacrifice! The registers with which Brady would liberate us! The registers that had killed Jorgen Jorgensen & for which I had risked my life & Capois Death had inadvertently given his life . . .

I rushed up & seized from her the book she was tearing up & throwing onto the flames, determined to fight to rescue at least one volume from her manic antipodean auto-da-fé, but to my surprise she offered no resistance to my sudden attack & instead just let go.

As I tried to pat out the book's flaring edges I noticed some of the words illuminated by the flames. In the firelight I read some sentences that made no sense whatsoever, about buying chairs as a futile act of atonement for unspecified but very real sins. Then the flame leapt up the page to my hand & the page, already loose, fell into the fire. I looked back up at her, but she was still staring down at the book, where I then read what was now its beginning, a half-torn page, the first legible words of which were:

'... for I am William Buelow Gould, sloe-souled, green-eyed, gap-toothed, shaggy-haired & grizzle-gutted, & I mean to paint pictures of fish & capture in them one more soul like mine . . . '

Suffering the dim sense of a skewed recognition, I flipped through more pages, leafing past pictures of fish & prose I found in several places to be recognisable as my work, & in other parts to be ludicrous nonsense though not without a curious & sometimes disturbing correspondence to reality on Sarah Island.

But it was not until my eyes alighted upon some lines at the bottom of a page in the front of the book that I experienced something like panic.

'William Buelow Gould,' read I, 'had been born with a memory but neither experience nor history to account for it, & had spent forever after seeking to invent what didn't exist in the curious belief that his imagination might become his experience, & thereby both explain & cure his problem of an inconsolable memory.'

Resolving to read no more of such fancy, I tore that offending page out & threw it into the flames, but I now felt my breath shortening into abrupt pants & on my back a prickly sweat of fear was rising & in my bowels my guts began dancing a watery jig.

Twopenny Sal wiped tears off her cheek & indicated that the far side of the pyre needed more fuel. I was infuriated by her total lack of interest in my feelings & was determined to read not another word, to begin there & then to try to erase this moment from my life.

I would recommence my search for Brady who would tell me that all I was now witnessing was simply the delirium of a man lost & starving in the wild woods of Transylvania. But it was no good—Billy Gould could not escape the growing suspicion that he had become entrapped in a book, a character whose future as much as his past was already written, determined, foretold, as unalterable as it was intolerable. What choice did he have but to destroy that book?

I tore out yet a dozen more pages with great energy & threw them in the fire, but the upward draught of the

336

flames picked the pages up & swept them straight back into my face. As I pulled a partly burnt page off my nose I could not help but read:

'Lying on the ground beside me, terminating in the smoking stump of a forearm, was a smouldering black hand . . . '

With great violence, I screwed the page up & threw it on the fire, only to see revealed on the next page a picture of a freshwater crayfish. It looked as if it had been painted in perfect imitation of my style. Trying desperately to avoid the conclusion that if this book of fish was a history of the settlement, it might also just be its prophecy, I then realised that the book was not near ended, that it contained several more chapters, & with mounting terror I read on the succeeding page of how—'I realised that the book was not near ended, that it contained several more chapters, & with mounting terror I read on the succeeding page of how—'

II

—STRANGELY, TO MYSELF no longer inexplicably, I then let the entire *Book of Fish* fall into the inferno, & proceeded to join with the black woman in tearing the other books apart & feeding the torn pages to the fire.

Onto that pyre those descriptions of so many individual pasts, their implicit idea of a single future, & how those hungry flames shrieked with delight! As Pobjoy so long ago told me, definitions belong to the definer, not the defined, & I no longer wished to have my life & death foretold by others. I had endured too much to be reduced to an idea. Onto that pyre I threw so many, many words—that entire untrue literature of the past which had shackled & subjugated me as surely as the spiked iron collars & leg locks & jagged basils & balls & chains & headshaving—that had so long denied me my free voice & the stories I needed to tell.

I no longer wished to read lies as to who & why I was. I knew who I was: I was the past that had been flogged on the triangle, but I am the flagellator dipping his cat in the sand bucket to give the tails extra bite; I was the past that fell with choked scream through the gallows' green wood trapdoor, but I am the hangman swinging on the dying man's legs; I was the past bought & chained & raped by sealers, but I am the sealer making the black woman eat her own thigh & ears.

Onto the fire I threw those books of betrayals, of fantastickal rumours, of stories a little true & mostly false, all with treacheries great & insignificant at their core hiding from us our shame at how we were made to be both gaoled & gaoler. Neither we nor our children nor their infinite progeny were ever to forget the shame, long after the memory of why had been lost. Onto the fire I threw *Crania Tasmaniae*—those beautiful lithographs of stolen skulls & they too danced around the charring corpse. Onto the fire & into its hungry heart we heaped them all, all those lies that obscured the mysteries & clues & echoes & questions & answers, in order to escape that prison finally & completely & forever; onto the fire we cast every last register, every loose sheet of paper, on & on, & on & on they burnt.

At first so much damp paper merely smothered the

fire, but soon the flames re-emerged & the fire leapt back into being like a huge ball, as if the System were a dragon that had just been slain, its dying breath apocalyptic, as though a thousand furious spirits were being released. The fire shrieked & cracked & threw geysers of sparks far into the night sky, the bush all around brightly lit by a dancing red glow.

The huge fire was wild with it all, & then the surrounding bushes spontaneously combusted from its banshee-breath & the night sky began to thrum to its growing banshee-wail. The fire began spreading & the surrounding pencil pines & then the forest beyond was in flames & then as far as I could see, everything was afire & without willing it or thinking it, I found myself joining the black woman in her dance, bathed in the wild red ochre light thrown by the inferno.

I dragged my withered, ulcerated legs in poor but definite imitation of her jumps & leaps, & together with her & the children I danced so many things that lay so deep within my soul it felt like a purifying fire itself. It was a joy & it was a sadness & it was inexplicable. It was the weaver & my poor mother, it was Audubon & all the birds he shot, Old Gould & Old Gould's daughter, Voltaire & Mrs Gottliebsen, the Surgeon & the fish, the Commandant & Towtereh, Capois Death & his beloved Tommy, the potaroos & the Tracker. We were dancing something beyond words. My body took on such wild life separate of me that I feared my wretched old bones might break & fragment in that ceaseless, strange furrowing of the earth.

After a long time, after the flames had departed to the

ranges & tiers far beyond & only warm cinders lay about us & the smoke billowed far below along distant ridges in the rising light of dawn, I watched the black woman gather up the ashes of the dead Tracker Marks & mix them with water to form a mud, grey & gritty, that she then smeared all over herself & her children. Thus attired in the night of their grief, they prepared to depart into a morning she seemed determined not to relinquish.

'No you worry, Tracker he go to England,' she told me. 'Tracker he numminer piccaninny now.'

'He's dead,' said I. 'When you are dead you don't get reborn as an Englishman.'

'Numminer!' cried she. 'Tracker numminer! Gould numminer, but long time before you were Palawa.' And with an outstretched arm she described a vast arc through the dawning sky above, her pointed finger beginning at me & ending at the other end of her world pointing down at charred earth.

'Long time before,' said she, 'you were us.'

I looked at her & then I couldn't look at her, & so I looked at the ash-strewn, dance-scuffed ground.

'Gould, you come,' said she.

I kicked my toes into the dirt, felt myself shuddering & swallowing.

Said she: 'Come back, cobber.'

III

BUT I WHOSE obsession had been the past & its chronicles, found myself without either the desire or the energy to follow Twopenny Sal into the future.

I had watched them walk off—this women whose name I had never known & her bedraggled children, of whom one may have been mine—into the charred, still smouldering forest. Before long their naked forms were indistinguishable from the burnt stags & saplings that spiked that beautiful blackened country.

I headed into the east wind, walking in the opposite direction to her & the westward surging fire, a lengthening wall of smoke receding from my back. I made my way up through an alpine country of heaths & small shrubs, still aiming for the peak of Frenchman's Cap. No longer encumbered by the sled & books, I found myself even in my weak state making much quicker progress.

Mid-afternoon I came upon a steep creek. It rose a few hundred yards further on in an alpine tarn, a little lake caught in the cupped palm of a small mountain valley. At that summer level the creek was nothing more than the gentlest of cascades playing around large river rocks on one of which was a creature, glistening greens & apricots, emerging out of a large shell a good yard long.

For some moments I was unsure what it was, until I recognised it as a freshwater crayfish of the type the convicts sometimes hunted in the rivers. It was shedding its carapace & emerging newer & larger, yet still the same. I looked at the translucent shell the crayfish was abandoning & marvelled at its metamorphosis, at the magical power it had to appear one thing & become another, its ability to leave behind an image of itself that was no longer itself.

I thought of trying to catch it, for its flesh is very fine eating. But the moment I threw a fist-sized river rock, the crayfish leapt backwards into the water. The rock landed with a futile thud where the crayfish had a moment before crouched, & all that remained were suggestions of what had once been: the shell in which it had lived, a damp shadow on the rock where it had stood, a vortex of bubbling water into which it had disappeared.

I gave up, and walked on. Beyond the tarn I passed a grove of pencil pines & entered a clearing in which sat a dozen or more dome-like buildings arranged in a circle. From their large beehive shape & the careful, intricate thatching of the tea-tree & grass, I recognised these as the cottages of the blackfellas, the tarn as the site as one of their villages.

But there were no blackfellas.

There was an old firesite at the village's centre, lichen scabbing the dirty ash, over which were scattered, as if in explanation, mounds of bones & a host of human skulls, long since picked clean by animals & birds & insects. Remnants of black women's ornaments rotting upon some bones, & of black men's ornaments on others. Skulls with one, or at most two small holes, I presumed from musket balls. Skulls with the back smashed out where devils had bitten through to get at the brains beneath. Skulls bleached white, & skulls with a gathering of green moss. Big skulls. Little skulls, toothless, translucent as parchment.

IV

I was lying on the ground, panting quickly, shaking uncontrollably with fear. The mountain earth was reaching around me with the sweet weight of death. My body heavier & heavier, my head a stone, & within an insistent voice wimbling away, dragging me downwards, urging me sleep—sleep, sleep Billy boy. Through eyes pearling, I dimly noticed a few yards distant an entrance to one of the larger dome huts, a low hole no more than a foot wide & no greater than double that in height.

I began a crawl away from that firesite of skulls, toward that narrow opening, a cruel, harrowing journey over ground strewn with the feathers of emu, & the broken bones of this stately bird as well as of kangaroos & possums. I hauled myself over intricately woven grass bags, crushing beneath me small plants growing out of their rotted thatch.

I halted my infinitely slow crawl to rest, & saw the letters of all my childhood prayers bounced back & reformed on the ground as some scattered leaves torn from the Bible, smeared with red ochre. On examining some of these leaves I found them to contain such passages as, 'I am black but comely, O ye daughters of Jerusalem' & 'Thy navel is like a round goblet which wanteth not liquor: thy belly is like a heap of wheat set about with lilies'; the sort of rot you might use to get your way with a bedswerver like the publican's wife. But I found it so peculiarly ill-adapted to me that I could not help blaspheming, & so without applicability to my situation that I blew my nose upon it. Given I had sent God 26 letters on numerous occasions—admittedly long ago—I thought God could have done a little better than this. The last page I looked at lay at the wombat-hole entrance to the hut. It was even more irrelevant. 'I said of laughter,' it read: 'It is mad: & of mirth, what good doeth it?'

Bugger all. I threw it away. Upon finally crawling inside the hut I was overwhelmed by a fecundity of smells—stinking human & animal odours, smoke & cooked meat, decay & growth, but mostly decay—which made my stomach clutch. I went to puke, but Tracker Mark's potaroos would not budge from my gut & instead my throat just burnt with bile. I rolled the wasted rack of my body onto its back. For a long time I lay not far from the low entrance, exhausted, crook, trying to empty my mind, my eyes adjusting to the darkness.

A capacious room, surprisingly comfortable, remarkable warm & dry, slowly appeared around me, large enough to accommodate perhaps twenty people, though presently home only to two potaroos & one tiger cat which had scampered out after I entered.

I felt as though I were nestling in a giant sea-eagle's nest turned upside down, for the dome's walls curved around me, covered with the sulphur-dipped feathers of cockatoos, the raven black feathers of evil-eyed currawongs. Here & there animal skins were pegged with sticks on the downy wall. Scattered around me sharp stones of the type the blackfellas use for tools, the back of a looking glass, & what appeared to be a flint-lock

344

that had been pounded into a small, sharp knife-like tool. As with my eyes, so too did my nose begin to adjust, & the strong smells at first so distressing, grew comforting, halfway between meat cooling & coming home.

I eased myself up into a sitting position. I stared at the dead firesite at the centre of the hut for a long time, lost in despair, for what was I to do now? To have come so far, only to have all my records burnt. To recognise I could go on no further. To no longer care if I lived or died, far less found Brady. My supplies, my strength, my very life seemed spent in a quixotic mission that had come to nothing but utter disillusionment.

My back spasmed, a mass of cruel knots ever more tightly tangled. The joints in my legs felt like river rocks grinding on each other. My head swam in a light fever. Cold, old, alone in a land no white man even knew on maps, far less in their heart, beyond any redemption in a blackfella's house of feathers. Though it was warm, a coldness, terrible & violent, crept over me. I felt very still, yet I was hurtling around in circles both inside & outside my body. With an unexpected clarity I knew that I was dying, & that, if I did nothing, before very long I would no longer care if I was dying. I found myself battling death &, worse yet, my desire to live.

I was so frightened.

I resolved to pray to God.

I resolved to confess to Him everything.

I cleared my throat with an awkward cough. I pulled myself into what felt like dignity & knelt. I would just let it all pour out, everything from

Castlereagh's drinking habits to Ackermann's awful teeth & a hundred & one other things, it really would be a terrific thing to finally say it all & not hold it down any longer.

'God,' began I & my prayer of confession went like this—

V

'A-B-C-D-E-F-G-H-I-J-K-L-M-N-O-P-Q-R-S-T-U-V-W-X-Y-Z.'

VI

IT WAS A wondrous ark that confession & I really did put everything I knew in it so they might live: all the plants & birds & fish & animals I have loved, not to mention the Commandant's bad breath & Mrs Gottliebsen's splendid areolae & Twopenny Sal's dancing & all of it was just 26 letters long.

But it did no good whatsoever—what prayer ever did? And not being able to kneel on the rock of the church any longer I was swaying falling dreaming embracing the earth.

VII

I PROBABLY WOULD have died very soon after if my fall had not been most uncomfortably broken by a small cairn of ochre stained rocks. When I rolled over, groaning with yet one more set of new bruises & aches, it was to notice that protruding from the now half-collapsed cairn was a book.

At that point there could have been nothing more likely to depress me than the dismal prospect of reading, for reading had become for me the source only of disappointment & disillusionment, of a measure that seemed to turn my entire life upside down, disturb & distress me beyond compare, & make me think everything I had hitherto taken for granted about this world was all cack-handed & wrong.

I understood how Mrs Gottliebsen would have felt if I hadn't discovered Voltaire in the nick of time. She would have felt like me with books. Cheated.

After all, it was reading all those romances & adventures as a young boy that had been the undoing of Jorgensen, making him think he could remake the world in the image of a book. It was reading Miss Anne's idiotic missives that had led the Commandant into his follies; & it was reading all those works by Linnaeus & Lamarck that had made the porcupine fish think he had a sacred role in reordering a world that was only ever going to reorder him as the supreme example of a degenerate black skull.

It was the nonsense of all their reading & then me in the Registry stupidly sticking my own beak into books that I shouldn't have, that had led me to this sorry pass where I was about to die alone in a nameless forest.

Thought I: only a fool would touch it.

My fingers stroked the cover's dusty invitation. I pulled my hand away, looked up at the ceiling, away from that wretched book sticking out of stones, taunting me like the publican's wife all those years ago behind the bar with her sultry silent come hithers. I rolled myself onto my side, pushed what remained of the cairn apart with my outstretched hand, & lifted the book out from the dry rubble.

It wasn't a large & grand tome like those in which Jorgen Jorgensen had reinvented Sarah Island, but a small & crudely made volume. Its pages appeared to be roughly bound with gut sinew, which I recognised as having been stretched & softened in the blackfella manner of chewing. Its cover—wallaby hide, like the rest of the book—was stained red with ochre like that which, I realised, touching my cheek, still remained on my face from where the black woman had rubbed it on.

Thought I: only a madman would open it.

The book fell open in my outstretched hand, & there at the book's front, written in what thought I a surprisingly childlike hand, was the name—

Matt Brady.

Thought I: I can't bear to read what follows.

When I had finished reading I breathed deeply for some time. I felt my skin prickle & breathing grow shallow. Then sobs, which I tried to stifle by pushing a fist into my mouth, erupted like odd, acrid bubbles bursting forth from a burning pot. I tried to stop my head shuddering.

I felt only an immense emptying. A great disillusionment. Time . . . well, what did I care about *time* now? Perhaps it halted or started or danced or fell asleep or went to the pub for several Larrikin Soups. My nausea abated a little. Hunger—incessant, unavoidable—came back upon me. I shoved the wallaby-hide cover of the book in my mouth & tried to eat the book, as much to be rid of it as to appease my belly.

But that proved pointless, for the book was as inedible as it was incomprehensible. How can I convey the utter futility of what I had read? It was, I suppose, best described as a kind of personal journal written in what the author claimed to be kangaroo blood, a small earthenware inkwell of which I noticed remained sitting amidst the stones from where I had grabbed the journal.

It was a rattle bag of things really. There were observations on blackfella ways & habits, which seemed pointless. There were vulgar jokes written out in great & tedious length, emptying their vehicles of what little humour they may have had. There were pieces of what I suppose amounted to a personal philosophy: various commonplaces on the theme of friendship such as 'Love cannot live without the forgiveness of sins continually' & similar such tripe. Recipes for bush poultices & medicinal draughts. Observations of animals & birds. The currawong. The quoll. The sea eagle. The tiger. Did he not have a gun? Could he not like Audubon at least have had the decency to shoot one or two & make some bad pictures? No. His style was too artless. 'The shrike-thrush calling lovely like he has lost an old cobber calls he Jo Witty? Jo Witty?' He had no ambition. Whenever a thought or observation overwhelmed him, rather than seek to conclude his idea he would instead just write, 'And on & on, & round & round', as though idiocy is the need for conclusions.

I searched in vain through those pages, sometimes stiff & thick, sometimes as thin & light as pressed flowers, for orders for a jacquerie, any mention of a rebellion, plans for a revolution, or even something that might amount to an outline for an orchestrated uprising, a draft declaration of independence for the republic—anything that might fundamentally threaten the System.

There was nothing.

Only page after page of more pathetick affirmations of love between a white man & a black woman, that left me feeling queasy. At one point the typically cryptic aside: 'To love is not safe.'

And what did that mean?

I had no idea.

The ink was dried up & the dreams were only of Brady's love for a black woman, of building a white man, black woman home, the whole something other than either in the merge, adorned with moonbird & black swan feathers, with a large vegetable garden where he & she might live knowing that place & each other & their family over the course of a long life, growing old together.

To love is not safe. Whole circle, black man. Circle bisected, white man. Really it was just like Descartes, or Descartes was really just like them, him thinking in whirlpools & them in circles, & all a similar nonsense. Love. Forgiveness. Love, love, love, thought I—is that all? Is that it?

Apart from a recipe for roo patties, it was.

I closed the book.

Who was this Brady?

It occurred to me that he may have been Tracker Marks. Or René Descartes. Or that he may have been the black woman whose name I never learnt. I even wondered if he was in the end just an idea, but then his story would properly belong in the realm of literature, & not here in a truthful account that deals only in real fish.

And what had happened?

Had he killed the blacks who lived in this & the other beehive huts? Or had he been killed with them? Was he now condemned to some nether world of the type Pliny the Elder had described in the book I had found impaled on the old Dane's sword, living with the Monocoli & the Astomi & all the other fabled people?

I rolled onto my back, exhausted beyond measure, all hope finally extinguished.

VIII

I READIED MYSELF to die.

For several hours I merely let my gaze wander the inside of that hut, staring at the texture of the tea-tree thatching, its feather cladding, so rough, so gentle, the whole hut I fancied like gnarled old hands grown into great wings cupping around me, & the dull-dun tobacco colour of it all, acquired, I suppose, from the fire smoke that must have once played in the now dead black coals at the hut's centre.

Skins of wallaby & possum & quoll hung on the walls at unusual angles, as if they might momentarily take back their original form as animals & leap down. I looked at the pictures drawn on these skins in fats stained with charcoal & red ochre, of tigers & devils & kangaroos, of hunting parties, of men & women dancing, of the moon in its various guises, which had, I had to admit, a certain mesmerising power.

I took the skins off the wall & placed them under & over me. I curled into a ball over which kangaroos & wombats & devils & dancers & hunters & the moon roamed in stories I had no way of understanding. In that serene dark of the beehive hut of feathers, covered in incomprehensible tales with Brady's book of indigestible love at my side, I finally fell asleep.

Like the crayfish leaping backwards into the water after abandoning its shell, I prepared to abandon the shell of who & what I was, & metamorphose into something else. As with my mind's eye I saw a shimmering arch of blue flame, smelling of singed fustian, being drawn out of my nostrils by those dancing animals & then sent hurtling out of the hut, I finally felt my soul taking flight.

Stories as written are progressive, sentence must build upon sentence as brick upon brick, yet the beauty of this life in its endless mystery is circular. Sun & moon, spheres endlessly circling. Black man, full circle; white man, bisected circle; life, the third circle, on & on, & round & round.

I dreamt I spat onto the crazed sepia crust of kangaroo blood at the bottom of Brady's ink pot, making a scarlet ink, the colour of a troubled dawn. Into that wet, dark demon I dipped the nib of an old quill with which

I then wrote in Brady's wallaby-skin journal where Brady's dreams ended & the clean, empty sheets began:
    Orbis tertius,
my first words rendering that third circle in Latin.

And then, finally, breaking apart the spider web of an infinite memory in which I had become enshrouded, I dreamt of the man whom I had been—a convict forger who called himself William Buelow Gould, & who, discovering that implicit in a single seahorse was the universe, that everyone had the capacity to be someone, something, somebody else, that Numminer were Palawa & Palawa Numminer, had painted a few queer pictures of fish, & then died.

IX

I HAVE STOLEN songs from God.

X

As I SLEPT on I began to wonder whether if all this were just a dream & I the dreamer, that the many strange forms of my dream might also just be me. Could it be that, though the Commandant reigned over me, I was yet the Commandant? Was it possible that though Mr Lempriere ordered me to paint the fish, I was Mr Lempriere? And that though I painted the fish, I . . . ?

But it was not possible to continue.

There were shouts, curses, the heavy sound of tramping, a cry of discovery, the sharp, ammoniac aroma of excited fear, the sudden clicking of flintlocks. I opened my eyes, saw barrels radiating from my head, as if I were a sea urchin & the levelled muskets my spikes. Brandishing the firearms were some lousy bottom-feeding soldiers, great galoots of gurnards with their huffy cheeks—redder than their rotten coats—& poppy eyes. In what felt a single movement I was roughly dragged from my bed of skins & heaved outside. I groaned, spat out the peat that had ploughed into my mouth where I had so rudely landed, & lifted my head.

To my side were a mangy tiger-skin cap & the dead eyes of one whose terribly bloodied head seemed familiar & the foolish & naked body beyond from which it was severed finally recognisable as that of the *banditto*, traitor, child-murderer, rapist & sealer, Clucas. I did not then know that having fulfilled his part of a bargain in providing several dozen barrels of gunpowder, Clucas had then been paid out in his own currency of death. But when I looked further up I did know, without seeing his face, the name of his murderer. For eclipsing the sun now rising beyond was the unmistakable & monstrous udderish outline of the great ball bag of Musha Pug.

THE SILVER DORY

*On the perplexities of time—Burning of Nova
Venezia—Betrayed by an opium-eater—Intimations
of immortality—A disembowelling—Mutiny—The
silver dory detonates—Sky rains dreams & hopes &
railway carriages—Tales of love, paid in
death—Reflections on Rembrandt van Rijn & sundry
other matters—Fish plot vengeance.*

I

BILLY GOULD HAD awoken startled. Shaking his head,
he ran his hand over his roughly bearded chin, scratching himself in all the awful places awful lice were biting.
Feeling a sudden desire to move, if only in order to be
momentarily rid of the itch of lice & the insolence of
dreams, Billy Gould leapt up & seizing hold of the
prison bars high up, hauled himself to the slit window
& looked out. Relieved, I saw the miserable magnifi-
cence of the Commandant's Nova Venezia all about, &
my heart swelled with gratitude toward Musha Pug for
having brought me back.

I should have known why I was there, but in truth
I didn't. To be frank, although I have painted all I
know, it's clear that what I know is two parts of
bugger-all. All that I don't know, on the other hand, is
truly impressive & the library of Alexandria would be

too small to contain the details of all my ignorance. I don't know, for example, why I am now to hang for two murders I never committed, yet why nobody is guilty of the firesite of skulls. Nor do I know why murdering the Pudding or Jorgensen is deemed a crime, while murdering a people is at best a question & at worst a scientifick imperative. There is much more I don't know. For example: why people read Bowdler-Sharpe & dismiss fairy tales as nonsense. Why an alphabet can be contained in a world, but a world could never be contained in an alphabet. These things & so many others are all mysteries to me. How boats float. Why we order our lives as ladders while around us the earth circles. How mortar works. Why a man quivers like a fish when a woman walks by. How buildings don't collapse. Why we can walk but not fly. Why I dreamt I had transformed into a forest but woke to find my gob ploughing the earth until it hit the stump of Musha Pug's boots.

Whatever their more clandestine purposes, Pug's party of traps had officially been on patrol with the aim of gathering information on Brady's movements, & for a moment had thought in my wasted sleeping form they had finally captured the great man himself. I told them that I had indeed met the one they sought, & pointed in the opposite direction to where Twopenny Sal had set out.

'Did you think Brady could save you?' laughed Musha Pug, kicking my head.

'Of course,' said I, because it was what he wanted me to say, but now I knew the truth was otherwise.

Even if he had all the histories of the world & its suffering open in front of him, Matt Brady, whoever & wherever he was, could not have saved us. Nothing could. Not the Surgeon's Science. Not the Commandant's Culture. Not God, who is infinite time. Nor could we save ourselves. There was no solace in the past. There was no solace in the future. There was no solace even in the idea of salvation. There were only Musha Pug's boots, & after they had landed one more blow on my cheek & were skating over my mouth I kissed them. I kissed them because they were all that I had left to love.

II

THE SLIT WINDOW from which I was hanging afforded a view I found both splendid & instructive: on the fish-netting gang's crude plank jetty below a gibbet was being erected, an incentive to us condemned souls watching from above to concentrate our minds upon repentance before all was finally lost. Below the jetty at low tide some washed-up skulls & bones of Lieutenant Lethborg's platoon were bleaching and breaking back into the sand. I had been brought to my new cell—a death cell—after my capture, to await my imminent execution eight days hence.

This new home was not without virtues. It didn't flood on a daily basis & its ceiling seemed unlikely to collapse. It was one of three slightly larger cells on the other side of the island to the main settlement, & I could have been almost happy with my imminent demise if it hadn't been for Pobjoy, who at that point took it upon himself to interrupt my splendid solitude.

I tried to continue hanging like Christ, but I wasn't really that interested in suffering on my own behalf, far less that of the entire world as the old priest had taught. My poor arms could not hold even such miserable weight as I was any longer, & I fell back into the darkness of my cell while Pobjoy, as ever stooping to new lows, announced that he was seeking the return of the oil-paint set. Until that point I had thought the self-interest of Pobjoy & his need for a continuing supply of convict-Constables might make common cause with my desire to live. Quite the opposite: he calmly told me that my impending execution no longer disturbed him.

'I feel—' said he, determinedly moving into the cell & grabbing the paint set & my most recent convict-Constable, then corrected himself: 'I *know* I am more than capable of picking up where you have left off.'

For once I looked up into his face. Though tall, he had a round red dial with a wall-eye, which may have explained his similarly bent illusions. He had a jutting lower lip & an angry red-raw jaw where he had shaven badly, like a silver dory's great ugly mug, &, though I can't tell you exactly why, I've never really taken to dories. They're trouble.

I should have guessed from the raffish way he had lately taken to wearing his redcoat partly unbuttoned that Urges Dreadful had come upon him. His desire was grand: 'I want,' said he, head jerking backward in a gesture at once haughty & nervous, as if disclosing an illicit passion that might prove his undoing, 'to become an Artist.' I told him there were worse ambitions, but at that moment I was unable to think of any.

The more he talked, the redder grew his face & the more his head jutted back & forth. The greater the head rocking & face ruddying, the longer his lips protruded as if overcoming some childhood handicap in talking. And the more his lips stuck out like the silver dory's infinitely-extendible mouth, the more I wondered whether he was telling me things, or trying to suck something out of me with his great gob, something fundamental that he might need to help nourish all that immense folly of aesthetick aspiration.

Then, perhaps overcome with nostalgia for happier times, he gave me a good kicking. Afterwards I assured him he had all the attributes necessary for a successful artistick career, though unfortunately my mouth was too swollen to list them for Pobjoy's benefit: mediocrity; a violent capacity with any potential rivals; the desire not only to succeed but to see your fellow artists fail; gross insincerity; & a capacity for betrayal. Fortune favours folly, I tried to say, but merely succeeded in dribbling some blood & teeth.

Then Pobjoy was weeping, saying he always had bad luck, he had bad luck being pressed into the army, then worse luck being sent to such a dismal outpost as this, & worst luck of all being made guard idiots like me. I managed to get my lips moving again & began telling him a story to try to console him for his bad luck, but this just seemed to make him angry once more & he told me to shut up.

'I'll have you drawn & quartered,' yelled he. 'I will

personally flog your back until there's nothing left & the cat's tails are sticking out the other side tickling your tits.'

He snorted snot from his nose back down his throat & from his great height gobbed on me.

'Are you such a half-wit, Gould?'

I knew better than to disagree with Authority, so while wiping my face with my hand, I humbly ventured I most certainly was.

'Shut up! Shut up you stupid bastard, or are you so stupid that you can't see I'm fed up to here with you & all your stupid stories? If you say a word more I'll kick you again.'

So I told him about how I once knew a certain Ned Hennessy who came from near Waterford, who was a simpleton & whose friends decided to play a joke on him. They pretended that one of their number had died & had him laid out in the coffin & asked Ned Hennessy to guard him through the night with a pistol in case the spirits from the other side came to steal him away. Then, in the middle of the night, up bobbed the corpse & said, 'Hello, Ned,' & Ned, who was frightened of the dark & had stowed a pistol in his pants, shot his prankster mate—bang!—dead through his forehead.

'Shut up', said Pobjoy dully.

'Ned Hennessy,' I concluded, 'was a right rumun.'

Pobjoy gave me a good clubbing all over this time, with his fists & his head & even a couple of wallops with the paintbox, but he didn't even bother with his boots & I knew his heart was no longer in such violence, poor Pobjoy!

'A man such as yourself,' I began, but my speech was slurring, blood was dribbling out over my words, & it was hard to see much lying on the floor, 'in the obvious prime of life . . .' But I could hear the cell door slamming shut, the bolts sliding, & as I spat the last of my teeth out, I had to admit that it hadn't been an entirely agreeable meeting, that I had lost my paints & this time it really might all be over.

III

THE FOLLOWING MORNING, as I once more hung from the cell's high barred window, gazing out, I avoided looking at the gibbet by focusing on the distant plumes of smoke that daily moved further outward from Frenchman's Cap & closer to us. The rest of the settlement at first thought little of the growing fire that was consuming the great uncharted forests of myrtle & pine that the Commandant had not sold & the Japanese not carted away.

No-one would have believed me if I had told them how the fire had started, & who, pray, was I to do the telling? Who was I to say that the conflagration was first fuelled by the poesy of the very System itself?

At the beginning we all saw the fire only as an extension of our own particular, peculiar vanities. For some convicts the accumulating dust in the air was one further oppressive element of a natural world that existed only as a gaoler, while through his gilded vision the Commandant saw the catastrophe as only another mercantile opportunity, & immediately sent envoys to several Portuguese colonies offering deals on charcoal which with mercury was used to smelt gold in the distant jungles of the New World; & on it went, with each of us remarking upon the fire only as a prolongation of our various worlds, rather than the ending of them as it was to become.

Five days before I was to hang, small pieces of ash began falling from the sky. When the wind arose, larger leaves of myrtle & fern fronds charred to a crisp rained upon us, perfect in shape & form, but entirely black in colour, harbingers of our fate fluttering onto our hair & noses & shoulders as if rejoinders from another place & another time that we had wrongly understood & hence irretrievably ruptured.

Three days before I was to hang, so much ash had fallen that in some places it had blown into drifts in which a man's leg would sink to his thigh, & by the following morning only the stakes of the compound, the top storeys of the taller buildings & the narrow lanes the chain gangs were made keep clear with an incessant labour remained as evidence that there had once been a settlement of any description on this island of mounting ash.

As the wind blew stronger & stronger from the northeast, as the fire grew larger & came closer, the convicts—whether in condemned cells or chain gangs or cosy billets—began to sense its magnitude & grow aware of its power & believed it must be Brady's doing, a part of his grand conception that would see us all freed—oh the genius of the man! That he would use the very Nature that had gaoled us to free us & destroy that Nature at the same time! And they waited for when he & McCabe & the rest of the grand gang would burst like those splendid horsemen of the Apocalypse out of that inferno dispensing a fiery judgement with muskets of thunder & flintlocks of righteousness.

Because they knew judgement was nigh the convicts cared not for the redcoats or the convict screws. One day before I was to hang, I heard the guards outside whispering how Ben Joshua refused to go bottom dog in the sawpit & said so to Musha Pug, 'Brady will have you too, Musha,' said he. 'Brady will truss you up, Musha Pug, & bind your bulbous ball bag & gag your filthy gob & hold it under water till you have pearls for eyes & flathead for friends a full fathom five down.'

Musha Pug hit him hard but it was a blow for a woman not a man, a backhand not a fist, & Musha Pug then turned his back & walked off on his three legs & everybody saw it was a slap not a punch. Everybody saw Musha Pug walk away & everybody knew why it had been a slap not a punch. Then chain gangs laughed at the convict constables when they ordered them to work, & then the convict constables refused to use force when the officers told them to maintain order. Rather than beat the convicts senseless there & then, the convict constables either disappeared to their sheds & haunts away from the convicts or tried to curry favour with them, offering tobacco & jokes & guesses as to exactly when & how & in what magnificent form & number Brady would arrive.

The pining gang refused to leave the island & head

up river. The shipwrights lay back in the hull of the cutter they were building & the coopers walked away from their half-finished barrels which with their unbound staves looked like flowers half-wilting, half-blossoming, & no amount of threats or pleading would have a felon move, & very soon the island was at a standstill & all—guard & lag alike—were simply waiting.

Then Musha Pug broke out a rum barrel, then another, & offered it round the convict sawyers & convict shipwrights & convict coopers in the shipyards, saying over & over that cobbers weren't dobbers. Later the redcoats came down, but only to commandeer a keg to take back to their barracks where they sat quietly & drank sullenly in a search for courage or oblivion. By sunset, the island was three sheets to the wind, the talk all a wild dreaming of a new country to be, & all eyes focussed intently & expectantly upon the mountains to the east for any sign amidst the smoke that might signify the imminent arrival of Brady, & even I, sitting in the almost complete darkness of the condemned cell awaiting my execution the following day, could not suppress the faintest surge of hope.

IV

NONE OF THE handful who were to survive could afterwards satisfactorily describe the strangeness of that time, so many images of horror around which the fires of Hell rose & fluttered like the Commandant's moonbird epaulettes.

Picture it, as I had to picture it on the morning of that eighth day after the fire had first been sighted—only a few hours before my execution—standing naked in my smoking oven of a cell, occasionally putting my mouth close to the door's dark edge where the slightest of fetid drafts was for me a welcome breeze, a mistral that brought images of horrors elsewhere in its sluggish wake.

Picture smoke-choked birds—the native swifts & grass parrots that had not been caught & painted & the jays that had not been caught & eaten, all the sea eagles & black cockatoos & fantails & blue wrens—dropping dead from the sky into that boiling sea. A tideline of their bodies ringed the island, a boom of birds against which our hopes began to beat ever more futilely for the island was even then starting to smoulder & there was nowhere to go, only dead blackened birds to throw at flames that were even then beginning to appear all over the island.

Watch the whole island transforming into a single furnace, one flame as infinite as Hell, an eternity of suffering in which nothing existed except to fuel the fire further, & then the fire finding its way into the heart of the settlement.

Over everything & spreading everywhere there is just fire & wind & smoke, smoke as acrid as sin, thick as dirt, heat blistering your skin, singeing your hair, & vilely tonguing through it all the ubiquitous redness.

Picture men shaping in & out of smoke as they run from the flame into the flame, all one & the same now the maelstrom had arrived. Pity the soldiers & the convicts who have ceased fighting the gathering firestorm, giving up their unequal struggle & with all the energy they can muster running to the wharf, a pied swarm of redcoated soldiers & yellow slop-coated canaries, a moving motley of terror, seeking protection under the piers, in the water, returning to the sea to escape the infernal heat, & all who are not yet dead wishing themselves so.

They run over earth scorching; they run past carts, barrels, half-built ships, jetties & even men self-combusting & exploding into fireballs, breath sucked out as flame before they can even scream their final agony; they run away from flame swirling in whirlpools of fire writhing up a hundred yards up into the sky; they curse & hate & run from that flame falling back down from the heavens in a yellow & blue & red storm with one thought inescapable: *run!*

V

BUT IF FOR a moment you dare pause to pant for breath, spare a thought for Billy Gould in his miserable cell. He couldn't run. Because you may suppose that all those prisoners locked up in solitary cells would have been released in order that they might also escape the conflagration. And in this you would be entirely wrong. Our guard had retreated to beneath the jetty, refusing to open our cell doors without an order from Pobjoy, & Pobjoy—for reasons I intend to explain—had been summoned to the settlement shortly before it turned into a complete inferno & was, though none of us yet knew it, never to return.

Left to roast in my cell, biting smoke so thick that it had become a rancid grease down my throat, eyes watering so wild that were I painting I would have been able to moisten my brush with my tears, I could only make myself feel better by dwelling upon the fortunes of one in an even more wretched state than me, the only other person on the island who wasn't running either, not because like me he couldn't, but because he wouldn't.

The Commandant was sitting up on the sofa on which he had for a time laid after he had abandoned the smouldering ruins of his cell & taken refuge in his palace, one of the last buildings still standing on the island. He felt the wet, Huon pine-oil scented towel peel off his mask & he resumed watching with unwearying pleasure the magnificent spectacle of his palace which had now also begun burning. He coughed. A few threads of blood ran in red rills over his black lips & onto his smudged mask.

Those few left around him offered every form of succour & consolation, telling him false news of successes in holding the fire back & serving cups of cold sassafras tea to cleanse his lips & soothe his consumptive-cough scoured throat, all of which only served to reinforce in him the sense of how utterly distant & ignorant they were of him & his true nature.

For in truth nothing had given him greater happiness since the time he had first met the Mulatto. He felt a great glee as burning roofs began caving in, waterfalls of flame. Then, as everything he had struggled & fought & killed for was gobbled up in front of his eyes by fire, he felt his glee transform into a great tranquillity; as into flame dissolved the unbearable weight of inanimate objects that had become a massive anchor chaining him for so long to a person—the Commandant—he no longer wished to be; to a place—Sarah Island—that he had at first endured only because there was nowhere else in the world in which he might remain safe & free; to a life—his own—which he now recognised as patently absurd.

The drawing room where he had received foreign dignitaries, the ballroom where the great parties & orgies had been held, where he had hidden behind the long green curtains of Japanese silk waiting to grab the Mulatto & take her there & then, the Great Hall of National History with its many full-length portraits I had painted of him as a Noble Sage, National Hero, Ancient Philosopher, Modern Saviour, Roman Emperor, & Napoleonic Liberator upon rearing white stallion, all now crackled & blistered & flared into flame, & as the canvas bowed outward with the intense heat, the figures ballooned as if suddenly animated & finally freed from their exile on those distant walls & able to escape with their maddened vanities & cracking desires into smoke.

Into those flames he now let fall an eight-month-old letter he had just received from Thomas De Quincey. The writer was grief-stricken: Miss Anne had disappeared & he feared greatly for her safety.

He had had an opium-inspired dream: 'At a distance,' wrote he,

as a stain upon the horizon were visible the domes
and cupolas of a great city—an image or faint
abstraction, caught perhaps in childhood from
some picture of Jerusalem. And not a bow-shot
from me, upon a stone, and shaded by Judean
palms, there sat a woman; and I looked; and it
was—Miss Anne! Her looks were tranquil, but
with unusual solemnity of expression; and now I
gazed upon her with some awe, but suddenly her
countenance grew dim, and, turning to the mountains, I perceived vapours rolling between us; in a
moment, all had vanished; thick darkness came on;
and in the twinkling of an eye, I was far away . . .

Try as he might, the Commandant, who understood
the curse of wishing to please an audience, felt De
Quincey could not write without sounding as if he
longed to hear the salon politely applauding his artifice
as on & on the London literato drearily drummed,
writing that he could not find her, that only rumours
remained—that she was dead, worse yet, that she had
never even existed but was only a character out of a
modern novel of whom the novelist had tired & had
made emigrate to the colonies. Had he, her beloved
brother, perhaps seen her there?

But the Commandant's tears could not hide from
his blurring vision what was so obvious: that De
Quincey's hand & Miss Anne's were identical.

His sister revealed as fake as her brother, his nation
ash, the Commandant threw away his scented towel &
inhaled so deeply of that great tumbling acridity of

fumes that he found himself retching. The notion of a golden age to come, of a fall only just hidden, of a utopia desecrated, of a hell that could be obliterated only by a determined amnesia, all this he finally smelt in the smoke of his burning palace as the folly of those who cannot accept life.

He was gripped by the sensation that he was awakening, not from a dream but its fearful, terrifying inverse, waking from reality to the sense that all life, properly understood, is a savage dream in which one is shuffled about, taken by the tides & winds & the knowledge—constantly in danger of being lost—that one is only ever an awestruck witness to everyday wonder.

He thought—don't exasperate me by asking how Billy Gould *knew* what he thought, for if it isn't obvious by now that he knew much more than he ever let on, it never will be—he thought several banal things, which I reproduce in no particular order.

—There is no Europe worth replicating, no wisdom beyond the flames consuming my palace. There is only this life we know in all its wondrous dirt & filth & splendour.

—The idea of the past is as useless as the idea of the future. Both could be invoked by anybody about any-thing. There is never any more beauty than there is now. There is no more joy or sorrow or wonder than there is now, nor perfection, nor any more evil nor any more good than there is now.

—I have lived a life of meaninglessness for this one moment of meaning & these things which I now know,

& the knowing of which will flee my mind & heart as abruptly as they have entered.

He wondered if even the perfumer Chardin would be capable of filling Voltaire's head with the aroma of such pungent enlightenment?

And he thought he knew all these things fully & completely, & he felt it as grace, the consummation of an otherwise entirely pointless life. Then he knew that his thinking was a final useless vanity & that like his palace, his thoughts were disappearing into the smoke, & he was left holding a cup of sassafras tea growing eerily warm.

When the burning roof of the palace collapsed into charring timber beams cracking & flames shrieking, the smoke-hazed sky above the Commandant's terrified eyes began darkening with thousands upon thousands of moonbirds returning to their sand-dune burrows. With the force of premonition the Commandant knew he was about to be enveloped by the night.

Thinking:

I have been everything, only to discover everything is nothing.

Guessing:

The rest is silence.

His cup of sassafras tea began boiling in his hand & even before he had dropped it in pain he sensed with horror his gold mask similarly heating & then running like treacle, & too late smelt it scorching his flesh, felt it searing his skin, & he suddenly screamed for he knew the mask was melting into his face, fixing forever his image in that of somebody who was not him but had now become so.

Alone in his palace knowing now that His Destiny & that of His Nation were one & the same, the screech of the fire the only sound now echoing up & down the lonely ash-defined corridors & was it his lungs or was it the fire or was it his destiny calling *slap-slap-slap* even now, calling him on, was it his own breath rasping *brady-brady-brady* or was it the shriek of the fire lurching, leaping, flying ever closer, was it the same nightmare of the sea rising & rising & rising, & *brady-brady-brady* coming ever closer & closer & the flames of Hell ever hotter . . .

VI

IN THE END lucidity returned. As the Commandant lay haemorrhaging on that bloody quarterdeck of the black ship, it was as he had long feared: he was immortal. He would not transform into a whale as some of his putative murderers later had it, but he would return to the sea whence he had come.

Earlier, when bound in a filthy calico straitjacket he was frogmarched by a large detachment of hand-picked soldiers through the dying flames & still glowing beams of what had been his palace, all who saw him through the coiling smoke knew that the writhing blubbering dwarf was not to be confused with the tyrannical visionary who had been our leader for so long.

It was not possible that this screeching simpleton —with the putrid stains in his pants where he had pissed & shat himself, with the frothy black mercury dribble flying from his whirling head; whose face like a raw beefsteak was hideously wounded from where the soldiers had with pliers pulled out the melted gold of his mask—could be mistaken for our feared & glorious patriarch who had once transformed ships into clouds before our eyes & invited us to take flight with him, who had changed, as he had assuredly told us, a penal colony into a new Venice.

Long before then & the coup d'etat led by Musha Pug, the signs of decay were already there for the alert to notice. Fungi was breaking up through the paving, ferns sprouting out of walls, blackwood seedlings dangling from spouts; but at first only a few had been prepared to acknowledge that all that vanity of activity, that glorious carnival of commerce, had been an illusion, a theatre of mercantile triumph to hide the despair of the island from its sorry inhabitants.

Yet in the months preceding his grab for power Musha Pug—pendulous ball bag swaying back & forth—chose to see none of it. He was to be seen hobbling everywhere, all over the island like some treacherous three-legged monster, whispering words of conspiracy & retribution, making duplicitous promises of the spoils of future power shared, as he set about assembling in the second floor of the windmill a secret armoury of modern American armaments & several dozen barrels of Chinese gunpowder, along with the two hundred & forty redundant mah-jong sets already stored there.

But all that Musha Pug coveted was already

crumbling. In the summer before the fire a destiny that did now seem inescapable once more asserted itself, as the devils & feral pigs took to wandering through the empty warehouses & the possums to nesting in the lofts of the clerks' & actuaries' rooms & eating their gold-brocaded purple curtains. As the bollards up & down the vast empty wharf were rusting from having no ropes winding back & forth to polish them, the slime of rotting geranium petals was underfoot everywhere, the scent of pink dissolving into brown, the carnal transforming into the faecal.

Shit, thought the Commandant when the men he derided as traitorous mutineers had surrounded him & ordered him on pain of death to surrender, *It's all gone to shit*. But said he nothing, & instead held up his hands in acknowledgment of the silence of an undeniable solitude that was returning forever.

They had the Commandant sit down, & at bayonet point sign several confessions, all of which were untrue & none of which came close in their litany of criminal intent to the Commandant's real achievement, but he understood authority's need for order & signed anyway, for the files were God's joke on memory, the only understanding of today that would remain tomorrow.

'History, the cruellest of goddesses,' said the Commandant, handing the quill back after condemning himself in the name of several fictions that surprised him only in their banality, 'rides her chariot over the corpses of the slain.'

'Slow,' replied his guard to the Commandant's subsequent polite query as to the manner of his death on the black ship as it sailed out of Hells Gates into a wild sea to there throw him into the deep, because they had to, there was no choice. The story was so mad, the crime so immense, the culpability of so many others at stake, for they had believed him & backed him & everyone was guilty & it was better a prophet die than his followers be punished. 'Not only because we have to,' said the sailor smiling, such a gentle, pretty mouth he had, 'but because there is a pleasure to be had in it also.'

In the end it was as the Commandant had long suspected: so that he might make no mistake as to the pattern of cause & effect & understand life is stupidly linear instead of mysteriously circular, on Marshal Musha's express orders (as the former constable now styled himself) they gelded him & had him pound his own balls to a mince with a hammer, & then failed to rip the first knife up his brisket & had to get a cooper's saw to finish the job so that they might wrest his heart out & wave it about, crying out in glee—

'You heartless bastard!—& who gave you this?'

—& none read the name of the Mulatto that was inscribed upon it so bold & clear so that all might see, none saw that the fatty heart was her, & that it was also hers forever & ever, they just laughed & laughed. But there were some in that carnival that day who were silent, not from pity or fear, but from wonder, for he was human & though he was monstrous what had made him so & what was it that separated them from him?

He wished to tell that finally he knew the answer to

the question that had for so long haunted him. The search for power, he concluded in his last remaining moments of clarity, was the saddest expression of all, of an absence of love, worse yet, of the capacity to love. He wished to cry out, *I am imprisoned in the solitude of my love!* To yell, *See, see, that is all there is & I didn't see it!* And indeed, he was not entirely sure that he hadn't done so, for his torturers first jumped backwards when a low moan came from his mouth, but then cried in glee upon deciding that this was just the final passage of some wind from the lungs being forced by the partial disembowelling that continued on the vinegared quarterdeck for a few more minutes yet.

VII

AT THAT SAME moment the Commandant was metamorphosing into a cetacean legend, Pobjoy, red-faced from more than just the growing heat, stood outside the windmill—as the headquarters of the coup d'etat, one of the few buildings still being adequately defended against the fire—beset by terror. He had a few days earlier sold Marshal Musha an authentic Constable—my very last work—for a considerable number of Bengal dollars. While being hung, there had been discovered on the back of the canvas a painting of a silver dory & Marshal Musha quickly guessed the nature & origin of the deception.

Inside his windmill, emboldened by the ease with which he had taken power without resort to any of the considerable firepower he had murderously assembled in the floor above him, Marshal Musha had spent the last hour angrily shouting at his new minions that he was much too absorbed in affairs of state to talk, while compiling a list of possible new titles for himself.

The title *Marshal Musha* had a barracks room familiarity he had first liked, but which now worried him. The Commandant's folly was to think you could turn a penal colony into a nation, whereas it was clear as day to Musha Pug that it would be far more successful as a company. He had crossed out the words *The Supreme, The First Consul, His Bunefience* (the spelling of which had taxed him considerably) and was circling *The Chairman* when Pobjoy was marched in to see him.

Wishing to impress on all present that *time was money* Marshal Musha stood up, went over to the wall where the convict-Constable hung, & before the gaoler's eyes ripped the canvas out of the frame & screwed it up. He threw the balled canvas at Pobjoy's feet & demanded double the sum he had paid for it by the following morning or Pobjoy would face a fate worse than that which was shortly to befall the wretched painter Gould. And with that, the interview was over.

After Pobjoy left, Marshal Musha ordered a detachment of guards make haste to the other side of the island & halt the execution of William Buelow Gould. Whatever a forged Constable was worth on Sarah Island, it was worth a great deal more in London. The Commandant's crime was to dream too much, thought Marshal Musha, Pobjoy's to dream too little. He, however, was determined to pursue a strictly mercantile line of moderate extortion, that had proven so successful with the likes of Clucas.

Outside Pobjoy let the crumpled canvas drop from his hands into the ash that now covered everything. In that ash a smouldering ember burnt a red hole into the canvas ball. Pobjoy spat in the palms of his hands. Reflecting that if he had lost a painting he had at least gained a pig, he took hold of the handles of the cart to which Castlereagh was strapped. As he grunted with the effort of lifting, he contemplated his successful theft of Castlereagh from his pen a short half hour earlier in the tumult of fire & mutiny, & never saw the swirl of angry hot wind that picked up the canvas ball at his feet & threw it dancing in the air.

In my mind I can see the fish, the pig, the Pobjoy in short, the whole calamity. There he goes now, & oh Lord look at him heading back up the Boulevard of Destiny away from the windmill, bowed & sweating & puffing & going green with all the unaccustomed effort, a wilting asparagus stick of a man pushing the firmly trussed & somewhat awkwardly tied down monster of a pig in a handcart unequal to its load, & both the pig & the Pobjoy entirely unaware that behind them the air gusting around the canvas ball has turned that glowing red hole into a flame.

Please don't ask how I know such things, please: where fish are concerned I know everything—or as good as—& besides, it's rude to interrupt when I am in the middle of telling you how that sorry crumpled dory began to flare up, transforming into a larger fireball, & how that growing fireball then leapt with the wind in all its fiery splendour, dancing up to the windmill's second floor & through a window into the Chairman's secret armoury, there to fall into the middle of some several dozen kegs of gunpowder.

VIII

I HEARD A massive boom.

I felt the air & earth pulse as if they were living swaying fancies.

What seemed a lifetime later, but which can have been no more than a second or two thereafter, came gasps from those who, unlike me, were able to witness the spectacular sight of a static world in sudden & complete majestick motion—here the Commandant's locomotive leaping heavenwards in roaring fragments; there carriages skyrocketing toward the stars like sticks for a dog; everywhere huge iron wheels flying like flattened cannonballs; plaster busts of Cicero & splinters of the Registry shelves; opened books flapping like dying birds; as well walls—pictures & mirrors still attached—billowing into the sky like sheets of paper tumbling in the wind; bowed bodies already limp impaled variously on pokers, banisters, chair legs & jagged floor joists rising like oddly-skewered autumn leaves toward the savage red sun; thousands of shreds of Miss Anne's letters singing Europe into being exploding into a thousand atonal notes & Marshal Musha's final scream atomising into as many particles as his exploding ball bag.

The sun was growing ever greater in size & redder in

colour until it was a monstrous bloody sphere the precise outline of which disappeared into that dark catastrophe of memories; & lost within it forever Brady & his great liberating army, ham hocks, Pliny's wonder, our hopes, the Commandant's vision of the Nation, letters of love, mah-jong pieces, the republic of dreams, pork knuckles & pieces of Pobjoy.

But in my cell how was I to know that others would rebuild the island, rewrite its histories, & condemn us all once more? For all that I could feel when I put my hand out through those bars was the gentlest of heavy black rains falling upon the land, all that I could see was our collective vanities returning to us now as so much ash, & what I could never know was that speckling the smoking sea was an exploded image of the one responsible for this final apocalypse: the charred remains of the silver dory.

IX

CAST-IRON COLLARS, chains & spiked basils, the smell of men's dying souls & living bodies, along with the true humour of suffering, the wondrous truth of contempt, the glorious freedom of neglect, the inarticulable fear of many fish & my unrequited love for them: these things I have known & will never know again. I was hurt by this world into making my soul transparent for all to see as words & pictures, but I was allowed to do it unbeholden & undazzled by anything other than that same shivering naked soul.

If my painting of such things had made me famous I would have known otherwise: I would have been courted, flattered, lied to, my preposterous opinions deemed significant, my paltry presence a blessing, my flap-dragon face attractive. The falsehood of honour, the po-faced seriousness of success, the prison of reputation; men wanting to cover my eyes with raining gold & women wishing to lie with me; all solicitous of my company or failing that the smallest token of my esteem, a sketch, a note, a hint of acknowledgment. All would have been mine. All mine & more than that mine & my name more than my work. My work would mean less & less, most particularly to myself. I would wish myself dead.

For many years I have been painting fish, & it is true that latterly I have been unfaithful. I abandoned them & I burnt them, but I never stopped loving them, I was like Voltaire who loved Madame du Chatelet so much that he was then able to run off with a whole host of other women, until finally she had a brief affair that resulted in her falling pregnant. Too late Voltaire realised what he risked losing, & returned to witness his great love dying in childbirth—which is why, after causing such misery, it was only right & proper he ended up an empty-headed perfume bottle used to bring women to pleasure ever after.

Outside the world glows red. Inside, with brown ink made from the last, most desperate of expedients—a slurry composed of spittle and a projectile normally reserved for the pleasure of Pobjoy—I now set down the final hours of both the settlement & myself in the convict's true ink, his poor man's umber that he uses to smear his protest, his rage and hate and fear of this shitty world, with shitty hands in shitty washes over cell walls in the hope he hopes not forlorn—that love will still at this last bid find him if he can but dig deep enough into his own decay.

Billy Gould, he would rather words & the remaining sheets of Pobjoy's paper, but it amounts to much the same thing: read his daubings how you will—an excuse for another hiding, as Pobjoy would see it; raging against the night, as a criticaster might have it; testament of belief, if you like; or, as he prefers, a confession of failure.

For many years I have been painting fish, & I would have to say that what once was an imposition—what started out as an order, became a cosy push then a criminal act—is now my love. At first, I tried, in spite of my artistick shortcomings, to create a record of this place, a history of its people & its stories, & all of it was to be fish. At the beginning it was to be every last one of them, all those faceless people who have no portraits, who only exist beyond their bodies as a sentence of exile, a convict indent record, a list of floggings, a tattooed initial on a fellow felon's chest or arms, gunpowder blue & hair-forested; a penny love token hanging around a heavy wrinkled neck recalled as a young woman's firm, sweet flesh; a memory fading quicker than hope.

I fancied I would paint fish finer than anyone in history; that Rembrandt van Rijn or Rubens or any Renaissance flashman would not hold a candle to Billy Gould, that my fish would be hung in the finest homes, the detail of the scale & gill praised by generations of periwigged professors.

I would fill a great London gallery with these transmuted images, so that people who came to view my paintings would soon find themselves swimming in a strange ocean they could not recognise, & they would feel a Great Sorrow about who they were & a Great Love for who they were not & it would all be mixed up & all clear at the same time, & they would never be able to explain any of it to anybody.

Then I came to see such was vanity. Far from caring whether they were hung, I no longer even cared whether my paintings were accurate or right in the way that the Surgeon & his Linnaean books of scientifick description wished paintings of fish to be accurate or right. I just wanted to tell a story of love & it was about fish & it was about me & it was about everything. But because I could not paint everything, because I could only paint fish & my love & because I could not even do that very well, you may not think it much of a story.

I grew older. My patron became a pig. I was condemned to death. We set the world aglow. I realised it was not fish I was trying to net, but water, that it was the very sea itself, & in the way nets cannot hold water, nor could I paint the sea.

Still, I continued making this *Book of Fish* because I could not laugh it or dance it like Twopenny Sal might have, because I could not swim it & live it like my subjects had, because this most inadequate form of communication—these images & words falling stillborn from my brush & quill—was all I was capable of realising.

Yet my paintings were—as the Surgeon on the first

day instructed me—to be of Life, not Death. I was to understand the manner of their movement of fin & flesh & gills to make the most accurate studies possible, & every time they were about to expire on the table, I was to toss them back in a tub of seawater in order to revive them so that they, like me, might maintain the terse stretch of life a little longer.

I wanted to tell a story of love as I slowly killed those fish, & it didn't seem right that I was slowly killing fish in order to tell such a story, & I found myself beginning to talk to the dying fish as their movements grew slug-gardly, as their brains slowly ceased working from lack of oxygen.

I told them all about me, about being a bad bastard who forged himself anew as a worse painter, but a painter nevertheless. I wanted to tell a story of love as I slowly killed those fish, & I told them how my paint-ings were not meant for Science or Art, but for people, to make people laugh, to make people think, to give people company & give them hope & remind them of those they had loved & those who loved them yet, beyond the ocean, beyond death, how it seemed when I was painting important to paint that way.

But such things weren't what people wanted in paintings, they wanted their animals dead & their wives dead, they wanted something that helped them to clas-sify & judge & keep the dead animals & dead wives & soon-to-die children in their place inside the prison of the frame, & this business of smuggling hope might make them wonder, might be the axe that smashed the frozen sea within, might make the dead wake & swim free. And that wasn't a painting worth twopence, but something more criminal than stealing.

I gulled myself with the hope that this death I imposed on each fish I painted might be a moment of profound release for them, something they might look forward to as I now looked forward to the gallows as a blessed release.

But the truth was that the fish sensed that I was dying too, that I was with each passing day finding it harder to breathe the air of that fetid settlement, that dense, smoky pall of oppression & degradation & sub-jugation. My movements too were growing sluggardly, my skin was also burning & my eyes dulling, & we all knew that the fish that had for so long been the object of my rapture were soon to have their revenge.

THE WEEDY SEADRAGON

Which treats of Brady's tragic death—A short battle—A dramatick escape from the gallows—On the company of fish—Lost at sea—The island of forgetting—Thoughts of heresy—The return of Mr Hung—A capture imminent.

I

MY TRAGEDY WAS that I became a fish. Brady's tragedy was that he didn't. For I am still alive & Brady is dead, I know he is dead, as I too feasted on his headless corpse (his head, unlike his life, clearly had a value to the governor) when they threw it off Constitution Dock into the Derwent River. There was for me no magick transformation, when hair fell out & skin slowly coarsened & divided into infinite scaling, when limbs seized & twitched & grew translucent & sharpedged as fins, no dawning sense of wonder when I began to feel the propulsive power & fine control of the long tail sprouting out beyond my arse; no sense of panic as gills erupted behind my mouth & my need for water became something altogether more torturous & profound than can ever be described by the mere & derisive word thirst.

I simply had spent too long in their company, staring at them, committing the near criminal folly of thinking there was something individually human about them, when the truth is that there is something irretrievably fishy about us all. One moment I was a convict forger, a Villain masquerading as an Artist, standing on the gibbet on the jetty, & the next moment I knew I had one last remaining piece of energy that I must summon. With an almighty jackknife I twisted out of the noose, glanced a jetty post, & fell from there into the sea.

But I must be more precise.

From the catastrophic events that had so quickly seized the island, we condemned inhabitants of the death cells & our twelve-strong guard had remained isolated. The fire had raced up the ridge immediately behind the cells; the mutineers had not sought the confidence or support of soldiers at outposts, & so we were left unburnt & unaware of the momentous events unfolding just over the hill on the other side of the island. But what with rumours variously of an invasion begun just the previous hour by the English Royal Navy, of a coup d'etat, of the Commandant's murder & miraculous resurrection, & the huge explosion which was, according to the bedraggled & wounded survivors who were just beginning to make their way to our part of the island, the mere beginning of the Commandant's vengeance, the small guard was nevertheless growing nervous. Their sergeant rallied them by arguing that they must continue as before or the Commandant would surely kill them, & that the first matter before them was to carry out that day's execution.

I had been led onto the wharf, I had climbed the

gibbet, I had looked wistfully into the smoke-salmoned sky & with my blindfolded eyes I sensed that the sky was not empty but full of dead souls waving me to come join them. I had listened to none of the priest's prayers, I had waved merry in the direction I had heard the small crowd of felons gather, obliged to watch. I had laughed with them, & I had bathed in their admiration of my white surplice with its long sleeves that fell below my hands, its splendid embroidered fish blessing my breast, its fine decorations of long bull-kelp streamers that the guards had thrown over me with derision—*Hey ho, King Neptune!*—& long before the others saw them, I knew that I had been condemned in a much more terrible way.

In my darkness I sensed them coming, felt the thrum of the earth beneath their heavy tramping feet & began in my mind writing a book, my very own 6-penny chapbook, which began like all good confessions of a condemned man at the beginning, like this—*My mother is a fish*; & which ends like that: *click-clack, rat-a-tat, silly Billy Gould, riding a seahorse to Banbury Cross.* This book of fish which I wrote in its entirety in my mind, word for word, which I painted brush stroke for brush stroke, in that instant between when I was of this flesh & when I was not, & which ended most unexpectedly with—

But just then a cry went up. I did not turn & run but faced them full on, to better focus all my senses upon my fate.

When they saw redcoats approaching with bayoneted muskets levelled, the small, formerly apprehensive & now terrified guards who were to hang me panicked.

They fired at the approaching soldiers, who in turn dropped to their knees behind a slipped whale boat & made ready to join combat. No shot was meant for me, of course, I know that now—these advancing soldiers were meant to rescue & free me, were they not?

But my guard took up positions using the gibbet as a barricade, & muskets, even at the best of times, are woefully inaccurate, & I, head still thrust through the loose hangman's noose, was the only body left exposed.

It was I who smelt the fiery scent of exploding gunpowder before the others had even seen their opponents' muskets levelled, aimed & fired; I alone who felt the slight ripple of breeze made by the motion of the musket ball rolling inexorably from the side of the whale boat through the air toward the gibbet as I calmly waited several lifetimes for the inevitable explosion in my chest.

So you see, it was both my fate which I accepted & against which I rebelled, that it was my destiny to willingly catch the bullet with my body but use its impetus to help topple myself backward & jerk my head out of that shoddily tied noose, to drive my sudden jackknife out of servitude & off the gibbet & onto the jetty. I knew my body to be bowing backwards, a sail bellying slowly outward when the wind first slaps & the journey into the unknown begins, filling & billowing I was as I rolled off the jetty & flopped into the ochre-red sea, & it was then my blindfold washed off & my dull eyes began once more to see & I knew my confessions were almost ended & my punishment just begun.

My body burnt with an immeasurable pain of penance. My balance was so badly affected by having been so long out of the water that at first I was floating side-on &, until I had taken a few deep breaths of water, I had no power to move whatsoever.

I heard the leader of the soldiers behind the whale boat yell:

'It's him we want, no-one else. It's Gould the painter whom we must bring back!'

I felt the trample of redcoats & crawlers rushing along the jetty to see & dispute the miracle that had just taken place.

I heard the shouts of confusion, though as queer low vibrations from above & not as shrill cries of disbelief. I felt the arguments of those who had seen with those who never would as a tepid pointless rackety rumble. With my restored sight I saw the musket balls fall slowly, the force of their explosion lost upon impact with the water, & only the weight of gravity dragging them downwards, a small drizzle of sluggish black hail, followed by oars futilely thwacking at the surface of the water, presumably trying to crown me, & then, a little more cunningly, a landing net swept close by.

Then I saw the gaffer hooks come down toward me & knew that they were trying to gaff me back up into slavery. With an agony that no human can ever understand & no fish can ever describe, I forced my body down, far, far, far from the light.

II

I WAS FLOATING, breathing water, falling, rising, my weight as nothing compared to what I had once known,

I was flying through water, dropping & soaring through dancing forests of bull-kelp, touching sea lettuce, coral, all the people I had known, pot-bellied seahorses, kelpies, porcupine fish, stargazers, leatherjackets, serpent eels, sawtooth sharks, crested weedfishes, silver dories & the sea was an infinite love that encompassed not only those I had loved but those I had not, the Commandant as well as Capois Death, the blacks who had killed Capois Death as well as Tracker Marks, the Surgeon as well as the machine breaker, & they were all touching me & I them as Tracker Marks had a lifetime ago reached out & touched me.

Who could be afraid of the sweetness of it?

Near the reef I came on the striped cowfish, & she told me her true name & I parted the fold between her buttock & thigh & licked her there, in search of the fulfilment of the promise of her scent, & then ran my tongue down her thigh & licked the muscles of her calves, the glorious arch of her insteps, the roly joy of her toes & in all of it tasted the thousand components of her scent that were yet not her scent & I gave tongue to her name & it was all water, I tasted the dried salt pan of her back, & she ever so slowly rolled over & looked away but I had eyes only for her wondrous breasts puddling & I felt the burden of their weight with my lips & I tasted her shoulders, I nuzzled the glorious hollow of her armpits & I found her movements which had at first been willing but stiff, grow long & languid & then she looked at me & close, her eyes closed & then her limbs blossomed out & I licked the part that was a little salt & a little sour & altogether something else again &

her breath was coming in hot hard rasps & I rolled her buttocks around & around & my nostrils began to flare on & on & I began to know the promise of the fulfilment of her scent & I recalled the story of the Astomi who lived on scent alone & how was I to know that for near two hundred years I too had lived so?—as Pliny had so long ago described, & as Amado the Reckless had searched the southern seas in vain for?—subsisting on nothing more than the smell of woman & then I was no longer licking or looking or smelling & I was riding her scent & she mine & then I was her scent & we were beyond her scent, & we were making our revolt our own way, & I thought,

Oh! My sweet how I have lived for this!

& I thought,

How will I die knowing this?

—all this that is beyond us, all this that goes on & on, ever outwards, world without end, this, our third circle.

III

THAT WAS LONG, long ago.

I live now in a perfect solitude. We fish keep company it is true, but our thoughts are our own & utterly incommunicable. Our thoughts deepen & we understand each other with a complete profundity only those unburdened by speech & its complications could understand. It is then untrue that we neither think nor feel. Indeed, apart from eating & swimming, it is all we have to occupy our minds.

I like my fellow fish. They do not whinge about small matters of no import, do not express guilt for their actions, nor do they seek to convey the diseases of kneeling to others, or of getting ahead, or of owning things. They do not make me sick with their discussions about their duties to society or science or whatever God. Their violences to one another—murder, cannibalism—are honest & without evil.

Some things become less clear to me though, the more I dwell upon them.

For a long time before I was a fish the only thing that mattered to me was that my pictures might speak to others, might express a feeling beyond the grave. To those who needed comfort. To those who were terrified.

Sometimes I must admit I long once more to have the power of human speech, if only for a few moments, so that I might explain how I once wanted to live as a rainbow of colour exploding, hard sun falling apart in soft rain, but had to be content instead with making grubby marks on cheap cartridge paper. So that I might say how I once wanted to rise into the sky & shake the heavens, sink into the sea & move the earth; know the beauty & wonder of this world, the beauty & wonder which I now realise is as limitless as its opposite, & how I wanted others to know it with me, & how it was all to no avail.

I wanted my pictures to speak, but was anyone listening? I lost my life to it, you see, my reason foundered owing to it. That's all right, I am not complaining—but what was the use? My feelings never ended their journey as a meaning others might as bread break & share. My pictures were so many mutes.

I opened myself up to everything. The more I felt &
the more I poured that feeling into my fish, the more
feeling I saw all around me. All that pain & all that sadness & all that hopeless love in every fractured life & in
every hidden heart, & then one day I couldn't bear to
see all that feeling & pain & love any longer & I burnt
my book of fish, wished it farewell & good riddance
hey-ho-the-diddly-o! I disguised myself so that I looked
like the others, grew seaweed leaves around my torso &
neck so that as I swam I would be indistinguishable
from the kelp & seagrass forests where divers occasionally now search me out.

Some have nets & wish to catch me & sell me to
Chinese apothecaries, those men of mystical medicine
who, in the manner of their forebears with whom the
Commandant once-upon-a-time did such a very fine
trade, would place my dried husk into a mortar & grind
my remaining essence to a dust to which they would
then attribute powers of fabled libido & a correspond-
ingly high price. They say it's nice to be wanted, but I
am not so sure. Any ambition, I was once told by Capois
Death, is good as long as it is realised, but in my more
aspiring moods I had hoped to amount to something
more than a passing erection.

Others have underwater cameras. They film & pho-
tograph me, for as a weedy seadragon I am regarded as
a primitive throwback whose species is on the verge of
extinction, & I, who was the Artist, have instead
become the subject; I, whose role was to assist with classification, have now become the classified. My small
filmy fins flutter like those of a fairy, & I stare at them

399

& they at me, awed by my colours wondrous, by my movements serene, & I wonder.

The question that haunts me as they chase me & as I chase brine-shrimp & lurk around the fish-rich reefs off Bruny Island that I have made my home, is this: is it easier for a man to live his life as a fish, than to accept the wonder of being human?

So alone, so frightened, so wanting for what we are afraid to give tongue to. Between the dead & the living—what?

And in the rolling diagonal pillars of light & dark that stripe my watery world, I wanted to ask these & other questions of those divers: Why is it that I am possessed of two entirely opposite emotions? Explain that to me? Because it can't be explained, but still I want to know why   why when all the evidence of my life tells me this world smells worse than the old Dane's bobbing corpse, why is it that I still can't help believing that the world is good & that without love I am nothing?

Sometimes I even want to tap with my long snout on those divers' goggles & say: You want to know what this country will become? Ask me—after all, if you can't trust a liar & a forger, a whore & an informer, a convicted murderer & a thief, you'll never understand this country. Because we all make our accommodations with power, & the mass of us would sell our brother or sister for a bit of peace & quiet. We've been trained to live a life of moral cowardice while all the time comforting ourselves that we are nature's rebels. But in truth we've never got upset & excited about anything;

we're like the sheep we shot the Aborigines to make way for, docile until slaughter.

Everything that's wrong about this country begins in my story: they've all been making the place up, ever since the Commandant tried to reinvent Sarah Island as a New Venice, as the island of forgetting, because anything is easier than remembering. They'll forget what happened here for a hundred years or more, then they'll reimagine it like the old Dane reimagined it, because any story will be better than the sorry truth that it wasn't the English who did this to us but ourselves, that convicts flogged convicts & pissed on blackfellas & spied on each other, that blackfellas sold black women for dogs & speared escaping convicts, that white sealers killed & raped black women, & black women killed the children that resulted.

So there you have it: two things & I can't bring them together & they are wrenching me apart. These two feelings, this knowledge of a world so awful, this sense of a life so extraordinary—how am I to resolve them? Can a man become a fish? All you divers who have come so far to fathom my mystery, these questions, this torment, this good & this evil, this love & this hate, this life, resolve them & it for me, make sense of my story, unite me with this life, tell me it is not an inextricable part of my nature—I am begging you . . .

For I am not reconciled to this world.

I wished to be & I was not & so I tried to rewrite this world as a book of fish & set it to rights in the only manner I knew how.

But my way was meaningless, my cries unheard, my

pictures spat on before they were lost for all eternity. Now I just watch & think the ridiculous, the improbable: the world is good, I think, & the world is good & the world is good.

None of it does anything, I know.

It is, at best, a thought of heresy for which punishment is inevitable & long overdue. Matt Brady's book of dreams was right: to love is not safe.

Behind the face mask of the diver coming toward me now with a net, I recognise the unmistakable visage of Mr Hung, out diving for more specimens for his aquarium, & I know it is only a matter of time before I am gazing out of that neon-lit tank that I once so intently stared into; that while the Conga & Mr Hung plot another scam, in which they will forge a convict's journal of two centuries ago & try to flog it off as authentic history, occasionally staring in at me, perhaps wondering what it would be like to be a fish, I will stare out at them wondering what it would be like to be like them, knowing that a scam is just a dream, & that a dream is a dangerous thing if you believe in it too much.

For out there, only just beyond our vision, the net is waiting for us all, ever ready to trap & then rise with us tangled within, fins flailing, bodies futilely thrashing, heading to who knows what chaotic destiny. Love & water. Sid Hammet stares at me for too long. I am not afraid, never have I been afraid. I shall be you. I am ascending from the night, rising, rolling, passing through glass & air into his sad eyes. Who am I? he can no longer ask & I—my punishment perfect for one who has taken a life but not gained another in return---can only wish for the certainty to answer: I am William Buelow Gould & my name is a song which will be sung, click-clack---rat-a-tat-a-tat, a penny a painting, silly Billy Gould riding a seahorse to Banbury Cross . . .

AFTERWORD

*From the Colonial Secretary's
correspondence file, 5 April* 1831

(ARCHIVES OFFICE OF TASMANIA)

GOULD, William Buelow, *prisoner number* 873645; *aliases* Sid Hammet, 'the Surgeon', Jorgen Jorgensen, Capois Death, Pobjoy, 'the Commandant'; *identifying marks* tattoo above left breast, red anchor with blue wings, *legend* 'Love & Liberty'; *absconded* Sarah Island, 29 February 1831. Drowned attempting escape.